LORI FOSTER

WHEN I FIRST MET YOU

MIRA

MIRA

ISBN-13: 978-0-7783-0624-5

When I First Met You

For questions and comments about the quality of this book, please contact us at CustomerService@Harlequin.com.

TM is a trademark of Harlequin Enterprises ULC.

MIRA
22 Adelaide St. West, 41st Floor
Toronto, Ontario M5H 4E3, Canada
MIRABooks.com

HarperCollins Publishers
Macken House, 39/40 Mayor Street Upper,
Dublin 1, D01 C9W8, Ireland
www.HarperCollins.com

Printed in U.S.A.

26 27 28 29 30 LBC 5 4 3 2 1

Praise for *New York Times* bestselling author Lori Foster

"Emotionally spellbinding and wicked hot."

—Lora Leigh, *New York Times* bestselling author, on *No Limits*

"[*No Holding Back* has] compassion, interesting family dynamics, troubled pasts, killer fight scenes, and of course, swoon-worthy romance. Highly recommended."

—Harlequin Junkie

"No one writes alpha heroes and sexy, swoon-worthy romance like Lori Foster."

—Jill Shalvis, *New York Times* bestselling author

"A must-read!"

—Fresh Fiction* on *The Dangerous One

"Hot enough to start a fire! A delicious and dangerous tale that proves why Foster is one of the best in the genre."

—RT Book Reviews* on *Fast Burn

"Count on Lori Foster for sexy, edgy romance."

—Jayne Ann Krentz, *New York Times* bestselling author

"Teasing and humorous dialogue, sizzling sex scenes, tender moments, and overriding tension show Foster's skill as a balanced storyteller."

***—Publishers Weekly* on *Under Pressure* (starred review)**

"Foster is a master at writing a simmering romance."

—USATODAY.com's Happy Ever After* blog on *Fast Burn

Also available from Lori Foster and MIRA Books

Family Ties

Let Me Be the One
When I First Met You

Osborn Brothers

The Dangerous One
The Fearless One

The Love Shack
The Little Flower Shop
The Honeymoon Cottage
The Summer of No Attachments
The Somerset Girls
Sisters of Summer's End
Cooper's Charm

The McKenzies of Ridge Trail

No Holding Back
Stronger Than You Know
Watching Over You

Road to Love

Driven to Distraction
Slow Ride
All Fired Up

For additional books by Lori Foster,
visit her website, lorifoster.com.

To lovely reader Anissa Hicks, who often visits my FB page. She shared info on her "dog-ter" with me—her sweet female dog—and allowed me to use the cute phrase in this book for Glory's adopted pooch.
Readers are the very best!
Thank you, Anissa.

1

With a deep bracing breath, Glory McCallahan got herself under control. She would not cry. Absolutely not. Crying made her nose red and her eyes puffy, so by God, she'd withhold her happy tears.

Because, damn it, she *was* happy. Never mind that things would never again be the same for her; her cousin, Callie, was now happily married to a perfect guy and they'd be starting their life together in her beloved hometown.

All good news. For Callie.

Unfortunately, Glory felt like she'd just lost the best piece of herself. No one had ever loved her like Callie did. Not the parents she'd lost, or the aunt and uncle who'd raised her. Definitely never a man.

Throughout the years, she'd relied on her cousin in so many ways, and now . . .

Now she was alone.

Or at least she would be once the wedding reception wrapped up, and she returned to her new home. Her new life. Her new . . . *everything*.

She'd only recently purchased the modest house in her cousin's hometown neighborhood so she'd be nearby but not underfoot. She couldn't bear being underfoot. Especially not now that Callie was so happy.

Damn it. *I will not cry*.

"I need a refill," her aunt called out to her, thankfully giving her something to do other than feel sorry for herself.

With a smile pinned in place, Glory hurried to flag a server for her. After Aunt Liz was settled again, her Uncle Frank slipped her some envelopes. "These are for the staff. See that they get them, okay?"

"Of course." She turned to the groom's mother, Addie. "Is there anything I can do for you?"

Addie, always a sweetheart, smiled at her. "You could sit down and take a break. I swear, Glory, you haven't been off your feet all night."

Before Glory could answer, her aunt added, "She's right, Glory. You're looking a little ragged with your cheeks flushed and your hair flying every which way. Maybe you should run to the restroom and tidy yourself up."

"She looks beautiful," Addie replied.

Leaning in, her aunt confided, "She's starting to get dewy."

Which was Aunt Liz's way of saying she was sweaty.

"She *glows*," Addie countered with an edge.

Glory almost grinned. Lately, she'd noticed Addie being her champion, even when it wasn't necessary. "I'll tidy my hair in a minute, Aunt Liz." Honestly, she looked forward to the moment alone.

Still smiling, Glory turned to follow the server toward the kitchen of the quaint event hall. Along the way she felt . . .

Well, she felt an unnerving tingle that traveled along her spine. Glancing back, she caught Kam Norwood, the groom's oh-so-hot and annoying younger brother, watching her intently. For a second, her breath caught—and then he looked away as if he'd merely been skimming the room and accidentally focused on her.

Heat rushed into her face and her lungs deflated. Of course, Kam wasn't checking her out. The man could barely stand her. Most of the time, if he looked at her, it was with a critical eye.

Well, screw him.

No . . . *wait.* She would not screw him. Not ever—even if she thought about it far too often. Seriously, what red-blooded woman wouldn't?

Another waiter passed her, giving her a barely-there smile.

Maybe her hair was worse than she thought.

Against her will, her gaze returned to Kam. Of course, he looked amazing whether he was in his usual jeans and a T-shirt or dressed up in a tux for his brother's wedding, as he was now.

Tall, lean, and strong, with dark chestnut hair, incredible green eyes, and a smile that could cause a girl's heart to stutter. As the best man, he'd been busy, too, and other than walking into the ceremony together, and the customary dance—which had been crazy-awkward, at least for Glory—she'd barely spoken to him. Maybe she should . . .

A young woman who was part of the staff drew Kam's attention. He gave her an immediate smile that flowed into easy conversation and a few laughs. The way they talked, Glory figured they were probably hooking up.

Refusing to acknowledge the envious kick to her heart, she got back to her assigned task. She distributed the envelopes to the available staff, leaving the rest with Dan Fellows, the owner of the hall, to share with those who were currently busy—like the pretty young woman engaging Kam.

With that done, Glory grabbed her purse off a table in the corner and darted out of the main room to the corridor that led to the bathroom.

The air here was cooler and a little fresher. Since Callie and Tanner—the bride and groom—had left nearly an hour ago, it was fine for her to try to wrap it up, too. She'd circle the room and make a few subtle gestures that would hopefully get everyone going.

"Only a few minutes more," she promised herself as she dampened a paper towel under the faucet and then patted it to her face, throat, and the back of her neck. She'd had too little sleep, not much to eat, and her emotions seemed to be in a blender.

She was fighting off the melancholy when she heard a text ding on her phone. Absurdly, she thought it might be Callie. Then she laughed at herself, because Callie was at home by now, with her husband, no doubt setting the sheets on fire.

Grinning at herself, glad for the distraction, she took the phone from her purse, swiped the screen—and froze.

Absurd that he still had this effect on her.

Through a haze, she read the message.

Can't wait to see you again. 😊

Those damned smiley faces made her skin crawl. They'd seemed cute at first, but they'd long since slid into sick territory.

Suddenly, she felt very alone. She breathed faster as she realized no one else was around—and a door to the parking lot was *right there*. Was it even locked—or could someone have come in unnoticed?

Thankfully, before the fear could dig deep, the laughter of approaching women reached her. Glory dropped the phone into her purse and left the restroom, smiling as she passed the women who were just coming in. She forged back into the hall, determined to get through the rest of her duties. Then she'd go home, enjoy a long hot soak in the tub, and crash for the night.

Tomorrow, her mood would surely be improved.

Kam did not mean to watch her so closely. In fact, he tried not to. Yet, he'd noticed when she left the room, and he'd watched for her return. For reasons he didn't understand, he noticed everything Glory did.

Even today, after a wedding and while hustling at the reception, Glory wore a mask of untouchable perfection. It bugged him big-time. The only time that practiced expression had slipped was at the end of the wedding, when tears had filled her eyes before she'd blinked them away.

Actually, that wasn't true. She'd been different during the slow dance they'd shared at the start of the reception. As the best man and maid of honor, it was expected. Traditional. Or so he'd been told.

It hadn't been easy for him to stay casual. Superficial.

Seeing Glory so perpetually composed naturally made him want to . . . What?

Tease her, fluster her, get her mussed so that her light blond hair was no longer so precisely styled?

Maybe steal the shiny lip gloss off her mouth—with his tongue.

Holding her during a slow dance, her body moving with his, led his thoughts to similar movements . . . while they were both naked. He imagined tugging down the front of her fancy dress until he exposed her breasts, until he could touch her and watch her pretty blue eyes go from wary to dark and vague . . .

"Ahem."

Jarred out of his sultry thoughts, Kam turned to see older blue eyes assessing him. Since adopting him years ago, Addie had caught him doing many things. In comparison to some of them, fantasizing about the maid of honor wasn't a big deal.

"Keep that up," Addie said, "and the girl's going to catch on fire."

He put his arm around Addie and hugged her close. "Have I told you how great you look?"

"Pfft." Addie smoothed her graying blond hair and lowered her voice. "I had to wear the dress since your brother and Callie insisted on buying it for me, but you know I'm most comfortable in my jeans and T-shirts."

Yeah, he felt the same about the damn tux he wore. Again, his gaze went to Glory. Her blue dress fastened over one shoulder, leaving her throat, upper chest, and opposite shoulder bare. Her skin was peachy and smooth. Unlike him and Addie, she seemed comfortable in the designer gown. "Callie's family is right at home in fancy duds."

Who knew his brother, also adopted by Addie, would marry the town princess? Her family had always owned half the businesses in Hoker, Kentucky, at least until they'd moved away years ago. Even back then, Tanner had been hung up on her.

Neither of them had ever met the cousin, although apparently Glory had been raised with Callie.

"Be nice," Addie admonished.

He realized he was frowning and deliberately lightened his expression when he said, "My feet are pinched in these shoes." Give him work boots or sneakers any day.

Leaning in closer, Addie whispered, "Mine are, too."

Sympathizing with her, Kam grinned. "Since the bride and groom are gone, we're allowed to head home, right?"

"I'm catching a ride with Callie's parents."

That took him back a step. "How come?"

"To spare Glory, of course." Resting against the outdated paneled wall, Addie glanced around the room, ensuring that the lingering guests couldn't hear her. "Drives me nuts how Liz keeps picking at her. That girl has worked her tail off setting up this wedding, and all Liz has done is complain."

"To you?" Kam asked, feeling his temper rile. Okay, so the wedding venue was small, but it was the only hall in town. Who cared if the chairs had plastic seats or if the linoleum floor had seen better days? Callie and Tanner were happy. Blissfully so.

Addie shook her head. "Of course not. It's Glory I'm worried about."

Right. Who could ever be rude to Addie? "So what do they say?"

She shrugged. "It's silly stuff, like telling her to slow down or she'll sweat."

Kam laughed.

"Or saying she needs to adjust the strap on her dress."

That sent his attention to her dress again. To him, that strap seemed plenty secure. Good thing, because if it slid down her arm, the entire top of the dress would go with it.

An intriguing idea.

"There was something about the flowers being wilted, and the cake being too sweet—"

He snorted. "In other words, just looking for things to bitch about?"

"It was a beautiful wedding," Addie said with a sigh.

"Don't start crying again."

"I'll cry if I want to." On a groan, she moved to sit on a chair, then slipped off her shoes and wiggled her toes.

Kam followed her. "You sure you don't want me to take

you home?" At seventy-two, Addie was still an energetic woman who didn't indulge a lot of idle time—but it was way past her usual bedtime. Early to bed, early to rise had always been her mantra.

"Callie's parents are just waiting on me." Her gaze slanted his way. "Figured it wouldn't hurt to let them wait a few minutes more. You need to hang back with Glory and see that she gets home."

Honest to God, he'd do anything for Addie. *Anything.* She'd literally saved his life when she'd taken him in as a kid—but he didn't want to take Glory home. "She's twenty-five, Addie. She knows how to get herself home."

"Kam," she said, her voice stern. "As the maid of honor, she needs to wrap up everything here, and as best man, you should lend her a hand, which means you two will be the last to leave. Do you really want her alone in a parking lot at this time of night?"

It wasn't a bad area. Hoker was mostly a quiet town. Except, okay, it was a weekend and things got a little rowdier, but still . . . "What's there to wrap up?" Admittedly, he didn't know anything about weddings or receptions. Seemed to him it was all taken care of.

Addie stood again, this time with her shoes dangling from the fingers of one hand. "Talk to Glory and find out." She went on tiptoes to kiss his cheek. "And Kam?"

"Yes, Addie," he replied dutifully.

"Be *nice*."

Smiling, he watched her walk off—barefoot, her long floral dress dragging on the floor behind her.

He waited there until she and Callie's parents had departed.

In short order, the last remaining guests also filed out. Kam looked around but didn't see Glory. His brows pulled together, dread settling in his stomach.

Maybe she'd already left, too. Damn it, Addie would have his ass.

He was about to search her out when Dan Fellows, the owner of the hall, approached him with a happy grin. "My, it was wonderful, wasn't it? Just wonderful." Sweat beaded on his brow as he took in the remaining decorations on the tables. "A great turnout. Lovely bride and groom."

"Yeah, it was nice." Where the hell was Glory?

"I guess I can close it up now, right? You don't need anything else?"

Honestly, Kam had no clue. "You're all taken care of?"

"Yes, yes. Paid in full and everyone was given a generous tip." He loudly confided. "We all love your in-laws. Generous people. Very generous."

"Not *my* in-laws," Kam said. "Jesus, don't start rumors."

Laughing, Dan gave him a sly look. "Sorry, Tanner's in-laws, then."

Kam was glad they hadn't scrimped on the tips. With rich people, you never knew. "So . . ." No sign of Glory at all. "I guess if you see anything, like anyone forgot something or left something behind, let us know." Kam offered his hand.

"Yes, of course, but Glory already made those arrangements."

Of course, she did. "Then I'll get out of here so you can wrap it up and get home." As soon as he stepped out, cooler evening air embraced him. Tension eased as he drew a deep breath, but it didn't entirely go away. *Where was Glory?*

Out of the shadows, the girl he'd talked with earlier sidled up to him. "Kam."

He turned to her, but he'd already forgotten her name. She was young, barely twenty, and while she was cute and obviously interested, tonight wasn't the night for him. It made him feel like an ass to acknowledge that he might have led her on a bit just because he'd known Glory was watching.

"Hey." Trying to keep it casual, he said, "Thanks again. The reception was nice."

"Your brother looked really happy."

"Yeah." Tanner had found that once-in-a-lifetime kind of love. It still amazed him. Before Callie had shown up and impacted them all, he hadn't even known something like that existed.

"So . . . you're heading home?" she asked, her suggestive gaze holding his.

Kam was trying to think up a good excuse when a new voice intruded.

"Sorry, but I'm not quite done with him yet." Glory stepped closer, her chin tilted up as if in challenge, shoulders back—which just made him glance at her boobs again—and a glint of determination in her pretty blue eyes.

He forced his mouth to curve in the semblance of a smile. "Is that right? What can I do you for?"

"I . . ." Confused, Glory asked, "What?"

His smile turned genuine. "What is it you need?" *Say me.* No, wait. *Don't* say that. If she did, he'd be all over her, and he didn't want that to happen . . . Did he?

The girl beside him put her arm through his. "But, Kam, we had plans."

Damn it, Kam couldn't even drum up her name. He patted her hand and attempted to free himself from her hold without much success. Giving up, he let her cling while he asked, "So what's the problem, Glory?"

Her gaze tracked over his arm, then over the girl attached to it. Smile tight, she replied, "I could use some help with . . . things."

"What things?"

Emotions flitted over her face, and stubbornness set in. "You know what? I just thought up another solution." She fluttered her hands. "You're free and clear to enjoy the rest of your evening." Pivoting on her heeled sandal, she marched away.

Damn it. To the other woman, he said, "Sorry, sugar," as he peeled her fingers away. "In case you couldn't tell, she was pissed, so I'd better see what's up." Without waiting for a reply, he broke into a jog to catch up with Glory, whose militant stride had already taken her around the corner and into the darkness of the back lot.

It wasn't until he got closer that he heard her low voice. "What are you even doing here?"

Another voice, a *male* voice, replied, "I'm picking you up."

Brows coming together, Kam took in the scene before him. Some guy was standing in the lot with Glory, but she was keeping her distance.

Without noticing him, Glory said to the dude, "No, you're not."

"You're alone," the guy crooned. "I'm alone."

"I told you I'm not alone."

With a smug smile, he asked, "Then, babe, where is he?"

"I'm not your babe, and he's delayed, but he'll be here any minute."

"Right. He's hanging out in the empty event hall?" He moved closer.

Pointing, Glory said, "His car is right there."

The jerk shrugged. "But he's not *with* you." He reached for her, and she jumped back, almost stumbling.

Kam debated on how to handle things: Stomp the guy into the ground, which was currently his preference, or try to use some tact.

"Come on, Glory. Don't be like that. I'm the only one here for you, your car is out of commission, and it's late."

Out of commission? Kam looked at her car—and saw flat

tires. Two of them, both the rears. Worse, he looked at his SUV and saw flats on it as well. "What the hell?"

Glory whirled to face him. *"Kam."*

"Sorry, babe." He relished saying that and was relieved when Glory didn't snap at him as she had the other guy. "I got held up." In a few long strides, he was at her side. Surprising her, he slipped his arm around her and drew her close for a soft kiss.

She did a great impression of a frozen pole, but he didn't mind. He still savored the press of his mouth on hers. Two seconds, three. Damn, he wouldn't mind doing that all night, turning his head for a better fit, teasing her stiff lips apart . . . but it'd probably be better if he got it together before she slugged him, especially since her pushy Romeo still stood there.

Keeping her snug against him, he nodded at her car. "What happened?"

"I—we—um . . ."

Clearly, he'd thrown her for a loop. A good thing, considering how many times she'd left him floundering.

Satisfied with her response, he gave her a little hug and a quicker kiss to her temple.

Finally finding her voice, she said, "Maybe we drove over something?"

Yeah, right. Kam cut his attention to the intrusive guy. He was tall, trim, dressed in casual clothes, and had obviously hoped to stake a claim on Glory. *Not happening, bud.*

"If that was so, Callie's parents would have had flats, too." They'd all taken the same route. "And how the hell are the flats only in back? If we drove over something, the front tires would have—"

"Hey, I'm Mike." The guy pushed forward, hand extended.

Kam had to release Glory to accept the handshake, but as he did so, he stepped slightly in front of her like a shield. "Hey,

Mike." The handshake, at least, was congenial enough. "I take it you two are friends?"

Affection softened Mike's smile as he looked at Glory. "We've been dating a while."

"No, we haven't," Glory said quickly, her voice a little too high. "It was three dates. Only three."

"Babe, come on." Looking at her over Kam's shoulder, Mike affected cool forbearance. In an aside to Kam, his voice low as if that might keep Glory from hearing even though she was right behind him, he confided, "We had a little disagreement. Guess she's still riled."

Mouth firming, Glory quickly moved away. Not closer to Kam, but away from Mike. As if the other guy wasn't there, she said to Kam, "We should get going."

Mike grinned and shook his head as if amused. "Guess I took too long to call. You know how it is."

"I'm not sure I do." Kam didn't know what was happening, but he didn't like it. Men who hassled women went instantly on the list of things he despised, right up there with child neglect and animal abuse. Never, under any circumstances, would he take part in such a thing.

It would make him too much like his parents, a fate he would never accept. Past accusations and his tainted bloodline was something he'd deny to his dying day.

With her composure slipping, Glory asked Kam, "Does the town have any kind of ride service?"

At first, he'd thought it possible that she was just teaching the dude a lesson. Maybe he'd let her down, or somehow insulted her and she'd hoped to use Kam to even the score.

Now, with the car tires flat and that look in her eyes, he knew it was more. "Normally in a pinch I'd call Tanner, but not on his wedding night. One tire I could have changed with a spare, but not two."

Mike held out his arms. "I can give you both a ride."

Glory's expression twisted his heart and expanded his uneasiness. Protective instincts, learned in his youth and honed in his maturity, rose up, urging him to study Mike more closely.

Just then, Dan Fellows joined them. "I was about to leave but heard you talking. Problem?"

Kam glanced around. "Where are you parked?"

"In the side lot for employees. Everyone has gone and I've locked up, but if you need something—"

"A ride?" Kam gestured to the cars. "Glory and I both have flats."

"Hmm. That's curious." Dan circled the cars.

They all ignored Mike—until he introduced himself. "I offered them a ride, so you can—"

"Dan Fellows." Around the handshake, Dan asked, "Your tires flat, too?"

"No, sir. I'm just here to give Glory a ride."

Glory sidled over next to Fellows. "I know it's a huge imposition, but if you're able to help us out, I'd be so grateful."

Fellows smiled down at her. "I'd be glad to. Plenty of room in my car." In a quick dismissal, he said to Mike, "Nice to meet you. Drive safely now."

Dumbfounded, Mike watched as Glory rushed to the driver's side of her car, opened the door and got out her purse before locking it again. Without glancing at Mike, she gave Kam an expectant look. "I'm ready."

"I'll call you," Mike said.

"That's okay." Again, she turned to Kam.

"I'll be right there, honey. Give me two minutes."

Her gaze shifted from him to Mike and back again before she worked up a smile. "Of course . . . *babe*." Her heels clicked on the blacktop pavement as she kept pace with Fellows.

"Take your time," Fellows said before he started a low conversation with Glory.

Fighting a grin, Kam turned back to Mike. "So." He walked to the back of Glory's red Mustang. "Hell of a thing, right?"

Distracted, Mike stared after Glory.

Kam didn't like the intensity in his gaze. "Don't you think?"

"What?"

Yeah, old Mike was very lost in thought there, and Kam was willing to bet none of those thoughts were appropriate, given how Glory had turned him down. "Flat tires on the only two cars still in the lot." He glanced around. "Where are you parked, by the way?"

"On the street."

As if that made sense, Kam nodded. "How is it you're here? Did Glory call you?"

Mike hesitated, then probably realized that Kam could find out the truth easily enough. With another happy-go-lucky grin, he said, "Nah, you see that she's upset with me right now."

"I noticed that, yeah."

"I was out with our group earlier today, making plans, when Tina called to see if Glory would want to join us. She said she couldn't, that she had the reception tonight."

"And somehow you got all the deets?"

"From Tina, yeah." All magnanimous and shit, he lifted a shoulder. "I knew she'd be alone because she hasn't dated since our disagreement."

"When was that, by the way?"

"I don't know. A month, maybe? Anyway, I figured I had let her stew long enough, so I came to save her."

Kam could barely suffer the ass. "Save her, huh?"

"Glory hates going to functions alone."

"She's not alone," Kam reminded him. Before Mike could protest that, he asked, "Did Tina tell Glory you were coming here?"

"No idea. I took off to play her hero, but you see how that worked out." He gave a little chuckle. "Shouldn't have wasted my time."

"Probably not." Kam made a point of looking beyond him, toward the section of street he could see, but there were no parked cars in view. "So you and Tina and other friends live nearby?"

"Not really."

Interesting. "How far was your drive?"

Congeniality faded from Mike's expression. "What is this? Why are you grilling me?"

"Seems to me that Glory has been clear." Kam watched him. "That should be the end of it."

Mike deflated. "It can't be. I love her."

"Sucks for you, but I'm telling you right now: leave her alone." He turned and walked away.

Mike said nothing else.

Having him at his back didn't feel right, so Kam glanced over his shoulder, and saw that the guy was already gone.

Gone where, he didn't know, but Kam had an awful feeling it wouldn't be the last he saw of him.

Glory wasn't sure what to do. Or where to go. She had hoped Mr. Fellows would drive her to her home, but the second Kam got in the car, he instructed that they should both be taken to Addie's. And really, she didn't want to be a bother, so she kept quiet. Except . . .

Did Kam expect her to sleep there? Long ago, she and Callie had spent a night in the finished attic, before Callie's home next door had been cleaned and refreshed. The attic was nice enough, sort of like a recreational space for when Kam and Tanner had been younger. Tonight, she didn't have anything with her—none of her toiletries, no makeup, no toothbrush . . . She didn't even have a change of clothes.

Other than Callie, no one saw her morning face, with puffy eyes and messed-up hair.

As far as she was concerned, no one ever would—definitely not Kam.

"I feel like a chauffeur," Fellows teased.

"Sorry." Kam, who'd gotten into the back seat with her for some reason, gave her a taunting grin. "Now that Glory has announced that we're together, I couldn't resist the opportunity to be near her."

"Ha!" Fellows said. "I knew it. I could tell when the two of you danced."

Glory sputtered. Kam knew why she'd fudged things just a little, hinting that they might be together, but Dan didn't.

"No one could miss it," he continued. "Just the way you two look at each other—very romantic. Reminds me of my own energetic youth."

Almost choking, Glory said, "But we don't—"

The way Kam squeezed her close stole her breath and interrupted her attempt to correct him. "And here we thought we were subtle."

Held too close to Kam's hard body, she stared into his green eyes and breathed, "What in the world are you doing?"

His gaze dropped to her mouth and stayed there. "This."

The heat of that whispered word teased her lips—right before *his* lips pressed to hers.

Unlike the surprising kiss in the parking lot where she'd been too stunned to feel it, this kiss nearly stopped her heart.

Too many times she'd thought about kissing him, but never would she have admitted it to anyone, not even Callie. It was too obvious that Kam disliked her.

Although, he didn't exactly kiss her with dislike.

And she didn't exactly reject him. In fact . . . she might have melted against him.

A few seconds later, when he ended the tantalizing contact, she opened her eyes to see he was smiling.

Of all the nerve! Glory shoved away from him, earning a chuckle from Mr. Fellows.

"Guess your pal, Mike, is out of luck," Fellows observed, clearly amused. "I could have told him he was wasting his time."

"Glory did tell him," Kam said, then added, "I'm just not sure he's listening."

"Natalie figured it out, too, or at least that's what she said when she came back into the hall."

Distracted, Glory asked, "Who's Natalie?"

"She's one of our waitstaff. Very nice young lady. Thought she had plans with Kam but I agreed she must have misunderstood."

"Damn," Kam said. "Sorry about that. I didn't realize—"

"It's my fault." Glory felt bad. *Sort of.* She really didn't like the idea of Kam with the pretty young woman, but she had no claim on him, either. If only Mike hadn't shown up . . . "I shouldn't have involved Kam."

Kam tugged her close again. "None of that. We're together," he teased. "Naturally, I'm involved."

She slanted him a look. Oh, he was definitely having fun. Not for a second did she think he actually wanted involvement. No, he just enjoyed her predicament.

As Fellows took a turn, he said, "Don't worry about Natalie. She'll be fine."

"I was just thinking . . ." *What am I going to do?* She definitely could not stay over tonight, but her home wasn't close enough for her to walk.

Kam spoke into her ear: "Relax. I have a plan."

If it was to confuse her, mission accomplished.

Just then, Mr. Fellows pulled into the driveway. There were no lights on inside, but the outside floodlights lit up the yard. Callie and Tanner would be in the next house over, enjoying their first night together as a married couple.

"Thanks, Dan," Kam said. "I owe you."

"Nonsense. After allowing me to host that beautiful reception, I'm thrilled to do it."

After Kam stepped out, Glory said, "The hall was perfect. Thank you for everything."

Mr. Fellows smiled back at her. "Never thought I'd see the day that Kam Norwood would settle down. You hold on tight to him, okay? He's a good one."

"Oh, um . . ." When Kam offered her a hand, she lost the opportunity for corrections. Sending Mr. Fellows a wan smile in return, she gathered her skirt and slid out.

Immediately, Kam put his arm around her. "Smile and wave, Glory. Don't confuse the man."

She smiled. She waved. And she badly wanted to leap away from Kam. He was far too tempting. Only the fact that he didn't actually like her, that this was all a joke to him—that *she* was the joke—kept her spine straight and her shoulders proud. When she got him alone . . . What? What could she do?

He'd assisted her, he'd gotten her away from Mike, so maybe she should just let him enjoy the moment.

2

It was dark out and with every fiber of his being, Kam was aware of Glory fuming beside him. She still looked perfect. Still smelled enticing.

Still annoyed him.

And yet he wanted her, damn it. Now more than ever.

Those two small tastes, measly perfunctory kisses, hadn't even come close to taking the edge off. "Come on."

She dug in, resisting his tug on her arm. "To where?"

"The house? Or did you want to spend the evening in the yard?"

"I wanted to go to my house."

"It would have been out of Dan's way to take you there, then take me here, and you still would have been without a car."

"Mr. Fellows might not have minded," she grumbled, and grudgingly allowed him to lead her along. Even lower, she said, "Sorry I ruined your night."

Interesting. So she was still willing to take the blame for that? Well, he wasn't above teasing her. "What's that, Glory? You said something?"

They stepped up to the door, and she inhaled a deep breath before facing him with the same enthusiasm she might have had facing a cockroach. "I said I apologize for ruining your evening."

Folding his arms and resting a shoulder on the exterior wall beside the door, Kam asked, "Why did you?" Would she admit she was afraid of Mike? If so, then he'd have reason to jump in. To get involved.

Instead, she shrugged. "It was a knee-jerk reaction to finding the flat tires, and then Mike showed up. Now, of course, I've thought of a dozen other ways I might have handled the situation. Unfortunately, they didn't occur to me in that moment."

"I occurred to you."

"Hmm, well, you do seem big enough and mean enough to discourage another guy."

Mean? He wasn't mean. At least, he didn't think so. Frowning, he wondered if that was how she genuinely perceived him. "Mike didn't seem all that discouraged to me."

"I know." Bothered by that, she looked away and stared out at the yard. "He's . . . persistent."

Kam touched her chin, bringing her gaze back to his. "How persistent?"

For a long moment, she just stared into his eyes—until she caught herself and stepped out of reach. Wrapping her arms around herself, she said, "It's not your problem."

He smirked. "Not what you said at the hall." Why he was so determined to help her, he couldn't say, especially when she seemed to constantly look down her nose at him.

Predictably, her shoulders stiffened. "I apologized. What else should I do? Bleed?"

Without changing his casual posture, he heard himself say, "Another kiss might cover it." The second the words left his mouth, his eyes flared. And he stared at her, waiting.

Her eyes narrowed. "Is that what you want, or is it another joke?"

"What do you mean?" Mostly he was intrigued that she wasn't ruling it out.

"Ha! You've made me the butt of your joke since I so stupidly asked for your help."

Is that how she viewed it? Okay, sure, he'd ribbed her a little, and he supposed he had enjoyed seeing her caught in her own scheme. Only . . . he didn't want her to feel bad for asking for help.

Dropping his head, feeling like a complete dick, Kam had to admit she was right. "Not what I'd intended," he said softly.

Glory turned slightly toward him. "No?"

It struck him that neither of them were rushing to get inside. At this time of night, without the scorching sun, the August air was muggy but tolerable.

Reaching out, Kam hooked one finger in a loosened hank of her silky hair, drawing it forward over her shoulder. "I only meant to tease you."

"But now I know you had other plans . . ."

"Not really." Time to fess up on that one, too. "I didn't even remember Natalie's name until Dan said it. I'd only been chatting her up to keep from watching you."

She bit her lip before asking tentatively, "Is that true?"

With a short quiet laugh, Kam said, "I'm many things, Glory, but I'm not a liar." He released her hair to slide his hand around her neck. "Now, about that kiss?"

"You actually want to kiss me? Because I've always gotten the impression that you don't like me."

"I don't *dis*like you."

"Kam," she warned.

His mouth twitched. For once, Glory didn't look quite so perfect, not with a mulish frown pulling her brows together. "Want me to spill my guts, huh?" He brushed his thumb over her cheek. God, she was soft. And she smelled so good, like subtle perfume, damp skin, and hot woman. "Fine." He tugged her a little closer—and praise the Lord, she didn't resist. "It bothers me that you're always so put together. Never a hair out of place, not a wrinkle in your clothes."

Flustered, she said, "That's not true."

"Mostly true," he said. "It makes me want to mess you up a little."

She had been subtly leaning toward him, drawn by the low tones of his voice, but now she abruptly straightened. "Mess me up? Why would you—"

"With a kiss," he murmured, drawing nearer. "Some touching." As he said it, he loosened more of her hair, stroking through it, enjoying the warmth and weight of it. Since she didn't object, he stepped against her, but instead of kissing her, he teased his nose up the column of her neck to her ear, then whispered, "A little nuzzling."

A sound of want purred out of her, and Kam knew he was a goner. He drew her close, and this time, he took the kiss he wanted—the kiss he'd been thinking about ever since meeting Glory McCallahan.

Whoa. Glory didn't mean to, but at the feel of his mouth moving over hers, she completely caved, all resistance gone as if it had never existed. Boneless, she allowed him to gather her close, from mouth to mouth, down to thighs to thighs.

Tongue to tongue.

Pelvis to . . . *Hello.*

Her fingers curled into his lapels to hold on since her legs weren't cooperating. Kam gave a growl of encouragement and turned his head just enough to kiss her deeper, hotter.

She forgot about everything except his hands on her body, one of them cradling her head, the other sliding down her spine to her backside.

Did she want that? Oh, yeah. She did. In fact, she wanted—

"Ahem."

They bounced apart as if a giant spring had magically appeared between them.

There, at the open door, stood Addie, an odd expression on her face, her arms crossed to hold her housecoat closed. Blu, Tanner's German shepherd, pushed his way out and, after a quick hello to Kam and Glory, went out into the yard to do his business.

Glory felt like all the oxygen had been sucked from her lungs. She couldn't draw a deep enough breath, couldn't think, and actually, she might've been panicking a little.

Apparently, Kam didn't suffer the same ailment. "Damn, Addie. That was rotten timing."

"How was I to know?" she said back with amusement. "Blu was in the room with me but he heard you right off. I kept waiting for you to come up—only you didn't." She turned to Glory, and her smile slipped away. "Good grief." Stepping out in a rush, she said, "You're hyperventilating."

Kam turned, too, and a touch of alarm filled his eyes. He reached her before Addie could. Catching her close, he shielded her with his body. "Are you all right?"

She nodded and wheezed noisily. Of all the people in the whole world, Addie was the nicest she'd ever met. Sure, she loved her cousin Callie, and they were close, but Addie was special. Kind to everyone, open and loving. Accepting.

Addie never judged her. No, she just accepted her.

Glory wanted her respect, and instead, she'd been busted

making out on her front stoop like a horny teenager, for crying out loud. She'd really like to sink into the ground and disappear.

Since that wouldn't happen, she needed to calm down.

"Give her some room." Pushing Kam aside, Addie eyed her critically and with some relief. "Better now?"

Better, when she now had the undivided attention of both Addie and Kam? No, but she could fake it with the best of them. She hoped. "I'm sorry we disturbed you." A quick scowl at Kam put the blame on him. After all, he was the one who'd started the kissing, but then she had no illusions about him trying to be perfect.

"Nonsense. I wasn't asleep yet. I was just in bed reading, unwinding, and enjoying being barefoot." She smiled. "How in the world you young girls wear those shoes I'll never know. Give me sneakers, flip-flops, or work boots any day."

See? Addie always knew how to put her at ease. Wrinkling her nose, Glory said, "I'm used to them, I guess."

"But don't you enjoy wiggling your toes now and then? Maybe when you're not working?"

Okay, seriously, she didn't want to discuss her toes. "I wanted to go to my own place, but Kam had Mr. Fellows bring us here."

Kam, who still had his arm around her, as if *that* was normal, filled in the details: "We both had flat tires. Dan brought us here. I was going to take your car, but I'd have left you a note, letting you know I'd have it back early."

So that had been his plan? He could have told her that. But wait. Why would he not have it back until early? Once he dropped her off, where did he plan to go?

Back to see Natalie?

Addie opened the door wider. "Come on in, and I'll get my keys."

"You two go on," Glory said. "I'll wait out here with Blu."

Kam gave her a look, whistled, and Blu bounded into the house. "Now we can all step inside."

His hand at the small of her back urged her in first. Now that Addie had mentioned shoes, Glory felt the ache in her arches. She didn't want to do any more walking than necessary, but more than that, she didn't want to complain.

As soon as she got home, though, she planned to strip off her clothes, take a nice long bath, and then sleep for hours.

Well, hell.

Kam saw the broken window the second he pulled into the driveway at Glory's new home. Since she was staring out the side window, doing her best to ignore him—which, he had to admit, she did well—she hadn't yet noticed.

He put the car in Park. "Glory—"

"Thanks for the ride." In a sudden rush, she unfastened her seat belt and picked up her purse. "I really appreciate it." She flashed him the briefest smile possible and opened her door before Kam caught her arm.

With a theatrical groan, she flopped back into her seat and asked, "Now what?"

Given that Mike might've had something to do with the vandalism, he shouldn't have been amused, but it was obvious she wanted to get away from him, so Kam couldn't help grinning. "All that, huh?"

"Yes, all that. You're being weird. And kissy. I don't understand it."

"Kissy?" His humor expanded.

"You know what I mean. For a man who only doesn't *dis*like me, there's no reason for kissing."

"I bet you can't say that again." She'd jumbled that odd sentence together so that few people would understand. He'd gotten her drift, though. "I like you fine—and you liked me kissing you." Would she admit it?

"Yeah, so? It's been a weird day, but it won't happen again."

Softly, he said, "Damn, girl, that sounds like a challenge."

"It's not!" She pulled her arm free and practically leaped from the car.

Sighing, Kam got out and followed her. "I can't just drop you off."

Heading to her door at a fast clip, she said, "Yes, you can."

He caught her again, then had to speak fast before she decked him. "Your window is broken."

Growling—like a literal *growl*—she snapped, "What is that supposed to mean?"

Damn it, she had him grinning again. "It's not a euphemism if that's what you're thinking." He turned her on the walkway and pointed to the main front window. Fortunately, it was a casement window and only one side was broken.

She gasped. "My window!"

When she started to charge forward, Kam snagged her once more. "Hold up there, speed racer. Let's think this through, okay? Earlier, you tangled with your asshole ex."

"He's not an ex. I didn't date him long enough for him to qualify as an ex."

Semantics. Not his point. "We both had flat tires. And now your window is broken."

"Mike doesn't know where I live."

Well, that was something, at least. "How about you let me go in first?"

She tucked in her chin and gave him a fierce frown. "How about we go in together?"

"I'll take what I can get." He took the keys from her hand and stepped around her.

"Kam! What does that mean?"

Seriously, he *would* take what he could get, but for now, he didn't want to debate it with her. "One thing at a time." She had double front doors, but only the right side opened. He stepped into a foyer with a built-in seat beneath a coat rack and cubbies for shoes or bags. Nice.

To the left was a small living room where broken pieces of glass glittered in the lights she flipped on. They both stopped to listen but didn't hear anything. Kam nodded at the rock in the middle of the shards. When he glanced at Glory, he found her mouth firmed and her expression stoic.

It infuriated him that some chickenshit bastard had done this to her. "Other than that little bit of mess, your living room looks really nice."

It relieved him when her tension eased. "Thank you. I decorated it myself, so I wasn't sure . . ."

Two stuffed couches in pale gray faced each other over a dark wood coffee table. Beneath the window was a simple bench with accent pillows. It seemed odd to him that the couches didn't face the TV, but maybe she didn't watch it much.

Beyond the foyer, still in the center of the house, he spotted the kitchen. "Want to give me a tour so I can make sure everything is secure?"

She gave another glance at the window, drew a shaky breath, and nodded.

He didn't yet tell her that she shouldn't stay here alone, that he should stay, too. She was already off-kilter. It'd be better if he eased her into the idea.

"I'll give you the quick tour," she relented, "but then you need to go." She started on her way, assuming he'd follow. "It'll take me a bit to clean up the mess, and it's already late."

Okay then, no time like the present. Right behind her, he stated, "I'm not going."

Just as matter-of-fact, she said, "Yes, you are." Gesturing, she said, "This is the kitchen."

It was nice and streamlined, with seats at a bar that held the sink. A person could clean a pan and still chat, or tidy the kitchen while keeping an eye on children.

With its location, there were no windows to worry about. "Be reasonable, Glory."

"That's my line to you." Another wave of her hand. "Dining room."

The dining room, with a cathedral ceiling, had a table with four chairs around it, and two more chairs, each of them with padded seats, flanked a window.

Kam lifted the simple blinds to check the lock, but it was secure. "I like your furniture." The gray cushions on the chairs matched the couches, which made sense, given that the rooms flowed together.

Surprisingly, there wasn't much in the way of wall decor and no plants to be seen. He couldn't imagine Glory decorating on a budget. After all, she was part of the McCallahan family. Could she be that different from her cousin? Callie loved plants and was forever adding a piece of artwork or a glass dish to every available surface.

He checked sliding doors that opened to a currently empty covered terrace. It, too, was secure. "I'm not letting you stay here alone."

Slowly, she pivoted to face him. "You're not *letting* me?"

"Time out. Let me rephrase that." God save him from difficult women. She'd known him long enough to know what he meant. "Addie would kick my ass if I walked off right now."

That softened her expression.

Aha! A toehold. *Everyone* liked Addie, so he'd use that to his advantage. "Can you imagine how she'd feel if she knew everything that had gone on tonight, how Mike had hassled you, and now a broken window?"

"Maybe."

"No maybe to it. She'd be pissed if you were here alone. Hell, Glory, she'd come here herself and insist on staying until it got repaired."

"No she wouldn't."

"Want to bet? I'll call her." Like a threat, he lifted his cell phone.

Her sigh of defeat gave him hope.

Leaning down to better see her expression, he promised, "You won't even know I'm here."

"Oh, I'll know."

Hmm. Though he didn't want to, he offered, "I'll sleep on one of the couches."

"Not necessary."

Full of hope, he said, "No?"

"I have a guest bedroom."

Well, hell. "Great."

She bit her lip, undecided, then looked back toward the living room and that broken window. "I have no idea how to secure it for the night."

"I do." Keeping his hands to himself wasn't easy. He wanted to touch her, smooth her hair, brush his thumb over her cheek again . . .

Kiss her senseless.

Instead, he looked into big blue eyes full of exhaustion. Yeah, he felt that. He, too, was tired to the bones. "Got any tools?"

"Oh." She brightened. "I do, yes." Hustling past him, she went through the kitchen, to the foyer and into a single-car garage.

Kam followed, then looked around in interest. Along every

wall, boxes were stacked. He saw a huge framed mirror, some other pieces of art, and three very large house plants.

Glory went to one box and unearthed . . . a pink tool kit.

Knowing it'd piss her off, he fought the grin. She looked so damned pleased with herself, he didn't want to hurt her feelings. Again. "Ah, you came prepared."

"I had the idea of hanging the art and the mirror, but it's heavier than I remembered."

He opened the petite tool kit to find a slender hammer, scissors, bit driver, measuring tape, pliers . . . Nothing all that sturdy but the hammer would do. "Nails?"

She went back to the same big box, dug around, and found a small pack of finishing nails. He looked around the garage again. "Are any of the boxes empty?"

"I, um . . . No."

"Is there one we can empty real quick?" To explain that, he said, "I don't see any wood, and we'll need to cover the window with something, or your house will fill with bugs." Not to mention that a creep could just climb right in.

Biting the corner of her lip, she surveyed each box, then said, "That one." With purpose, she headed for it. "My small appliances are in it. I can unload the stuff here and—"

"How about I just carry it into the kitchen, since that's where I assume the stuff will go?" Without waiting for an answer, he hefted the box into his arms. "You can grab the tool kit for me."

Taking charge seemed easier than waiting for Glory to figure it out, so that's what Kam did. She stuck close, following him as he went back to the living room to measure the size of the window, then back to the kitchen, where he cut the cardboard.

Every time he moved, he nearly bumped into her. He could tell she was nervous, and clearly, she had no idea how all that body contact was getting to him. "Look." He set everything aside and, giving into an urge, put his hands on her shoulders. "Why don't you go have a shower, get changed, and get comfortable while I finish up here?"

The second he'd touched her, she went perfectly still. "You're almost done, aren't you?"

He made the concerted effort not to pull her closer. Not to look at her mouth. A deep quiet inhale helped. "I'm getting there. Once I get the cardboard tacked up, I'm going to move a few things in the garage, so I can park Addie's car in there. I don't trust lover boy not to come around and dick with it."

"He's your lover boy? Wow, you work fast."

Grinning, Kam said, "Love your wit. I never realized you were so funny."

"You bring out the irony in me."

See, that made him lose the battle. Keeping it quick, he bent to press a kiss to her mouth, and before she could react, he said, "Don't worry. I'll be careful not to leave any visible nail holes around your window. And I won't ding anything when I pull in the car. Once you're done with your shower, you can show me the rest of the house and then we'll turn in."

She stepped out of reach. Color tinged her cheeks, but she kept her chin up. "The order of all that doesn't work for me. Instead, why don't you pull in the car, then put up the cardboard. When that's done, we can check the rest of the house together, and then I'll get ready for bed."

"We need to talk, too."

Her smile was faint, there and gone quickly. "In the morning. Tonight, I'm zoned."

Yeah, she looked it. Again overstepping, he stroked a hand over her hair. "All right. Stay here and guard the window while I get the car in. Won't take me a minute."

"Guard it from what?"

"Bugs? Bats? Anything."

Voice squeaking, she asked, "Bats?"

That made up his mind. "Window first, then." While she protested, he quickly got the cardboard up, then sealed the edges with painter's tape. It wouldn't keep out an intruder, but it would keep out prying eyes and insects.

After he pulled in the car, he ensured that the garage window, and an exterior door, which led to the backyard, were also locked.

Within ten minutes, he was back. He found Glory wavering on her feet. "How many rooms are left?"

"My bedroom, the main bathroom, and the guest bedroom."

One shower? That could be tricky, but he'd deal with it. "Okay, let's do this."

Her eyes flared comically.

"Don't put ideas in my head, honey. I meant let's finish checking out the house so you can get some sleep."

She let out a breath. "You must be sleepy, too."

"I'm beat." But he'd leave his door open and listen for her annoying Romeo, just in case.

Her bedroom was nice. The bed and two nightstands were flanked by windows, both locked and covered with curtains. "I notice a neutral theme going on here."

Fingers laced together, she looked around the room as if seeing it for the first time. "I'm a little afraid of color."

"Yeah? Why's that?"

"I'm not great at decorating and—"

"That's a joke, right? Everything you've done so far looks amazing. Like a designer did it or something."

She flushed. "The sales clerks helped." Together, they stepped into the bathroom.

Kam whistled. "Wow, this is a showstopper." A beautiful free-standing slipper tub was positioned smack-dab in front of floor-to-ceiling windows, thankfully covered by long drapes. The separate shower was enclosed in glass. Wooden shelves held towels. Opposite the tub were double sinks and the toilet. Everything was in cream-colored ceramic trimmed in bronze-toned brass.

"I really like this bathroom. It's what sold me on the house—well, that and the proximity to Callie." She lifted a shoulder. "She's staying in Hoker, so I'm staying in Hoker."

"The two of you are close, I know."

"We are, but I like the town. It's grown on me."

Kam remembered how much she'd hated it at first. Everything about it had put her off, including his brother, Tanner. It was nice that she'd softened on things—for Callie.

"It's the only full bathroom, but you can see that it not only opens into my bedroom, but also the hall." She stared worriedly at the hall door.

Using only two fingers, Kam lifted her chin. "Once I clean up for the night, I won't come in here again. Don't worry about me busting in on you."

She blinked fast. "I was just thinking, I'll have to remember to knock on the door before I come in. If you wouldn't mind doing the same?"

He could have teased her, and God knew all sorts of scenarios ran through his head, but in that moment, more than anything else, he wanted to reassure her. "I'll be sure to knock. When I'm in here, I'll lock both doors, then I'll unlock them before I step out."

She smiled up at him. "Good idea. I'll do the same."

Her sweet expression, which was rarely aimed at him, felt like an invitation—until she bolted past him and said, "The guest room is right here. It has a half bath, but that's all."

He peeked in and saw a toilet, pedestal sink, hand towels over a rail, and a matching rug on the floor. "It's nice."

"I'm sorry it's small, but the bedding is all clean and the pillows and quilt are new."

Kam trailed behind her, his thoughts everywhere they shouldn't be. Damn, but it was like Tanner had gotten married and now everything was different, including Glory—and how he felt about her.

"It'll be great, thanks." At least it had a full-size bed. Nothing fancy, which suited him. As she'd said, pillows, sheets, a quilt, even a small lamp on the nightstand . . . "It's everything I'd need."

Sleeping with her would have been better, but he'd make do. Tomorrow, they'd have to figure out how to get their cars fixed, get her window repaired, and share the workload for Callie and Tanner so they could enjoy a few post-wedding days off.

It was going to take some juggling, but he'd have all night to figure it out. It was certain he wouldn't be sleeping.

Glory turned over, trying to get comfortable without much success. She sank into the soft mattress she loved so much, closed her eyes . . . and stayed awake.

She could still hear Kam moving around. Subtle sounds that made her wonder what he was doing. One thing that was different though: She didn't notice the usual sounds of the house settling.

Every sense she possessed was on him.

Listening to him shower had been a revelation. Even with the door locked on her side, she'd stared at it, wondering if it'd suddenly open and he'd be standing there in his naked magnificence.

Hey, a girl could dream. And she did, with her eyes wide open, just in case.

Until moving in here, she'd never slept alone in a house.

After her parents had died, she'd grown up as part of Callie's family. When she'd gone out on her own, it was to an upscale apartment with people living above, below, and on either side of her.

Being alone in a house meant she usually heard every little thing: the settling of the house, the wind outside, the rustling of a branch against the roof . . . Tonight, all she heard was Kam finishing up in the shower, then the click as he unlocked the door from the bathroom side.

Her heart went into her throat and stayed there, but a moment later, she heard the hallway door close, and then his footsteps as he went to the guest room.

Vivid images of him naked continued to plague her. Not that she knew for a fact how he looked, but she'd seen him shirtless and that gave her a little to go on.

Blowing out a slow breath, she willed herself to sleep. On the one hand, knowing Kam was near was enough to keep her blood rushing through her veins. On the other hand, she wasn't alone tonight and so she didn't have to worry about Mike.

Tomorrow, she'd have to figure out her car, so she could get to Callie's and tend the animals. Her cousin had inherited chickens and goats, along with a little ratty house that she'd turned into a cozy home. For now, Callie and Tanner were staying there for a little privacy, but after a mere two weeks, they'd move in next door to Tanner's home with Addie.

It was a much larger place with plenty of room. Callie's house would be remodeled, so it could be used for at-risk teens, as a safe place for them to learn a trade, feel secure, and be guided into adulthood. Glory loved and respected that Tanner had devoted so much of his time to helping others.

In every way, her cousin's new husband was incredibly awesome.

Once they moved in with Addie, Kam planned to move

out. Supposedly, he already had an apartment rented and was just getting it set up. Thinking about Kam, his future plans, and wondering if he'd still be nearby, or too far away for her to see him often, Glory gradually fell asleep.

When she opened her eyes again, dawn was creeping in through the window. Like a kid on Christmas morning, excitement gripped her the moment she remembered that Kam had stayed over.

She sat up, listened, and heard a few faint, distant rumblings. Kam was already up. She left the bed, crept to the door, and peeked out. A light was on in the kitchen, and she could smell coffee.

Quietly closing and locking her door again, she slipped into the bathroom, made sure to lock both doors, and went about making herself presentable. She didn't want to look like she'd done much, but obviously, she had to do *something*.

Liz had told her many times that with her pale lashes and brows, she looked best in full makeup. That would seem too obvious, so after washing her face, cleaning her teeth, and brushing her hair until it was smooth, she put on just a touch of blush, lightly lined her eyes, and applied a single coat of mascara.

Not great, but not bad, either.

She looked down at her comfortable sleep shirt. Callie would walk out wearing it and not think a thing of it, but she wasn't Callie. Not only was the shirt shapeless, making her look shapeless, but the loose neckline showed the thin pale scar left on the top of her shoulder despite plastic surgery. Same with the top of her thigh.

Thinking about those scars automatically sent her hand to her nose, and then her jaw. So much pain, so many surgeries . . .

Because Callie was the best, she'd deliberately chosen a beautiful bridesmaid dress that covered her shoulder. Callie didn't think the scars were a big deal at all, but for multiple reasons, Glory felt very, very differently about them.

Shaking that off, she darted back into the bedroom and chose skinny jeans and a loose summer top. She ruffled her hair a little, so it wasn't too smooth, and left her feet bare to lend credence to her "just woke up" vibe.

Trying to be casual, she went down the hall, stepped into the kitchen, and . . . What? *How?*

Awe put her head on a swivel as she took it all in, from one end of the room to another. Her very basic kitchen, which had been only functioning, now looked like a designer ad. Her beautiful matching canisters were on the counter, the mug rack was set up by the coffeepot, and a lush plant was near the window. In a daze, she drifted to the dining room and saw her large pictures placed near where they'd hang, more plants, and her gorgeous centerpiece—the one she'd taken days to choose—was assembled and placed in the middle of the table with a runner. Unable to take it in, she moved to the living room. Everything she'd bought, each piece she'd so painstakingly selected but had left packed up in her garage so she could concentrate on the wedding, was now showcased.

Everywhere she looked, she found more of the same.

She also found a very shirtless, barefoot Kam in the foyer. Bare shoulder propped on the wall, tux pants hanging low, he spoke quietly into his cell phone.

"No, honey, not happening." With a smile in his tone, he said, "Because I have other shit to do. No, not a woman. Come on, we've been through this."

Glory bristled. Who was he talking to so early?

"Enough of that," he murmured low. "I have work to do. Will you be able to help or not? Great. I owe you—and no, don't say it. I'm not paying you like that."

Whatever the mystery woman said in response caused him to laugh softly. "Thanks. You're a doll. See you then." As soon as he pocketed the phone, he got busy unpacking another box.

This was like waking up in a fairy tale—but instead of facing singing animals, there was one very big hot, sexy—*shirtless*—guy hanging out, decorating her house.

Since he hadn't seemed to notice her, Glory decided to slink silently back to her room.

The second she moved, he said, "Looking is free, but feeling will cost you."

3

"You big faker!"

"Me?" Kam turned with a smile, but it froze when he saw that she'd not only dressed, but also wore makeup. And here he'd thought he might see the real Glory for once. He'd been anticipating it, damn it.

Glory, soft and sleepy, her hair messy, her defenses down. Sign him up.

Instead, she'd put on all her usual armor and looked ready to take on the world.

He couldn't recall ever seeing her when she wasn't fully put together. The woman did not allow herself to be anything less, and it pissed him off. If she kept herself elevated above mortal man, how could he get close? If he wanted close, of course. And he kind of did.

"It's barely seven a.m."

"You can tell time? Bravo." Her eyes narrowed. "Most would consider it far too early to be finagling dates."

"Finagling, huh? Well, Ms. Snoopy, what you listened in on was me turning down a date."

She huffed. "As if that could be called a date."

Starting to enjoy himself, Kam asked, "What does that mean?"

"You know you weren't talking about dinner or a movie."

Forgetting about the box he'd planned to unload, Kam stalked closer to her. "No? What do you think you heard, Glory?"

Her gaze stayed desperately locked on his. "You know."

"Afraid I don't." When he was close enough to touch her, he stopped and looked down into her wide eyes. He also breathed in the scent of toothpaste, floral lotion, and warm woman. "Spell it out for me."

Indecision appeared first, then her chin notched up and she stated in a whisper, "Sex."

"Sex?" he whispered right back.

"You and that woman."

"Her name is Ronna."

Glory's eyes flared even more. "I don't care what her name is."

"She works at the hardware store."

"I have no idea why you're telling me—"

"Her brother is a glazier, so she's hooking me up."

"With her brother?" Glory looked ready to smack him.

"No." Biting back a grin, Kam explained, "They're coming by to replace the broken glass in your window."

Her mouth opened, then smashed shut again. In her eyes, irritation warred with gratitude until, finally, she gave a brisk nod. "Thank you. I could have handled that."

"Oh? You know who to call in Hoker to get home repairs?"

"Well . . . Normally, I would have asked Tanner, but since he's obviously busy—"

"Obviously."

"I would have asked Addie."

"Ah. Anyone but me, huh?" He held out his arms. "Even though I'm right here?"

Her gaze took a quick trip along one arm, over his torso, to the fingertips of his other arm, with some lingering in between, before she cleared her throat. "I can't think when you're standing there like that."

"Shirtless?"

"Flaunting yourself." Half turning away, she waved a hand at his body. "And with your pants undone."

He glanced down. No, he hadn't completely fastened the tux pants. They weren't comfortable. "I'd have been happier just hanging in my shorts—"

Incredulity fueled her loud gasp.

"But since I was in and out of the yard, I figured you'd want me to put on something, and the stiff tux pants are all I have."

In slow motion, she turned to face him again. "You were in my yard looking like that?"

He took evil delight in saying, "You have some nice neighbors."

Hot color crept up her neck to her cheeks and then to her forehead. In a barely there rasp, she asked, "You met Mrs. Simmons?"

"Yeah. She came over to talk to me."

Glory closed her eyes. "I'm sure she did."

Enjoying himself, Kam inched a little closer still. Already, he craved her closeness. "She has to be mid-seventies, right? Yet she was awful curious about you having a man over."

Her throat worked when she gulped.

"Kept staring at my chest, too. Practically made me feel naked."

Lashes lifted, and the blue of Glory's eyes glowed like a flame. "Know why? Because you're *practically naked*."

Those last two words had ended on a high note, making him grin.

After throwing up her hands, Glory took a moment to collect herself.

It was something to see, the way she inhaled, slowly exhaled. Smoothed her already-smooth top. Shook out her hands. Flexed her neck. And finally curved her lips into a smile that conveyed mere curiosity. "Why, exactly, were you in the yard?"

Kam couldn't imagine having that much control. She'd gone from near implosion to cool composure. "Neat trick," he said, even while wishing he'd seen her really let go.

Without her lips moving, she said, "Kam," and there was no missing the warning.

"I had to back out the car so I could unload your garage."

Her eyes nearly crossed. "Why, if you don't mind me asking, did you unload my garage?"

Funny. For a woman who could irritate the hell out of him, she suddenly seemed really . . . cute. Frazzled, for sure. Annoyed, absolutely. But also a little unsure, and the fact that she couldn't keep her gaze off his body spurred him on.

"You know what, Glory? You look like a woman who could use a cup of coffee." Opening a hand to the small of her back, he guided her past the garage door entrance to the hall that led to the kitchen. "Take a seat and I'll serve you."

She propped her sexy rump up on a barstool and put her head in her hands. "What did you tell Nosy Old Lady Simmons?"

Struck by that description, he paused. "That's great. Nosy Old Lady Simmons. It suits her. She grilled me as if she'd found me using a battering ram on the door. I played nice, though—Addie would skin me if I didn't. I explained that someone had broken your window, and I'd camped out to ensure you'd be safe in case the vandals returned."

"Naturally, she saw you as a hero."

"Of course. She also said another neighbor had recently had a tree papered, and someone else had eggs busted on their door."

"A tree papered?"

"Glory, don't tell me you've never indulged in knuckle-headed youth pranks? No? So you've never taken rolls of toilet paper and thrown them all through the branches of a neighbor's trees?"

Fascinated, she shook her head. "Have you?"

"Ha! You think I'd chance you tattling to Addie? Even now, she'd get after me. Once, though, Tanner and I busted some assholes who were throwing eggs at the house."

"Did you call the cops?"

"We're not snitches."

She leveled him with a stern look. "I won't believe you didn't retaliate."

"Naturally not. We chased them down and pounded on them."

"How many were there?"

"Five."

"Five kids your age?"

"Two were Tanner's age, the others a year younger." Which had made them all older than him—not that he'd let that slow him down. Back then, he'd always been looking for a reason to brawl. Punks egging the house? Good enough for him.

Her disbelieving snort tickled him.

"You don't believe me?"

"Five against two?"

Lifting a shoulder, he made it clear it hadn't mattered. "A pissed-off Tanner is worth three men. And I held my own."

"Braggart."

He doctored her coffee the way he knew she liked it. "One of them started crying. Can you believe that? I let him go. Addie would have—"

Interrupting, Glory said, "Do you realize that anytime you do something nice, you blame Addie?"

"Because it's her fault."

"Or to her credit."

"That, too." He slid the mug of steaming coffee in front of her, then took the stool beside her, angling her way so that his knees almost touched her thigh. "Let me know if that's sweet enough."

Cautiously, she turned her head and eyed him. As if deciding he was sincere, she gave her attention to the coffee, sipped, and sighed. "Perfect, thank you."

"Low-fat creamer is nasty." But it was all she'd had in her fridge.

She'd just about taken another drink, but at his comment, she dropped her head and laughed. "You do that on purpose, don't you? Mix in an obnoxious comment with a nice word or act."

"Keeps you guessing." Because he knew she liked Addie, he said, "I have to constantly fight my demons, but these days, they're easier to battle because of Addie."

Curious, she half turned to face him, too. "You have demons?"

Oh, that gentle curiosity mixed with understanding. "Don't we all?" He figured Glory knew a thing or two about that, otherwise she wouldn't always be so defensive.

"I know she adopted you and Tanner."

"Guess God figured I could use an angel, so he sent Addie my way."

She hesitated so long Kam found himself wondering what she'd say.

Reserved, cautious, she asked, "Is that because you had a rough childhood?"

"It sucked, yeah." And that was as detailed as he was going to get. "I dealt with it by being a nonstop asshole. Got me knocked around a lot, but that was easier than thinking, even for a minute, that things would improve." He smirked a little, remembering when Addie first took him in. "She already had Tanner, so I felt like I was horning in, even though Addie swore they both wanted me." That memory got him caught up in a chuckle.

"What?"

"Sometimes I'd catch Tanner giving me the side-eye, you know? Hell, he was a kid, too, and he wasn't sure what to make of me." Years later, Tanner told him that it felt like Addie had brought a rabid raccoon into the house. Thinking of how he'd been back then, the description was apt.

"But now the two of you are close."

"Yeah." These days, he'd die—or kill—for Tanner, if necessary. Addie, too. Having the worst of families first had taught him to recognize the best of families once he had one. "How about you?"

"What do you mean?"

"You were raised with Callie and her folks, right?"

In a flash, Glory turned her attention back to her coffee.

Gently, he said, "Don't want to talk about it, huh? I get that. How about we leave it alone for now?"

"I just . . . I don't know how . . ."

Kam slipped his hand under the cool weight of her hair to the back of her neck, and for one brief moment, he touched his forehead to her temple. "Hey, I get it. Too many times I feel the same." Memories could be a motherfucker. Sometimes they had the power to transport a person right back to a fiery hell.

Surprising him, she clasped his forearm and moved closer, until she was practically in his embrace. Unfortunately, the moment of vulnerability lasted only for a second. When she straightened, she wore a smile that didn't quite hide the wealth of sadness in her eyes. "How did you do all this?"

Confused, he asked, "All what?"

She waved a hand. "The decorating."

Kam glanced around at the house that now looked more like a home. "None of it was a big deal." It had bugged him, seeing it half finished.

He hadn't yet told her that he had an apartment within walking distance of her. Once he got moved in—something he was anticipating—then he'd drop it on her. Until then, fixing up her place had given him an outlet.

"I did a lot of guessing, based on what you had, so if you want any of the plants moved, just let me know. I can hang the pictures too, as long as they're in the right places."

"They're exactly where I wanted them to go."

"I figured since the sizes fit." She had great taste, and the artwork would add a little more color to an otherwise neutral setting. He nodded up the hall toward the mirror. "I'm guessing it's for the foyer?"

"It is, but it was too heavy for me to . . . Kam, I didn't ask you to do any of this."

"Friends don't have to ask, right?" And while he was the topic . . . "Friends also don't need to doll up at the butt-crack of dawn just to say good morning."

Her lips twitched. "I didn't doll up, and dawn came and went."

"About five minutes ago." He studied her face, all the smooth curves and delicate bone structure. "I bet you're really pretty without the war paint."

"War paint?" she sputtered, half in umbrage, half in humor. Then with a wrinkle of her nose, she confessed, "My eyelashes are as pale as my hair, which means they're almost invisible. Without mascara, I look really washed out."

Silly Glory. "I doubt, under any circumstances, that you could be anything but pretty. One of these days, I'll see you a little messy."

"Honestly, you should hold your breath while you wait."

She said it so sweetly it took a second for the taunt to sink in. When it did, he grinned. Hell, around her, he did a lot of grinning. "So . . . It seems we need to talk."

After a sip of her coffee, she asked, "About what?"

"I think you know."

Like a rabbit who just spotted a wolf, she went still, before oh-so-cautiously turning her face to see him. In a mere whisper, she asked, "About the kiss?"

Okay, sure, he could talk about that, too. "I meant your persistent ex."

She deflated. "Oh." With palpable dread, she squared her shoulders and firmed her jaw. "He's not my ex. Like I said, I only went out with him three times, and the first time, it was a group thing."

"Like an orgy?"

When she swatted at him, he ducked out of reach, and she nearly fell off her stool. He caught her with a laugh. "Settle down, slugger. It was just a joke."

Slapping away his hands, she straightened. "Not funny."

No, it really wasn't. "Sorry. You're right. He's a creep, so I should be serious."

As if she didn't trust his about-face, she continued to eye him. "I don't know if *creep* is the right word, but he makes me uneasy. He's just . . . I don't know. He kept trying to move at Mach speed."

Kam waited, and when she didn't say more, he asked, "Care to expound on that?" Mentally, he was already cracking his knuckles. "Like, did the asshole pressure you?"

"Not the way you mean. See, that first time we were all at a party. I'd driven there, and when he asked about leaving together, I declined. He kissed me goodbye and that was it." She held the mug in both hands, her gaze averted. "I didn't particularly feel anything with the kiss, but I liked him okay. He'd been easy and fun, so when he called to ask me out on a second date, I agreed to meet him at a restaurant."

Kam struggled to block the image of Mike kissing her. Of her liking him enough to see him again. He had zero rights to jealousy, but he felt it just the same. Made no sense at all, but there you had it. Most of his time spent with Glory made no sense.

Too much time slipped by while she silently gathered her thoughts. Kam had a bad feeling about things, but then, he'd met Mike—and instantly disliked him. "Did the second date go okay?"

She gave an indolent lift of one shoulder.

No enthusiasm. Great. That relieved him.

"The restaurant was nice. Our booth was private. Candlelight and champagne." Her teeth nibbled at her bottom lip. "I'm not much of a drinker, but he had a few glasses, and he poured on the compliments."

Yeah, Kam hated him, and yet, he had to be fair. "That doesn't sound too bad."

"I know, but it felt off. I mean, no one compliments me like that. It was . . . weird."

Good thing he kept most of his thoughts to himself and chose to tease her instead of telling her how sexy her big blue eyes were, how badly he wanted to tangle his fingers in her hair, how even a hint of her cleavage got his imagination steaming.

What it was about Glory, he didn't know, but from the start, she'd intrigued him, annoyed him, and turned him on.

"What kind of compliments?"

Suddenly animated, she turned to face him, closer, more intense. "He went on and on about my eyes at first, until I was afraid to blink. He kept saying that he could tell how I really saw him, that I had truth in my eyes."

Odd, but . . . "You do have beautiful eyes, Glory."

"Thank you," she said dismissively. "But truth? My eyes don't hold truth." She snorted at the idea. "Then he started in on my lips. I don't remember exactly, but he said stuff like my smile was pure sunshine, and when I smiled at him, he felt like a warrior or something."

Okaaay. "Your lips are nice."

"They're lips. Not sunshine, for crying out loud. I got self-conscious and didn't even want to smile, because he acted like every smile was a gift to him or something."

Rubbing the back of his neck, Kam said, "I can see where that'd be uncomfortable." Especially since he'd rather her special smiles were for him—no, wait. He wanted to sleep with her, not cherish her damned smiles. "Go on."

"It gets worse," she warned.

"You lived it, so I think I can take hearing about it." When she stayed quiet, he nudged her. "Seriously, Glory. I'm here. I'm curious. And I want to help."

"How can you help?"

"I can keep him away like I did last night." Although really, Kam wasn't sure he'd convinced the guy of anything. The dude sounded rabid, like he was obsessed with her or something, and that worried him.

Glory fortified herself with the rest of her coffee. "All I

wanted to do was leave, but then he was so wounded about it. He apologized." She stared into her empty cup and her voice lowered. "He said he knew he'd come on too strong, and he wanted me to forgive him."

Getting up to refill her coffee gave Kam something to do so Glory wouldn't see his building anger.

Anger at Mike, not at her, but he didn't want her to misconstrue his mood. "Did you?"

"I felt like a jerk," she said miserably. "I'm sure you've noticed that I'm . . . awkward."

He wanted to deny it, but she was opening up to him. They were having their first serious conversation, relating without the usual sniping or defensive humor. So he gave her the truth. "Maybe a little, but not in a bad way." At least, he didn't think so now. Getting to know Glory was as difficult as pulling hen's teeth—maybe more so—but he was getting there. "Seems to me that sometimes you're unsure what you're supposed to do, when you could just do what you feel like doing."

A smile teased over her lips, and she tipped her head. "What?"

Yeah, that had sounded confusing even to him. If he told her she was full of artifice, that'd sound too insulting. "I think, occasionally, you try too hard." Likely because her aunt found fault in everything she did. "You could just be yourself."

Flustered, she took the coffee he offered, then burned her mouth when she tried to gulp a drink. "Damn it," she muttered. "See! I shouldn't curse, but when I'm not being careful, I say and do the wrong thing."

"I'm gravely wounded because you said *damn*. I may never be the same." He put a hand to his chest. "Look, I'm getting a bald spot." He circled a finger around his left peck. "Right here."

The quick averting of her gaze didn't hide her amusement. "You just want me to look at your awesome chest."

"It is awesome, isn't it?"

She sputtered a laugh.

"Better," he said, as her lightened mood sank into his heart. "I like it when you relax, Glory." A profound thought struck him. "Actually, I like it when you give me hell, too."

"I like it when you're shirtless." She put a hand over her mouth. "Now you see what you made me say?"

When was the last time he'd had this much fun with a woman? That is, without sex involved? Never that he could remember. "I won't tell if you don't."

Her pleasure lingered as she took a more cautious sip.

"So . . . Mike talked you into another date?"

Along with her nod, she sighed. "It was a massive mistake. At least I hadn't let him pick me up." She shot him a look. "I'm not big on that. I prefer to have my car so I can escape whenever I want."

"Good planning." Yet, the idea of her needing to escape got him riled all over again. Her effect was an assault on his senses—one second wringing a laugh from him, then stirring up unfamiliar tenderness, and always mixed with the other emotions was the edgy lust.

"You're staring at me," she said.

With a mental shake, he asked, "Where did the two of you go?"

"An outdoor market, which seemed harmless enough. It was near the river. Lots of vendors and small restaurants. We did some shopping for kitschy stuff, ate samples for a lot of different foods, walked along the river with a steady stream of other people."

"Where did it go off the rails?"

"During the walk. He took my hand and told me how perfect

we were together. We liked the same food, the same flowers, we both enjoyed the live music." As if shamed, she looked away and her voice dropped. "Everyone likes live music, the food was different, and I didn't even remember flowers."

"Glory." Cupping a hand to her shoulder, he offered comfort. "He had no right to pressure you. Or to make you uncomfortable."

"I tried to pull my hand away, but he held on."

Son of a bitch. When Kam felt her slight trembling, protectiveness surged, stronger than ever. Hell, it leveled him. "You should have nutted him."

Choking on a laugh, she swatted his arm—and then allowed her hand to linger a few heavy heartbeats before she withdrew. "There were people all around us. I didn't want to cause a scene."

"Fuck that. If he didn't turn you loose, it'd be him causing the scene, not you."

Guilt flashed over her face. Her smile disappeared as she looked down at her hands. "Maybe you're right, but at the time, I didn't know what to do."

Damn it, now he was the one making her feel bad. He scooted closer. Knowing her as he did now, he should have kept his big mouth shut. She second-guessed herself enough as it was. "Hey, I get it. It's tough to know what to do when someone takes you by surprise like that."

"When he started detailing how perfect our lives were going to be as a couple, it more than surprised me; it blindsided me. I had just started thinking that he wasn't that bad, and boom! He detailed our lifetime commitment. *On a third date.*"

Being this close to her played havoc with his system. Kam wanted to tug her into his lap, wrap his arms around her, and tell her that she didn't have to worry about Mike.

Instead, he said, "You're right to stay away from him. I'm sorry I didn't immediately back you up at the reception." Gently, he touched her chin until she faced him. "It won't happen again."

"That's a big promise to give."

Yeah, it was. Maybe misguided, too. Glory had a great job, social connections, a well-to-do family looking out for her—even if her aunt was often a pain in the ass—and she had a great education and a plan for her future.

What did she need from him? Nothing really.

But a few times now, he'd gotten her to laugh.

Last night, he was able to help her out with Mike.

In the long run, though, he couldn't offer her anything she didn't already have.

And good God, now he was thinking like Mike!

"Callie is now my sister."

"Sister-in-law."

"Same thing to me, so that makes you . . ."

Brows lifting, she waited.

Given how badly he wanted her, he had to search for the right word. "Important."

Deadpan, she said, "Well, I'm glad I'm not in the sister category."

"Or even the cousin category." He leaned closer. "Not with the way I've kissed you."

"There is that."

"And the way I want to kiss you again."

She looked at his mouth.

Time to regroup and fast, before he accepted her innocent invitation. "So what did you do with Mike? How'd you get away from him?"

"I agreed that I'd had fun—but I made it clear that it was

only in a very casual way, that I wasn't thinking about more, and he shouldn't be thinking about it, either."

"And?"

"Because he seemed strangely volatile, I nicely asked him to let me go. He gave me a smug smile and told me he could be patient. When he stopped squeezing my hand, I made sure he couldn't get a hold of me again. I kept us in the middle of the crowd, and I made a beeline for my car."

She'd been truly spooked; Kam could see it in her eyes—in how she held herself now. "Guess he didn't get the message."

She shook her head. "Since then, he's called or texted me a dozen times. It's like I can't shake him."

"Have you been outright rude to him?"

"You heard me in the parking lot! I told him it had been three dates. Only three. I've turned him down ever since—or I've ignored his calls or texts. The last time I spoke to him, I said I was moving, I'd been assigned a new job, and I wasn't interested in any involvement at all."

"Then he showed up here."

Storm clouds gathered in her eyes. "I hadn't told him where I was."

Needing her to know, he said, "I wasn't doubting you, but he still found out."

"I can't believe Tina told him, but then, I'd never told her what a pain he's been because he was her friend. I figured I'd just leave and never see him again."

"I hate to say it, I really do, but the guy sounds deranged."

Worry lifted her shoulders and amplified her uncertainty. "I know."

"Do you think he messed with our tires?"

"No idea—and that's the truth. All in all, I don't even know him that well."

"You know he's got his sights set on you and that he's determined." Kam stroked her hair again, then tunneled into the warm silk and curved his hand around her nape. "I told him to leave you alone, but he said he couldn't because he loved you."

Closing her eyes, she groaned. "Just as I don't know him, he doesn't really know me. If he did, he'd know . . ." She gave a firm shake of her head. "Never mind."

What had she been about to say? "Whatever it is, you can tell me."

The sound she made disproved his assertion. "You don't know me, either, Kam."

Not as well as he'd like to. "I'm trying."

"It's absurd, all of it."

That he was interested? Maybe a little absurd, given when he'd first met her she'd been aloof. "Have you told Callie any of this?" If Callie knew, Tanner probably knew, which meant Glory wouldn't need him at all.

"No way." Giving him the full force of her stare, she added, "Callie just got married. She's taking a week to celebrate. One lousy week. I'm not about to intrude on that, so promise me right now that you won't say anything."

Since he'd rather be the one helping her, he agreed. "No problem."

His easy agreement threw her, until he added, "So here's what we need to do."

Glory drew back. "We?"

Did she have to sound so skeptical? Sure, he'd already ingratiated himself into her life—not in a sick way like Mike the Stalker, but still. He had her best interests at heart, and unlike Mike, he wouldn't pressure her.

Except he might pressure her a little to accept his help.

If she insisted that he get lost anyway, then he'd talk to Tanner and Callie and let them know what was going on. But he wouldn't coerce her, and he wouldn't manipulate her.

That meant he needed to use good old-fashioned persuasion.

Kam couldn't remember the last time he'd had to deliberately turn on the charm with a woman. Hopefully, he hadn't lost his edge.

4

Glory was almost relieved when a knock sounded on the door. Not quite, because the play of emotions over Kam's features had fascinated her. At first, he'd appeared annoyed by her doubt.

Here's what we need to do.

Other than Callie, no one had ever offered her that kind of backup, as if they would tackle a difficult issue together. Mike most definitely wasn't his problem. She didn't even want him to be her problem. Why she'd unloaded on him, she wasn't sure, except that she was used to sharing everything with Callie, and with her cousin out of the immediate picture, she felt adrift in a big way.

That didn't mean she should burden Kam, though. Hadn't he already done enough?

Feigning relief, she stepped away from him and said, "Oh, what do you know? A surprise visitor."

Kam kept pace with her until she stopped in the living

room and looked at him over her shoulder. "What are you doing?"

"Going with you to get the door."

"You're not dressed."

"Dressed enough." He stepped around her. "Besides, it's probably Ronna and her brother."

Suffering some bizarre form of possessiveness, she all but jumped in front of Kam, barring him with her open arms. "At least fasten your pants."

"You're hissing at me. This ferocious side of you is worth experiencing."

"Decency isn't ferocious," she pointed out, while trying to erase all emotion from her face. Where was her cool detachment when she needed it?

His sexy mouth did that little twitching thing again. "Coming from you, it is."

With a long deliberate sigh, she gave up and dropped her arms. "Can you at least button up?"

"Yes, dear." With great fanfare, he snugged up the zipper and fastened the button. "Better?"

Ho, boy. Her gaze couldn't seem to move away from that tantalizing area around his fly. Seeing his hands right there, touching that firm abdomen, did funny things to her. Kam wasn't muscle bound, just very fit. Lean and hard. And she liked how that happy trail of dark silky hair disappeared beneath the waistband . . .

Kam crossed his arms. "I feel like I should be hanging off a meat hook."

Instead of acknowledging her faux pas, she spun away and raced to the door, aware of him chuckling behind her. The sexy jerk.

After pulling open the door, she said in a brisk and friendly tone, "Good morning."

Clearly, Ronna was disappointed that Kam hadn't answered, but it was Glory's house after all. It was past time she got control of herself and her life.

And the sensible side of her knew, without a doubt, that Kam wasn't in the equation.

Never before had she thought she'd enjoy feeding goats, but her cousin's goats were special. Callie knew their names, not that Glory could remember. Same with the chickens. Farm animals who were like beloved pets.

Her cousin had taken to country life easily. Glory had needed more time, but eventually the slower pace, the fresh air, and the people had won her over.

It helped that she'd gotten a promotion in the company with Callie's parents. No more nonstop flying from destination to destination. Now she could mostly work remotely from home, with trips to the office twice monthly, or when special needs arose.

Getting the animals out of the pens was easy. They were ready to fill the yard. As she'd been taught, Glory double-checked that the gates were all secure, then released them. Next, she refilled water reservoirs with fresh water and put out feed.

The chickens still worried her a little; she did not want to get pecked.

And the goats, with their creepy eyes and their eerie wailing spooked her.

Okay, so she'd never be good at this. She did well enough to give her cousin a break, and that's what mattered.

Fortunately, Addie said she'd handle gathering the eggs.

"You're getting good at that." As if she'd been summoned, Addie stepped up behind her with a basket.

Praying she wouldn't blush after everything that had happened with Kam, Glory smiled at her. "Good morning."

"Morning yourself, Sunshine."

Was Addie's smile a little more knowing this morning? The bump of a goat kept Glory from wondering about it too long. With a laugh, she awkwardly patted the goat's head and, keeping a wary eye on it, stepped aside. "Any sign of the newlyweds?"

"Not a peep." Glowing with happiness, Addie glanced at the house. "I can't tell you how pleased I am to have Callie for a daughter."

That's how Addie looked at it, but then, she'd claimed Callie almost from the day she'd moved in. "Callie feels the same."

"My Tanner deserves the best, but I'd almost given up on him ever settling down. He was always so driven, so determined to make a difference in our town and to help others, that he never slowed down enough to really help himself."

Glory had learned how dedicated Tanner was about helping underprivileged kids, especially those from neglectful or abusive homes. "He's amazing, but then he had you to help guide the way."

"I'd like to think I loved him enough to show him a better way than he'd known, but even if I hadn't, I think Tanner would have found his path. From the day I saw him walking down the street with a broken arm . . ." Her voice faded beneath memories, stealing her smile with it. "God gave me such a gift when He guided me to Tanner. Then to give me Kam, too? I've lived such a blessed life."

When the world blurred before Glory, she realized tears had filled her eyes, and she had to quickly blink them away. Since the wedding, she'd been far too emotional.

"I love how you talk about them." It was something she'd never witnessed from her own parents, and never with such depth from Callie's folks.

Catching herself, Addie gave a soft laugh and shook her head. "Listen to me, going on and on. Sorry about that. Guess I'm just floating on a cloud these days seeing my boys so happy." She went into the henhouse to get the eggs, leaving Glory alone with her thoughts.

The hot sun baked down on her, and she inhaled the scents of the surrounding woods, with the richer scent of the animals. It wasn't unpleasant.

Leaning against a large oak tree, she let her thoughts wander. She knew a little about Tanner's wretched home life, and that he'd moved in with Addie when he was thirteen. Kam had joined them later, when he'd only been ten. In such a short time, Addie had gone from lonely widow to single parent of two unruly, needy boys.

Glory never heard much about Kam's background, about what might have sent him into Addie's care, but she believed no one could love him more than Addie. Few people could be as special as her.

As Addie stepped back out, she asked, "Where is Kam? I figured he'd be with you."

Since she had Addie's car, Glory automatically apologized. "I'm sorry. When we got to my house last night, we found a broken window." Willing herself not to blush, Glory told a simplified tale. "With the flat tires and then a rock through my window—"

"A rock?"

"Kam said he didn't want to leave me alone."

"Of course, he didn't! Who would do such a thing, though?"

Unwilling to speculate about Mike, Glory shrugged. "Ronna and her brother came out to fix the window, so Kam stayed behind and here I am. I hope you don't mind, but I was going to use your car to go back and get him when I'm done here, and then we'll get our cars fixed."

"Hard to believe Kam agreed to stay behind."

Glory was still a little surprised by that, too. He'd been so friendly with the oh-so-helpful Ronna that Glory had only wanted to escape. "My understanding is that Ronna did him a special favor by getting to the window repair so quickly."

Waving that off, Addie said, "He's friends with a lot of girls, but don't let that bother you."

The forced laugh came out a little louder than Glory meant it to. "Why would it bother me?" Just because he'd kissed her, and teased her, and talked with her so earnestly over coffee . . .

He'd even gotten the boxes from her garage unloaded. She still didn't know what to make of that. "We couldn't be in two places at once, and neither of us wanted Callie and Tanner to have to work today."

Just then, the back door opened, and Callie strolled out, barefoot, in an oversized T-shirt and cutoffs. Her hair was in a high ponytail, and she wore no makeup. Despite, this, she glowed.

"You were supposed to take the day off!" Glory smiled as she opened her arms.

"When I have a chance to see my two favorite women in the entire world? No way." Stepping into the hug, she squeezed Glory tightly.

"You're in a good mood," Glory teased. "Wonder why that is."

"Because she loves my son, that's why. Now you two behave. Mothers don't need details."

"You summed it up anyway. I'm happy." She turned to hug Addie, too. "Deliriously happy. With Tanner—who is the most amazing man in the world—but also with my family."

Glory and Addie glanced at each other.

"Oh, come on," Callie said. "I have the most beautiful, spirited, trustworthy sister ever, and now I have a mother-in-law who blows me away with her kindness and generous spirit."

Glory loved that Callie considered her a sister more than a cousin. Being mostly raised together had made them close.

"Such praise," Addie teased. "But thank you."

"I am so ready to embrace my new world." Callie turned to Glory. "But first, you're going to tell me what's wrong."

Startled by the demand, Glory opened her mouth to deny any problems.

Callie didn't give her the chance. "No fudging because I know you too well." With a nudge, she said, "I'm married, but still interested in anything that concerns you, just as I know you would be with me."

"But you have a new husband waiting on you."

"No, I don't." Callie hooked one arm through Glory's, the other through Addie's. "Tanner just left."

The day after his wedding? "To go where?"

"The reception hall. He's going to pick up Kam, Liam will meet them there, and together, they'll get the tires changed."

Addie laughed while Glory sputtered.

Liam, too? She hated the idea of imposing on his day. "But how did you . . . Who told you . . ."

"We're part of a small town now," Callie said. "You should know that nothing stays secret for long."

Once her brother drove off, Ronna was on him. Laughing, Kam held her back. "What are you doing?"

"Getting you to pay up." Damp lips landed on his neck, followed by a hot tongue.

"Ronna," he chided, wondering how the hell he was going to get out of this one. "I told you, that's a no-go."

"I'll convince you." With no more warning than that, her

small hand cuddled his crotch through the tux pants, making him jump.

"Hey now." Getting his jewels well out of reach of grabby hands became a priority, good manners be damned. He felt molested. With more force, he stepped away from her, keeping her at bay with the length of his arms which, thankfully, were long. "Haven't you ever heard that no means no?"

"From you?" Her smile promised wicked things. "You never say no."

He hadn't before, but everything was different. "I'm saying it now."

Finally catching on, she scowled up at him. "Is that a joke?"

"I was clear, Ronna."

She studied his face. "I thought you were playing around!"

Had it come off that way? Maybe. "I'm sorry if I confused you."

Being a genuinely good person, Ronna gave up with a smile. "Well, damn. I already had my motor revving."

Relieved that she wasn't mad, or still grabbing for him, Kam relaxed. "I have no doubt there are ten guys lined up and waiting who would be thrilled to help with that."

"Probably twenty," she shot back with a cocky grin. "So is it the homeowner? What was her name? Glory?" Her gaze went over him. "Of course, it is. You're still in your tux from the wedding."

"Don't jump to conclusions, hon. My brother married her cousin, so she's family."

With a snort, Ronna let him know what she thought of his logic. "Sell that somewhere else. I know you too well. And so we're clear, you still owe me."

Forging past most of what she'd said, he agreed to owe her. "As long as you understand that I can't pay up the way you wanted."

"Don't worry," she said on the way to her car. "I'll think of something else."

Since Glory had already paid for the work, there was nothing for Kam to do but thank Ronna again and wave as she left.

While he waited for Glory to return, he hung her pictures and mounted the heavy mirror. He liked it. It looked good there.

Other boxes remained in the garage, and he thought they might go in the bedrooms, but without Glory's explicit direction, he wasn't going in there. It'd cross a line, and he knew it.

He'd just finished putting away the tools and was stuffing himself into the uncomfortable tux shirt when a knock sounded on Glory's front door.

Hoping it wasn't Ronna returning, while idly wondering if Mike the Dick would dare to show up, he went down the hall with a purpose. When he swung the door open, it was Tanner, and he didn't look happy.

"What the hell?" Leaning out the door, Kam looked around and quickly realized that Tanner had come alone. "Where is your wife?"

"At home with her cousin." Tanner muscled his way in, then shoved a bag of clothes at Kam. "Get changed so we can go."

Lost as to what was going on, he said, "Sure, thanks." He closed and locked the door, stepped into the living room, and stripped off the tux pants. "Want to tell me where we're going?"

"Dan Fellows was in a car wreck last night."

In only his boxers, jeans held loosely in his hand, Kam straightened. Misgivings swamped him, with anger hot behind it. "He gave Glory and me a lift."

"I know. He was on his way home when someone almost hit him. He veered to avoid the collision, slammed into a light pole, and now he has a concussion and a broken arm."

"Jesus." Kam's thoughts scrambled down a dangerous path. "The other driver?"

"Never stopped." Tanner loomed over him. "Do I have to dress you myself?"

Stepping into his jeans, then pulling on the T-shirt, Kam dressed with alacrity. "Dan's home now?"

"Yes." Looking around, Tanner took in Glory's home. "This is nice."

Kam refrained from volunteering his part in the decor. "She has good taste, doesn't she?"

Gaze coming back to him, Tanner said, "Her car was fucked with, and then the guy who gave her a ride was run off the road. I don't care how good her taste is, she can't stay here alone."

"I don't disagree." He should have known Tanner would hear of the trouble. Though he might have started life as an outcast in the town, as he'd matured, his brother had made alliances along with friendships. People respected him, and many looked up to him.

After pulling on his socks and sneakers, Kam folded the tux pants and shirt, stuffed them in the bag, then went to the bedroom he'd used to gather up his shoes, socks, and jacket. He turned and nearly plowed into Tanner.

"This is where you slept?"

Rolling his eyes, Kam stepped around him. "I got the feeling you were in a hurry."

"I have a new wife at home, so yeah."

"Glory and I didn't want to bother you. We had a plan for the day."

"I know, but I have a better plan."

Giving up, Kam turned to him and said, "Enough of the big-brother act, dude. We're both grown men."

For only a second, Tanner grinned at him. "I like the role, so sue me."

Yeah, other than their shaky start so many years ago—when Kam had been a complete pain in the ass—Tanner had always embraced the idea of having a brother. "Want the quick tour?"

"Sure."

It didn't surprise Kam that Tanner was as impressed with the bathroom as he'd been, though the entire house was nice. As they headed back to the living room, Kam asked, "So why are we rushing?"

"Liam's meeting us at the hall with spares." He gave Kam a quick glance. "We'll take them to the garage and inspect the damage. With luck, they can be repaired."

"It was late when we found them flat." With Mike hanging around. "I just wanted to get Glory home."

"I understand that."

Disgust at himself kept Kam frowning. "Damn, Tanner, it's the day after your wedding." And instead of enjoying his new life, he'd shown up to lend a hand. "I would have figured it out today, you know." But it would have been afternoon at the earliest.

"I don't like the idea of your and Glory's cars in the lot that long, not after the flats and then Dan being run off the road."

Kam nodded at the living room. "Her window was broken, too."

Speculative, Tanner wore his own frown, but short on time, he didn't linger. "Come on. We can talk on the way."

"Glory was coming back to pick me up."

"Callie doesn't know about Dan yet, but she knows you need help with the cars, so she'll spend the morning with

Glory and Addie." He slid behind the wheel, and once Kam was in, he added, "I made her promise they wouldn't go anywhere until she hears from me."

"You think it's that serious?"

Rolling one shoulder, Tanner said, "Got a bad feeling about it."

"I'm not feeling too good about it myself." And they never discounted their intuition, not since they'd learned to trust Addie. "I'll make sure to pay Liam for his time."

Tanner nodded his thanks.

Liam was an almost twenty-year-old who'd gotten out on his own after a rough start in life. Overall, Tanner, Kam, and Addie treated him like extended family. Wasn't hard to do when Liam was so appreciative of everything ever done for him.

After a quick debate with himself, Kam said, "Some dude named Mike was hanging around last night, hoping to give Glory a ride. She didn't want me to say anything to you, but you already know most of it now."

"Did he see Dan?"

"Yeah, he was there when Dan offered us a ride."

"This gets more interesting by the second."

It got more . . . something. Because of his promise to Glory, he wouldn't go into any details about Mike, but with Dan being run off the road, he had to make sure his brother was on guard. "Mike could be a problem. He's pushy and doesn't seem to take *no* for an answer."

"No to you, or to Glory?"

"Both." Keeping it simple, Kam added, "Keep an eye out. I don't know if he's still around, if he's staying in town—"

"If he's the clown who broke Glory's window."

"Exactly." How far would Mike take it, and just how dangerous could he be? "Right now, he's an unknown, and I don't like it."

"Isn't your new apartment supposed to be around here somewhere?"

Supposed to be? Kam had no doubt that Tanner knew exactly where the place was. It was only because of the wedding that Kam hadn't yet moved in.

Knowing his brother liked to bait him, and that he'd get to the point soon, Kam nodded at a cross street. "It's right there, in that four-family." Close enough that he could be at Glory's in two minutes, tops. Sooner if he ran.

Seconds ticked by before Tanner gave a disgruntled huff. "I still don't understand why you're leaving."

"I'm not *leaving*." Wasn't like he was abandoning his family. "I'm twenty-six. Past time I get my own place."

The flexing of Tanner's hands on the wheel gave away his mood. "Callie thinks it's because of her, because she's moving in. She's worried that—"

"For God's sake. I hope you told her that was nonsense."

"I did."

Since Tanner's tension didn't ease, Kam's annoyance grew. "Callie is a sweetheart. I enjoy her company, and more than that, I love that you have her and that she has you. I could happily live with her around—if I hadn't already decided that I wanted my own space."

That didn't appease Tanner. "I like having my family together."

Laughing with frustration, Kam ran his hands over his face. "There's together, and then there's together. I will always be there for you and Addie, and now Callie, too." And Glory, though he wouldn't say that out loud. "Always."

Because he understood Tanner, Kam knew he wanted to keep the people he loved close at hand. The start that each of them had had in life . . . It was the sick, twisted kind of hurt that crawled deep and lived with you the rest of your days. By taking them in, Addie had literally saved them, showed them the type of unconditional love they hadn't known was possible, and taught them the meaning of family.

It was important to Kam, too, but equally important was his need to prove he could make it on his own. "I'm not you, Tanner. I'd appreciate it if you gave me space to do my own thing."

Exhaling, Tanner ceded with a tight nod. "You're right. I guess with our backgrounds, I like having everyone close together and accounted for—a tight family, know what I mean?"

"You're protective by nature and like to keep an eye on everyone." Kam knew it well. He'd rarely had to fight a battle on his own once Tanner became his brother. "We'll still be tight. You'll see me every day if you want. Addie's already made me promise to come back for dinner."

That further loosened Tanner's shoulders. "Yeah, you can't be missing her food. It'd make her sad."

That's something he'd never want to do. But he hated the idea of disappointing Tanner, too. For ten years, before Addie had taken him in, Kam was told the type of man he'd one day be. The worst type of human.

So many times, he'd been punished for something he hadn't done, but for what others assumed he'd one day be. *You're just like your father. A no-good bastard.* Remembering put a lead weight on his chest. *You're in his image. Hateful, mean—every woman's nightmare.*

Solemn, Tanner reached over to clap him on the shoulder. "You're a good man, Kam."

Christ, he hated it when Tanner read his mind. The grin cracked, and he shook his head. Yes, it bugged him, but at the same time, he appreciated it. "I'll still be around helping with the tree farm, and you know you can count on me to stay involved with the kids."

A new type of peace showed in Tanner's smile. "Callie's ready to pitch in, too. She's actually looking forward to it."

See? How could he not love Callie? Not only did she embrace Tanner's work with at-risk kids, she wanted to do her own share.

"I have some welding classes set up with them, and a few field trips planned to visit the shop. A couple of the boys, and one of the girls, have shown interest." As a welder, Kam worked on everything from farm equipment to artistic sculptures, and a lot of stuff in between.

"You need to be close to Glory."

"And I will be." He could multitask as well as Tanner. "That is, if she'll let me. I'm working on that."

"Work harder. If you can't convince her to let you stick around, then Callie is going to insist that she comes to stay with us."

Ha! "Won't happen," Kam warned. "She wants you two to have some privacy since you didn't take an official honeymoon."

"I was willing, but Callie wanted to stick close to home as much as I did."

She was *so* perfect for Tanner.

"If it doesn't work out, you know Addie is going to ask to stay with Glory, and I'll be damned before I let that happen. Until we sort out if this Mike creep is plaguing her, I don't want Addie involved."

"I'll figure it out," Kam promised. And somehow, he'd make that come true.

Electrified by his plan, Mike rode beside Jones, the tow truck driver who would earn a small fortune today. Once

Glory's car was loaded up, Mike would give her a call and ask her where she wanted it delivered. He'd not only be her savior, he'd get to spend quality time with her.

Burning contempt filled him when he thought of how she'd dismissed him last night. After all the trouble he'd gone through, she should have been grateful. Then again, he'd known from the start that Glory McCallahan was different. Too often she looked down her pert nose at him, only sparingly doling out scraps of affection. Goddesses were like that.

Her resistance only made the rewards sweeter, especially since he knew how it would end. For now, she could pretend she didn't want him. He'd play along until the time was right.

And then he'd end the games.

The memory of her surprise curled the corners of his mouth. She'd jumped when he'd first spoken to her in the dark parking lot, the two of them all alone. Her obvious anxiety had excited him. He could have given her a taste of their inevitability—but the other guy had intruded, all cavalier, as if he had the right to interrupt when he absolutely did not. *He* didn't matter.

Unless he got in the way one too many times. Then Mike would have to deal with him.

"Turn here," he told Jones.

Silently, the driver did as he was told.

Mike knew that when you paid enough, there were no questions.

The hall was empty right now; he'd already checked their online schedule of events. Nothing was happening until tomorrow afternoon.

"Her car is in the back lot."

The driver whistled as he pulled in. "Slick ride."

"Yes. For such a sedate woman, she has a flashy side." The red Mustang felt like a show of rebellion. Most in her position would have driven something less sporty. Something classic that showed off her station in life.

Not his Glory.

It thrilled him, that wild streak she tried so hard to hide. It was something they could work on together, once he'd cemented their relationship. With his guidance, she'd be as perfect as she always tried to be.

In ways Glory couldn't yet understand, they were made for each other. He felt it down to his soul and eventually she'd feel it, too.

One way or another, he'd make sure she did.

"Motherfucker," Kam rasped, sitting forward in his seat and glaring at the tow truck ready to hook up Glory's car. Tanner had barely slowed the truck before Kam was out, anger carrying him forward in long strides.

Having already spotted him, the startled truck driver tried to get it in gear to drive forward, but Tanner had the foresight to block him in.

Kam reached the truck, jerked the door open, and around the cringing driver, he grabbed the keys.

"Hey," the driver said. "You can't—"

When Kam's glare landed on him, the driver raised his hands. "I'm just here for a job."

The job of stealing Glory's car? "Did she give you permission?"

"No, but he did."

Just then, Mike stepped forward and said, "Kam, hey. It's good to see you again." He'd come around the back of the tow truck, all smiles, as if he hadn't been trying to manipulate Glory again.

Fighting the urge to remove Mike's smile with his fist, Kam got to his first question. "What the fuck do you think you're doing?"

Confusion filled Mike's expression. "Why are you angry?" Then with dawning horror, "My God. Did something happen with Glory? Is she okay?"

Taken aback by that reaction, Kam clenched and unclenched. "Glory is fine." Better than fine; she was safe with family. "Did you have permission to move her car?"

Blowing out a deep sigh of relief, Mike slumped against the tow truck. "Don't scare me like that. The way you were acting—"

"Answer my question."

With a conspiratorial smile, Mike leaned toward him. "I was going to surprise her. You know how women are. They don't want to have to deal with stuff like this."

That sentiment mirrored his own a little too closely for Kam to correct him, but he did say, "Glory is resilient. She'd have figured it out." Studying the other man, Kam watched for any telltale signs of deception. "As it happens, she doesn't need to—and she doesn't need your help. I'm here to take care of it for her."

"Oh?" Mike's smile tightened. "She gave *you* permission?"

No, she hadn't, but only because he hadn't asked. Now, of course, he realized he should have. He'd apologize for that as soon as he saw her. For now, he just fudged things a bit. "I had to come for my car anyway."

"But I already have the tow truck. Jones has been paid and he's ready to handle it." Arrogantly generous, Mike offered, "I'll even have him come back for your car, if you'd like."

"No thanks. It's already handled."

"But—" The rebuttal dropped off when his attention caught on something—or someone—behind Kam's shoulder.

The way Mike fell back a step was a clear sign that Tanner had joined them.

Looming large and angry, Tanner asked, "Is it already hooked up?"

"No, but in another minute or two, it would've been gone."

Jones said, "I haven't touched it, I swear!"

"Count yourself lucky." Tanner stepped up alongside Kam. "This is the guy?"

Somewhat recovered, Mike lifted his eyebrows. "The guy? If you mean Glory's boyfriend, then yes, I'm the guy."

Tanner made a rude sound. "Odd that she's never mentioned you. Even odder that she'd dodge you." He took another step forward. "But she won't have to do that anymore, right?"

Far as threats went, Tanner's was clear. Kam scowled. Damn it, he could handle Mike on his own. To Tanner, he said, "See what's keeping Liam. I've got this."

Reluctantly, Tanner stepped toward his truck to make the call.

Knowing he wouldn't have much time, not with the way his "big brother" liked to oversee things, Kam moved toward Mike. "Let's talk."

Amicable in the extreme, Mike smiled and followed along. "Of course."

He went only as far as Glory's car. "You know anything about Glory's broken window?"

Showing only enigmatic concern, Mike regarded her car. "One of the windows is broken?"

Animosity heating, Kam had to admit that Mike was either one hell of a liar or certifiably unhinged enough to believe his own bullshit. No way was he innocent. "At her house."

"She has a house?" Affecting the look of a proud boyfriend, Mike said, "I shouldn't be surprised. She's a hard worker and she has a great job with a supportive family. I just never pictured her in a home of her own. She's always enjoyed an apartment." He grinned. "I assumed the responsibilities of a house didn't interest her."

Done being nice, Kam said, "*You* don't interest her. Last night, Glory was clear." Mike started to speak, but Kam crowded closer, cutting him off. "She doesn't want you around, and she damn sure doesn't need your favors. I told you once already, so this is your last chance. Leave her alone."

Finding his spine, Mike stiffened. "You're threatening me?"

"Just giving you pertinent details."

"Sounded more like a threat to me. So spell it out. What are these dire consequences?"

The thing was, Kam had dealt with every kind of person in existence: bad, ugly, mean, misunderstood, and dangerous. Where Mike fell, he didn't yet know. The urge to strike him was there, tightening his hands into fists, causing his shoulders to bunch.

His father had settled disputes, and in just about every other situation, in that exact way, but by God, he was not his father.

He considered himself smarter and more controlled, so he knew not to state his intent upfront. It was always better to hold on to your ammunition so it couldn't be used against you.

If it became necessary, he'd take Mike apart and probably enjoy it, but for now, he didn't want to give the prick a reason to call the cops.

Filling his smile with evil intent, Kam pressed closer, close enough that Mike shrunk back, tucked in his chin, and turned his face away to keep from touching.

"She's not alone, Mike." Without raising his voice, Kam put steal into his tone. "I'm in the picture and I'm telling you flat out: Stay. Away. From her."

5

The turbulent ire churned within Kam all the way home. He'd thought the drive would give him a chance to cool down, but instead his thoughts played an endless loop of all the ways a man could plague a woman. Never before had he felt such an overwhelming need to ensure a woman's safety.

Yet, he felt that for Glory.

Tanner had agreed that Mike reeked of danger. Not just pushy, not just lovesick or annoying. Something was off with Mike, something dark and desperate.

And the guy wouldn't quit. So far, Kam had seen him in three different modes: full of boisterous teasing when he tried to convince Glory to let him give her a ride, sad despair when he confessed to Kam that he loved her, and now this over-the-top shit with trying to commandeer her ride.

What mood would he be in next?

Thinking about that bothered Kam enough that even driving Glory's flashy Mustang didn't distract him.

Worse, the second he pulled in to Callie's driveway, he saw all three women hanging out on the front porch, drinking iced tea and eating cookies as if they didn't have a care.

He wished that were true, but both he and Tanner had decided that extra precautions were in order.

Starting with getting Glory's consent to let him stay close. If he had to, he'd sleep on her front porch.

Smiling, Glory walked over. "You got my car."

Trying for a lighter mood, Kam stepped out and ran a hand along the glossy hood. "She's a beauty. I enjoyed being behind the wheel."

Glory beamed at him. "I love her, too. She was one of my indulgences when I got a nice bonus back when I turned twenty. Even though she's not new anymore, I can't imagine trading her in."

So only five years ago? Another way in which they differed; to him, a five-year-old car was definitely still new.

"I've kept her in good shape."

Okay, so his teasing didn't work if Glory also considered the car a "she."

"Callie told me Tanner was going to lend you a hand." She turned her face up to his. "Were you able to get your tires fixed, too?"

Nodding, Kam handed over the keys. "Liam showed up with some spares and helped get them changed out. We took the cars to the shop—it was only a couple of miles—and got the tires repaired. Tanner's driving his truck and Liam's bringing my SUV home. I'll drop him off when—" *when I head back to your house* "—I wrap up here."

Missing his verbal stumble, Glory asked, "Repaired? I didn't need new tires?"

This is where it got tricky. "The air was deliberately let out of your tires without doing any damage to them."

"But . . . how?"

With the others looking on, Kam didn't want to drag this out. Liam would arrive soon with his SUV, and he still needed to talk to Glory about future arrangements. "Easy enough with a tool. If you compress the valve stem . . ." Yeah, given her expression, she didn't need a lesson on tire pressure.

Dread showed in her eyes. "What about your tires?"

Rolling a shoulder, he gave her the truth. "Someone sabotaged mine."

Far too defeated, her eyes sank shut.

"Hey, none of that." Kam cupped her face, always aware of her warmth and softness. Manfully, he resisted the urge to kiss her.

Others were watching, or he'd have given in.

"They're just tires, Glory. Not a big deal, I promise." In the grand scheme of things, he was far more worried about her well-being.

"I'll pay you back."

Oh, hell no. Instead of making him angry, her offer left him comically bemused. "Absolutely not. I won't take money from you."

"But—"

That did it. He kissed her, quick and firm, and ignored the whispers he could hear coming from Callie's porch. "So you assume Mike was behind the flats, too?"

Subdued, she admitted, "It seems likely."

More than likely. "He didn't want me to be able to offer you a ride." Bending his knees made it easier for him to look her in the eyes. "He wants to get you alone, Glory."

"He offered us both a ride."

"What do you want to bet he'd have insisted on dropping me off first?" Without waiting for an answer, he added, "The guy is unpredictable." *As in demented.*

She stepped closer. "So you don't think I overreacted?"

"I think you're astute, with good instincts, but for now, I need you to shake this off so we can go somewhere private to talk."

Belatedly remembering her cousin and Addie, she glanced that way. Both women waved, grinning.

Flushing, Glory lowered her voice. "I can't just leave. You don't have to wait for me, though. I'm sure you have other things to do today, especially after taking care of my issues all morning."

Kam scrubbed both hands over his face. "Actually, the only thing on my agenda is you."

One slender eyebrow lifted. "Me?"

Did she have to sound so incredulous? "Hate to break it to you, but Mike was there."

Her lips barely moved when she breathed, "What?"

"Yeah, my reaction exactly."

Liam pulled up to the curb with his SUV, so Kam attempted to hurry her along. "I've got a lot to tell you, and it's better shared in private, so how about you gather up whatever you need and we'll head to your house to discuss our plans."

"But—"

He pressed a finger to her mouth, then didn't want to stop touching her. "Yes, it's still *our* plans. And so you know, Tanner and I discussed it. He met Mike, and he's all set to insist you stay with him and Callie."

"I would *never*!"

"Told him that. But if you disagree, he's sure Addie will come calling on you, because she won't want you alone right now, either."

Issuing a growl of frustration, she turned away, then turned right back. "Callie told me I was in a small town now, and things were done differently."

"She's not wrong." *Bless you, Callie.* "So what do you say? Want to grab a late lunch with me and we can strategize?"

Something softened in her expression. "Strategize, huh?"

"Over food. I'm starving."

"All right, but only if it's my treat." This time, she smashed her finger to his mouth. "You took care of my tires. It's the least I can do."

In reply, he licked her finger, causing her to jerk back. Eyes wide with disbelief, she cradled her hand to her heart. *"Kam."* Scandalized, she darted her gaze around. "Behave."

One quick look and Kam saw Addie, Callie, and Liam making no pretense of watching on. Shit. He wanted—needed—Glory to accept him. He hadn't felt this damned desperate since he'd been a kid, uprooted from hell and dropped into heaven with no idea how to adjust, afraid to accept, and more afraid not to.

"Lunch," he said, ordering himself to ignore the wash of pink color in her cheeks. "Time for us to head out." Time for him to get it together.

Past time for him to decide what he wanted, and how he was going to work it out.

"I can't believe I didn't know this place was here." The small diner seemed to be run by two older men, one in the kitchen cooking and the other on the floor ensuring the customers were pleased. They were both balding, both big around the bellies, and both good-humored in a coarse but jovial way.

When Kam had walked in with her, the man on the floor had called out to him, saying, "Steppin' up your game, boy? I approve."

Kam had muttered, "Ignore him," then said louder to the man, "Don't heckle her, Ted."

Ignoring him was easier said than done when Ted came to

seat them personally, then hung around to ask Glory her name and if she'd be in town long.

Of course, she'd clarified that she lived in the area now and apologized for not knowing about the restaurant sooner.

"New blood. Just what this town needs. You'll certainly pretty up the place." He'd clapped Kam on the shoulder. "Not that our boy doesn't always have a looker hanging on."

She saw it in Kam's set face, how he expected her to be insulted. Instead, she laughed. "Please note that I'm *not* hanging on. Just having lunch, that's all."

"Give him time, give him time. Ain't that right, Kam?"

"Stow it, Ted, before you embarrass her."

"Huh. She's not the one looking embarrassed."

Kam gave an eye roll and then did introductions, explaining that she was Callie's cousin. Plenty of heads had turned. It seemed everyone knew Callie, but then, it was big news that Tanner had married.

Now, with their meals almost gone, she realized Kam was watching her eat. "What?"

He sat back in his seat, smiling at how she finished off her loaded cheeseburger. "It's good, right?"

"Delicious." She hadn't indulged in this type of food in forever.

A sensual smile curved his mouth. "Told you you'd like it."

"Liking it isn't my problem." She liked it a little too much.

"Then thank you for indulging me by splurging a little."

If she indulged too often, she'd have to deal with the consequences of unhealthy eating. Pretending to share a great secret, she put a hand to her mouth and whispered, "Just don't tell Liz." Callie's mother had more than her fair share of opinions on everything.

Folding his arms on the tabletop and leaning in, Kam said just as quietly, "Or, you could tell Liz to mind her own business."

Shocking. Never in a million years would she do that. "Liz means well. She always has my best interests at heart."

Kam didn't bother to hide his doubt. "If you say so."

In a bid to change the subject, Glory pushed her empty plate aside and got serious. "You said we need to do some planning?"

"We do." Full of grave concern, he reached across the table and took her hands. "I think Mike hoped to find you alone, convince you to let him help with the tow truck driver, and then you'd have to give him your address."

Just the thought of that had her grip tightening on his. It was so nice of him to lend her some of his strength.

It'd be nicer still if she could find her own store of fortitude. "If that's true, then you don't think it was him who broke my window?"

"Didn't say that."

"Then . . ."

"He'd have been cleared of the window, able to say he'd only just learned your address."

She hadn't thought of that.

"Good old Mike would look all benevolent and shit, caring only for your well-being, only wanting to help."

"I guess that makes sense." Just how far would Mike go? The fact that she questioned it scared her. The idea of being alone at night bothered her even more.

Maybe staying with Addie wasn't such a horrid idea—except that she didn't want to bring trouble to anyone else. "I've considered calling the police, but I don't know what good it would do me. Mike hasn't actually done anything—at least nothing I can prove."

When Kam's thumbs moved over her knuckles, she realized they were just sitting there, holding hands, and half the diner was glancing at them.

"We've been putting on spectacles all day it seems."

His mouth hitched. "Ed and Ted have sure taken notice."

"Ed?"

"Ted's brother, the cook."

Oh. She looked toward the kitchen, and sure enough, the two brothers stood there, on opposite sides of a serving wall, gossiping.

"Come on." Abruptly, Kam slid out of the booth. "Let's get out of here. I think the rest of what I need to say will be better said in private."

"Okay, sure." What did he have to say? Glory opened her purse to get money for a tip, then slipped the bills halfway under her plate.

They had to go to the corner counter to pay, and Ed himself came strutting out. "How was your burger?"

"Delicious, thank you."

"And those fries?"

"It was all wonderful. Next time I'm in, I want to try the club sandwich."

Beaming, Ed leaned close and confided, "I have a special sauce. Top secret. It's so good, you'll like it more than—"

"Damn, Ed." Kam stationed himself in front of Glory, as if to shield her from the jest. "Curb it, will you?"

Ed drew back. "None of your other girls minded a little raunchy joking." He slanted a look at Glory. "She's not like the others?"

"No."

Grin widening, Ed turned to his brother. "Ted, she's not like the others."

"Already figured that out on my own."

Glory waited for him to say that she was like family, but he didn't, so she quickly reached around Kam and handed over her credit card to pay. That got the brothers going again, and had her quickly explaining. "This is payback."

Laughing even more, they elbowed each other.

Kam glared at Glory. "You see what you caused?"

Trying and failing to subdue her smile, she shrugged. Perhaps she should divert their attention. "This place has a great atmosphere."

Incredulity had Kam turning to face her. "You like nonstop ribbing and inappropriate chatter?"

"I like friendliness and a laidback attitude. The diner would be a great place to incorporate into Tanner's efforts."

All three men gave her blank stares, but it didn't deter Glory. To the brothers, she asked, "Are you aware of Tanner's community work?"

As he went back to cooking, Ed said, "Everyone knows."

Ted added, "But it's not only Tanner. Kam does his fair share of pitching in. Addie, too."

"And soon my cousin will be helping out." Glory wondered if there was a way she could also take part. Not that she knew much about it, and she wasn't sure she could offer much, but she'd love to try.

Until recently, her job within the luxury travel agency, owned by Callie's parents, had been to ferret out new locations for leisure activities at vacation destinations. For a while there, she'd been traveling nonstop, so there hadn't been time for her to consider pitching in. She'd never really had time to enjoy any of the locations because she was too busy analyzing, making reports, and sharing her findings. Now, though, she realized her expertise might offer some value.

"This place—" she lifted a hand to indicate the entirety of the small diner "—along with the two of you, could teach a lot to a young person."

From the grill, Ed said, "I'm not sharing my secret sauce recipe with no one."

"Naturally, not. But look at the experience you have at timing things. You just cooked and chatted simultaneously, and I know nothing will be overdone. That's not something just anyone could do."

Giving it some quick thought, Ed nodded. "I can also tell you the most popular meals, and ways to cut corners without losing any flavor."

"Brilliant," Glory praised.

Eagerly watching her, Ted asked, "What about me? I manage this place."

"You have a real knack for knowing your customers, for putting them at ease in a way that makes them feel like they're dining with friends or family."

A blush crawled up the big man's neck, his jowls, and even over his ears. "That's just me," he blustered. "I've always been chatty. Kam will tell you so."

But a new, more aware expression had dawned on Kam's face. "She's right. The two of you run a great business. Hell, you've been here for . . . what? Fifteen years?"

"Twenty-two." Tucking his thumbs into his waistband, Ted rocked back on his heels. "I'd just turned twenty-nine and Ed was twenty-six when we inherited the place. It was nice then, but we had plans."

Ed looked up with a smile. "Boy, did we. Spent two whole nights up thinking of things we'd keep the same and things we'd update."

"Took a lot of elbow grease to get it exactly as we wanted it."

"Didn't have a lot of money to invest," Ed added. "Had to do a lot of the work ourselves, but others in the neighborhood helped out."

Full of pride, Ted put back his shoulders. "They wanted to keep it around, and God love 'em all, they cheered us on."

"We're part of the community." Ed lifted his spatula in a salute, then slid two full plates onto the counter for the waitress to grab. "Been around too long to just let it disappear."

"That's my point." Hoping they'd go along with the idea, Glory smiled at the men. "You two would make great mentors."

Kam immediately backed her up. "You guys really would. You know you could use the extra help, and Tanner and I would appreciate it."

"Well, now." When he glanced back at Ed, Ted got his nod of agreement. "I reckon we could take on two young people. One could spend some time working with me, seeing how I do the books and such, while the other was with Ed. Then after a few weeks, we could trade."

"That way," Ed called out, "they'd know the entire business."

"Not just for restaurant work," Glory clarified as she caught their enthusiasm. She didn't want the young people to feel pigeonholed, and at the same time she wanted Ed and Ted to realize the valuable lessons they could teach. "They'd be learning good management skills and organization."

The men agreed.

Totally on board now, Kam promised to share the info with Tanner and said one of them would be back in touch very soon.

"Looks like Kam was right," Ted commented.

Unsure what he meant, Glory cocked her head to the side and waited.

"You really are different." He clapped Kam on the shoulder again. "We expect you to bring her around more often."

"I'll bring myself around." Glory didn't want Kam put on the spot. "Thank you. Both of you. This has been . . . enlightening."

With a broad knowing smile, Kam put his hand to the small of her back, and together, they walked out.

Glory liked the diner. She enjoyed Ed and Ted. The entire town was like a breath of fresh air, a different pace with fewer expectations.

Most of all, she liked Kam, more than she'd thought possible.

When had they gone from silent adversaries to allies against a potential risk?

Mike's obsession was scary, but her new relationship with Kam was the best thing to happen to her in a very, very long time. All in all, she'd call it a win.

Relieved that he didn't need to finagle an invite inside, Kam followed along as Callie continued their conversation on mentoring programs. She had great ideas that would benefit the kids without intruding on their privacy.

They'd discussed it on the drive, and during a quick stop at the grocery store.

"Many of the kids are withdrawn, angry, antagonistic." Just as he'd been. "It takes a little work to get them to open up enough to want to try." A few of them would rather spit on a friendly hand than accept it.

"That's so sad." After unlocking the front door and stepping inside, Glory took one of the grocery bags from him. "It's sometimes hard to trust when you've been hurt."

Just because Kam knew that firsthand didn't mean he wanted Glory to be the same. "Some of them only know disappointment, never acceptance. Others . . ." For others, it was far, far worse.

Busying himself by closing and relocking the door, he considered the right way to say things.

When he turned, he almost slammed into Glory. She hadn't budged when he'd thought she'd gone into the kitchen. The bag fell from her hand with a clatter, vegetables and fruits falling out. He had to do some quick juggling to catch her and hang on to his own bag of groceries.

Breathless, she stared up at him. "Sorry. What you said just caught me."

Taking his time, Kam lowered the bag to the floor so his hands would be free. His palms tingled even before they touched the bare skin of her shoulders, up to her throat. As his gaze took in every nuance of her alert expression, he slipped his fingers into her hair.

Giving up with a groan, Glory went on her tiptoes and pressed her lips to his.

Heaven. No other woman could pack the same emotional and physical punch. Kam gathered her close, immediately scooping one hand beneath her bottom and lifting her so they were pelvis to pelvis.

Her arms wrapped around him, her mouth open and hot. Damn. She caught fire fast and that caused him to go up in flames, too. Nearly tripping over the groceries on the floor, Kam turned to pin her to the wall, almost displacing the large mirror. "Sorry," he muttered.

She caught his mouth again, her tongue tasting as she rolled her hips into him.

There were no words. None. He needed her right now.

Absently, he booted aside a head of lettuce and what might have been a tomato so he could plant his feet. Her summer top lifted easily, making it easy to cup a breast. Firm, round, and just the right size for his hands.

Freeing her mouth on a deep inhale, eyes closed and skin flushed, she tilted her head to the side. No objections, and in fact, her fingertips dug into his shoulders, spurring him on.

"Feel good?" The silky material of her bra added a little extra slip and slide to the movement of his thumb over her nipple. He kissed the side of her throat, nuzzled against her, and breathed in her stirring scent.

"Are we going to have sex?" A drowsy sort of arousal sounded in her tone.

It ramped up his already-racing heartbeat. "Yes." Absolutely. He whispered against her skin: "Right here, Glory. Right now."

Three labored breaths later, and she reached beneath her shirt to open the front closure of her bra. "Good."

That did it. Kam went on autopilot, lifting the shirt higher so he could see her. He'd seen breasts before—plenty of them. But this was Glory and seeing her left him scorched with need.

She held the shirt up with one hand, letting him look his fill, and with the other, she unsnapped her jeans. Then her slender fingers teased down the zipper, exposing the pale flesh of her lower stomach.

He wanted to say something witty. *Keep going.* Or *nice show.* Anything clever that would prove she didn't have him off balance, but nothing came to mind except having her. Tasting her. Licking her.

Branding her as his own.

Not Mike's. Not any other man's.

His and his alone.

Even while reminding himself that he wasn't the possessive type, he had to get his mouth on her. Mindful of her delicate skin, he kissed down her throat to her chest. Shoving the shirt higher, he drew in one nipple.

Her fingers clenched in his hair, and she pressed closer on a soft moan.

Yeah, she liked that. Using both hands, he shoved down her jeans. They were tight, and it wasn't easy, but he had enough determination to get it done in record time. Her small throaty laugh proved that she enjoyed his urgency.

He didn't care. When his fingers moved over her, then in her, he found proof that her need matched his own.

If Glory hadn't been every bit as frantic as him, maybe he could have slowed down. Maybe.

But it was the snap of his jeans she attacked now, so as long as she was with him, he wouldn't slow down. Couldn't slow down—God. Especially not when her warm fingers squeezed around his cock. Laboring for breath, they both paused.

"Now," Glory said, hurriedly shoving her pants lower. "Right now."

"Yeah." The guttural agreement gave him away—and he didn't care. Once she'd kicked out of her jeans and panties, he caught her ass with both hands, lifted her against him and pinned her to the wall. Without hesitation, she wrapped her legs around him. "Hold on to me."

Her arms tightened around his neck. In a haze of lust, he reached down, guided himself to her, and pressed home.

At almost the same time, he felt her sharp little teeth on his shoulder and heard her reverberating moan.

So good. So fucking good he couldn't see straight. They moved together, a little wild, a little rough. Hot kisses, harsh sounds, building pleasure, tighter and tighter . . .

"Kam." Putting her head back, she clamped down on him, coming hard.

For once, her expression was raw and real. More beautiful than ever. He got lost watching her, experiencing her, catching every shift of pleasurable expression until she shakily released a breath.

The second she relaxed, he let himself go.

Nothing had ever felt so right.

A minute later, slumped against Glory, their boneless bodies more or less propped against the wall, he heard a snicker.

It made him smile. "Careful," he warned. "It's only by sheer force of will that I'm supporting us both."

"You could let me go."

Never. That's what he wanted to say. It'd be far too serious for their first time, though. "You mean to tell me you've recovered when I haven't?"

He felt her teeth again, this time in a gentle love bite followed by a soft lick, then the press of a kiss. "You did all the work."

"So what you're saying is that I'm a stud?"

Another snicker, another kiss, then a more serious, "Kam, let me down. We're . . . messy."

That made him smile, too. "I like being messy with you." That could become his new favorite euphemism for scorching hot spontaneous sex. "Okay, easy now." One at a time, he let her slender legs slide down until she stood on her own feet, shakily, but she stayed upright. Good thing, because he had to use a hand flattened to the wall to help support his own legs.

Glory was one massive surprise after another. Sex as soon as they walked in the door? Nope, that hadn't been on his bingo card. He'd damn sure be putting it there from now on, though.

Unable to resist, he nuzzled her neck. "You smell good."

"So do you." Sticking close to him, Glory tugged her shirt over her breasts—and then kept on tugging until she had it stretched down enough to cover most of her backside.

Suddenly shy? "Glory." Reinvigorated by her modesty, Kam bent his knees to see her face, but she turned away. "Hey, what's up?"

"Nothing. That is . . . I need to, um . . ." Darting around the fallen groceries and stripped-off clothes, she padded quickly down the hall and into her bedroom. The door closed, and then he heard the click of the lock.

Well, hell. She'd literally just run from him. Bare-assed, except for a shirt not meant to cover those curves.

Was she now appalled that they'd gotten it on in the hall, up against a wall, while she'd still worn her shirt and opened bra, and he hadn't taken off a single piece of clothing?

Disgusted, he looked down at himself, at his jeans barely shoved below his hips. Her jeans and a silky little pair of panties were in a twisted pile on the floor.

What a debacle—and it was rightfully her fault. Around her, he wasn't himself anymore. For him, sex was playful and uncommitted. Indulging lust in a fun way, making sure the woman enjoyed herself, teasing her afterward with overblown compliments—that's how he rolled.

He did not forget where he was, *who* he was, while losing himself in the hottest pleasure he'd ever known.

Guilt settled onto his shoulders and made his temples ache. What to do?

He supposed tucking himself away was the first order of business. Stomping into the kitchen, he washed up and dried using paper towels.

A first for him, but then, he'd lived with Tanner and Addie and no way would he have been caught having sex in the foyer. Now . . . Well, he wouldn't mind trying out a few other places with Glory. Like the couches in her living area, or that nice-sized dining room table.

Even better: that big deep bathtub she had . . .

Knowing he had to get his mind on other things, he put away the groceries.

When he was finished, Glory still hadn't emerged, so he snagged up her undies and jeans, strode down the hall with a purpose and, using one knuckle, tapped at her door. Very aware of the silkiness of that tiny pair of panties, he waited. And waited some more.

Okay, now he was feeling insulted. “Glory, open up.”

Seconds later, the doorknob turned and the door crept open. Standing there in a different pair of jeans, her hair tucked behind each ear, her makeup a little messy, she looked like sex personified.

Every male instinct he possessed sat up and took notice. “Hey.”

She blinked fast.

For lack of anything else to say, he thrust her discarded garments toward her. “Here.”

Eyes widening, she snatched them from his hand and held them behind her back.

Humor slipped in. Done resisting her, he ran the back of one finger over her warmed cheek, actually feeling the heat of her blush. “Come here.” He scooped her close, his arms loosely draped around her. “Don’t be embarrassed, okay?”

Awkwardly, she tossed the jeans and panties aside, then melted against him, her forehead to his sternum. “I’ve never done anything like that before.”

Then they were even, because he’d never been so charmed by a woman. Out of control, spontaneous sex, followed by this sweet uncertainty—it was a combo guaranteed to melt his cynical heart.

Without thought, Kam kissed her temple, then her ear. “Will it help if I admit that it wasn’t exactly routine for me?”

Her quiet sound of disbelief had him smiling. “I’m flattered you think I’m such a sexual dynamo I can cause women to drop their groceries—” *and their pants* “—in unconventional places. I mean, we barely had the front door closed. Can you imagine how Old Lady Simmons would’ve acted if she’d seen us?”

This time her snort was louder. "Listen to you, embellishing everything."

Glad that she'd loosened up a little, he held her tighter and said quietly, with great sincerity, "That was a fantasy come to life. Hottest moment of my life. I have no regrets, Glory. I don't want you to have any, either."

"I don't. It's just . . ." She tipped back to see him. "I shocked myself."

Kam had to kiss her, but he kept it light, just brushing his mouth over hers. "There's something going on between us."

She nodded, but asked, "Like what?"

So many things he couldn't put into words, which was okay because telling her the depth of his own emotions would sidetrack them. Besides, he wasn't sure he could adequately describe the turbulent mix of feelings she caused.

Settling on the simplest explanation, he said, "I want you. Again."

"Now?" she whispered, a little appalled by the idea.

Yeah, now would be good, but he didn't want to spook her. "When you're ready. What do you think?"

Cuddling close again, she hid her face. "I want you, too. But not right now."

Damn. Talk about stirring the embers. His heart started popping hard and fast against his ribs. "Let me stay."

"For sex?"

That was sure as hell his preference. "I vote yes, but I will never pressure you." *I am not Mike*, he wanted to say, but if she didn't know that by now, it was already too late for them.

"So you want to stay the night?" Her eyes searched his, measuring his intent.

"Tonight, tomorrow—until we know Mike has hit the road and things calm down?"

Her lack of objection encouraged him.

Shocking him, pleasing him, she said, "Okay—but even if it's only a day, I have some ground rules."

As long as she didn't tell him to take a hike, he could deal with anything. "Let's hear it."

"You sleep the whole night with me."

That's how he wanted it anyway. "Done."

"There's more."

He wrestled his tone into calm moderation. "Go ahead."

In a sudden rush, she went through a list. "Lights out, some clothes on, no questions, and . . . and we can't tell anyone."

What. The. Hell. Pulling back, Kam stared at her serious expression and was lost. "Want to tell me why?"

Shoving away from him, her voice high and thin, she reiterated, "No questions!"

Kam took in her panicked stance and knew nothing else mattered except reassuring her. Whatever she hoped to accomplish, he'd work past it soon enough. Then they could move on to better arrangements.

Lifting his hands in the universal sign of surrender, Kam said, "Sorry. I forgot that rule."

She was breathing too quickly; her entire body tensed. "I know it sounds absurd, but I don't want sex to ruin things."

Absurd covered it. Tension gathered in the back of his neck. "Should I be insulted? I mean, just because it was my fantasy, doesn't guarantee you feel the same."

She assured him, "I do." Those two little words, which sounded too much like wedding vows, had her spinning away again. Arms hugged around herself, she moved into the kitchen until the bar separated them.

"Slow down, babe." To help put her at ease, he took a seat at the bar. "Whatever it is, we'll figure it out." *Somehow.*

"I love seeing Callie so happy, and I love Tanner because he gave that to her. I love Addie, too. I've never known anyone like her."

She threw that word out like confetti, leaving love scattered everywhere. Normally, hearing it just once would make him twitchy. This time, with Glory, he didn't have a problem with it. "Addie is special," he agreed. But what Tanner and Addie had to do with anything, he didn't know.

"You know my parents died when I was younger." Needlessly, she straightened the canisters beside the stove. "Callie's parents have been wonderful—"

He snorted. Liz and Frank were a unique type of obtuse critics, especially when it came to Glory. To be fair, it was more Liz than Frank, but Frank didn't intercede, and in Kam's book, that made him guilty, too.

Moving past that, Glory said, "I appreciate everything they did for me, but I've never quite measured up to them."

Unable to bite off the words, Kam said, "They set impossible standards. Ignore them."

When she looked up at him, she wore a gentle smile. "That's what Callie always says."

"I knew right off that Callie was an insightful woman."

The smile flickered a little more, before it disappeared. "Addie just accepts me as I am."

Like a ton of bricks, it hit him. She'd found acceptance here and she didn't want to risk it. "Glory." Fuck the distance between them. He strode around the counter and tugged her back into his arms. Right now, that's where she belonged. "I would never do anything to hurt your relationship with Addie or Tanner. I couldn't. You're family now and that's not something either of them would take lightly."

Resting her cheek to his chest, she slid her arms around him and gave him a tight hug. "Still. Promise you won't say anything to anyone."

"They saw me kiss you earlier."

"One kiss. That's all. But this . . ."

Yeah, this was definitely more.

"No one needs the distraction right now."

So he was a distraction? He supposed he'd been worse things in his lifetime. Pressing a kiss to her lips bought him a little time. He cupped her face, tipped it up, and deepened the kiss. Once they were both breathing hard, he lightened up. "I promise."

Glory let out a grateful breath. "Thank you."

There she went, charming him again. "You're welcome." Hopefully, once he settled down with her in a bed, she'd forget her silly rules. "People are bound to notice that I'm staying here, too."

Dismissing that as insignificant, she said, "You're protective, so that's fine."

She honestly thought anyone would believe they were beneath the same roof and not doing anything?

"Just don't mention the sex."

Right. The sex. *Lights out. Some clothes on.* "I'm not an asshole who brags, so no problem." He thought of how she'd stretched the shirt so low and wondered what she was hiding. He'd held her ass in his hands and as far as he could tell, that sweet part of her anatomy was perfection.

Though for sure, he'd never approached sex with a list of rules laid out first. Especially not minutes after ungoverned carnality in a foyer.

Then again, nothing with Glory felt standard. It was all new and different—and more exciting because of it.

6

Well, now that she'd made a complete fool of herself, Glory wondered how to proceed. Deflecting seemed her best bet. "I should head back to Callie's. I promised her she wouldn't have to lift a finger."

"How about we go together?"

"Because . . . why?"

"You agreed to let me stay for a while, right? Well, I'll need some clothes." He put up a hand. "I know. You'd prefer I go around in just jeans, but really, Glory, think of Old Lady Simmons. What if she has a weak heart?"

Though she knew he was teasing, he wasn't wrong. She'd love to have Kam strutting his goods for her from dusk to dawn. That could be *her* fantasy, except that reality intruded. "We could drive separately." That would help to quell suspicion.

"Trust me, Callie, Tanner, and Addie, all three would think that was silly. There's no reason to take both cars, so how about I drive? I have more room."

"How much stuff do you need?"

"I have the essentials boxed up already." He leaned back against the counter. "But you need to understand, I'm not moving in on you. You won't have me underfoot forever."

Bummer. Since she couldn't say that, she lifted her brows in silent query.

"I have my own place. An apartment. Very near here, in fact. When we head out, I can show you."

Very near sounded good to her. Not as good as him being *underfoot*, as he'd said, but still. "I'd like that." For now, she needed to understand the scope of his . . . Well, *not* a proposition. "So what will you be bringing here?"

"Some clothes, toothbrush, razor. That sort of thing."

That was *not* excitement zinging around in her heart. "Sounds reasonable."

"I'll get everything moved to my apartment over the next few days, then while I'm here, if I need something, I can easily run over there and grab it."

Glory nodded. "Okay, then."

A new sultry, suggestive light came into his eyes. "I'll be handy to have around. I cook, you know—not like Addie, but you won't starve."

"I'll want to see Ted and Ed again, too."

"We'll go together." He stepped away from the counter. "Tonight, though, I think Addie would like us to eat with her. What do you say?"

"I say we have a lot to get done in the next few hours, so how about you show me the apartment now?"

Dazed at how easily he'd convinced Glory to let him stay over, Kam unlocked his apartment door and walked in. Had she agreed because Mike scared her? Because she'd enjoyed their frenzied hallway sex?

Or was she starting to care for him?

Not knowing kept his thoughts churning this way and that. *He* cared, damn it. Far more than he'd expected. In a single night, everything had changed. The threat of another man hurting her—and yeah, that awesome sex against the wall—had conspired against him, making him face up to unfamiliar feelings. Things he didn't want to feel. Emotions he hadn't known existed.

He'd gotten the apartment for independence, to prove—to himself more than anyone else—that he was more than others had so often claimed, more than the genetic makeup of an absurdly awful father.

More, damn it, than either of his parents had expected.

Seeing the apartment now, he accepted that it wasn't much. Not big. Not open. Not new. Nothing like her stylish house, but he refused to be self-conscious about it. "Once I get more furniture in here, put some stuff on the walls and things like that, it'll look better."

Keen interest took Glory's gaze everywhere, scrutinizing in minute detail. "It's nice."

Scoffing would only make him feel more absurd. "I haven't done much yet. Just got furniture dropped off and sort of shoved around." The couch was against a wall with end tables shoved up against it. His TV, the only new item, sat across the room on a peach crate. "We had the wedding, and Addie's been so emotional about it . . ."

A smile preceded her teasing, "Forever blaming Addie."

Skipping past that, especially since he knew it was true, Kam concentrated on the living space. "You've given me some ideas."

"Sexual ideas?"

Her quick wit continued to amuse him. "So you always have sex on the brain, huh?"

"I . . . What? No."

The flustered denial certainly gave *him* ideas. "So only around me?"

Folding her arms, she pinned him with a direct look. "Ideas for the apartment, Kam?"

"A mirror and table just inside the door. Maybe with a bowl or something to drop my keys and change. New bedding? I don't know. I never much thought about pillow shams and all that goofy shit but seeing your place so polished put the ideas in my head."

"You don't have nice bedding at Addie's?"

"A navy blue corduroy bedspread, probably ten . . . no, thirteen years old." Mouth twisting to the side, he admitted, "It was a big deal when I got a full-size bed instead of the twin I'd been sleeping on." And that had been better than anything he'd had before coming to live with Addie and Tanner. "Addie went all out, getting me new sheets and pillows. Damn, those pillows were big and soft." Such a great memory, one he hadn't thought of in a while. "I can still remember that first night, settling my head back, pulling up that soft corduroy spread . . . I was on top of the world."

Somehow, his reminiscing brought her back to him, now with her gaze soft and misty. "I love seeing your life in the way you tell it." Her small palm settled over his heart. "I can almost feel it with you."

Seeing her like this did crazy things to him. It was such a contrast to his first impression of her, when she'd seemed too perfect, icy and untouchable. "How was it when you first moved in with Callie?"

The gleam faded from her eyes. She ducked her head, hiding her face from him. "They were really kind. Before I ever got there, they converted the guest bedroom for me. It was this huge room with a massive walk-in closet and my own bathroom. Everything was brand new. I could smell the newness, know what I mean?"

Just as she'd felt his description, he felt hers, and his heart cracked a little at what sounded cold, too formal, and detached. To lighten the mood, he asked, "Was everything pink and fluffy?"

"Of course not. It was stylish, like something out of a designer magazine. Beige with accents of black and gold."

For a kid's room?

"It was really beautiful . . . but it kind of overwhelmed me."

"Were your folks well-to-do like Callie's?"

"No."

The simplicity of that answer said a lot, all of it adding to the ache in his chest. "Did you—"

Stepping away from him, she faced the living room and asked with a deliberately brightened tone, "So what are you envisioning here?"

Never call him insensitive. Questions bombarded his brain, but he put them on hold so she could relax. "I couldn't pull off anything as nice as what you've got going on at your place, but I wouldn't mind some finishing touches."

"You're the one who put it all together for me."

"Not all of it." Just a few things she'd already bought but hadn't gotten around to unboxing.

"I could help you." Diving in with enthusiasm, she started a tour around his space. "It would be fun, right? You can tell me your ideas, your preferences—"

"In bed?"

This time, she only said, "Ha!" and proceeded into his bedroom to gaze at the white walls and a window. "I'm guessing you're a neutral color scheme kind of guy, but pops of color are always great." Turning to him with eagerness, she asked, "What's your favorite color?"

"I've never really thought about it."

In response to that, she touched his chest. "You wear dark green a lot."

Did he? At the moment, with her looking at him like that, he couldn't recall.

"T-shirts, sneakers, even a few button-down shirts."

"Noticed that, did you?" How long had she been noticing him?

With a nod, she glanced around again. "I have some great ideas."

"Hate to break it to you, babe." His hand over hers kept her close. "We have very different budgets."

"I understand that, but that's another thing we could work on."

Skeptical, he asked, "What?"

"The budget. You already have the bones in place. Nice neutral couch and some tables, bedroom furniture, blinds on the windows. We could work on one room at a time. What do you think?"

Testing the waters, he said, "That could take a while."

Her chin notched up. "I'm patient. Are you?"

Patience wasn't the issue. What she suggested was more of a commitment. Not necessarily romantic, but he wouldn't mind any excuse to lock down more time with her.

Lacing his fingers through hers, he led her back out of the room. "I was thinking of a round dining table here, in front of the patio doors, since the kitchen is so small."

The sight of her top teeth sinking into her bottom lip told him that wasn't the right idea.

"Or," she said judiciously, "you could set up a narrow rectangular table that could act as a divider between the living room and this space. It would naturally lead people to the kitchen, or the hall to the bath and bedroom. Then when you decorate the balcony—"

"I was just going to put out a lawn chair."

"You could bring just a few elements inside, so the space feels like it flows from the outside in."

"Yeah . . . I have no idea what you're talking about." But he enjoyed her animated expression as she shared it.

"I have an idea."

The way she said that alarmed him. "No."

"It'll be my gift to you!"

"Hell, no."

"But you're playing bodyguard!" Jerking free of his hold, she propped her hands low on her hips.

"Also bed companion. Fantasy fulfiller." Snarky grin in place, he overly enunciated, *"Lover."* Closing the space between them made him feel better, even if it caused her to stiffen. "You don't see me asking for compensation for *that*."

She went soft and sweet. "It would cost me a fortune."

"You little flatterer." Now he had all kinds of ideas, like getting her on his bed, and she could even keep her silly rules in place.

"Be serious, Kam."

"I am serious." Serious about having her again, knowing waiting until tonight would be excruciating.

"You'll be staying with me when you could be sprucing up your own place."

"Not really, because I ran out of spruce-up money already. It'll be a few paychecks before I do more."

"Oh."

She looked so crestfallen he smirked and shook his head. "I'm not broke, Glory. I won't have to survive on broth and crackers. That budget you mentioned? I started one when I was fifteen with my first real job."

"You had a job at fifteen?"

He almost asked, *You didn't?* Not a good idea, though,

given her reaction. "Lawn care. I worked with a great guy who had his own equipment. Not just cutting grass, but trimming bushes, edging driveways, working on flower beds. I got my first paycheck and . . ." It had leveled him. His own money. *His.* To spend or not spend however he wanted. Yet another memory to make him smile. "I took Tanner and Addie out to a restaurant, with both of them bitching endlessly because they didn't want me to spend money on them."

"Oh, Kam."

"Damn, babe, don't look like that." Laughing, he cupped her face, then pressed a quick kiss to her mouth. Weird, how quickly he'd gotten used to doing that. "It wasn't a sad thing, I swear. They weren't complaining about me, they just . . ." *Loved me enough that they wanted me to keep it all.* His throat got so tight that he had to swallow before he could continue. "Addie was everything I'd never had before, like a mom and dad, grandparents, caregiver, encourager, and teacher all rolled into one superwoman. Before her, I didn't even know someone could be like her."

Glory smiled, and that was much better than her upset.

"I wanted to treat her to something since she'd treated me so many times." Without thinking about it, he brought Glory against him, one hand coasting up and down her back. "Tanner was always looking out for me. Even when I first showed up and was a total dickhead."

She hugged him close. "I think you maybe had reason?"

"Maybe." He'd been so afraid to trust in anything good. Anything that didn't hurt or insult. "But Tanner stuck with me. Knocked me around when necessary, too." Usually when Kam wouldn't stop attacking him. Remembering that brought out a short laugh. "I used to go after him just because." Just because he was bigger and better grounded. Older and more comfortable. Just because the idea of having a brother as awesome as Tanner had scared him to death.

Back then, he'd felt unwanted and useless—things he'd always been told.

"Once they got seated at the restaurant, they settled down and enjoyed the meal. Addie told me it was wonderful, and then she explained that I didn't need to take her out to show her I cared." She'd had tears in her eyes as she'd spoken, but no sadness. By then, Kam had learned to tell the difference. "She said I showed her love every time I helped out around the house, whenever I gave her a hug or let her hug me, when I enjoyed the food she cooked, or appreciated the clothes she bought."

"She knew you loved her."

He nodded. "She knew. She didn't need me to buy her dinner to prove it. But then Tanner jumped in and took my side. He made it all sound so logical, saying I should be able to treat the people I cared about if I wanted to—as long as I saved one third of each paycheck."

Glory gave a startled laugh. "A little push and pull, huh? Smart. So did you?"

"Yup. Every paycheck since that first one. But I talked with Tanner a lot, too. He was only three years older, but man, he seemed so grown up. He had all these plans, things we'd talked about before, but since I was making money, too, I felt more a part of it. We'd sit at the kitchen table together and go over things. College and cars, repairs to the house. I can't remember a time when Tanner wasn't planning, looking for a way to make things better—for himself, for me and Addie."

"And now for every kid who needs a helping hand."

"Yeah." There was no man he admired more than his brother. "Tanner is forward thinking, you know? He knew Addie couldn't do it all on her own, so together, we worked on that."

Emotion glazed her eyes again. "You worked as a family."

How special was it that Glory really got it? "Family was, and always will be, a priority for us."

"I love that, Kam. Thank you for sharing with me."

Never had he known a woman to so freely throw around the *love* word. Glory never gave it a thought, he assumed, because she wasn't looking to tie him down, not like the other women had. Shara, especially, had come after him hot and heavy. She'd seemed so nice at first, though—much like Glory. Polished, pretending to adore his family . . .

"What?" Glory drew back. "You're looking at me like I insulted you."

"No, sorry. I was just thinking."

Sympathizing, she stroked his shoulder and asked with concern, "About something unpleasant?"

"Doesn't matter." He did his best to get the image of Shara out of his head.

"You can tell me. Or not. I mean, I won't pressure you, but if you want to talk, I don't mind."

"So magnanimous."

Hurt by that, she withdrew—and he hated it.

Hitching her purse strap over her shoulder, she glanced at the door. "We should get going."

Damn it. They'd been connecting before he'd tripped up. Not that he'd meant to go into his past. Usually, he wouldn't have. Sometimes with Glory, it just felt right.

Hoping to bring her back around, he moved closer. "I've spent some of my savings. College, my car, the remodel Tanner and I did for Addie—but those were big things I'd planned for. Always, no matter what, I make sure I have enough for emergencies."

"And new plans?"

"Sure."

As if she, too, felt the loss of harmony, Glory grew hesitant. And quiet.

"What?" he teased, almost desperate to regain the moment. "Don't hold back now."

Serious eyes took his measure. "All right. I just wondered what other big plans you might have, if not now, then later."

Way to hit him with the big stuff. The roll of his shoulder didn't quite hide his uneasiness over the things he craved. *A woman who loves me enough to be my wife through good times and bad, kids I can coddle and protect, a home of my own, and a future to embrace . . .* Not about to spit that out, he removed the significance and spoke in hypotheticals. "The usual stuff, I guess. House, security, and all that."

She, too, lightened up in a deliberate bid to remove the tension. "A retirement plan?"

"Sure. Hey, I can't stay young and healthy forever." He thought of Addie, now in her early seventies, and it scared him like nothing else could. She might be a little slower these days, but she was still going strong. He wanted to be able to pamper her, so she'd last through the rest of his lifetime.

Of course, Addie knew that wouldn't be possible, and that's why she'd spent so much time talking to him and Tanner about finding the right one, the person who would make you feel whole even when problems tried to tear you down. She'd had that once, but her perfect someone had passed away too soon. According to Addie, she'd had a lonely life until God had given her Tanner, and then Kam.

He liked how she looked at it, as if they'd been special gifts instead of burdens.

Absently, he crushed Glory closer, pressed his cheek to the softness of her hair, and then kissed her temple.

"You okay?" she asked.

"Yeah, fine." *But somehow holding you has become a habit.*

"Tell you what. Write out what you think I should get, and how much you think it'll cost, and I'll figure out what I can get and when."

Showing her pleasure, she pressed back to clap her hands. "You'll let me help?"

"With choosing and arranging if you want, but not with buying."

Her playful pout was cute, making him grin.

"Take it or leave it, babe."

She put up her nose and said, "I'll take it—for now. But don't think for a single moment that you can boss me around, Kam Norwood."

No, he wouldn't even try. But neither would he let her get away with flaunting her money. Not for him anyway. An upbringing of wealth showed in her decorum, how she moved, and the ease with which she indulged her life—but that wasn't him. Hell, he'd crawled from the sewer, and now he preferred to make it on his own.

Yes, Glory had chosen a moderate house, and her Mustang was sporty, not a luxury car, but he doubted she had to budget very often.

Working for Callie's parents, he assumed she had a high income. Liz might criticize her too often, but she'd raised Glory alongside Callie, so she had to consider her a daughter.

That probably accounted for a lot of financial pampering.

Kam preferred making his own way. As much as he loved Addie, he was ready to embrace complete independence.

If he got to embrace it with Glory, that only made it better.

Dinner, Glory soon discovered, wasn't just with Addie. They arrived a few minutes late and found the driveway full of cars.

"Looks like a party," Kam said, as he got out to circle the

SUV. It was obvious by his careless tone that the idea of a crowd didn't bother him at all.

Unfortunately, Glory didn't feel the same. She recognized Frank's BMW, meaning Callie's parents were joining them. Overall, she'd had a nice day, but now the glow faded and a chill left her stiff.

She should have changed her clothes and touched up her makeup. Too late now.

Painfully self-conscious, she got out when Kam opened her door. Dreading the evening, she allowed him to tug her along until, near the large garage, he paused and looked down at her.

"Hey, what's wrong?"

A smile and stiff lips didn't mesh well. "Nothing. I'm fine."

"Bull." Scrutinizing her, he curved his hand around her jaw and lifted her face. "Tell me what's going on."

He had a bad habit of wanting to look her in the eyes. Usually, she didn't mind, but now, while she was feeling cornered, she didn't appreciate it. "We're running late. I hope they didn't hold dinner for us."

"Five minutes is not late."

She could debate that with him.

"Besides, Addie always waits. It won't be a problem."

Somewhere behind them, Callie said, "Good to know, because I'm starved."

Together, Glory and Kam turned to see her cousin and Tanner, hand in hand, coming around the line of wild honeysuckle bushes that separated the two properties.

With a wicked grin, Tanner said, "She's worked up an appetite."

Now this smile was real, because Glory noticed that Callie was really dressed down, wearing only cotton shorts, an oversized T-shirt, and flip-flops. Her hair was up in her now-patented messy bun, which looked amazing on her.

"Aren't you two supposed to be off enjoying matrimonial ecstasy?"

"Yes," Callie said, leaving Tanner behind to hook her arm through Glory's and lead her toward the door. "But a girl has to eat, and Addie's cooking is too scrumptious to pass up."

God bless her. Glory tilted her head in, Callie did the same, and it felt like old times. Aware of the men behind them, Glory asked in a barely there whisper, "You knew they were here, didn't you?"

"Yup," Callie whispered back. "And since you're all in on living your own life, I decided to come along and encourage you."

Independence from her aunt and uncle; it was something Glory really wanted, and yet, old habits were hard to break. "I've made strides," she promised. Independent living in her own house, and a new position in the company that kept her from constantly interacting with them. Those were huge deals, at least for Glory.

"I know and I'm so proud of you." At the front door, Callie turned to face her. "Now you just need to keep it up."

Since that was the plan, Glory nodded. "I should feel guilty for interrupting your pseudo honeymoon." But she didn't. She was too relieved to have Callie with her. Confrontations were never easy for her, at least not with family.

Callie hugged her close. "You never ever have to feel guilty with me. We're here for each other, right? Always."

"Always," Glory swore.

Tanner held Kam back. "Let them talk a moment. I want to ask you how things went."

If Kam could get his gaze off Glory, it might be easier to answer. Faced with seeing the people who'd raised her, she'd morphed into a different woman. The perfect, icily polite mannequin he'd first met. He didn't like it, but he wasn't sure what to do about it.

"Kam?"

"Yeah," he said absently. "I'll be staying with her. We ironed that out." He wouldn't tell Tanner about Glory's rules; they were private and intimate, not something to spread around. In broad terms, though, he didn't keep secrets from his brother, so he admitted low, "She doesn't want anyone to know."

"That you're staying with her?"

In answer, Kam lifted a shoulder. "She's worried Addie won't respect her or something." He glanced at Tanner's bemused expression. "She doesn't want to be a distraction."

"You boys done gossiping?" Callie asked. "We gals are hungry."

Standing there, side by side with his brother, Kam grinned. Glory and Callie were like mismatched bookends, one a little rumpled and cute, the other polished to a high shine and rigid, but they were both lookers.

Tanner nudged him forward. "Let's go. The sooner we get this over with, the sooner I can put my in-laws out of my mind once again."

Death by a thousand pricks. That's what dinner had encompassed. If Glory moved, Liz made a critical comment. Then Addie would counter it with a compliment while Callie sniped at her mother. Liam, who often joined them at dinner, had brought along Nell. They had silently taken in the strife, but Glory could tell that it bothered Nell.

She was such a sweet girl, still so young, but a tough life had matured her well beyond her years. She and Liam had that in common. Nell had spent time with the family while grooming Tanner's dog and Kam's cat, and now she often visited, but the dinners were usually much calmer.

Both animals currently rested under Nell's seat.

When they pulled into her driveway later that evening, Glory was finally able to let out a tense breath and relax her spine.

"There you go," Kam said. "'Bout time, too."

The satisfaction in his tone confounded her. "What do you mean?"

"It tortured me seeing you being so stiff and prim." Before she could take umbrage at that, with a little heat, he added, "Why don't you tell Liz to mind her own damn business?"

"Should I have interrupted Callie?" Her cousin had done a fine job of nipping at her mother's every comment. "Or spoken over Addie's praise?" She'd supplied an endless stream of admiration on everything from Glory's hair to her posture and how she lifted a fork. It was ridiculous—and sweet. Liz would make note of something, and Addie would immediately counter it.

If it hadn't made her feel so awkward, she might have laughed over it.

"And poor Nell, stuck in the middle of that. Didn't anyone else notice how uneasy it made her? I think she's probably been stuck in similar uncomfortable situations." More than anything, Glory had wanted to take Nell's hand, lead her outside, and sit and chat. About *everything*. Life, dealing with family, being a woman . . . All the things she and Callie had grown up discussing.

Pinning her with a stern frown, Kam discounted everything she'd just said. "None of that should have kept you from standing up for yourself."

There it was. The worst of the insults. Glory fought back the hurt and glared at him. "Liz took me in when I had nowhere to go. She gave me everything she could. And now she employs me." Shoving her door open, she stepped out into the muggy night. At nearly 8:00 p.m., the sun was a fiery yellow ball resting on the horizon, turning the sky a dusky orange. Pretty—but not enough to lift her sudden ire.

She spun to face Kam when he strode toward her with a purpose. "Why haven't you brought your cat home?"

That drew him up short. "What?"

"Percy is your cat, right? Yet, you've . . ." She couldn't say *abandoned*. "You left him behind."

"Case you haven't noticed, I'm not settled into my apartment yet. Addie insisted he should stay with her until I am. Besides, he's bonded with Blu. He and that dog love each other."

That made sense, but she wasn't ready to be reasonable, not after the nasty things he'd said to her. "So you're happy to dump one more responsibility on Addie?"

For a long tense moment, he studied her, then the heat left his eyes. "I would never do that." He approached cautiously, like he thought she might flee.

And damn it, she felt like it. She hated being weak, hated letting Liz walk all over her. And she especially hated knowing she'd never been loved. Not by her parents, not by Liz and Frank.

Only Callie had ever truly loved her, and now Callie had a husband. A wonderful husband. The perfect man for her.

It was only right that he'd take precedence. Glory wouldn't have it any other way. Sooner or later, she'd get used to the new dynamic of being . . . less important. Again.

God, could she be a more selfish bitch? Almost hating herself, Glory deflated. Especially because she'd taken out her pity party on Kam, and he didn't deserve it.

Faking an intense interest in the sunset, she kept her gaze averted. "I'm sorry."

"Ah, babe." His strong arms came around her, crossing over

her breasts as he snuggled close behind her. "You stole the words right out of my mouth. I deserved to be blasted."

"No, you didn't." Resting her hands over his forearms, she dropped her head back to his shoulder and simply relished his nearness, the delicious scent of him, how his touch energized her and comforted her at the same time. "I think Liz just has that effect on everyone."

"She's fine when she isn't nettling you."

Meaning they all got along well when Glory wasn't around? Great. One more way to make her feel—*no*. Damn it, she would stop being pathetic right now.

"She sure had Addie riled," Kam noted.

The corner of her mouth quirked. "I'd like to know how Addie came up with all those silly compliments so quickly. I think she praised everything about me, including my eyelashes."

"They're pretty eyelashes," he said, his voice huskier. "So you know, Percy is my cat, but I guess he's Addie's, too. He's always lived in that house, and when I was away at school or work, Addie was there with him. Blu, too."

"It's a big wonderful house. I'm glad Callie decided to move in with them so they could all stay together."

That observation was met with silence. Glory turned to face him, spotted Nosy Old Lady Simmons peeking at her through her curtains, and decided it was time to head in. "Come on. We're entertaining the neighbors."

"Simmons?" he asked, keeping her in place.

"She thinks she's being sneaky, but I can see her."

Cupping her face, Kam whispered, "Then we might as well give her something to gawk at," right before he put his mouth over hers in a kiss guaranteed to send her foul mood packing for good.

7

"Titillating the neighbors is nothing new for me."

"No? But I thought you didn't have any close neighbors, just Callie's uncle on one side."

"I meant . . ." As they headed inside, he wanted to kick his own ass. Now was not the time to delve into the past.

She flipped on a few lights as he relocked the door.

"Meant what?" She waited, then realization dawned in her eyes. "Or it's something you don't want to talk about?" Hand to her forehead, she apologized again. "I'm sorry. I keep pushing when I don't mean to."

When she started to turn away, Kam caught her hand. Here, where they'd gotten carried away earlier that day, seemed like as good a place as any to bare his soul. "It's not that. My past . . . It's an ugly memory."

"I'm sorry." As if to shield him, she slipped her arms around him. "I knew that, or at least I've assumed, since Addie adopted you."

"My parents died, but it wasn't a big loss to anyone." Though it had still crushed him. With his nose against her hair, breathing in her gentle fragrance, he confessed, "I used to think of paybacks. Like one day I'd be big enough to beat the shit out of my dad, or when my mom picked up a belt, I'd turn it on her." Her arms tightened, and though she didn't make a sound, he felt her distress.

He needed to shut up, but the words kept coming.

"Neighbors were forever spying on my dysfunctional family. I'd stick out my tongue or flip them the bird."

"Trying to prove you didn't care."

Her quiet whisper felt like an understanding stroke, making it impossible for him to deny. "Something like that."

Often he got a harsh punishment from his mother for doing it. Not that it stopped him.

He'd gotten tough because he'd had no choice. It was either fight back or break, because his folks had enjoyed a wicked game that always put him in the middle. His dad would smack him around, saying he had to toughen up, which doubled his mother's determination to beat out all resemblance to his father.

He'd found following his father's advice easier. If he was going to get hit, he might as well swing back. Didn't do him much good, but it felt better than just taking it.

All along, he'd told himself that one day he'd run away, that he'd go where no one would find him: A place where he could make his own rules.

A place where what *he* wanted mattered.

"So many times, I'd wished my parents dead—and then one day, they were." And he'd been so fucking lost he'd wished for death, too. "Sometimes they'd lock me in my room."

Glory squeezed him tighter.

"For my own good, they'd say." Many times, Kam wondered

why they'd even kept him around. "Occasionally, they'd be gone so long I'd have to crawl out the window to use the bathroom."

"Where did they go?"

"Dad liked to hang out with his friends, usually at a bar. Mom would go to my grandmother's house." Continued anger and hurt put a cruel smile on his mouth. "The night they died, I thought they'd forgotten all about me and I'd considered just running away. I figured I could get pretty far before they ever returned. I was hungry, pissed off . . . and a little afraid." *Afraid to stay—and afraid to go.* "I went out the window again and a neighbor saw me. He tried to talk to me, but I told him to fuck off."

"Kam."

Prim Glory. If she stuck around long enough, she'd hear worse from him. He'd been cursing since he was five years old—encouraged by dad, beaten by his mother. Then again, he could usually curb it for Addie, so he should probably curb it for Glory, too. "He called the police, concerned because he hadn't seen any signs of life from my parents for a day and a half. The next thing I knew, cops were talking to me through my window, then they broke down the door, and I was being hauled off to someplace new."

Sympathy showed in her furrowed brows and the trembling of her lips. "Your parents?"

"Bizarre tale, really." For the first time, talking about it wasn't devastating. Other than telling Addie and Tanner once, skimmed-over versions at best, he'd refused to talk about it. With Glory, he felt like a man, not that overwhelmed boy with no control of his life. Stepping back, he lifted Glory's face and pressed a kiss to her mouth. "You pack some powerful juju, lady."

A sad smile teased her lips. "What do you mean?"

Powerful, and she didn't even know it. "You make things easier."

Complimented by that idea, her eyes brightened. "I do?" Then she teased, "Or are you just hoping to get busy against the wall again?"

"A guy can always hope, right?" Bending his knees, he looked into her eyes. "But hey, I know you have preferences, so no pressure from me."

"Come on." She took his hand and led him toward the kitchen. "You're leaving me in suspense, you know."

"About sex? Rest assured, it's guaranteed."

With a laugh, she slid her sexy rump up onto a barstool. "No, I meant about your parents." In a gentler tone, she added, "Or would you rather not share?"

"It's weird, but I don't mind." He, too, took a stool, angling toward her so that their knees touched. "How about I keep it brief?" Then they could move on to better things. "I guess Dad had run out of cash, so he tried to rob my grandmother. He grabbed some cash she had hidden, but she must have busted him because he tore out of the driveway in a rush." Deadpan, he explained, "My granny carried a revolver in her housecoat pocket. She'd have shot him if she could."

Incredulous, Glory stared without blinking.

"Anyway, she and my mother chased after him. That was all on the door cam, him hightailing it out of there, the two women jumping in my mom's car and screeching after him. Neighbors watched them racing up the road. Dad was going too fast when he tried to take the turn, almost hit a big garbage truck and rolled. Since he wasn't buckled in, he ended up in the roadway, his head and neck mangled. Granny and Mom hit the truck. They weren't buckled in, either. Mom was crushed inside the car. Granny was half in, half out of the vehicle. She died from internal bleeding. Fortunately, the truck driver was okay."

"Do you miss them?"

"Addie asked me that once, too." Maybe Glory had more in common with Addie than she realized. "Tanner answered for me, because he already knew."

Looking into his eyes, she guessed, "No?"

"I'll never forget Tanner's exact words." Affecting Tanner's bossy tone, he said, "*No, and if he did, he'd deny it, same as I would.*"

She grinned with him. "He can be autocratic—but was he right?"

"Yeah, and that was the day I decided to lighten up on him, to maybe be his brother instead of his adversary."

Just above his knee, she lightly touched his thigh. "I think, even when things are awful, our parents manage to find a little place to live in our hearts."

He shrugged. "Like a cancer or something." At least, that's how he felt about his parents. He wondered how she felt about hers.

"Maybe. I guess not everyone is cut out to be a parent."

"Truth. That's why Tanner does so much to help kids now."

"You help as well."

How could he not? If it hadn't been for Addie, he'd have never known what family should be. Even when he was a jerk, she loved him. When he got into trouble, she protected him, but she also lectured him.

And not once, even while giving him guidance, did she insult him.

Ever.

She taught him and Tanner about loyalty and honor, but she'd taught them about family, too. She brought into his life things he'd never dared to hope for, like birthday celebrations, a Christmas tree with presents under it, fun outings . . . Jokes over dinner, the ability to discuss anything, ask questions without being ridiculed, reprimands that weren't demeaning, praise he never expected . . . All things that he'd come to cherish. "Every kid deserves to feel valued."

"Even when they screw up," Glory agreed.

That made him even more curious, especially with the way Glory withdrew. "How Addie treated me had a lot to do with it, but it helped that she knew how to make a house a home. Not that it was big or fancy or anything. Before Tanner and I helped expand and remodel parts, it was just a midsize farm-house."

"It's a home in a way few places ever can be."

Very true. "Even when it was run-down, the place had warmth and love." He grinned. "And Addie cooking. Most of the time, I'd wake in the morning to the smell of something good coming from the kitchen."

"That sounds really nice."

To an underfed kid, it had been heaven. "Tanner said he'll never leave it, so I'm really glad Callie agreed to move in."

"And yet, you wanted to leave."

It would have been easy to stay on at Addie's home with her always pampering him, to get comfortable with Tanner sharing his workload and his worries. "One day, I might go back." After he'd proven that it was a choice, not a need.

It wasn't until that very moment that it hit him: Was it a need, not for him, but possibly for Addie and Tanner? Did they need him to help pay the bills? From the time they'd gotten jobs, he and Tanner had always pitched in, financially and with the upkeep of the house. Christ, had he been a self-ish ass?

"What?" Concern brought her closer. "You don't like the idea of going back?"

He shook his head, unwilling to share all that right now

when he'd rather focus on getting her to bed. That meant lightening things up a little. "I doubt I'll ever take Percy from there. Addie and I both give it lip service, but . . ."

"It's his home, too."

"Percy was a scruffy little thing when I got him. All fluff with a nonstop meow that about drove me crazy." He watched her lips curve in a tempting smile. That made his lips curve, too. "He showed up in the woods one day, skinny, hissing, covered in burrs. Tanner and I got him inside, but man, he was a pissed-off kitty, at least until I fed him. He growled the whole time he ate."

"I bet that was sweet."

"Sweet, and a little threatening. Kittens have super-sharp claws. Luckily, he settled down after that. Addie kept an eye on him while Tanner and I went out to search for other kittens, but we didn't find any."

"So no idea where he came from?"

"Nope. He was old enough to be weaned, but a runt from living on his own."

"He's such a big lug now."

"Yeah, he is. Lazy, too. Occasionally, he likes to prowl outside, but he never goes far. Plus, he's chipped and has a GPS tag on his collar, so I'd always be able to find him."

"I've never had a pet," she suddenly said.

Kam took her hands in his, coasting his thumbs over her knuckles. "Did you want one?"

"I don't know. I like Blu and Percy, and I'm getting used to Callie's goats and chickens."

Her lack of enthusiasm over the farm animals made him want to grin. "You've met the horses, too, right?"

"Once." Wrinkling her nose, she said, "They're awfully big."

"Callie and Tanner go riding often now."

Immediately, she shook her head. "No way will I ever get on a horse."

If he got her to try it, she might change her mind. Few things were as peaceful as riding out, the sun on his back and the wind in his face, with nothing to distract him but the sounds of nature and the horse's hooves meeting the ground. "We'll see."

Dismissing that, she slid off the stool, stepped up against him, and gave him a slow-burn kiss that quickly had his mind on other things. It was the first time he could recall her initiating things, and damn, it was hot.

As she eased up, she said, "I'm going to take a quick shower before we turn in."

He hoped her idea of quick meant two minutes, because he wasn't sure he'd last longer than that.

She gave him another kiss, this one a light brushing of her lips over his. "You're not sleepy, are you?"

Ha! "No."

"Remember, there are rules."

He wasn't likely to forget, but all he said was, "Whatever you need, Glory."

That earned him a very sweet smile before she turned and headed to her bedroom.

The second her door closed, he launched into the hall and out to the SUV to grab one of the boxes he'd brought from home. It held his toiletries and a few changes of clothes.

The whole day had gone from one extreme emotion to another, but what he felt now—extreme lust tinged with tenderness—yeah, he liked that best. Lust he knew, but the deeper caring . . . That added a new dimension to things.

And it beat the hell out of strolling down memory lane.

After locking the front door again, Kam strode into the guest room to do his own quick washup, brush his teeth, and change into loose pajama pants.

They didn't have pockets, so the condoms he grabbed remained in his hand as he left the room. Bare chested and barefoot, he stopped outside her door and heard the shower turn off. It sent his heart thundering.

The way his body reacted, you'd think he'd never had sex before.

Glory had a unique effect on him, and he was starting to like it.

When her door opened, he went still.

She peeked out, looked startled to see him waiting right there, but her surprise quickly settled into a gentle smile. That was all the encouragement he needed.

He couldn't recall ever arranging sex quite like this. Usually it was more impulsive or expected. But not . . . arranged. A kiss led to a feel, which led to removing clothes and—*ta-da*—sex happened. On a couch, a bed . . .

Against a wall.

Somehow, in some indefinable way, this excited him even more.

The second he reached her, he pulled her into his arms. With the blackout blinds down and not a single lamp on, dark shadows dominated the room. From what he could feel, she wore a sleep shirt . . . and nothing else.

Oh, yeah. That worked for him.

One of her rules was him staying the whole night with her. A lot could happen in the dark, under the sheets, during sex.

Like a starving man, he took her mouth.

Showing her own lack of patience, she ran her hands over his chest, his shoulders, and down to his ass.

Okay then, fair play. He reciprocated, using his free hand to reach beneath the night shirt and encountering nothing but her warm silky skin. He groaned.

Glory pulled her mouth away and said, "The bed," as she quickly led him to it.

He tripped over something, maybe a shoe. "Damn."

"Right here." She tried to tug him down to the mattress with her, but he held back. "Let me put the condoms on the nightstand."

"Condoms, plural?"

"Three."

She said nothing, and that worried him. He found the nightstand, made sure he wouldn't knock over anything, and dropped the condoms there.

"You could lose the sleep pants."

Kam paused. "You said some clothes?"

"For me. I'm all for you being naked."

Before she'd finished talking, he had them off. "Done."

Voice lower, sultry, she said, "Come here."

Wow, this was new. Breathing hard, grinning, too, Kam reached for the bed, encountered her thigh, and used that touch to guide himself down beside her.

When he slid a hand to her hip, she caught his wrist and instead redirected him to her breast.

She'd already pushed the nightshirt up, leaving everything from her shoulders down bare. In the middle of rioting senses and burning lust, he wondered, *Why the rules?* But he kept the thought to himself. He wasn't about to say or do anything that might cause her to shy away.

Besides, one of her rules had been no questions.

While he kissed her, caressed her, she lifted her leg over his hip.

Even immersed in the most intense sensuality, a small part of Kam's brain went on autopilot. He was aware that she kept the nightshirt bunched above her breasts, and she didn't want him touching her left hip. Right hip was fair game, kissing and touching—anywhere, everywhere—she loved. But it was her left hip, and possibly something to do with her shoulders, that had inspired her rules.

Kissing his way down her chest to her breasts, he plumped her up with his hands, then teased one nipple.

Glory arched hard against him.

Testing her, just a little, he asked, "You like that?"

"*Yes*," she said, her voice a low vibration.

So that question was fine. He smiled as he circled her nipple with his tongue, then lightly caught it in his teeth.

Her breath shuddering out, she tangled her hands in his hair and held him closer until he drew her in. When she arched hard against him, he trailed a hand down her waist, near to her left hip—until she stiffened—then he bypassed that tempting area to press his fingers between her legs. He found her hot and wet, ready, and given how she moved, anxious.

At that point, he forgot his curiosity and wanted only her pleasure.

Moving to her other nipple, he licked twice, then sucked at her while he slowly pressed a finger deep. Her hands were all over him, her breathing choppy.

Adding a second finger, he found a rhythm she liked and soon she was on the ragged edge, saying his name, gasping. He'd erred once, taking her without a rubber, but going forward he wouldn't put her at risk. For him, it was now or never because her pleasure heightened his own.

"Let me grab a rubber."

"Hurry."

Sitting up, he felt for the nightstand—damn, he hated this clumsiness in the dark—and finally felt the small packet. Glory hadn't moved, so once he finished, he settled over her, between her legs.

He couldn't resist saying, "I wish I could see you." His mouth on hers stopped any protest she might have made. "I love looking at you, Glory." Without thinking about it, he kissed her neck . . . on her left side.

Wiggling, she got his mouth back to hers and said with urgent worry, "Now."

Brushing his lips over hers in soft agreement, he aligned them, opened her, and entered in one long slow thrust. Glory gripped him, her legs around his hips, arms around his neck . . . She even squeezed his cock.

He'd meant to make it last this time, use a little finesse, drag out her enjoyment, offer a counter-perspective to their frenzied rush against the wall.

Wasn't happening. In a nanosecond, he forgot his plans and only responded to her cues. Bodies entwined, he rocked with her, heat and pleasure coiling tighter. The second she tipped her head back on a long low groan, he let himself go, too. God, it was sweet. And hot.

And special—because this was Glory.

One day, he promised himself, he'd know all her secrets. For now, this was enough.

Sitting at the small bar located within three miles of the hall where he'd hoped to reengage Glory, Mike stewed. He'd changed his appearance as much as possible. His brown hair was now black, with added mousse to make it messier. His clear contacts had been changed out so that now his eyes looked chocolate brown. Much as he detested being unkempt, he allowed itchy beard scruff to cover his face. Instead of his usual tidy polo shirts, he wore plain dark T-shirts and jeans with sneakers.

Even his own mother, if she were miraculously brought back from the dead, wouldn't recognize him now. Not that the bitch had ever paid much attention to him, anyway.

That was a lowering thought, and he quickly scrubbed it from his mind.

Instead, his thoughts veered to Jenn . . . and he didn't like that, either. His mother no longer mattered. Neither did Jenn.

All that mattered was his Glory. She was his soulmate. He knew it, and soon she would know it, too.

If he were the type to get drunk, he might actually enjoy slumming at the not-so-quaint establishment. Instead, he sipped his second Manhattan and calculated his next move.

He'd have preferred a brandy but, of course, the little hicktown bar didn't carry it. Not a surprise, really. Everyone else in the place appeared to be swilling longneck beers.

It had been a miserable week since he'd attempted to take Glory's car and he'd yet to locate her again. She'd even blocked his number so he couldn't call or text.

The games were getting ridiculous, but he wouldn't give up. A man did not give up his heart.

"Oh, now look at that long face. Drinking alone is never fun, is it?"

He didn't want to have fun, but at the throaty purr, Mike looked up to see a tall, slim woman, beautiful really, smiling down at him. Long straight light brown hair hung over her shoulders. Not styled the way Glory preferred, but he supposed there was a certain appeal to the unkempt look. Her dark eyes took his measure.

Fine. He checked her out, too.

"Mind if I join you?"

Rude, to slide into the booth without an invitation. "And if I do?"

"Guess I'd have to convince you."

Reviled by the prospect, Mike indicated the seat she'd already taken. "By all means, make yourself comfortable."

"Already did." Laughing, she noted, "You sure are uptight. Whiskey not helping?"

"I don't look to alcohol to solve my problems." He had a brain for that. "Is that what you're hoping to do?" He glanced at her drink—thankfully not a beer—and lifted his brows. "Are you hoping to unwind . . . ?"

"Shara," she said, supplying her name, and even reaching over the table to offer a small hand, her long nails painted a glaring red.

Never would he give this woman his actual name. "Leon," he said, bringing back the alias he'd used once before, when it was necessary to hide his real name.

With this woman, he'd be Leon again.

Her hand felt rough, making him wonder at her occupation. Glory's skin was always soft, pampered, and never would she paint her nails such a garish color.

"Actually," Shara said, "I found out a guy I liked has hooked up with someone else. Pisses me off, you know?"

The crude language annoyed him. "I'm sure it's his loss."

Her glossy lips curled. "I thought maybe I'd retaliate. Have my own fling and then tell him about it."

Whore. Mike barely kept his revulsion hidden. "I'm dealing with a similar situation, but I won't sully myself with anyone else. I love her and that's what matters." It *had* to matter. Eventually, Glory would realize it.

Once before, he'd met a woman he thought would do . . . but she'd let him down. Getting rid of her hadn't been easy, but he'd done it. The same way he'd gotten rid of his mother. In this world, he'd discovered that there weren't many women like his Glory, a beautiful beacon of gentleness, the perfect counterpoint to his turbulence. Around her, he could find calm moderation.

Away from her, the tempest raged.

Shara's laugh broke into his thoughts. "Sully yourself? Are you for real?"

Tight with anger, he stared at her until she ended her giggles. "Love is a serious emotion. I assume you don't actually love this man or you wouldn't be offering yourself elsewhere."

"Love Kam?" she asked. "I certainly loved things about him. I would have married him. Still would, I guess, but—why are you staring at me like that?" She snapped her fingers in his face. "C'mon, man. You okay?"

Belatedly, Mike remembered to inhale. This foul woman knew Kam? It had to be the same man. Surely, this tiny backward town didn't boast two men with that exact uncommon name.

"Excuse me," he said, taking a moment to sip his drink and quiet his rioting instincts. Patting his mouth with his napkin, he finally met her gaze. "So Kam is the one you want?"

"Yes," she purred. "He's delicious."

"He sounds like a small man." Gently leading her, he said, "Probably pale."

"Ha! You couldn't be more wrong. He's over six feet tall, ripped from his work on a tree farm and machine shop. Not at all pale—not with his brown hair, dark brows and lashes."

Dreamily, as if she'd slipped into a mental fantasy, Shara smiled. In his head, Mike locked down the details she's provided: tree farm, machine shop. If either of those establishments were in the actual town, they'd be easy for him to find. "Whatever lurid things you're envisioning are likely best kept to yourself." Doing his utmost to hide his disgust, he folded his hands on the booth tabletop. "So who is your Kam seeing now?"

"Some snooty bitch."

The vicious squeeze of his hands caused his knuckles to pop. How dare this miserable slut insult his Glory? Through his teeth, he asked, "Have you met her?"

"No, but I've seen her. She polishes herself up like a piece of fine china. Never a hair out of place, never a wrinkle in her designer duds. I doubt a woman like her has ever cut loose."

"Of course, she hasn't."

Brows lifted in surprise, Shara stared at him.

He quickly recovered. "That is, I assume by the way you've described her that she wouldn't . . ." *How to say it without insulting her?* ". . . ah, let down her hair and . . ." At a loss, he gestured to Shara, to her body displayed in an extremely low-cut tank top. "Do that."

Knowingly, Shara smiled, then shimmied in her seat.

It caused her fleshy breasts to jiggle. Despite his love of Glory, Mike looked. That was the way of men, and why each needed his perfect woman.

For him, that was Glory.

Mike assured himself that attraction had nothing to do with it. He was a man. Breasts, by way of nature, appealed to his carnal nature.

"I think you're going about this all wrong." Sitting forward, Mike was ready to put a plan into action. "If this other woman is as demure as you claim—"

Barking another obnoxious laugh, Shara repeated, "Demure? Damn, dude, where did you come from?"

"Not," he stated through clenched teeth, "from around here."

"No kidding. I could tell that right off."

Again, to hide his identity, he said, "I recently moved here from Canada."

"Don't Canadians have an accent?"

"Have you met many?"

"Well . . . no."

He had doubts that she'd ever stepped outside of this absurd town. "So would you like some excellent advice or not?"

She held out slender arms. "Lay it on me."

Getting right to the point—*his* point, that was—Mike said, "Go after him. Make yourself accessible as often as possible. Men are not good at resisting temptation." Some men. Men who weren't truly in love. "He'll crack, and when he does, this other woman will realize he's not honorable. If nothing else, she'll be out of the picture and that will give you an opening."

She wrinkled her nose. "It'll make me look desperate."

"More likely it'll flatter him." Didn't matter that Kam had acted all cocksure of himself, so full of confidence. All men suffered weakness of the flesh.

Once Mike had Glory, he'd do better. He *had* to have her—and he would. Very soon.

Now to manipulate Kam's weakness. "Look at it this way: You could do it for payback. He spurned you, so egg him on, get him enticed, and when the other woman catches the two of you, you can spurn him."

"Spurn him, huh? You do have a funny way of talking, but I get your meaning. I would enjoy a little sweet revenge."

Yes, Mike thought, *revenge would be very sweet.* Once Kam showed his true colors, Glory would naturally turn to him for solace.

Once he had her again, he wouldn't make the same mistake he'd made with Jenn.

He'd never let Glory go.

Until then, he decided that loud and uncouth Shara could be a fount of information. If nothing else, she could tell him where to find Kam.

Breaking Glory's window hadn't frightened her enough to bring her back, but more trouble would come her way. He'd see to it. When it added up, when she got jumpy and possibly clingy, as all women did, Kam would tire of the drama.

Smiling, Mike lifted his hand to get the attention of the waitress. He'd get a few more drinks for his unexpected and largely unwanted guest. Since she was here, he may as well ensure she was useful.

No reason for her to spend her entire life as a waste of humanity.

In fact, given that most of the town looked to be of very moderate means, there were likely others in her circle that he could engage. Why should he do the dirty work himself?

As the drink was set before Shara, Mike decided to get her contact info, and to learn more about some of her friends. If, like her, they were foolish and desperate, he'd have a reliable network set up in no time.

8

For the first time that Glory could remember, life felt magical. She was practically floating through her days—and her nights. Mmm, the nights were beyond incredible.

No doubt her uplifted spirits were the result of a week-long sexual marathon. Not once had Kam pushed beyond her rules. In some subtle ways, he'd made it clear that he'd prefer to have the lights on—that he'd love to see her completely bare.

He definitely wanted to touch her all over.

But he didn't make a big deal of it. On the occasions when she darkened the room, when she held him back from removing her top or redirected his hands, he didn't say a word.

All he did was scorch her with amazing sex.

She'd never felt anything like it. Were they that compatible, or was he just that good?

In comparison, the sex she'd had with other men now seemed mediocre, so she assumed it was his skill.

"Glory," he said, his lips hovering near her ear. "What are you thinking? Or should I guess?"

"Hush." With Kam's family and her cousin within earshot, she worried that someone might overhear. "Behave please."

"For now," he agreed. "But when I get you alone tonight, all bets are off."

What a wicked tease! With Addie, Callie, and Tanner all close, she struggled to keep a friendly smile in place. So far, no one had questioned Kam's presence in her home, likely because they knew about his streak of protectiveness. But how was she supposed to keep their relationship under wraps when he said things that turned her pink?

As if she'd sensed the tension, Addie said, "We'll have beautiful weather next week."

"Good. I'll be able to get caught up." Tanner put his arm around Callie. "Not that I'm complaining about my recent diversions."

Callie, who didn't seem at all embarrassed by the comment, only laughed.

Yes, she and Tanner were still celebrating their marriage, but yesterday, they'd each gotten back to work. Tanner claimed orders were piling up—even though Kam had done his best to stay on top of everything with his own job and the deliveries from the tree farm while Addie handled all the paperwork. It had still been a busy week, but none of them had minded.

In one breath, Callie had thanked Glory for taking over her duties with the animals, and in the next, she'd swore the chickens and goats missed her. It didn't matter that, the first botched day aside, Glory had managed her exact routine; Callie loved the animals, and they obviously loved her, too.

"You two are creatures of habit," Addie said. "Happiest when you're busy."

"Look who's talking." Tanner sent Addie a salute.

"It helps that we love our work." Callie picked up a dish to carry to the table. "But it sure works up an appetite."

Tonight, the dinner would have been immediate family only—Addie, Kam, Tanner, and Callie—except that Kam insisted Glory come along.

It made no sense. He shouldn't still be worried. An entire week had gone by with nothing else happening. Not a peep from Mike. It was Glory's fondest hope that Mike had given up and gotten back to his own life.

Except . . . Kam had an apartment waiting for him, and she hated the thought of him leaving her house. It was so nice having him there, sleeping with him each night, sharing coffee each morning. Even when they spent hours apart, he kept track of her, and at the same time, he checked in so she'd know how to reach him. He'd text her before driving out a delivery, call her during his lunch break, and let her know when he was heading "home." On the occasions when she was busy, he was understanding about it.

Neither of them had said it, and she definitely didn't want to share, but they were a couple. At least, she thought they were. There wasn't extra time for him to be seeing anyone else. He hadn't actually declared they were together—but how could he when she'd sworn him to secrecy?

As sexually active as Kam had been, no one would think they were truly involved unless they were sleeping together. Looking at Tanner and Addie . . . No, she still wasn't yet ready to make that admission.

Avoiding Kam's knowing gaze, Glory carried a pitcher of iced tea to the table. "We talked with Dan Fellows today."

"How is he?" Tanner took the pitcher from her and began filling drinks.

It was nice how everyone worked together—how they let *her* work with them. She loved the relaxed atmosphere.

Whenever she was there, in their family home, she truly felt a part of things.

Not an interloper, not an awkward extra. She almost felt like family, too, except that, other than Callie, they weren't her family.

But a girl could wish.

If they knew she and Kam were sleeping together, would it change things? Honestly, she just didn't know—and she wasn't yet ready to take the chance.

"He's great, considering." Automatically, Kam took the seat beside Glory. "He'll have the cast on his arm for a while yet, but the concussion still has him down, anyway."

Putting a hand to her stomach, Glory tried to quell her sudden uneasiness as she recalled seeing Dan, his battered face and broken arm. "He's still covered in bruises. All around his forehead, his temple, and one of his eyes." No matter what anyone said, it felt like her fault. "His poor nose . . ."

"His glasses broke from the impact." Without looking at her, Kam reached beneath the table and retrieved her hand for a gentle squeeze. "Dan was all smiles during our visit, but this one—" he tipped his head at Glory "—looked ready to cry when she saw him."

"It's awful." The worst part was imagining what might have happened. "He could have been killed."

"But he wasn't." Addie passed the platter of pork chops to Tanner. "Fortunately, he's at home being pampered by his family. He'll recover, so let's focus on that."

Giving her a sympathetic glance, Tanner said, "Callie and I will stop in and see him, too."

"I asked if he needed anything." It would have made her feel better to do something for him. "He swears he doesn't."

"He has his family." Briefly, Callie put her head on Tanner's shoulder. "For most of us, that's enough."

Tanner kissed her forehead.

They were so close, so in love, that it was hard to believe her cousin had almost married someone else. Thankfully, the loser had shown his true colors before that happened. *Sometimes*, Glory thought, *things happened for a reason*.

Callie had busted her ex cheating, and now she had Tanner. A perfect outcome to what had started as an awful situation, especially with how everyone had tried to pressure Callie into marrying the ex, anyway.

Wearing a big warm smile, Addie glanced around the table. "It's so nice having all of you here." Her gaze landed on each of them, one by one, until it stopped on Glory. "My heart is full."

That started a round of gratitude with everyone telling Addie what a treat it was to get both her food and her company.

"Thank you for including me," Glory added last, "even though I'm not related."

"Bull." Callie tossed a napkin at her. "You're my cousin who's more like a sister, and when I married in, I made you part of the deal."

"True," Tanner said. "You're officially stuck with us."

That earned him a big smile from Callie.

"We're not so bad," Addie said, teasing her. "But they're right. You're family, honey. Don't ever forget it."

Oh, God. What if things went sideways between her and Kam? No way would they feel the same, it'd be too awkward. Naturally, she'd be on the outside again.

Exactly where she didn't want to be. It was too nice being included. Too special. If she screwed it up . . .

Using his shoulder, Kam nudged her out of her worry.

She had to grab the table, so she didn't fall off her seat. "Hey."

Callie and Tanner laughed, while Addie swatted at him.

Devilish amusement glittered in his green eyes. "I'm the worst of the bunch, you know. But I'm not so hard to get along with, right?"

Heat rushed into her face. She got along with him just fine—especially in bed. Feeling guilty, and probably looking it, too, Glory struggled to find something to say.

Bless Callie, she started up a conversation about the renovations to her small home. Though Glory chose to stay silent, the others chatted through the rest of the meal.

She was saved by the ringing of the doorbell. Since she was the closest and anxious for a reason to escape, she said, "I can get it."

Tanner got up before she could move. "Stay put." He shared a male-inspired glance with Kam. "I've got it."

Wondering what that look had meant, she relaxed back in her seat. "Is something going on?"

"Men conspiring." Callie, who had a mouthful, lifted her napkin and hastily chewed. "They're still worried about that creep, Mike."

"Rightfully so." Kam stared toward the muted voices at the door. "Until we know where that jackass is, you have to be careful."

"He wouldn't come *here*." At least, she hoped he wouldn't.

"Maybe not." Kam rolled one shoulder. "But we'd rather not take chances."

Good grief, what did he think Mike would do?

"Leave room for dessert," Addie said, switching the topic. "I made blueberry cobbler and it'll still be warm. I have vanilla ice cream to go with it."

"Oh, that sounds good, doesn't it, Glory?"

"It sounds like pure temptation."

Kam grinned at her.

Just then, Tanner reentered the dining room, an unmistakable expression of irony on his face. "Kam, you have a guest. I told her you were eating, but she was . . . persistent."

On his heels was a woman Glory hadn't met. Tall, model-slim, with long fawn-colored hair and dark eyes, she breezed in with familiarity—until she spotted Callie and Glory. That drew her up short and she glared at each of them.

After coming to his feet, Kam put a hand on the back of Glory's chair. "Shara. What are you doing here?"

"You didn't call me back, so I came by to see you."

First Natalie at the reception hall, then Ronna from the hardware store, and now this woman? Kam certainly got around.

Done with her meal, Glory stood. Pride kept her voice even and friendly. "I'll just take our dishes to the kitchen."

Callie jumped up. "I'll help you."

"Here, now," Addie protested, scrambling to join them. "I'm the host."

"And as such, you should relax." Glory urged her back to her seat.

"You fixed the meal, now let us clear the table." Callie gave Tanner a kiss, whispered something to him, and then filled her arms with stacked dishes."

As she was walking away, Glory heard Kam say, "Sorry, Shara, but I've been busy."

"With her?" The other woman laughed. "Get real."

It didn't help that even when they reached the kitchen, Glory could still perfectly hear the conversation in the dining room. It consisted of Shara making not-so-veiled insults toward her, and Kam clearly becoming irked.

Callie glared back toward the dining room. "Kam should tell that woman to shut it."

"Shh." That hearing thing went both ways. "I'm sure he doesn't want to be rude."

"Well, I don't mind throwing her rudeness right back in her face."

"Callie," she hissed. "Please don't embarrass me."

Taking one look at her cousin's expression, Callie relented and lowered her tone. "She's a nasty woman. I don't like her."

"Neither of us really knows her."

"I know you and Kam have something going on, so stop trying to hide it."

"I . . . It's just . . ."

"Glory, you know you can't fib to me. There's a sister code or something, I'm sure of it."

"We're cousins."

"You only say that when it's convenient."

From the other room, they both heard Shara say, "Why is Miss High and Mighty hanging out here?"

In a tone rife with irritation, Tanner said, "She's my wife's cousin—"

At that, Glory raised a brow as if to say, *See, we're cousins.*

"But they're more like sisters."

Callie gave a muffled, "Ha!"

"And they're both lovely women," Addie insisted, her own voice bordering on hostile.

"Fine, she's nice," Shara said to Addie without much conviction. "Do you honestly think she's interested in Kam?"

"Why wouldn't she be?"

"She comes from money, that's why. She walks around with her nose in the air as if she's better than us."

"Us?" Tanner repeated, his tone flat. "Glory likes me just fine."

"And me," Addie said.

"Ha! She's up to something, I tell you."

The strangest thing happened. Glory didn't mean to intrude, and in fact, she hadn't wanted to. But anger propelled her to the dining room, and suddenly, she was there, face-to-face with Shara, and she heard herself say in silky menace, "Are you somehow insinuating that this family is beneath me?"

"Beneath *us*?" Callie said, as she slipped her arm through Glory's in a show of solidarity.

"Because you couldn't be more wrong." It took a lot to get Glory riled, but insulting this wonderful family, in any way, certainly did it. "I've never met finer men or a more beautiful, generous woman."

Surprised by the direct confrontation, Shara moved closer to Kam.

Folding his arms over his chest, his mouth tipped in a very small smile, he waited. So did Tanner and Addie, and they all three looked . . . pleased.

Oh, Lord. Glory couldn't believe she'd started this.

"Well," Shara said. "I guess you're slumming, then?"

"Slumming?" Glory was right back to being enraged. "I doubt I deserve to be here with them, not the other way around!"

"So you're . . . what?" Shara sneered. "Genuinely interested in Kam?"

Put on the spot like that, Glory floundered.

Callie, unfortunately, did not. "He's staying with her." She dusted her hands, as if that settled it.

"I . . . That is, Kam and I are friends."

Curling her lip, Shara suggestively asked, "Friends with benefits?"

Glory took a step forward. "How dare you be so crude in front of his mother?" She turned to Addie. "I'm so sorry for her insensitive remarks."

"Oh, um . . ." Addie blinked over the defense. "Yes, you're right." She tried, and completely failed, to look shocked. Overall, she appeared fascinated by the entire clash.

Callie snickered. Tanner grinned.

Of course, having raised Tanner and Kam, Addie had likely heard a lot worse over the years.

Glory didn't care. "It's incredibly rude to enter someone's home and sling around insults and accusations."

Suddenly unsure of herself, Shara turned to Kam. "I've always thought you were all awesome. You know that, right?"

"Sure," he said with disinterest, then he took Shara's arm and said gently, "Come on, I'll walk you out."

"But I wasn't leaving."

"Yeah, you are." He urged her along.

As the silence descended, Glory wished for a quick way out. "Kitchen. I'm, um, yes. The kitchen." She spun away and rushed back to the dishes. Why was it she could never find the right way to fit in? Every time, she ended up saying or doing something that made her feel foolish. She certainly knew better. If Liz were here, she'd be scandalized. Over and over, Liz had stressed that scenes were to be avoided.

Wallowing in her own humiliation, Glory hoped no one would join her, not even Callie.

Then she heard the sudden roar of laughter. She glanced back to see the three of them hanging onto each other, cracking up. Putting her hands over her face, Glory wondered if she could sneak out the back.

But before long, she, too, was grinning.

Maybe she fit in better than she realized.

The second they were through the door, Kam was on Glory. Damn, it had been hard keeping his comments—and his hands—to himself, while they were visiting Addie and eating cobbler.

Not for a second did he think Tanner or Addie were dense enough to overlook the obvious. He and Glory had some powerful chemistry going on, and even when she tried to hide it, the sparks ignited.

Pinning her to what he now referred to as his favorite wall, Kam took her mouth like a starving man. Even better, she reciprocated in kind. Hands to her backside, he lifted her against him so he could grind his erection against her softness.

When he kissed his way to her throat, she said, "You taste like blueberries."

He growled. "You taste like heated woman." To punctuate that, he gave her a soft love bite that had her groaning.

In a rush, she pressed him back, but snagged his hand. "Come on."

What she meant was: Come to the bedroom, where I can make it too dark for you to see. God, he wanted to explore every inch of her body. He wanted to reassure her that she had nothing to hide.

Night after night, those damn rules stood between them; a brick wall he couldn't scale and couldn't ram through, not without hurting her. She'd come up with them for a reason, and until she trusted him enough to share those reasons, he'd keep respecting her wishes.

In the bedroom, he found the blinds already closed. Glory flipped on the small lamp on her nightstand, using the low light to fold back the plush bedding, then setting out two condoms.

"Love your faith in my stamina."

Hitching her chin, she smiled. "You've given me reason to have faith."

He'd given her reason to trust him, too, but apparently she needed more time.

Coming toward him in a sassy walk, she said, "Give me three minutes in the shower."

Kam caught her hand and drew her around to him. "Sorry, babe. I can't wait." Stealing any chance she had for a protest, and hoping to chisel away on the trust issue, he lifted her in his arms, took two steps toward the bed, and lowered her to her back.

It wasn't easy to ignore the way her eyes flared with worry. He slipped off her shoes and tossed them toward her closet. He wouldn't want her tripping over them later when she tried to move around in the dark room.

Standing again, he reached back with one hand and grabbed his shirt, stripping it off over his head and tossing it toward a corner. He kicked his shoes in that general direction, then opened his jeans.

Glory came up to her elbows to watch.

That's right, girl. A little stripping can be sexy. He didn't mind giving her a show. Eventually, she'd repay the favor. He had to believe that.

Without a speck of modesty, he pushed down his jeans and boxers, and without looking, threw them in the general direction of his shirt and shoes. *Trust*, he reminded himself. That's what he needed from her.

Breathing deeper, Glory tracked his every step as he moved to the nightstand to pick up a condom. He flipped it a few times, enjoying how her focus stayed on his dick, then he handed it to her. "Why don't you put it on me?"

As she sat forward, her chest rose on a deep breath. "The light . . ."

"Can go off when you're done."

Briefly, her gaze met his—with apology, and maybe a touch of gratitude, too.

Kam touched the side of her face. "It's your show, Glory. Whatever you need, remember?"

A flush rose in her cheeks, warm and enticing, followed by a sultry smile. With one hand, she held the condom packet, and with the other, she reached out to stroke his hip. "You devastate me."

That husky timbre in her voice hit him hard. "Back atcha."

Shaking her head, she said, "I'm just me. But you . . ." She leaned forward to brush her nose against his torso, which nearly stopped his heart. "You smell so good."

Damn, much more of that and he'd lose it. "You smell good too, Glory. Waking up with you against me, my nose in your hair or against your neck, is one of my favorite things." While he spoke, he brushed his fingers through her hair. "Right up there with hearing you laugh." Serious, hoping she'd understand, he added, "You don't laugh often enough."

"I'll try to do better." The whispered words, said absently, preceded the bold curl of her fingers around him. He barely had time to drag in a breath before he felt the soft press of her lips.

Closing his eyes didn't help, so he opened them again to watch her. Nothing in this world could be hotter than Glory's blond hair falling forward, half hiding her face while her pink lips parted, followed by the slow stroke of her tongue across his dick.

"God," he growled, trying to find the words to encourage her, to hurry her along.

"I'm glad you left the light on for this."

Yeah, he was glad, too.

With no other warning, she drew him into her mouth, damp heat closing around him.

"Glory . . ." His muscles locked, but he kept his hand gentle as he stroked her hair, her shoulder, the side of her face, where he felt the way her cheeks hollowed on a slow suck. For two minutes more, he enjoyed the slow torture before he accepted he was at his breaking point. "Enough, or the night will be over without a single condom used." After uttering that nonsense, he had to catch his breath. "Condom on, babe. No more playing."

Eyes half closed, she slicked her tongue over her bottom lip, then smiled up at him. "You have promises to keep." She rolled the condom onto him, then stretched over to turn out the lamp.

Damn. He'd half hoped she'd moved beyond it, but he wasn't about to slow things down now. Blindly, he reached out, felt her leg, and then tracked his fingers up to the closure of her jeans. "Okay for me to get these off you?"

Her hesitation hung in the air. Kam held his breath, waiting.

"Yes."

Yeah, that about did it. Her small quiet agreement had the impact of a vow. To keep her from regrets, he lectured himself about ensuring his hands were on safe ground—at least, the ground she deemed safe. Meaning off her left shoulder and hip.

When he stripped off her jeans, he took her silky panties, too, dropping both to the floor. Moving over her, he held her face and kissed her urgently, because she needed to catch up.

Fortunately, she was already there, her hands in his hair, her legs wrapping around him. Damn it, she still wore her shirt and bra, and as much as he wanted them gone, it was her call.

"Now, Kam. I can't wait."

Worked for him. He reached down to move two fingers over her, feeling her wetness, her heat. He positioned himself, and they both pressed together with need.

Nothing with Glory was conventional.

That was just one of the things that made her so special.

A few hours later, they were both still breathing hard—after round two.

Smiling, Kam drew Glory atop him. He might have rushed her to bed, but she'd kept him there. She still wore her shirt, but at least her bra was open now, the cups tangled up under her arms. She hadn't yet removed her makeup, and when he tried to imagine how she might look, he laughed.

Every time with Glory was hotter, and he figured that might be because he constantly got to know her better.

"What's funny?" she murmured.

Earlier, her defense of his family had warmed him from the inside out. In some indefinable way, that feeling of contentment had transformed into need. Since needing anyone made him antsy, he'd deliberately shifted it to lust. "Just thinking of how your eye makeup must look right now."

"Jerk." Sluggishly, she thumped her fist to his shoulder, but there was no real anger behind it. "You'll never know."

"Spoilsport." He pressed a kiss to her damp temple. "You don't need to worry about Shara, you know."

With a little less lethargy, she asked, "Is that so?"

"We used to date, but it was never more than that."

Time ticked by, nearly half a minute, before she asked, "Had she called you?"

"A few times." Overall, he'd been ignoring her and assuming she'd catch on.

"You didn't mention it."

"Why would I?"

Glory shoved up, and if it hadn't been so dark, he assumed he would've seen her glare.

Bringing his hands up her shoulders to her neck, he stroked his thumbs over her silky skin. "It's cute that you're jealous, but—"

"Cute?"

Good thing she couldn't see his grin. "I've been jealous of Mike, too."

"That's ridiculous. I want nothing to do with Mike."

"Ditto. From me, I mean, about Shara."

"Or Natalie? Or Ronna?"

"What?" he teased. "Are you keeping a record?"

With a huff, she settled against him again. "Are there any others?"

He shrugged. "Do you honestly think I want any other woman right now?"

"Right now," she repeated, "maybe not."

The unspoken fact that they weren't locked down, not in any way, annoyed him. "You're the one who wants everything kept private. I have no problem sharing." Hell, he'd happily shout it to anyone who listened.

"Thank you."

That made him lock his teeth.

"Do you think I could have just a little more time?" In a rush, she raised herself up again, kissed him, and said, "I love being included with your family." Abruptly, she moved to the side of him. "Oh, not that you *have* to include me. I don't mean that. But it's nice, and I—"

Grabbing her, Kam managed to roll her under him, kissed her hard, and stated, "You. Are. Family. Believe it, please. No matter how it rolls out with us." Though he certainly had his preferences.

He could practically feel her thinking before she whispered, "That's what Addie said."

"She means it."

"But if things went poorly, and you were angry with me—"

"Won't happen."

"You walked Shara out." Her arms went around his neck and she hugged him tight. "I wouldn't want to be walked out."

Kam groaned. "It's not at all the same thing." Shara had never been in his life. Mostly, she'd been a hookup for sex—which had worked for both of them. She knew his family only because they all lived in the same area. Everyone knew everyone else in Hoker. That was the curse—and often the blessing—of a small town.

Glory pushed at him. "I need that shower now."

He didn't want the night to end like this, but she was already scrambling away.

Kam flopped back, one arm over his eyes. Not like he'd be able to see anything, anyway. "I'll shower after you and then we'll get some sleep."

"Okay." When the light flashed on, it startled him enough that he came up on one arm.

Glory stood in the bathroom doorway, her shirt tugged low, her hair a little wild, her eye makeup leaving dark smudges.

And she stared at him. "Thank you for letting me enjoy you tonight."

A cocky grin came despite his effort to stave it off. "Thank you for enjoying me." That sounded goofy enough that he laughed.

She grinned, too, then backed two steps into the bathroom and shut the door.

"Only with you, Glory," he whispered. In his heart, he knew that was true.

Now that he'd been with her like this, no other woman would do.

Three days later, Mike had a peon on his payroll. It was easy to spot the kid Shara had described. Kirby—Mike didn't remember his last name—looked to be sixteen or seventeen, lanky, with the weight of the world on his skinny shoulders. Oh, boo-hoo. Mike half rolled his eyes in a distinct lack of pity. Whatever trouble this kid had, he'd probably brought it on himself.

As Mike had promised—anonymously over an untraceable

phone—the kid found the hundred dollars taped to the bottom of the bench in the park.

Kirby stared at the money with undiluted greed, even rubbing his mouth a few times and then glancing guiltily around him, as if it were stolen cash.

Mike was far enough away that Kirby wouldn't notice him, but with the binoculars, he could see the kid just fine. After pocketing the money, Kirby looked around again, then retrieved the note that had been taped next to the money.

Half smiling, Mike saw the apprehension grow as the kid read. "Do it," Mike said quietly. "Do it, and there will be more."

Kirby didn't put the money back. No, he just firmed his mouth, shoved the note in his pocket, too, then headed to a junker car and left the park.

If he followed through, if he did as he was told, Mike would give him the rest of the promised money, in a new location, of course. And he'd give him new instructions. Soon, very soon, Glory would be back where she belonged: with him. Once he had her, he'd make certain she understood the futility of resisting.

Unlike Jenn, he and Glory were meant to be. She belonged to him.

Willingly . . . or otherwise.

9

Kam had barely finished a single cup of coffee when the call came in. As was their new pattern, he'd quickly showered and then started the coffee. Glory was still in the shower. While he waited for her to finish, he rushed through dressing.

She was just stepping out of the room when he'd lifted his hand to knock.

Seeing him there, his fist raised, she backpedaled on a laugh. "You startled me."

Drawing her out, Kam put a quick kiss to her mouth, using care since he hadn't taken the time to shave. "Sorry, but I have to head out. There was a fire at the shop." He headed for the front door where he'd left his shoes.

"What shop?" she asked, hustling to keep up with him.

"The machine shop where I work."

"What happened? How bad is it?"

"A big trash receptacle caught fire; I don't know how yet. There was damage to the front of the building, but . . ." That's when it hit him. He turned to stare at Glory. "Are you ready to go, too?"

"I will be in five minutes. Why? Did you need something from me?"

He was starting to think he needed *everything* from her. That silent admission put him on guard, but he wouldn't take chances with her safety.

"Kam? What is it? You look . . . well, enraged."

Probably because his instincts were kicking hard. "It didn't occur to me at first, but what if Mike is behind this?" Running a hand over his messy hair, he considered all the possibilities. "He could be distracting me so he can . . . I don't know. Try something." *With you*.

Bottom lip caught in her teeth, Glory stared at him. Finally, she said, "That seems unlikely, right? We haven't heard from him in over a week, and how could he even know where you work?"

"Small town, babe, remember? He could ask the cashier at the local grocery and find out all he needs to know." He didn't want to scare Glory, but damn it, now he was divided.

"I'm going to the office today. I'll be surrounded by people."

"The office your folks opened here in town?" If so, he could follow her there and be around before she headed back home.

Apologetically, she shook her head. "In Bowling Green. It's only a little over an hour away." Touching his arm, she placated him. "I'll be on I-165 most of the time. It's always congested. No reason for you to worry."

"I don't worry," he grumbled, even as he looked at the time. "Shit. I've got to go. It's all hands on deck so we can clean up the damage and still stay on track." He was due to finish up a custom job on an especially old tractor, so it'd be ready for a sale. "I'd rather we head out at the same time."

She hesitated, then nodded. "I was going to grab a bagel, but I'll get something at the office. Just let me get my purse." She darted off and was back in less than a minute.

As they stepped out together, Kam looked up and down the quiet street. "Am I rushing you off too early?"

"No, it's fine. If I get to the office before the client, I'll just visit with the other employees. I haven't seen them in a while, so it'll be nice to catch up."

Spotting Old Lady Simmons coming out her front door, Kam grinned. He cupped Glory's face. "Will you please call me once you're there, and then again when you're heading back?"

"See, that's called worrying." Unaware of her neighbor's scrutiny, she went on tiptoe to kiss him. "But no, I don't mind calling—as long as you do the same. After all, it was the shop where you work that had a fire."

"I assume you can call hands-free?"

"I can. I'll keep my cell phone in the cup holder instead of storing it in my purse."

"Thank you." He initiated the next kiss, then whispered against her lips, "Want to give Simmons something to see?"

"What—Kam!" Pressing him away, she glanced over and saw the woman scowling at her. Fashioning a false smile, Glory waved. "Good morning, Mrs. Simmons."

"I'm sure it is, with that young man all over you."

Blank-faced, Glory asked from the side of her mouth, "Erm, Kam, was that a joke, do you think?"

"The way she keeps her eyebrows together, I can't tell." Just for the heck of it, he waved too as they headed for their separate cars. "Remember: Call me. Often. Definitely before you go anywhere."

He'd still worry, but he felt better knowing she'd stay in touch. And if it turned out that Mike was targeting him instead, that'd work fine. Given half an excuse, Kam would take the other man apart and enjoy doing it.

On the road, he thought about Glory, about the things he felt—things he'd never counted on. Overwhelming things, or they should be, but when he was with her, he mostly felt at peace.

He considered his apartment now that it was slowly coming together, except that it was still unoccupied. One of these days—soon—he'd need to make a decision on that. After he made a decision on Glory.

Driving by habit, he allowed his thoughts to wander, and as they often did, they took him back to a painful time. *You're no good. You'll never be good. Every day you look more like him.*

Then his father would drag him out for an evening of bar hopping, all the while telling him that he had to toughen up, that all women were hateful and mean.

He encouraged him to fight back. When he'd been ten years old, he was supposed to punch it out with his mother.

How was a kid to understand any of that? Hatred from a mother? And if she detested his father so much, why the hell had she married the man and stayed with him?

For a father to encourage physical retaliation? Yes, his father had slapped her around, even punched her a few times. Kam had always hated it.

He'd hated her . . . but he hadn't liked to see her bruised and bleeding.

Memory of the emotional sickness twisted Kam's stomach. A semitruck full of past baggage parked on his chest, making it tough to breathe.

The questions, so many of them, would always go unanswered because now they were both dead. The only choice Kam had was to prove them wrong.

He'd be a good man, and never in his life would he raise an

angry hand against a woman. He'd know the truth, even if his miserable parents never would.

Glory's trip to the office turned into a nice break in her routine. She visited with familiar employees and a few new hires. The client, who'd brought along his fiancée, was friendly, knew what he wanted, and already had an established plan. She felt certain they could do business together.

For lunch, she joined office friends at a nearby restaurant, carpooling to get there, so Kam wouldn't worry. Back at the office, she caught up on paperwork, lent her expertise to the new hires, and fielded more phone calls than she could recount.

It was a full day, and by the time she was nearing home, she was ready to kick off her shoes, take a nice long shower, and then share time with Kam. It was later than she realized when Callie called.

"What's that noise?" Callie asked.

"Sorry, I'm just getting into town. You probably hear the traffic."

"You're not at home?"

"I went to the office today but I'm on way back now. I'll be there in another thirty minutes. Did you need anything?"

"Yes. The full scoop on Kam."

"What do you mean?" While Glory wouldn't lie to her, she didn't want to outright confirm much, either.

"Fine," Callie said. "Keep all the juicy details to yourself. Just remember, I'm married to his brother, so I have high expectations. Very high. Skyscraper high."

Unable to resist, Glory said, "To the moon and back."

"Aha! I knew it. You've had that good-sex glow." Before Glory could say a word, Callie continued, "Good for you. I'm thrilled. You deserve the best—in sex and men, and even though Tanner is the best, Kam is probably a close second. Or wait, he could be the best *for you*, right?"

"Callie—"

"Wouldn't it be amazing if we married brothers?"

Her hands clenched on the steering wheel. "No one is talking about marriage!" As she said it, a car got close to her bumper, making her nervously glance in the rearview mirror.

"Just think, you'd be an actual sister. Well, a sister-in-law, but also a cousin who's like a sister."

Deadpan, Glory said, "You like me more now that you're married to Tanner."

"More so than if I had married Sutter, that's for sure."

"Very true." For the fiftieth time, with full sincerity, Glory added, "I'm really sorry about my part in pressuring you—"

"Look at how it all worked out. Because I'm so happy now, I'm not sorry about any of it—and I don't want you to be, either. Promise me you'll let that go."

Impossible, but she said, "I'll try." Now that she was off the highway, the car trailing her got closer. Glory couldn't see through the darkened windows, but her pulse was starting to leap in that pre-panic way.

The car eased back, allowing her to release a breath.

"While you're doing that," Callie said, regaining her undivided attention, "try giving Kam a chance, too. It would be amazing if we turned into one big awesome family."

Mouth open, Glory prepared to let her down, but Callie didn't give her a chance.

"Love ya! Bye."

Just like Callie, spewing all that and then disconnecting before Glory could get a word out. Surely, she wouldn't share any of those thoughts with Tanner. If she did, Tanner would tell Kam, and Kam would go running in the opposite direction.

The man had an apartment. He was preparing to live on his own.

He was not interested in marriage.

Glory was happy to have him for now, and for however long it lasted. But she refused to look too far into the future. Like Kam, she was starting a new phase in her life. She had her own plans.

Sure, Mike had put a kink in the works, but she was still determined.

When the car reappeared again, this time hanging back, Glory wasn't sure what to think.

She was dividing her time between watching the road and glancing in her mirrors, so when the phone rang, it startled her. Liz wanted an update on the meeting she'd just attended, and how the work from home was going. Her strident voice put Glory even more on edge. The second she thought it, she felt guilty.

She owed Liz a lot and she would never forget it, so she made sure her tone was light and friendly as she answered Liz's questions and updated her on new business.

"You're not overworking, are you?" Liz asked. "I already have one daughter running around like a raggedy farm girl. I don't need both of you coming unraveled."

Locking her jaw to keep from defending Callie, Glory said, "I'm not unraveling, I promise."

"Good. You know we depend on you."

Huh. That was as close to a compliment as Liz ever gave, and it pleased her. "Thank you. I depend on you as well."

That blasted car pulled up even closer and Glory decided it was time to worry. "Sorry, Liz, I'm driving on those old winding roads so how about I call you tomorrow morning? We can talk more then."

"You should never answer your phone while driving. Those roads, especially, are dangerous. They all need to be repaved and there are too many trees blocking the road signs. It's a wonder people don't get killed there every day."

Glory slowed, hoping the car would go around her, but instead, it just continued to follow her. "We'll visit soon to catch up. Bye now." She disconnected and, even though she thought she might be overreacting, she called Kam.

He answered on the first ring. "Hey, babe. Where are you? Getting close?"

"I think someone is following me." She tried not to sound frantic because it wouldn't help anything, but still she knew her voice was a pitch too high. To moderate it, she cleared her throat. "I can't see the driver because he has tinted windows, but the car's been behind me for a while now."

"Where are you?"

His calm, take-charge tone helped. "I'm still on Mill, about five minutes from Bloom Road." A largely deserted stretch of road surrounded by woods.

"I'm on my way. Already in my car. Stay on the line with me."

Now she really felt absurd. "I didn't mean to have you—"

"Don't piss me off, Glory. I told you we're not taking chances."

The touch of anger actually reassured her that she'd done the right thing. "Okay, thank you."

"You have both hands on the wheel, right?"

"Yes, of course."

"Tell me about the other car. Make, model?"

"Um . . ." She knew next to nothing about cars so this would be one of those times when she felt horribly self-conscious. Callie would laugh it off, but Glory looked in the rearview mirror and spotted the car again. "It's white, midsize."

Without ridiculing her lack of knowledge, Kam asked, "Car, SUV, or truck?"

"Definitely a car." As she slowed even more for a curve, it got closer again.

"Two-door or four-door?"

"I think . . ." She looked at the car again. "Four-door?"

"I don't suppose you can see the license plate?"

"He's close, but not that close." She clenched her hands on the wheel, horribly afraid that Mike was in that car.

"I'm only a few minutes away from you now, babe."

"I don't think I'll have—" From the woods along the side of the road, a small dog ran out in front of her. Glory half screamed, hit her breaks and tried to swerve to avoid the dog, but instead, the car spun. The driver of the white car barely missed her as she went off the road and came up against a tree with teeth-jarring impact.

"Glory!"

She tried to move, but something pinned her in place. "I . . . I hit my head." She realized her voice was faint, sort of hazy, and everything was spinning around her. "I can't move my left arm."

She knew Kam couldn't hear her when he shouted her name again.

"Kam?" Her left arm ached and felt impossibly heavy. When she tried to move it, indescribable pain coursed through her torso and stole all her breath. Something liquid dripped into her eyes and she had the awful thought that she might be dying.

No! She wouldn't . . . Oh, God. She'd been through this before.

That time, her mother and father had died, and she'd just been . . . damaged.

I don't want to be damaged again.

Neither did she want to die, damn it.

What if the man following her came after her now? If it was Mike, at least he was familiar. Unhinged, but still, better a known threat than an unknown.

The sudden screech of tires, then the slamming of a door, filled her eyes with tears. She couldn't die, not when she was so happy with Kam. Not when she was finally coming into her own, learning to speak up for herself—albeit slowly, but still, she was making progress.

Callie would be devastated. How unfair for her to have to deal with this when she should still be celebrating her new marriage. "No," she whispered, her voice barely there. "I don't want to die."

"Glory," came a gravelly, emotional voice. "Jesus, honey, hang on. An ambulance is on the way."

"Kam?" She couldn't see very well through the film over her eyes.

"Don't move, okay? Your driver side door is smashed and the airbags deployed." A loud screech proved that he'd wrenched open the passenger door. "I'm right here, okay?" His rough, broken voice was closer, as if he sat right beside her now. "Callie and Tanner are on their way."

"Don't tell Liz." The last thing she wanted was more surgeries. No more, not ever again. "Promise you won't—"

The backs of his fingers touched her face. "It's okay, baby. I won't tell."

She suddenly remembered. "The other car!"

"No one else is around. Whoever did this is long gone. The police will be looking for him."

"Kam." With new desperation, she remembered the dog. Dear God, had she hit it? A sob tried to edge up her throat. She couldn't quite swallow it back, but breathing and speaking hurt, so she could only imagine how bad crying would be. "There was a dog. A little dog. Maybe a puppy."

"I didn't see a dog."

"You have to find it! Find the dog."

"Shh. Calm down."

No, she wouldn't. Tears leaked out and she knew she was a terrible crier. The ugliest crier ever, but she couldn't get it together. "Please." Gaining strength, she tried to move, but dear God, it hurt.

"Be still, honey."

"*Please* find the dog."

"Listen to me. Tanner will find it, okay?" He was quiet a second, then he said, "Hear that siren? The ambulance is here and Tanner's right behind it. He'll find the dog, I promise."

She didn't hear anything. Actually, darkness was closing in around her. There was more she wanted to say, but she couldn't catch her breath. Couldn't speak . . .

"Don't leave me, Glory." His voice, now ragged, emerged deep and desperate. "Don't you dare leave me."

Her last thought was that Kam sounded awfully sad, and if she could, she'd make him smile.

Never in his life had he been more agonized. His eyes burned and his throat ached with the need to shout. If only shouting would help anything.

Tanner clasped his shoulder. "Shouldn't be much longer."

That promise didn't help much when too many hours had already passed. He kept seeing her again, crumpled and bloody, squashed in that fucking car. Blood had covered her face and pale hair. The door pinned her in place as she'd labored to breathe.

"She'll be all right," Callie stated with firm determination, her eyes swimming with tears, her nose bright pink. *"She will."*

Tanner tugged her into his lap and wrapped himself around her.

Kam felt mean, like he needed to destroy something—or

someone. Like Mike. He knew that miserable puke had to be behind this.

When Callie stood, both Tanner and Kam looked at her.

Her face showed her strain and her voice broke when she said, "I can't sit here. I'm going to—" she gestured at the small waiting room "—move. Before I explode." And with that, she began pacing the perimeter of the room.

Helpless, his jaw locked, Tanner watched her.

"You can walk with her, you know. You don't need to babysit me."

"Right now, she looks in better shape than you."

"Fuck you, Tanner," he said without heat. He pressed the heels of his hands against his eye sockets. "Christ, this sucks."

"I know, but she'll be okay." He shared a crooked smile. "At least I found that pup."

Dropping back in his seat, Kam lowered his hands and closed his eyes. "Yeah, that's something, I guess." Opening his eyes again, he pinned Tanner in place. "She begged me to find the dog—and not to tell Liz."

The shifting of Tanner's gaze showed guilt.

The rage of fear rose again. "You know why that is, don't you?"

"Glory will tell you."

"I want my *brother* to tell me."

Lifting his brows, Tanner said, "So we're kids again?"

Right. Not since he was an angry youth put in unfamiliar circumstances had Kam sneered *brother* in quite that mean, insulting way. It was meant to degrade the relationship, because back then, he hadn't trusted in anything good. Now he did. "I'm sorry."

"Understandable." Tanner kept his gaze on his wife as she tried to outrun her worry in a room too small for the mission. "Years ago, Glory was in another accident, the same one that killed her parents. She had a lot of injuries then, and my understanding is that Liz, in trying to help, offered one plastic surgery after another."

Horrified, Kam sat forward, his every muscle clenched tight. "She was a kid."

"Very much so, and she almost died with her parents. She had a broken shoulder, leg, ribs, nose, and jaw."

Crushing pain settled around Kam's heart. "To think what she went through . . ." He couldn't bear it.

"You've met Liz. She's not the overly maternal type. My guess is that she was trying to help in the only way she knew how."

"By removing the scars." And putting Glory through more pain, more stress.

Tanner shrugged.

Glory's bedroom rules were starting to make sense, and he was so damned grateful that he'd never insisted, never tried to coerce her into showing more. His heart thrashed in his chest, hard enough to rattle his frame. Or maybe that was anger and pity shaking him.

Being a big brother, Tanner draped an arm over his shoulders. "You thought she was too perfect when you first met her."

"Physically, she still is."

Tanner nodded. "Now that we've gotten to know her, she's as real as any woman can be. Flaws and all."

Kam tried a deep breath, but it snagged in his throat.

Tanner clapped him on the back, and offered him a moment of privacy by saying, "Sit tight. I'm going to grab colas for us."

Just then, the waiting room door opened and a woman wearing a white coat over her scrubs stepped in. "McCallahan family?"

The three of them rushed her, Callie arriving first.

The doctor smiled. "Let's sit." She moved to a chair, then waited while the three of them reclaimed their seats. Kam was so anxious he couldn't take his eyes off the doctor.

She held out her hand to Tanner. "I'm Dr. Sydney."

"Tanner Patrick. This is my wife, Callie. She's Glory's sister."

Kam doubted any of them would bother clarifying that Glory was a cousin. In all the ways that mattered most, Callie and Glory were sisters.

"And my brother, Kam."

She nodded to each of them. "First off, Ms. McCallahan will be fine."

Grateful that he was sitting, Kam felt his legs go boneless. He actually gasped a breath. "The blood?"

"A laceration on her forehead and cheek, another on her thigh. None of the cuts were dangerously deep—that is, they didn't reach critical structures like major blood vessels or nerves—but they were still significant enough to need numerous sutures to close properly and heal well."

So much blood had covered her face, running into her eyes, that he hadn't been able to tell much. Now relief left him limp.

"She also has two rib fractures, and a rotator cuff tear. All on her left side. She said that was the side of her car that impacted with the tree."

The damned car had bent around the tree. It was a wonder she hadn't been crushed.

"She's going to be in a lot of pain."

Callie covered her mouth on a sob. Tanner quickly hugged her closer.

Nodding, swallowing, Callie said, "Sorry. I'm okay. Please, go on."

"I'm including a referral to an orthopedic specialist for the shoulder. I would suggest she see one right away."

Tanner, the only one not shaken, asked, "Anything else?"

"She has numerous contusions, especially on her left side. You'll notice it immediately on her face and forehead, and the discoloration will get worse before it starts to lighten. But I see no signs of a concussion. She's clearheaded, worried about a dog, and worried about all of you." A frown marred her brow. "She's against surgery for the injury to her shoulder, but I'll leave that to the specialist."

"When can she go home?" Callie asked.

Dr. Sydney smiled. "She's anxious to be on her way."

Kam stiffened all over. "She can leave the hospital?"

"I understand your concern, but her condition is stable, and the fractures aren't severe enough to require inpatient care. She'll heal just as well—maybe even better—at home where she can rest without the usual disruptions a hospital brings. It'll also be better to avoid risks like infection." She looked at each of them. "She shouldn't be alone."

Together, they stated firmly, "She won't be."

The doctor smiled again. "She can manage her pain with ice for her shoulder, along with the OTC meds I've recommended. Her ribs will be most painful for the first week, but then should start to get better."

"How long?" Callie asked.

"Four to six weeks to heal. We'll follow up outpatient if needed, but there's no benefit to keeping her here."

Callie said, "She can come home with me."

What? Kam leaned around his brother. "No, I'll be with her at her house."

Tanner stood up between them and again held out his hand to the doctor. "Thank you. How soon can we see her?"

Understanding the predicament, something she likely saw often with the families of patients, the doctor said, "A nurse will let you know shortly. Oh, one more thing: She's anxious to get the blood out of her hair. She'll need help to do that without a shower. After twenty-four hours, if she attempts a shower, it should be brief because of the sutures, without water directly hitting those areas."

"She has a handheld shower nozzle," Callie said. "I can do it and be really careful."

Kam locked his jaw. He wanted to help Glory, but he supposed he should let things go for now. There'd be plenty of time to iron out who could do what after he got her home. But he *was* taking her home.

The second the good doctor was gone, Kam took a stance. He kept his tone gentle, but he wasn't about to be swayed. "Glory is going home with me."

"You have to work," Callie said. "If she goes with me, Addie or I can always be with her."

A quick glance around the waiting room showed they were still alone. "There was a fire at my shop today."

Slowly, Tanner turned to face him. "How bad?"

"It was set in a big garbage bin where we tossed out cardboard boxes, plastic and some wood. It singed part of the front exterior wall on the shop, but luckily, Robby, from the landscape shop, saw the flames and ran over with his fire extinguisher. No major damage done."

Tanner ran a hand over his mouth. "Hell of a coincidence, though, your jobsite dealing with a fire and someone tailing Glory."

No shit. Kam had been thinking about it nonstop, along with his fear and worry for Glory. "I don't think the driver tailed her all day. From what she said . . ." He had to stop, to clear his head and fight back the alarm he'd felt when she screamed.

Tanner and Callie waited, not pushing, but he could feel their concern, and it bugged him. Hell, everything was bugging him.

He needed to see Glory.

"It wasn't until she was on Mill Road that she noticed him."

Nodding, Tanner drew Callie into his arms. "I agree with my brother. He needs to be there with Glory. She'll be most comfortable in her own home, and," he said, when she tried to object, "we'll take turns helping out. All of us."

That was one of the million perks of having a brother. To Callie, he said, "Thank you for understanding," even though she hadn't yet offered her understanding or, from her expression, accepted the decision.

A male nurse stuck his head in the door. "Family of Glory McCallahan?"

Once again, all three of them surged forward.

"Sorry, but only one at a time," the nurse said.

Tanner, doing him a solid, held Callie back at his side so that Kam was the first in the room. Dread smothered him as he saw the pulled curtain and heard the beep and buzz of hospital machinery droning in the background.

He hesitated only a second, then said, "Glory?" as he eased the curtain aside. Thank God he'd braced himself. The sight of her nearly sent him to his knees. One eye was practically swollen shut beneath a neat row of stitches that cut through her eyebrow. Her cheekbone was swollen, split, and the side of her nose was bruised.

She tried to turn her face away.

"Don't. I need to see you. To know that you're going to be okay."

Her lips, her beautiful lips, drew him, quivering a little as he bent and very gently touched his mouth to hers. "You scared a decade off my life, babe."

The back of the bed was raised so that she was practically sitting. *Her ribs*, he thought, wondering if that position was easier for her. "Are you in pain?"

Her eyes grew liquid. "I didn't want you to see . . . see me."

The break in her voice wrenched emotion from him. "No one could have kept me away."

"The dog?"

A laugh strangled out, and then he did kneel, unwilling to chance hurting her by sitting on the side of the bed. "He's with Addie and I'm sure he's a happy little camper. I think he'd been on his own for a while, but now he's in good hands."

"He's my dog," she whispered, her tone fierce.

"Okay. That's fine." He'd have the dog brought to her if it'd make her feel better. "Tanner and Callie are here, too, so we had to leave him with Addie. She wanted to be here as well. She told me to tell you that and to give you her love."

Glory gasped, then winced, closed her eyes and swallowed.

"Easy," Kam said. If he could take the pain for her, he'd have accepted it gladly. He loved her. He knew that now. Nothing but love could hurt this much.

"I've been thinking about him," she said once she'd gotten her breath back. The words were low, carefully moderated. "I want him. I've never had a dog." Her lips trembled again. "Oh, God, I look so ugly."

"You are the most beautiful thing I've ever seen in my entire life. Please believe me."

"Get up off the floor."

Her strangled whisper had him smiling despite the awfulness of the moment. "I'm going to take some time off work."

"No."

"I want to be there with you, to help you, to do anything I can. You can't tell me no because that would be cruel, and you aren't cruel, Glory."

Tears tracked down her cheeks. "I have scars."

"We all do, baby."

"If I could smack you, I would."

"I'll keep count and when you're better, you can deliver all the smacks at one time." As carefully as he could, he brushed the tears off her cheeks.

"I was so scared," she whispered.

"Me, too."

"I shouldn't have panicked, but I was in a wreck once before . . ."

Should he tell her he already knew that? Or would that bother her more? "I imagine anyone who'd ever been in a bad wreck would fear it happening again."

"For years, I would feel paralyzed whenever I had to get in a car. I did my best, but it would feel like my lungs were seizing up."

She'd been a kid, with Liz sending her off to additional surgeries. His throat thickened until he couldn't speak without her hearing the pity in his voice. Instead, he leaned forward and gently kissed her knuckles.

"For years now, I've been better about it. I didn't really have a choice. Kids travel in cars. Adult women drive."

"I understand." He really did. How hard would it be for her to get back in a car again? He'd figure it out. Somehow, he'd make things all right for her.

"I don't want to go backward. As soon as I can, I have to get back to driving."

"We can do that together." He'd be with her every step of the way. "There are old country roads around here, where all you'll see is a horse or a cow, maybe a farmer on a tractor."

Her lips trembled. "You're going to hate me."

"No." Coming up next to her again, he stole another soft kiss. "Why would you even say that?"

She turned her face away, and he saw tears tracking down her bruised cheeks again. "You're going to hate me and so will Addie."

Her upset just about killed him. "Never, Glory. That will never ever happen."

"Damn it," she rasped low, without much breath. "I am such a pathetic mess."

"You're not pathetic and you're not a mess. You're hurt, and I wish I could somehow make it better." He got as close to her as he could without bumping her, without causing her more pain. "All I can do is swear to you that no one will hate you. Not for any reason."

The shuddering breath she drew made her freeze, stark agony on her face. "Oh, God."

They both went still for several seconds.

"I think it's the medication," she finally whispered. "It's making me whiny."

"But it's clearly not helping enough." Kam wanted to find the nearest nurse or doctor and demand they do something—but what? The doctor had said her ribs would hurt the worst for the first week. Seven days of this? He had to remind himself that Glory was strong, a fighter, who'd already come through one wreck, then the multiple surgeries that followed.

"You impress the hell out of me." He touched his mouth to hers one last time—for now—then said, "Callie is anxious to see you."

"This shouldn't have happened when she's supposed to be celebrating her new marriage."

Through the door, Callie said, "I can hear you, Glory, and you know better. Now kick out Kam, so I can have a turn."

Wasn't easy, but he came to his feet. "I'm taking you home, and I'll be taking care of you." He lightly brushed his fingertips over her jaw. "Don't let Callie convince you of anything different."

"I can manage on my own."

"Cruel," he murmured, trying to sound light instead of tormented. "I know you won't be cruel." Not wanting to hear anything else, Kam stepped out to give Callie a turn. He didn't look at her or Tanner, or any of the medical people coming and going along the hallway. He went to a wall, braced his arms against it, and lowered his head.

Far as he was concerned, Mike was a dead man, and if that made him like his father, he didn't care.

10

Mike had never been so panicked in his life.

Injured. His beautiful, perfect Glory was injured, and he didn't even know how badly. If he tried asking around, he might implicate himself.

Half an hour ago, he'd called Kirby on the burner phone and gotten the awful truth. While he'd been following her, as close as he dared so he wouldn't lose her, she'd swerved to avoid hitting a dog.

That had led to her crashing into a large sturdy oak, her car mangled around it. Kirby had taken off. Mike hated that she'd been left alone on the long deserted road, but he had to agree that Kirby was right. If he'd been found and questioned, it might have—somehow—led back to him.

Mike couldn't very well love Glory, worship her, and possess her if he was tossed in jail.

Stark fear left him shaking. All Kirby knew was that her car was in a ditch, smashed around the tree, and blood was on the windshield.

Blood. His Glory's blood. *Is she dead? Is she disfigured?*

At the same bar where he'd met Shara, Mike knocked back a whiskey. It burned all the way down his throat and landed like fire in his stomach, but it didn't offer any relief. His hands were shaking, his eyes itching.

He had to find out if she was okay, but how?

He should kill Kirby, the fucking idiot. Obviously, he'd done something wrong. Mike had only wanted Glory followed. He'd wanted her worried.

Not injured.

How could she come to him if she was hurt?

Just then, he heard someone say, *"You hear about that wreck out on Mill Road?"*

Hands gripping the edge of the booth, Mike strained forward and listened.

"Young woman was driving. They had to cut her out of the car."

The words slammed into him like physical blows from a sledgehammer. He weakened, slumping in his seat, his heart thudding heavily, his guts twisting.

"Is she okay?"

"Don't know, but they took her to the hospital in an ambulance."

She had to be okay. No other outcome was acceptable.

"Good thing the hospital is close, I guess."

A clue! He could do a search to see which hospital was closest to that road.

Did he call to ask about her? What else could he do? He needed to see her, to hold her, to know for a fact that she was all right, that she was still his perfect Glory.

And if she wasn't?

He swallowed convulsively, sweat breaking out on his brow, but he knew the truth.

If he couldn't have her, no one would.

Back in her own home, set up on one of the sofas, Glory felt like the biggest fraud in the world. Yes, she hurt. The kind of hurt that worsened if she breathed, if she blinked, if she even moved a finger. Her hair was sticky, she could smell antiseptic on her skin, and the idea of trying to change clothes—or use the bathroom—made her shudder.

But that wasn't the reason for her moodiness and hopeless worry.

"Are you okay? Can I get you anything?"

Sweet, loving Addie. Just looking at her filled Glory's eyes with fat salty tears. "Don't be nice to me," she frantically ordered. "I'm too ridiculous right now."

The ice on her shoulder kept her shivering. A rolled-up towel under her arm kept it separated from her body, which helped to take pressure off the injured rotator cuff. The stitches did burn, and she idly wondered if she'd have new scars. At the moment, she couldn't work up a lot of energy to care.

Addie smiled in that special way, then touched her hand to Glory's uninjured cheek. "If you want to cry, I'll get a damp washcloth and keep your tears mopped up so they don't bother your cuts and scrapes."

Glory gave a doleful laugh that caused renewed pain to cinch around her chest.

"Sorry," Addie said, all businesslike now. "Let's just look at this adorable pup, okay? I think he's worried about you."

One look at the dog's big soulful brown eyes and her heart melted. No matter what came of this whole ordeal, she had this sweet little dog now, and that was something special. "Hey, Peanut Butter. I'm okay."

The dog's ears twitched and his skinny tail started swinging.

"Peanut Butter, huh?" Addie grinned. "I like it."

"I ate lunch with friends at this fancy restaurant, and I kept thinking I would have rather had peanut butter on toast."

"I love it, too, plus it's a great name for this one, with his light brown ears and that mask over his eyes."

"The rest of him could be bread." She grinned, too. The dog was so pretty with his off-white coat and the splashes of honey-brown. In a whisper, Glory said, "I'm going to love him so much."

"I know you will—when you can move. Right now, I don't want him jumping on you."

No, she didn't want that, either. Even lifting her right hand, oh, so slowly, to tickle the dog under his chin, caused her sharp pain. But it was worth it.

Wanting no misunderstandings, she said to Addie, "You're amazing with animals." With people, too. "But I'm keeping him. He can't go back home with you because then he'll love it there and not want to come back."

After a long look, Addie nodded. Voice soft with understanding, she said, "Thank you, honey. That's an amazing compliment." As Kam reentered the room, she added, "I'm so glad you like it there."

Addie didn't see Glory's surprise because she'd already stepped away, the pup held in her arms. Yes, she supposed it was a compliment. Glory loved visiting Addie's home, because it *was* a home—in a way she'd never experienced before. Every room held memories, good ones that Kam, Tanner, and Addie loved to share, and some bad ones, too, that they could thankfully laugh about now. Everywhere Glory looked, there was warmth, even in a framed photo, or a cherished gift—like the wall hanging the boys got Addie for her birthday one year that said: *Now I know what home means.* Addie had gotten teary-eyed when telling Glory about it.

Glory had, too.

That sense of warmth was even there in the worn material of an older love seat where Addie used to snuggle up with the boys on either side of her for movie night. They'd share popcorn, drink milkshakes, and take turns picking the movie for the night. Addie had told her that on the nights when it was Kam's turn, he often wanted action movies. Tanner enjoyed horror, and she would choose comedies.

It was such a wonderful family thing to do.

Glory heard some whispering, then Kam carefully sat beside her. "Callie and Tanner are taking the pup out for a bit. They want him to be able to get used to your backyard. Addie's fixing you something to eat." He touched her cheek. "How do you feel?"

Selfish, sad, scared . . . and a little excited. She couldn't, wouldn't say any of that, though, so she said, "I'm fine." Seated on the couch, an ice pack on her shoulder, the probable repercussions making her head swim, she felt . . . completely lost. "I'm fine."

"If by fine, you mean safe, then yes you are."

Honestly, she hadn't thought much in terms of safety, but she probably should. "Did the police talk to you?"

"At the hospital. They stopped by the waiting room with a bunch of questions, but there wasn't much I could tell them. None of us know of any specific white cars with tinted windows."

"They talked to me as soon as the doctor had finished stitching me up."

His jaw flexed as if he'd clenched his teeth. "Shitty timing on their part."

"No," she said. "It was understandable. They wanted to

find out if I thought the wreck was deliberate, if I recognized anyone, or if the car was familiar." She shifted, felt the pain in her ribs, and immediately stilled. "Thinking back on it, it's possible I overreacted. Mike has me spooked, I guess."

Appearing tired and tense, Kam rubbed both hands over his face, then huffed a breath.

So far, he'd been incredibly gentle with her, and she missed his snarky, comedic side, his quick comebacks and wicked teasing. "Don't hold back. If you have something to say to me, say it." She'd welcome a return to normalcy.

He slanted her a look, his brows together, before he shifted to face her. "You didn't overreact, okay? Get that out of your head."

Such an order. It made her smile despite all the complications churning for attention. "Yes, sir."

"I mean it, Glory. This was Mike. We both know it." As if gauging her reaction, he said, "I told the cops about him."

"Good. So did I." His surprise made her smile widen. "What, you didn't think I'd mention it? I gave them what information I could, and they said they'd check up on him. I don't know if they'll get back to me or not, but I hope they keep me updated."

"We'll check in with them in the morning."

Addie returned with a bowl and a fork. "I have homemade mac and cheese for you. It wasn't easy to think of something you could eat with an injured shoulder and broken ribs. Hot soup was out—I didn't want to chance you getting burned on top of it. Tomorrow I'll bring some other dishes for you." She handed the bowl to Kam. "Things that will be easy to eat."

The mention of food made her realize how hungry she'd gotten. "Thank you. It smells delicious."

Kam lifted a bite to her mouth.

No way did he expect to feed her. "I can—"

The bite went into her mouth. Scowling at him, she had no option but to chew and, oh, heaven, it was good. "Mmm, that's amazing."

Beaming, Addie said, "Oh, good, here comes Callie and Tanner with PB."

Yapping, the dog bounded in, turned a circle, and then tried to jump up on the couch with Glory.

Four people lunged at the poor animal, startling him, and making Glory flinch. Kam got the pup first, holding him close so he couldn't wiggle free while he tried to calm him.

PB stared at Glory the whole time, and to her exhausted eyes, he looked loving. Damn it, she'd start bawling if she wasn't careful. "He's okay."

Kam looked at her like she was nuts. "Babe, listen to me, please. We can't do this tonight."

"We?" she asked first, and then, "Do what?"

"The pup needs to go with Addie. I know, okay? We all get it; he's your dog. But it's already going to be near impossible for you to find a comfortable position to sleep in. Trust me on this, okay?"

Stubbornly, feeling desperate even, she insisted, "He's *my* dog."

"We'll bring him back in the morning," Callie promised.

Tanner said, "Come on, Glory. The last thing you need is to trip over him. He's young and energetic. Let's give it a few days."

Pinched with worry, Addie watched her, and Glory knew the exact moment she settled on a plan. It was there in her shrewd blue eyes. With all the innocence she could muster, Addie sighed. "If you don't trust me with him, remember that Callie and Tanner are in the house, too."

It cost her, making her ribs aches, but Glory snorted. "Nice try, Addie, but I see right through that ploy." Giving up seemed to be her easiest option. "I trust all of you, I just don't want PB to be confused."

"He's no longer wandering the woods, he's tick-free, and he has a full belly. One step at a time, okay?"

Glory nodded. "All right, as long as I get to see him every day."

"With someone around to run interference so he doesn't hurt you." Kam leaned in and put a soft kiss to her cheek.

With Addie, Tanner, and Callie right there, the affectionate gesture made her blush. Trying to brazen her way through it, she reached up with her right hand to touch her hair. "I don't know how I'm going to sleep with my hair still so yucky."

Kam's mouth twisted. "It's your ribs and shoulder that concern me, not your hair."

Callie, who better understood her, quickly said, "One more day for your stitches, and then I can help you shower. Tomorrow, I'll try sponging it off again. It is better, Glory. No more blood, so it's mostly clean, just not styled."

She wasn't about to snort again. "I'm wrecked from head to toe, so I guess styling doesn't matter." She gave them each a firm look. "It's time for everyone to head home. I'm going to feed myself this amazing mac and cheese, and I want to move without you all gasping, then I need to brush my teeth, figure out how I'm going to sleep, and hopefully tomorrow, I'll figure out . . . everything else." Like her life, her upcoming and overwhelming responsibilities—and the lurking danger.

As carefully as possible, she sat forward. Yes, it hurt, a lot, but the ice pack was starting to drip on her and she had to pee.

Tanner hastily removed the ice, saying to Kam, "Remember, you need to time it. Fifteen minutes on, then off for a while. Always put a thin towel or something between her skin and the ice bag."

"Got it," he said, and tried to offer her another bite of food.

She wasn't about to let Kam feed her. "No."

Sheepish, he put the fork back in the dish.

"I want to snuggle my dog before he's taken away."

Hedging, Callie moved closer. "Tomorrow, I need to tell Mom."

Which meant Liz would make a well-meaning visit. Not something she'd anticipate with gladness, but she'd deal with that, too. "I understand. Thanks. Just tell her that I'm okay and not to worry. Now, I want to see PB, so he won't forget me."

For the most part, Kam controlled the dog. Still, he landed several swipes of his tongue across her chin. Dodging him made both her shoulder and her ribs thrum with pain, but it was worth it. Glory stroked him, kissed his furry little head, and felt the softness of his floppy ears. There'd be no way to keep the others from hearing, but she kept her voice low, anyway. "Thank God I didn't hurt you, PB." She kissed him again, already missing him even though she and the dog weren't well acquainted.

Kam stroked the back of her hair. "Pretty sure he's some sort of beagle mix."

Tanner said, "I'll set up a vet appointment. Until then, Nell could take a look at him. She's good with animals."

"Great idea." Glory really liked Nell and wouldn't mind having a reason to pay the girl.

Since no one was budging, she gripped the edge of the couch with her right hand, braced herself, and struggled to get to her feet. Hurt. Like. Hell.

Kam hastily handed the dog over to Callie and helped support Glory until she was fully upright. "What are we doing?"

It took her a second to catch her breath, then she said, "I'm going to the bathroom. You can see everyone out." Deliberately, she didn't make eye contact on her way out of the room. If she did, she'd get weepy again. Or worse, she'd spill her guts, and she'd already decided that this was one secret she needed to keep for a while. At least until she'd healed and could think rationally, without all the emotion brought on by the pain and the residual fear from the wreck.

In her bathroom, she closed the door, then locked it for good measure. With a few winces, she removed the towel from under her left arm and set it on the sink. One glance in the mirror and she almost laughed. Seriously, her hair was the least of her worries as far as looks went. How any of them could stand to look at her, she didn't know. The sight certainly turned her stomach.

Her own clothes had been ruined, so at some point, while she'd been prodded, stitched, x-rayed, and examined, Tanner had called Liam. That young man, who was always dependable, had driven to Addie's and collected the mismatched outfit she now wore. Addie had put it together based on comfort and ease, and while Glory knew she looked ridiculous in one of Callie's long elastic-waist summer skirts with Tanner's roomy button-up cotton shirt, she was thankful she wouldn't have to deal with the slacks and form-fitting shirt she'd worn to work.

Getting on and off the toilet was an ordeal. Who knew simply sitting and then standing could make everything hurt so much? While she had some privacy, she dampened a washcloth and did a more thorough job of cleaning her face.

If she could count a blessing out of the recent mishaps, it was that her left arm had been injured, and not her right.

Well, and the fact that she now had a dog she already loved.

And . . . the hospital tests had revealed things she might not have known for quite some time. Monumental things. Life-altering things.

She'd just placed her hand on her midriff when the tentative tap sounded at the door.

"You okay in there?"

Guiltily, she dropped her hand and then winced. "Yes. I'll be out in a minute."

She heard a thump that might have been Kam's head against the door. "I would love to help, Glory. You know that, right?"

It was his tone that really got her. Kam was always so take-charge, but right now, he sounded a little lost.

She opened the door, and wow.

Stark emotion showed on his face. Did he care so much about her? If so, she could definitely build on that.

Hope took root. Dangerous, scary, impossible hope. But what else did she have?

She already loved him; she knew that. Loved him enough that she didn't want to complicate his life, to impossibly twist it up with hers. And yet, that's what she would do.

He wouldn't object. Kam wasn't the type to shirk responsibilities ever, plus it was half his fault. Not that she'd think in terms of "fault." More like unexpected blessings.

Immediately, he stepped in, cupped her face in his hands, and touched his mouth to hers. "What can I do?"

Darn it, the blasted tears she'd held at bay suddenly welled up and spilled over. When she saw his alarm, she released a shaky laugh. "I'm fine—no, Kam. I really am. Bruised, sure, and still a little shaken from the wreck, but I'm absolutely okay." She glanced at the mirror. "Although, I look like a banged-up clown from a cheap sideshow."

He kissed her again. "You look like a survivor to me."

What a sweet thing to say.

"Tell me something I can do."

Carefully, she allowed herself to slump into him. Though her ribs protested and her shoulder thumped, it felt good to be this close to him again, to feel his arms slide around her. Against his chest, she asked, "You're sure you don't mind? I'm hideous."

His big hands, warm and gentle, moved over her back. "God, babe, you can't know."

"Can't know what?"

"How it feels to want to fix things for you when I can't. How fucking awful it is to see you hurt and know there's nothing I can do about it."

She felt his sincerity, and it worked like a balm to her frazzled thoughts. "You're doing a lot, actually. Being here with me, suffering my moodiness, handling other people—even people I love."

He pressed a tender kiss to her ear. "Speaking of people we love . . . do you want to finish up your mac and cheese?"

So he wouldn't question her love of his brother and Addie? Maybe she could call that progress. "I'm starving, so yes. After that, I need to change into something that doesn't look absurd but is still comfortable for sleeping." She had so much to think about, but lethargy pulled at her. "I won't be sleeping in a bed, though."

"I know. I have an idea." Using a lot of caution, he eased her away. "But first, food."

"I guess there's no reason to hide my scars." Nervously, Glory shifted.

"No reason at all." Pretending he hadn't noticed, Kam continued to unbutton her shirt while emotions bombarded him. That she allowed him to undress her proved her level of physical discomfort. She'd been so strict about covering parts of herself, staying in the dark, and yet now, he'd see all of her.

He wanted that. A lot. But not like this. Not from a lack of options.

His breathing was a little too deep, his gaze too intent as he opened the last button.

They stood very close together, both their heads down until their foreheads touched.

"I mean, you've seen worse now, right?"

If he could find the words to reassure her, Kam would, but he'd already said everything he felt, everything he knew. Without her looking at him, it was easier to speak his mind. "You matter to me, Glory. More than you know. A few scars won't change that."

In the silence of her bedroom, he heard her swallow. "It's silly. I mean, now it is. It's just that, in my head . . ." She gave a small gasp, curved her uninjured arm around her middle, and went still.

"I'm sorry." He was still now, too. The idea of hurting her devastated him. "What did I do?"

"It wasn't you." Two more slow easy breaths, and she opened her eyes again. "Sometimes, even a tiny movement just gets me."

"Ribs or shoulder?"

"Shoulder that time, but I'm okay now."

The sooner he got her comfortable, the sooner they could try to get some sleep. She needed rest to heal. Hopefully, with the new day, she'd be more open to seeing an orthopedic doctor.

Taking her right hand, Kam kissed her palm and then moved her arm to the side, so he could ease the shirt off her shoulders. His heart was a thundering drumbeat. The overhead light was on, and he could see all of her. Every inch of her skin.

No bra, just some bruising, and underneath it all, there on her left shoulder, a scar that ran from her shoulder toward her collarbone. She'd been hurt in so many ways over the years that he just naturally bent forward to put a healing kiss to the mark, to show her it didn't matter, couldn't matter—not between them.

"Kam," she whispered, with a touch of embarrassment.

Made sense, because here she was, breasts showing, and his gaze was snagged on her shoulder. "Your shoulder has taken some abuse, hasn't it? First as a kid and now again."

Not really expecting an answer, he eased the shirt down her arms, thankful that it was Tanner's shirt and therefore roomy enough to remove easily.

In a small voice, she said, "It was a lot worse back then."

"A broken bone versus a rotator cuff injury?"

"I guess, but also, I was young and so scared."

Not giving her a chance to think about it, he stretched the waistband of the skirt and, lowering to a knee, brought it down over her backside, her hips and thighs, down to her feet. "I can't imagine," he said, but he could. He, too, had lost his parents—under very different circumstances. "Did you have to stay in the hospital?"

"For a few days."

That thin voice had him looking up at her. She'd closed her eyes, not in pain this time, at least he didn't think so. A rosy flush covered her cheeks and throat.

Without thinking about it, he said, "You're so fucking sexy. You know that, right?"

Her eyes shot open and a short laugh, devoid of humor, escaped her. "With all my scars? And now so many bruises? No, I don't think so."

"As a man who wants you, I'm telling you that you are. Not that I'll do anything about it right now. You're hurt and that's my top priority. But once you're healed, we'll have this conversation again."

"I don't understand you."

"I know." Directly in front of him was the scar that slightly curved from the front of her thigh to the side and down a few inches. It had healed, but he could see that it had been gruesome at one time. The thickness of it, the jagged line, gave an indication of the agony she must have suffered.

He coasted his lips over this injury, too, wishing kisses really could heal because he knew she still felt pain—emotional pain. And sometimes that was worse. "How bad was this break?"

Around slightly choppy breathing, she said, "Bad, I guess. They called it a femoral shaft fracture."

Despite her injuries, old and new, she had an incredibly beautiful body, and he wasn't immune. Softer emotions helped to blunt the sharp-edged lust gnawing beneath the surface of his control. She wouldn't be up to anything physical for weeks, maybe even months, so he'd keep it under wraps and concentrate on helping her. Didn't mean he wouldn't want her.

Looking up at her, he asked, "What does that mean, exactly?"

"The bone came through the skin. It's why that scar is so gross."

He didn't want to, but Kam came back to his feet. "Nothing about you is gross. *Nothing.* You're a beautiful woman who's lived a difficult life and has a few scars to prove it."

"It's ugly."

"It's a part of you." Carefully, he cupped her face, willing her to believe him. "You're not perfect, Glory. No one is. But know what? I think that makes you better."

"Better?"

"Real. Sexy. Strong. I not only want you, I admire you. So damn much."

"You shouldn't." Visibly struggling with her thoughts, she stared at his chest. "The hardest part wasn't being hurt, it was being alone, knowing my parents were gone." Her breath hitched. "And knowing it was my fault."

That small shaky confession hit like a sledgehammer. To give himself a moment, Kam picked up the soft robe she'd chosen to wear. Light blue with small yellow flowers, as soft as a T-shirt but thicker, with wide sleeves and a tie belt, it'd be the easiest thing to get on and off her. Still, he used extra care as he bundled her up.

Now, with her covered, he smoothed back her hair. "Panties?"

Looking past him, she shook her head. "Aunt Liz would be scandalized, but for once, I don't care. They're not worth the trouble of getting them on and off."

"We're going to talk in a minute, okay? Not for a single second do I think a kid could be responsible for her parents' actions. But first, I want to get you as comfortable as possible. So how about some aspirin?"

"I took acetaminophen when I brushed my teeth."

He nodded. "Good. For sleeping, I'm thinking the couch would be easier—"

Emotion brought her brows together, but she didn't make a sound.

"For us both to fit."

That brought her gaze to his.

God, he wanted to hold her, to make outrageous promises that wouldn't fit the moment.

If she thought he'd sleep away from her, she was in for a surprise. "Your two couches will be convenient, though I wouldn't mind being right beside you, our feet propped up, if it won't cause you any discomfort."

A wealth of gratitude filled her wide eyes.

Going for a casual vibe that he hoped would help put her at ease, Kam pointed out why the couch might be better. "It's firmer, and I can rearrange things so you're reclining a bit but not attempting to lay flat. Plus, you can use the armrest to take pressure off your shoulder."

Flustered, she nodded. "Okay, sounds good."

"You won't mind if I stick close? Because, babe, I need to

be there—for me, not you. You've already proven that you can handle it. Me? I'm caught between wanting to kill Mike and the urge to wrap you in cotton padding and keep you secreted away so no one and nothing could ever hurt you again."

Her lips inched into a smile. "No killing, okay?" Slowly, she began shuffling her way from the room.

Kam stuck close to her, ready to support her if she needed it.

"You can't wrap me in cotton padding, either. That doesn't sound very fashionable at all."

Relieved that her tone was now teasing, he grinned. "I bet you'd make it look hot."

"Well, I would try, or at least, I'd want it to look stylish, but I doubt it'd be possible the way I look right now. It's a sweet thought, though."

"For me to keep you all to myself? I would never be so selfish—tempting as it might be."

At a snail's pace, they made their way to the living room. "You know you're wicked, right? I can barely move, so no matter how awesome you looked kneeling in front of me when I was naked, I can't take advantage of it."

"Did I look awesome? I was going for concerned and caring." *Loving.* "You have no idea how difficult it was to stomp down my baser instincts. Naked, babe, usually means a lot of touching, kissing." He glanced at her profile. "Licking."

"Eh, probably not when the woman is so banged up and gross."

"Babe, are you fishing for compliments?"

Appalled, she said, "No!"

"Then stop putting yourself down. I keep telling you: You're hot. No matter what." Even when her face and hair had been covered in blood, her left eye nearly swollen shut, his overriding thought had been that she was his. "I can't deny the banged-up part, but I swear, that makes me want to go all caveman on you. Shelter and protect you—that sort of thing."

"Caveman, huh?"

"That territorial tendency is as powerful as lust, but with you, I felt all of it. Every sharp-edged, raging instinct. I want to keep you safe. Once you're healed, I want to make love to you—with the lights on. But until you've recovered, I'm definitely someone you can rely on." And after that, too.

Pausing, she turned to face him, her expression so vulnerable it hurt.

Kam drifted his fingertips over her cheek. "I want all that. I know it's asking a lot, but—"

She laughed, gasped, and caught her hand to her ribs. "Yes, to all that, and a big *thank-you* as well. Now I really need to get off my feet."

Yes, to all that. The constriction in his chest lifted. He stepped around her, arranged the cushions the way he thought would work best, and helped to ease her into her seat. "Don't move. I'll be right back."

Practically running, he went down the hall to fetch multiple pillows and a couple of blankets. Ten minutes later, with a lot of small adjustments, Glory settled comfortably with a small sigh of relief.

"Okay?" he asked, stretched out along her right side with a soft pillow between them so he wouldn't accidentally bump her.

"It's as perfect as it can be, but will you be able to sleep?"

"Better than I could apart from you." He shifted to half face her. "Swear that if you need anything, even a drink of water, you'll let me know."

The room was dim with only a small light from the kitchen filtering into the room, but he still saw her slight smile. "I swear." She turned her head toward him. "Thank you for being here with me."

"It's where I want to be." He'd pulled her coffee table close to the couch, and then gently lifted her feet up on a pillow. She was reclining as much as she could, which wasn't much. A lounge chair might be better for her, but she didn't have one, and if he got one, then he wouldn't be next to her. "Are you sleepy?

"A little."

Sleep would be the best thing for her—but her confession was still out there, and he didn't want her to think he'd dodged the topic, or worse, that he didn't care. "Do you feel like explaining what you said earlier?"

"About how my parents died?"

Maybe, with it darker now, it'd be easier for her to share. "Yes—if you feel up to it. If you'd rather sleep and talk in the morning, that's okay, too. Just know that everything about you interests me." He wouldn't blame her, never that, but if she blamed herself, getting it out there might help her rest easier.

"There are things that happened that day that I've never shared."

"Never? Not even with Callie?"

"There was no reason to. Mom and Dad were dead, and nothing would bring them back. Others had heard them arguing, especially at the gas station when Dad stopped to fill up. The weather was bad. They'd both been drinking."

In other words, no one had questioned the wreck? "I'm sure everyone was busy taking care of you."

"That, too." She kept her head turned, her gaze on him, as if that gave her comfort.

He reached out to settle his hand on hers, holding her fingers loosely.

She returned the touch, not so loosely. "I was bad, Kam."

Just as quietly, he said, "You were a child."

"I was eleven. Older than you when you went to live with Addie. Old enough to know better."

"What happened?"

"It was pounding rain, the wind blowing really hard. Mom and Dad had both drank too much, but they weren't drunk. Not like they sometimes got. They'd argued all day over everything. Mom was mad and telling him he was a lousy driver. He yelled back that she was a lousy lay." She let that land, cleared her throat, and continued. "She slapped him. He shoved her. I was already a little freaked out from the storm, and I guess I lost it."

"Lost it how?"

"I started screaming."

That last word came out higher, thinner, and Kam knew she was crying but he didn't know what to do about it. He wanted to hold her, but she was hurt. He wanted to reassure her, but she needed to let it out. All he could do was rub his thumb over her knuckles and keep holding on. Listening. Being with her.

Caring. And he did. He cared far too much.

"Dad tried to look back at me, not understanding." Her words broke, and she gasped.

"Memories can cause more pain than fractured ribs. I know that, babe." Hell, his own eyes burned. "I understand, okay?"

"Mom leaned over the seat to grab me, to tell me to shut up. Dad was swearing." Swallowing her tears, she whispered, "And we crashed. I was screaming because I hated them, hated hearing them fight all the time, hated being stuck with them—and a few minutes later, they were gone." Rushing the rest of the explanation, she said, "We went off the road, hit something, maybe a guardrail, then over a hill. Or something. I don't remember much of that. I just remember flashlights coming through the windows, an ambulance, and people talking—but the storm never stopped. I guess I passed out, and when I woke up in the hospital, everything was different."

Needing to be nearer, he scooted closer, close enough to feel her warmth. "Okay? I'm not hurting you?"

"You could never hurt me."

Those words fisted around his heart like the tightest of hugs. "No, I never could. Not on purpose. I would never lie to you, either." Using ultimate care, he kissed the tears from her cheeks. "Now you listen to me, Glory McCallahan. You were a child, and you reacted as a child would. That's on them, not you. Kids do and say things because they're kids. That's how it should be. You're not at fault, so don't think that."

"But—"

"Liam was a mistreated kid, you know that right?"

"I assumed."

"He felt the same shit you're feeling. I felt it. Tanner felt it. The difference is, Addie taught us it was okay to be a kid. Tanner teaches that fact to at-risk kids all the time. I believe it now, and I want you to believe it, too."

After a sniffle, she admitted, "It's not easy. My brain knows you're right, but my heart tells me that by screaming, I changed everything."

Sitting forward, Kam retrieved a tissue from the side table. "Can I do this for you or—"

"Ha!" As if in slow motion, she took the tissue from him, mopped her face, and then blew her nose.

Tomorrow, he'd get her better set up with everything she'd need close at hand, but for now, he grabbed another tissue, wrapped it around the one she held, and pitched it toward the kitchen. "I'll get that when I get up."

She half smiled. "Okay." After a moment, she gave him a long look. "I don't know why, but I feel better now that I shared, so thank you for listening."

"Thank you for sharing with me." The distance was killing him, so he moved that damned divider pillow, placing it on her lap and getting up next to her. Now he could breathe in the scent of her skin and feel the warmth from her body. "Will this work?"

"It's better." Tipping her head to his shoulder, she shifted enough to ease into his side. "Much better."

"For me, too."

"We've shared a lot of secrets, haven't we?"

"Yeah, and it means something important." Did she sense that, too? "It's like we have a pact or something, right? I trust you; you trust me . . ." He left that hanging out there, waiting for confirmation.

Softly, she gave him what he needed. "I trust you."

"So no more secrets." The second he said it, he felt her go still with new apprehension. "Hey, I'm not asking you to bare your soul or anything." He needed her relaxed, not tensed up.

Damn it, he must have pushed her too much. She should have been asleep an hour ago. "Do you need anything?"

Faking a yawn, she closed her eyes. "No, I'm ready to sleep. How about you?"

Not a chance, but all he said was, "Can barely keep my eyes open." He kissed her temple, then waited, listening to her breathe until, finally, she really did fade out.

Kam looked at her face, pale in the dim evening light, her hair leaving shadows over her cheek that mingled with the bruising. *I could have lost her.*

How could she have become so important to him when he had so many goals? Seeing her like this, battered but still gentle, scared but concerned for a stray dog, loving her family and his and yet wanting privacy—with him—it touched him deep inside, forcing an alignment of all the things he considered important.

Family, independence, proving he was nothing like his father . . . The shift had been creeping up on him, but the wreck had changed everything in minutes and now Glory topped his list.

In her sleep, she moved, flinched, and somehow cuddled closer to him. Using extra care, he rearranged her so that she didn't put undue stress on her shoulder, and so the pillow helped to cushion her ribs.

This, he thought, was where he was meant to be. With Glory. For sex in the dark—and against the wall. Morning coffee and silly flirting. During easy times with his family, and when she needed him the most.

The next few weeks would be rough for her, but he'd be with her as often as possible, and when he had to work, his family and Callie would fill in. Glory loved his family; he knew that now. What she didn't yet understand was that they loved her right back.

11

After a week, Glory felt better. Not fully recovered, but she'd adapted enough that she desperately wanted to reclaim part of her normal routine.

With Callie's help, she managed a regular shower. Her hair, while not styled exactly the way she preferred, was clean and soft. Her shoulder still ached but she'd learned which moves to avoid and found a regimen of OTC pain meds and ice that kept it tolerable.

Her ribs were another matter, but even they had lightened up. Unfortunately, her bruising had turned several ugly shades of green and yellow. No matter how it shocked Aunt Liz, she wasn't about to attempt makeup. Kam didn't seem to care, and no one else mentioned it.

"Well," said Aunt Liz, as she fretted around her. "If you're sure there's nothing I can do for you . . ."

It still surprised Glory that Liz came by every other day to sit with her for an hour. That first day had been horrid, with

Liz nearly falling apart. Streaming tears—which had destroyed her own makeup—Liz wanted to embrace her, but everyone stopped her. She'd tried to dramatically drop down beside her, but Kam quickly cautioned her to go easy.

Finally, Liz had gone behind the couch to lean down very closely. She'd stroked Glory's bloodstained hair, carefully kissed her cheek, and begged to know if there was anything she could do.

It had unsettled Glory enough that she'd scrambled for a task, ultimately settling on asking her aunt to figure out some prettier clothes that she could easily get on and off.

Her aunt had nailed it. The very next day she'd come by with three outfits, and since then, she'd brought over three more.

"You've already done so much, Aunt Liz." Glory glanced down at the cotton wide-legged drawstring pants she wore. Nothing could be more fashionable and comfortable for her injuries. The roomy buttoned-up tops certainly looked better than any other choices she had. "Thank you again for the clothes."

"Of course. You're like a daughter to me," Liz stated. "I don't cook as Addie does, and I know you prefer for Callie to help you with your showers."

"You're all wonderful to me, and I appreciate it."

Liz gave her a funny look, then very delicately sat beside her and took her hand. "You do realize that we all love you?"

Never before had Liz spoken like this. Glory wondered if it was Addie's influence, or if the wreck had upset her that much. "I do know it, and I love you, too, Aunt Liz."

They both smiled, and then Liz asked, "Does the padded brace around your torso help? The pharmacist told me that many people with broken ribs use it when sleeping."

"It helps a lot. I'm still sleeping on the couch—" she didn't know when she'd be able to fully recline without pain, only that it wasn't in her immediate future "—but now I don't wake up as often."

"Excellent." Touching her face, Liz frowned. "You're sure you don't want any makeup? Maybe just enough to cover the horrific bruising?"

And there was the aunt she knew and adored. Smile widening, Glory said, "You've all already seen me like this, and I don't plan to venture out anytime soon. Putting on makeup would just mean having to take it off." Brushing her teeth was enough of an ordeal. "Plus, we both know nothing is going to cover all this discoloration. I'll just have to look wretched until it fades."

Liz bit her lip, her brow creased. "It's just that you look worse now than when I first saw you."

Poor Addie had just entered from the kitchen and she gasped. "Liz, what in the world are you telling her?" Frustration and worry brought her rushing forward. "Don't listen to her, Glory. You look fine."

Glory and Liz both snorted—then looked at each other and laughed.

Okay, yeah, that hurt—the snort and the laugh. But how could she have resisted?

Her grimace was enough to have both women suddenly fussing over her.

And in came her own personal hero. "Can she breathe?"

Addie twisted around to face Kam. "Well, of course, she can breathe. Why would you ask such a thing?"

"With you two smothering her, I wasn't sure." His gaze met hers and he smiled. "Pretty sure we need to give her some room, okay?" To help accomplish that, he added, "Liz, would you mind getting her some juice? Addie, how about you grab her ice pack?"

After both women jumped to do his bidding, Kam eased down beside her. "You look worn out."

"You and Aunt Liz, full of compliments today."

In reply to that, he kissed her forehead near her healing cut, then her cheek, and finally, the corner of her mouth. In a whisper, he asked, "Want me to clear house?"

"Is that possible without hurting feelings?" While Kam had worked, she'd had visitors on and off all day.

Once the women finished their tasks, Kam managed to get them on their way with little fanfare.

"I'll be by again soon," Liz said. "I ordered you a beautiful quilt, one that will match your living room since you're practically living in here now. It should arrive soon."

"That's so nice of you, Aunt Liz, but you don't have to—"

The kiss Liz landed on her cheek wasn't quite as gentle as Kam's, but it didn't hurt much.

Next, Addie said, "I hope you enjoy your dinner. Now that you're able to move your arms a little more easily, I fixed you something hardier. Roast pork and dressing with all the sides. Don't hesitate to have Kam cut up the meat for you."

"Thank you, Addie. I'm sure it's delicious." Everything she made was amazing. "Please don't go to so much trouble, though. I don't mind ordering from a restaurant every now and then."

"When I love cooking for you? Don't be silly." Lightly, she touched Glory's right shoulder, gave Kam a big hug, and then she walked out with Liz.

Kam locked the door behind them. "Alone at last."

This was her favorite part of the day, when she had Kam all to herself. How long that could go on, she didn't know. "Everything go okay at work today?"

"Yup." He headed into the kitchen, saying, "I'll get our food together."

While he was occupied, she worked her way up from the couch. "Let's sit at the table. I'm tired of the couch."

He straightened from the oven where Addie had left the food to warm. His gaze swept over her, tracking her progress. "I thought you were going to ice your shoulder?"

While carrying the ice pack and her juice, Glory did her best to make her walk smooth and easy. "I don't need it right now. I really am feeling much better."

Stepping around the bar, he relieved her of the juice to set it on the table, then took the ice pack from her and put it on the bar.

When she reached for a chair at the dining table, he pulled it out for her. "Can I at least get a pillow to put behind your back?"

"That's okay. It feels good to move a little." Not a lie. So far, her views had been from the couch or the bathroom. Every day she felt stronger, though that probably had as much to do with her emotions as it did her healing injuries.

"I was thinking about that. I wonder if you could manage a lounge chair outside? Not for long, but for a bit of fresh air."

"That sounds like Addie talking, and yes, I'd love a break from being cooped up indoors. I'll order one online today. Never in my life have I watched three movies in a single day, but now it's becoming a habit. I've read two books, listened to an audiobook, and I've become a pro at online solitaire."

He grinned as he set the table. "I watched two of those movies with you, and I enjoyed it. A lazy day on the couch is good sometimes."

Did he really feel that way? "Wouldn't you rather be fixing up your new apartment?"

Pausing in the middle of serving the food, his smile paled to enigmatic scrutiny. "Is this your way of saying you want some time alone?"

"Not exactly."

That answer didn't appease him. "Am I crowding you?"

Absolutely not. She was so glad not to be alone that it scared her, especially at a time when she really needed to learn to stand on her own.

What scared her more was hogging his time, stealing him away from his obligations, interrupting his plans. Kam was a good man with a busy life—a life he'd put on hold for her. "I like having you here," she offered, as a way to ease into things.

"I've moved in on you." With the food on their plates, he took a seat across from her. "I didn't really give you much of a choice, though."

Moved in when he still had an apartment? "It's not a problem for me."

"You'll get a break tomorrow, though."

His set expression kept her uneasy. "Oh?"

"I know it's Saturday, but I have to head in to work for a few hours to finish up a custom order, then I'm taking a bunch of kids to play Putt-Putt golf. Liam and Nell are going along."

How ridiculous was it that she felt left out? She didn't begrudge the kids having some fun, and she respected Kam so much for the time he spent with them. "Liam is still involved?"

He nodded. "Nell, too. It helps, because the teens know them and trust them, at least to a point."

Liam was nineteen and Nell was seventeen, but they were remarkably mature for their ages. They were also a couple, though not everyone knew that. Until Nell had turned seventeen, Liam had viewed her as hands-off.

"Nell still spends some nights at the halfway house." Kam's mouth firmed. "I worry about her, but it's better now that she and Liam are together. At least when she needs a place to go in the middle of the night, she's comfortable with him."

"I think they're in love." Using only her right hand, she forked a few peas on her plate. "She had to grow up fast, didn't she?"

"Afraid so. Her grandma tries, but . . ." He shook his head and changed the topic. "How did your visit with Callie go?"

There remained a cautious distance between them, but Glory wasn't sure what to do about it. "PB was with her. Nell gave her a clean bill of health, by the way."

"She took her to the clinic where she works?"

"Yes. PB is now up-to-date on her shots and Tanner got her a very pretty collar." For the next few seconds, they both stayed busy eating. "Mmm. Addie has outdone herself."

"When I first came to live with her, I couldn't believe the food." A genuine smile showed not only on his mouth, but in his eyes. "There was always something cooking or something sweet on the counter. Addie would ask me what I'd like to eat, and I never knew what to tell her. Everything she made was great."

"I'm not much of a cook." Once she said it, she glanced at him, feeling a little defensive. "I mean . . . Addie definitely has a talent."

"She does, and even better, she enjoys it."

"I can read a recipe."

Unlike her, Kam didn't seem to think anything of it. "Same. I don't do too badly, but food always tastes better when someone else cooks it."

Glad that she wouldn't be compared to Addie, Glory tried to relax. "Putt-Putt golf sounds fun. I wish I were able to join you."

Lifting his gaze from his food, he took in her left arm, carefully held to her side, then the bruising on her face. "I wish you could, too, but you have a lot of healing to do before you'll be up for something like that."

The look in his eyes conveyed more than his casual response. "I'm okay on my own, you know. If there are things you need to do, don't feel like you have to arrange for someone else to be here with me."

"Ha! It's all I can do to keep them away."

Given the enthusiasm from everyone when they visited, that might be true. "I'm not used to so much attention. It's overwhelming." And exhausting. Being the center of attention didn't suit her. She wanted to groan without anyone hearing it, wanted to get off the couch without others seeing her struggle. She wanted to be herself, not someone who endlessly garnered pity.

Kam set aside his fork. "So you want some time alone?"

Not from him, but she could see that he'd taken it that way. Damn, she was butchering this. "I'm going to be blunt."

"Sure, let's try that."

Her frown snapped into place and with the stitches still in her forehead and cheek, she imagined it looked as angry as it felt. "You say that like I've kept things from you."

"You're hedging around about something. Just spit it out."

Fine. "I like having you here. I want you here."

Kam started to relax.

"As long as it's convenient."

He stiffened right up again. "For me or you?"

No man could be that obtuse. "I don't want you to feel obligated." *And I don't want to feel like a nuisance.* Cue pity party. Maybe if she slept better, she'd handle him better, too—if anyone could *handle* Kam. It didn't seem likely. He had a streak of honor that would always guide him. Admirable, as long as that wasn't what kept him with her. "You have a life away from me; I know that. Work at the shop, a family who adores you—"

"Tanner might object to that description."

"And your volunteer time with kids in the youth program.

Plus, you still help out with the tree farm." Addie and Tanner depended on him. The at-risk kids needed him. She did not want to hog all his time. It made her feel needy and selfish, when she'd been well on her way to changing her life.

If he lived with her—permanently, without that perfectly good apartment going to waste—she might feel differently. He'd kept the apartment, though, and now he was stuck here with her.

Firming her chin, she tried to sit a little straighter, to look less like a wounded victim. "I can get around on my own now."

His brows leveled over his eyes. "Sure, from the couch to the table."

"So I'm a little sore, big deal. You wouldn't let that slow you down. Neither would Tanner, and I'm guessing Addie would forge on no matter what. Callie was hurt and she still went out to feed her chickens. Remember that?"

With a distinct lack of humor, the corner of his mouth lifted. "Do you remember that Callie didn't have broken ribs and a torn rotator cuff?"

No, but she'd fallen from her attic, and she'd been bruised almost as badly as Glory was now. "Hurt is hurt," she said, refusing to give up her point.

"There's hurt and then there's injured. Besides, if you think Tanner and I wouldn't be pampering Addie, you haven't paid attention."

Maybe it was from being cooped up, but Glory felt like throwing her fork at him. "Callie and I would dote on her, too. That's not what I'm saying, and you know it."

Kam rubbed a hand over his face. "Actually, yeah, I get it. You want to normalize your life as much as you can."

Recognizing that he did understand took away some of her starch. She relaxed her spine again, shifting to get as comfortable as she could in the hard chair. "I have weeks to go yet before my ribs are healed. The idea of nonstop visitors is daunting."

He nodded in acceptance. "Want me to talk to them?"

"We could do that together." With a moderated inhale, she prepped herself for the next battle. "I want PB back here. For good."

"Babe—"

"Don't *babe* me, Kam. She's my dog. My dog-ter." Yes, she liked that term. "You know the longer she's with Addie, Tanner, and Callie, the more attached she'll be to them."

This time, it was his mouth he rubbed, but still when he dropped his hand, real humor showed in the tilt of his mouth. "Dog-ter, huh?"

"Yes. My dog-daughter." Glory had so much love to give—love she wanted to lavish on others. Kam wasn't ready for that yet, so PB was it. Well, and Callie. But that was different. Usually, Callie tried to take care of her—as much as Kam did. With PB, she'd love her and care for her . . . and baby her. Instinctively, she rested her hand over her abdomen. "I want her established here and that's that."

"I get your point. PB will probably bond with the pets, too."

Very true. Blu the dog and Percy the cat would become PB's friends, and then she'd lose the dog for good. "It's not right to leave her there."

"Fine, I'll work on it." Getting cagey, he pointed at her. "But only if you're okay with me staying, because you're in no shape to be constantly bending down to attach a leash when she needs to go out."

"No problem." She wanted him to stay—and seriously, she couldn't imagine trying to bend like that. Feeling like she'd won that round, Glory smiled at him. "I told you I wanted you to stay—but only if you want to."

"I want to."

Because she still needed so much help. "What about your work with the kids?"

"I've been thinking about that. You're right that it's important—to them and to me—so I'll fit it in."

"You promise? It would mean a lot to me if you could. I never want to interfere with that."

Some strange expression overcame him. Like a mix of tenderness and admiration. "First, you could never interfere. Second, as long as I know you're not overdoing it, I'll make sure I keep up with them."

After that sweet comment, Glory felt like tallying up another win for herself. "And your apartment?"

"It's not going anywhere."

Such an unsatisfying reply. Did that mean he wanted to eventually get back to it, or just that he still had time to decide. Payments were due the first week of each month and she hated to see him spending his hard-earned money on a place he wasn't using.

At the same time, she didn't want him to give up his plans just because she'd been caught off guard. "So . . ." She forked up another bite of succulent pork, buying herself some time as she ate. "Pretty sure this is going to tick you off."

"Now what?" He sent her a long-suffering look. "So we're clear, I don't expect you to tiptoe around about things." He, too, went back to eating. "If you've got something on your mind, I want to hear it."

She finished a few bites first. No reason to waste Addie's delicious meal. While she did that, she reevaluated.

"Dragging out the suspense, huh?"

"No, it's just . . . I'm bored." That was it in a nutshell; a way to get to her pertinent point.

His brows lifted. "I imagine so."

"Your apartment is empty."

The unnecessary reminder tightened his jaw. "I know, but it doesn't matter."

That did it. No longer under control, all the words just rushed out. "It matters to *me* because I'm the one keeping you from it. You're here playing nurse, and housekeeper, and personal servant, which," she added with a somewhat snide and suggestive laugh, "is one hell of a fabulous fantasy, so you know. All the other women would love it, believe me. But it shouldn't be all about me, not when you're so incredible and you're missing out on so much. You had plans, Kam. Good plans, even though I know Addie would disagree. But that should be between you and her, and instead, I'm messing up everything."

"You've been fantasizing about me?"

Throwing her fork became a real possibility. "That's all you heard?"

The curve of his mouth wasn't all that friendly or amused. "I'm flattered, so yeah, that part stuck with me. It was more interesting than the rest of that nonsense you're spewing."

Nonsense! She's just opened her heart to him, and he dared to act put out?

He sat back in his chair and waved a hand at her. "You're dying to tell me, so what does my incredibleness have to do with my apartment?"

Since the wreck, it seemed her emotions had boarded a roller coaster and hadn't gotten off yet. It was enough to make a woman dizzy. One minute, she wanted to tell him she loved him, the next, she wanted to confess that they'd be tied together, and right now, she wanted to tell him to go away.

Except that she didn't really want to be alone. She wanted some peace and quiet, yes, but she wanted it with Kam.

Dreaded tears burned her eyes. "You're doing all the giving, I'm doing all the taking, and I don't like it."

"You just said you liked it enough to fantasize over it."

At least glaring at him didn't hurt.

Hitching his shoulder, he said, "Fine. We'll move past the fantasizing part since we can't do anything about it yet. Plan to revisit that topic when you're healed, though."

No other man could be so outrageous. To get it said, Glory waited until he put a big bite in his mouth, then rattled off the words she'd rehearsed in her head. "I'm buying some things for your apartment. Fun things. Things that will look great." She lifted her right hand to stop any complaints. "I'm doing it. I need to do it. You can't stop me."

He dropped his fork with a clatter. "I can refuse to accept it!"

At least he'd lost his patronizing tone. "You can try. But then you'll make me sad, and I'll . . ." Her heart clenched, but this was important. "I'll have to make you leave when I'd rather you stay."

Anger gathered his brows together and added fire to his green eyes. "Blackmail?"

"That's an impressive look, sexy really, but I know you won't lose your temper on me." Plus, she wasn't above fighting dirty.

"Damn it, Glory—"

"Oh!" Utilizing theatrical drama, she put a hand to her ribs.

"What?" Galvanized, he came around the table, his arguments disappearing with light speed. "Are you all right?"

"Yes, I keep telling you I am." Despite a few real twinges of pain, she rose from her seat. "I just wanted your attention." Getting out of a hardback chair was trickier than rising from the couch.

He stood there, fuming. "Did you fake that just to shut me up?"

"It's possible." She picked up her mostly empty plate and shuffled her way toward the kitchen.

Angry footsteps followed her. "I won't be manipulated."

She refrained from pointing out the obvious. "All right, but I have to be fair. If I can't do for you, I can't allow you to continue doing for me."

A string of curses singed her ears. He couldn't see her face, so she gave in to a smile. He was so stubborn, and so proud—but then, so was she. "My independence is as important as yours. You might want to keep that in mind."

"Fine." With his concession out there, he took the plate from her. "I insist on limits."

"I don't know that I can agree with that. After all, our ideas of limits are different."

Shoulders rigid and neck stiff, he scraped the plate into the garbage with more energy than was necessary. "Because I'm blue collar and you're part of Hoker's most upscale family? Believe me, I know you have deep pockets. It's not something I'll ever forget."

So they'd always have that issue between them? Not a good start. "I wouldn't have put it quite like that."

"No? Let's hear your take on it." He got to work on his own plate.

The churlish attitude was stealing all her fun. She wanted to get him gifts . . . and she wanted him to like them. "I work for a living, the same as you. Yes, my aunt and uncle are generous. I would never deny that. In many ways, they've treated me the same as Callie."

Exasperation brought him around to face her. "Not where it matters most."

"We're talking about financials right now." Yes, her aunt's expectations were high, but she'd taken care of Glory. "They covered my expenses for college."

"And expected you to be top of the class?"

Well . . . yes, they had. "I expected that of myself." *The absolute truth.* "They gave me a great job in the company—"

"And ran you ragged."

Not quite ragged, but yes, her aunt had definitely twisted Glory's schedule to her advantage. "I love—*loved*—my job and was good at it, but when I said I wanted to cut back on travel, they didn't complain." *Too much.* "They gave me the new position I have now, and it's perfect for me." Especially since she could stay close to Callie. "They've always included good health insurance with employment. It's why I can afford to be off work now." Saying it all out loud really drove home the advantages she'd been given.

Advantages Kam had done without.

For a few silent seconds, they simply stared at each other until Glory admitted, "I forgot the point I was making."

"Don't expect me to remind you."

No, in his soured mood, he wouldn't want to be agreeable. "I make my own way, Kam." *Mostly.* Hadn't she just detailed all the ways she'd been helped? "I've been working on being better. Less pampered." *More like Callie.* "I won't backslide just because of a few injuries."

He snorted. "Broken ribs are a big deal."

Yes, but so was her future—especially because the future would no longer be hers alone. She'd have a big responsibility, and she was determined to do her best. "It's been a week, and I'm feeling better. I can't just stay parked on the couch. I'm already restless." When she inhaled slowly, keeping it shallow, the discomfort was minimal. "I'm going to help in the kitchen."

"No way."

"I need to move. My butt goes numb from sitting so much."

Slowly, his antagonism converted to humor. "Want me to rub it?"

"Yes—after I've helped."

In a lightened mood—maybe because he was thinking of her

backside—he said without heat, "You're the most infuriating woman."

If he considered her infuriating, she might as well go for broke. "Once we've gotten everything put away, know what I want to do?"

"Get your butt rubbed?"

His wolfish grin made her snicker. Here she stood, battered and bruised, her hair messy, her clothes baggy, looking absolutely horrid, and still, he flirted. "Yes, but there's something else, too."

The buzz of his phone interrupted. After a single glance at the screen, Kam ignored it.

Glory didn't. She gave him a look. "Aren't you going to answer it?"

"Nah."

Suspicions crawled in. Clearly, it wasn't family, because he never ignored their calls. "Why not?"

Brushing past her, he went for more dishes. "I'm busy right now."

Too busy to answer his phone?

The buzzing stopped—and then started again. "Answer it."

"Why?"

"Why not?" she countered.

Grousing under his breath, he stalked past her with their glasses. "It's Shara, and I already explained things to her."

Shara! Now she was irked. "Maybe you need to explain again."

He tried frowning, but Glory just gave him an imperturbable stare. She trusted him; that wasn't the issue. At the moment, she wasn't sure of the issue, she only knew she didn't like it.

"Women." Despite his grumble, he took the phone from his pocket and answered with, "Not a great time."

Whatever Shara replied had him looking up at the ceiling.

Deciding not to hover, Glory went into the kitchen, which was all of five feet away, and put the lid back on the food containers Addie had brought over. Though she was slow, she had them into the refrigerator just as Kam ended a low and somewhat private conversation.

Before she could even turn, he was back and carefully slipping an arm behind her. "Will you please sit back down now?"

"Everything okay?"

"I can tell you're dying to know, so yes, things are fine. Shara is just being persistent. I told her—again—that it's not happening."

"How'd she take that?"

"If you're asking if that's the end of it, probably not. She came by the shop yesterday. She's called a few other times. No idea what's gotten into her, but Addie said she's probably jealous because of you."

A dash of cold water wouldn't have been as jarring. "Addie knew she's been after you, but you didn't bother to tell me?" That hurt. They were practically living together. Or actually living together, except that his apartment was very nearby. Whatever. Even if she was out of commission, he still shouldn't have kept it from her.

"You," he said after a peck to the end of her nose, "had enough to deal with. I wasn't keeping secrets, but I didn't think it was necessary to update you on a pesky ex, either."

No, probably not, but he should have, anyway.

"Glory, Shara doesn't matter." He put his big warm hands on either side of her face, then bent his knees to look into her eyes. "We have plenty of things we can debate, but this shouldn't be one of them."

Wrinkling her nose, Glory said, "Guess I'm a little jealous, too?"

The warmth of his gaze told her he liked it. "You have no reason to be."

Didn't she? If she hadn't gotten hurt, would Kam even still be with her? Glory's heart said yes, but her head questioned everything. The automatic sigh caused a twinge in her ribs.

He stopped, stepped around to the front of her, and then carefully settled his hands on her backside. "Okay?"

Um . . . "What are you doing?"

"This." Warm and gentle, his hands carefully massaged her. "Tell me if I hurt you."

Oh, *heaven*. Needing the support, she rested her forehead on his chest. "That's wonderful."

"Fantasy-inspiring?"

With a grin, she said, "Most definitely."

His lips touched the side of her neck. "No reason for jealousy, okay? This? With you? It's enough for me."

So many internal battles left her weary. "How can that be?"

"Because it's you. With me. And you're alive and getting better, and I won't ever take that for granted, not after almost losing you."

Those blasted tears filled her eyes again. She didn't know if it was the new life growing inside her, the low-level pain that never quite left her, or the uncertainty of the coming months that kept her emotions rioting, but to her, that almost sounded like a vow. "I wish I could put both arms around you and squeeze you real tight."

"We'll get there, babe. I promise."

She'd hold him to that. "Your magic fingers are both making me sleepy and making me wish I could do more."

"For me, too." Moving his hands to safer ground, he coaxed her out of the kitchen.

Allowing it, she sighed. "I have a lot to figure out."

"Like?"

"Many things, actually." When should she spell it out to Kam? Soon . . . but not tonight. "For now, there's something I want to do." When they reached the couch, she hesitated. "I want to call Mike."

First blank-faced, then irate, Kam stated, "Fuck that."

"Your language is deteriorating."

"I want to deteriorate that prick with my bare hands, so yeah, the language is sure to follow."

Understanding how he felt, Glory stared up at him. "My life is currently on hold. I've been working on myself for a long while, doing my best to be independent, to not rely so much on Liz's approval, and just when I think I'm making progress, I'm supposed to let Mike slow me down again?"

"You were in a bad wreck."

"I'm well aware. It took me a long time to get comfortable in a car after the first one, but I overcame that fear once and I'll do it again. I've lived for years with self-conscious dread over my scars—"

"Glory," he said tenderly, helping her into her seat.

She'd have to tell him about the baby soon. Keeping it bottled up inside was too difficult. "You helped me get over that. Sort of. I'm still uncomfortable with them, but since I'll now have scars on my face, too, I guess people seeing them is unavoidable. I'm not about to do more surgery . . . of any kind."

He positioned the pillow behind her, then lifted her feet to another pillow on the coffee table. "Your shoulder might need it."

"Around endless TV, books, and a surplus of visitors, I've done my research on that. A tear in my rotator cuff might not heal, but if I could build up the muscles around it, I should be able to get by with only occasional pinches of pain. I could live with that. It's not like I'm a super-physical person, anyway."

"You're physical with me. We'll get physical again as soon as you're up for it."

Her heart softened to mush. "I'm counting on it, anticipating it, too, but that'll happen sooner if I don't get shoulder surgery."

He held up his hands, not to give up, she was sure, but to put off the discussion for a while.

"If I call Mike," she persisted, "I can put it on speaker, and between us, we might be able to figure out if he had anything to do with this."

"You know he did. First Dan Fellows is run off the road, and then you are. Two car accidents since Mike showed up in town."

"Oh, my God, I'd almost forgotten about Mr. Fellows!"

"It's okay, Glory. He's doing much better. I was just pointing out the obvious."

It did seem obvious. Still . . . "I'd like it confirmed. I thought you'd want to listen in, but if you'd rather not—"

"Haven't you insulted me enough for one day?" His tone was mild, and he even leaned forward to give her a soft kiss. "Give me two minutes and I'll be back, then we can make the call."

Had she been insulting? "I'm sorry."

"Under the circumstances, you're allowed."

"Misery loves company?" She'd never want to make him miserable. Just the opposite.

"Sorry if I snapped, too. Two minutes. Until then, just rest."

Could she and Kam make it for the long haul, eventually becoming a couple like Callie and Tanner? Would he share her house with her?

Would he be happy about the baby?

That thought took her hand to her middle, where she thought of the tiny life already growing. It was cowardly not to tell him, and until she did, she couldn't tell anyone else. Kam would be the first to know.

Thank God she wasn't suffering morning sickness, because she couldn't imagine throwing up with her injuries.

"What's wrong?" Frowning, Kam came to her side with a glass of juice and two OTC pain pills, thankfully the ones the doctor had approved. "Are you feeling nauseous?"

Glory slipped her hand away. "No, just thinking." He was such a stunningly handsome man with his chestnut hair and vivid green eyes she couldn't help staring at him a moment. "Seriously, I'm surly and I know it, but I didn't mean to take it out on you."

Gingerly, he sat beside her. "Here, take these."

She tossed the pills back gratefully. The second she lowered the glass, he took it from her and kissed her. An easy kiss, light and gentle, because he worried about hurting her.

"More?" she asked on a soft breath.

Just like that, he carefully held her face and came back for a more thorough kiss, not quite as steamy as she wanted, but still pretty hot.

He smiled. "Better?"

"Mmm, yes. It'll do more for me than the pills."

"Then I'll be sure to dose you every day."

Silly Kam. He always had an answer. For the rest of her life, she wanted to hear his teasing, taste his kisses, enjoy the quiet times together, share a movie in the evening, and wake up to the scent of him.

She truly loved everything about him: the easy way he chatted with the diner owners, Ed and Ted, how he doted on Addie, backed up Tanner, and teased Callie. The ease with which he handled Liz and the proficient way he ran interference for her.

Leaning forward the tiniest bit—all she could manage, really, but it was an improvement—she pressed one more kiss to his delectable mouth. "In case it seemed otherwise, I appreciate all you do, not just for me but for everyone, your town, and family . . . and my family, too."

"All that, huh?"

"Don't downplay it, Kam. Not to me."

His brows lifted. "If you want to idolize me, I won't argue—as long as you're not kicking me out."

Never. But saying that might pressure him, and she didn't want him that way. She wanted his love, because he had hers. "I'm not kicking you out, but please tell me if you need to spend time somewhere else."

"Deal."

Much more of that and she'd be telling him everything, making confessions better saved for another time. "Are you okay with me calling Mike now? I really will feel better knowing how he reacts."

Bracing himself with a big breath, Kam handed over her phone. "All right. Go for it. I'll do my best to keep my mouth shut, but let me know if you want me to step in."

She wouldn't, because he'd already stepped in enough. It'd be so easy to let him handle her problems, but it was past time for her to take charge.

Removing Mike from the block list didn't take long. With one press of her finger, she called his number. It might not prove anything, but right now, it was the only proactive move she could make.

12

Endless worry kept Mike pacing around the midsize house. Far from the swankiest place he'd ever been, it was clean but outdated. The maiden aunt decor was atrocious, enough to turn his stomach, but at least it wasn't the dive motel room he'd had to suffer in Hoker.

Plus renting the house outside of town helped ensure that no one could easily find him. Pending traffic, he could still be back in the small town in ten minutes. He knew because he drove through there every day, hoping he'd run into Glory. He'd see her, she would see him, they would laugh, and he'd finally know that she was okay.

Or at least he'd get a glimpse of her, enough to be reassured that she was up and about, not lying broken in a hospital bed.

That vision consumed him, gnawing on his peace of mind, keeping him on the edge. *She's mine.* That would never change. If she was hurt, he should be with her.

It displeased him that she still held on to her snit. Not at all the trait of a perfect woman. It had to be Kam's influence. That no-good trespasser should find his own woman instead of trying to steal Mike's.

Once he reunited with her, she'd learn not to act out so impetuously.

Thinking of all the ways he'd school her deepened his breathing. Jenn had let him down. Her perfection had only been skin-deep, and once she was pitifully begging, even that was gone.

Glory was different, pure through and through, and smart enough to learn what was expected of her. They were meant to be together; she'd understand that soon enough.

The sudden ring of his phone jarred him from that favorite fantasy. He didn't want to talk to anyone. He didn't want to have to be social. He wanted Glory, back with him where she belonged.

Out of sheer habit, he glanced at the screen, and his heart nearly stopped. Hands fumbling, he grabbed up the phone, dropped it, then fell to his knees to snatch it up. He swiped his thumb over the screen and, at almost the same time, shouted, "Glory! Oh, thank God. Do you know how worried I've been? I didn't know what happened or how badly you were hurt, and no one would tell me anything because I'm not a member of this godforsaken town."

When she didn't reply, his excitement died. *"Glory?"*

"Um . . . Mike?"

That uncertain voice took the strength from his bones, and he sat back on his ass with a raspy laugh. "Of course, it's me, sweetheart. I'm so glad to hear from you."

More seconds ticked by before she asked, "You said you were worried. Does that mean you know I was in a wreck?"

"Yes, and I've been going insane worrying about you." Dropping his voice, he rebuked her. "You shouldn't have blocked me. You can't know how hard that was for me."

"*How*," she interrupted, her own tone sharpening, "did you know?"

"Everyone knows. Apparently, nothing happens in this town that isn't reported and shared and gossiped about. I've been so frantic I've barely been able to sleep. I called different hospitals in the area, but no one would tell me a thing."

Again, she took her time in replying. "So you overheard something?"

Hadn't he just said so? Her distinct lack of concern for him, especially after he'd worried himself sick over her, left him peevish. "I was in a . . ." No, he wasn't about to tell her he'd been in a bar. She might frown on it because they both held such high standards, plus it was where he met Shara. God knew that woman had been a disappointment. She hadn't been able to make any headway yet with Kam. He'd be happy just to be done with her—and he would be, soon.

Amending his explanation, he continued with, "I was in a store and overheard people talking. I don't know of any other woman driving a cherry-red Mustang in this town, so I was immediately concerned and started listening in."

"You eavesdropped?"

"Believe me, the ramblings of quaint country people normally bore me, but I felt sure it was about you. When they said a blonde woman had been taken away in an ambulance, I almost died."

Bypassing any concern for his mental anguish, she asked, "Was it you following me when it happened?"

Immediate rage washed through him, clenching his heart—and his fists. How dare she blame him? How dare she be so cold? "You're accusing me?" The words snarled from his throat, but he couldn't help that.

"Are you denying it?" she countered.

Oh, she'd definitely be reprimanded for her impertinence.

Breathing hard, he came to his feet and gave her a hard dose of truth. "I would absolutely follow you if I thought you needed me. I would dog you day and night to keep you safe."

Her voice emerged, equally low and mean. "I don't need *you*."

"And I *didn't* follow you." Knowing he had to get control, he stiffly paced—from one end of the room to the other, then back again. *I don't need you*. The hell she didn't!

Now more than ever, she needed him. She was straying off the path, becoming embroiled with hillbillies, and growing far too lippy. "I thought you had been hurt. I feared you might have died."

Deadpan, she quipped, "Well, obviously, I'm not dead."

Blood thundered in his ears and heat scorched up the back of his neck. "Don't even say that." Rasped out around the constriction in his suddenly tight throat, the words were faint, scratchy. "Don't you ever say that. I couldn't live without you. You're a part of me."

"No, I'm not—and I never will be."

She was wrong, and he'd prove it to her. She'd beg for him. He only hoped she wouldn't wait until it was too late.

He heard a faint grumbling before she continued. "I was hurt, Mike. I have two fractured ribs, a torn rotator cuff, and a lot of colorful bruises."

There went his legs again. "Jesus." Macabre scenes filled his imagination. His Glory, broken and bruised. "Baby, what can I do? How can I help?"

Without thanking him for the offer, she said, "I don't need your help. I only called because I wanted to know if it was you following me. That's why I went off the road. I was spooked by a car tailing me. I was watching the rearview mirror and then a dog ran in front of me, and when I tried to swerve, I lost control."

"No," he breathed. Hearing it from her was even worse than hearing it from Kirby.

"I hit a tree."

And she could have died. "Glory . . ."

"The person following me—you, I assumed—took off."

New rage coalesced, cinching his muscles and burning his eyes. It was a good thing the little witch wasn't here right now to suffer his temper. How dare she malign him like that? "You actually think I would do that?" He sounded pissed and didn't care. "You think I would watch you crash into a tree and then just drive away? Do you fucking know me at all?"

"Don't curse at me."

Emotion exploded from him. "I love you! I would never leave you like that. You're my life, Glory, a part of me. My soulmate. We belong together."

Oddly, his anger worked to calm hers, leaving her tone flat. "We're nothing to each other. I've told you that numerous times now. We were never together and we never will be."

Shaking his head didn't clear away the fog of her denial. "You don't mean that. We're meant to be. You're mine."

The sound of two slow, strained inhales came through the line. "I mean every word. Go back to your life and forget about me. As soon as I end this call, I'm blocking you again and that's the end of it."

"Don't you dare—"

But she'd already disconnected.

It took everything he had not to smash the phone against the wall. Only the very strong belief that she would come to her senses and call again kept him from the violence. Glory needed him, whether she realized it or not.

Forcing his hand to slowly loosen, each finger peeling away, he was finally able to drop the phone to the table.

He knew what he had to do. Kirby, the one who left her

there broken and bleeding, would have to die. He'd take pleasure in killing him, so that Glory would understand: He would always protect her.

Shara might have to go as well. She'd proven herself useless.

But first, before he disposed of them, he'd make use of them one last time. It was the least they owed him.

And then he'd stop playing with Glory.

Taking her with broken ribs might be difficult—for her. It'd be a warning not to waste what little patience he had left. He'd indulged her long enough. Too long.

It was past time for her to come to grips with reality.

Never would he let her go. Not for any reason.

She'd learn her first lesson soon enough.

"I don't want to leave you." Kam hadn't stopped stewing since that fateful call.

Mike was certifiably unhinged, so he'd insisted on calling the local cops. It wasn't something he did often, not after the way they'd hassled Tanner when he was younger, as if he'd been responsible for his father's death.

But that was years ago, and now, with a lunatic on the loose, he wouldn't take chances with Glory's safety.

Not that they'd been able to help much. They promised to keep an eye out, and someone would attempt to contact Mike, to ask him pertinent questions.

Good luck with that, Kam thought. They hadn't been able to reach him after the wreck, and odds were they wouldn't get ahold of him now.

Glory gave Kam a smile. "I'll be fine."

If that were true, why did he feel like things were unraveling around him? "I know you wanted less company, but Callie insisted she would be by." Something he'd encouraged. No way did he want Glory to be alone. He'd prefer she had a houseful of people, but he also understood her need for privacy.

At least Callie would have PB with her. "When they can find the time, Nell and Liam will stop by long enough to get a run set up for the dog."

"I have it all planned out," Glory enthused. "I'll call PB up on the couch with me, hook the leash to the collar, so I don't have to bend, and then we can step outside for a bit. The fresh air will be nice."

I love you. The words burned in his throat and in his heart. If she hadn't harked on yesterday about his apartment, he might have given in and said them.

Then again, he'd spent a long time last night thinking about how to proceed. It seemed to him that he had to show Glory a few things.

First and foremost, he needed her to know he was nothing like his father. He wasn't abusive, wasn't lazy, and would definitely pull his own weight.

The only way he knew to do that was to stick to his original plan. He'd fix up his apartment, and once she was better able to get around on her own, he'd move into the damned thing, too—just long enough to show her that he'd rather be with her.

He'd move in, but he wouldn't stay there. By joining her in the morning for coffee, taking her to dinner—to restaurants and to visit his family—he'd prove to her that he wanted to be with her. Shower alone when he could shower with her? Leave an empty apartment when he could instead kiss her goodbye in the morning?

Hopefully, she'd get the message soon enough.

Sucked that she was trying to find ways to pretty up the place for him when he no longer wanted it. His overall plan had been to rely on no one but himself. And he could—except the thought wasn't as appealing as it once was.

Sure, he didn't have the same financial status as the McCallahan family, but he wasn't destitute, either. He had a good job, a comfortable savings account, not a lot of bills, and a retirement portfolio. He'd never be rich, but he'd ensured his future as much as he could, he had a solid plan, and now he wanted to prove to her . . . What?

"Kam," she teased. "You've gone awfully quiet, and if you don't get going, you'll be late."

Gently taking her face in his hands, he kissed each bruise that remained, then gave her another of the kisses she enjoyed, putting his whole heart into it.

"Well," she breathed when he let up. "I know what I'll be thinking about all day."

He smiled with her, but the worry remained. "The stitches will dissolve soon."

"I know. I'll be glad to be done with them." Wrinkling her nose in that now familiar way, she said, "They itch."

God, she was precious to him. "I'd take them for you if I could."

"Don't be a martyr." A peck to his chin, then his throat, followed by a soft nuzzle, took away the insult. "I shouldn't complain so much. And you shouldn't be late. Now go on before I get whiny."

Concerned, he tipped up her face. "Are you feeling whiny?"

Her grin said otherwise. "Not really. I feel pretty good today, and I think it's because I took action."

"Don't believe Mike." Sure, the prick had sounded convincing, as if he'd been dealt the worst insult ever. Kam wouldn't buy it. In his gut, he knew Mike was involved in some way.

"I don't. Not entirely. I'll always be cautious when it comes to him, I promise. But at least I stopped sitting around worrying and actually did something. I have some other ideas, too—and no, I'm not going into them now. We'll talk about it soon."

Slowly, in halting steps, she urged him toward the door.

"Anxious to get rid of me?"

"To do some online shopping, actually."

Unwilling to dim her smile, he took that one on the chin. "Do you need anything before I go?"

"I need you to stop worrying."

"Let me worry. Let me take care of you." *Let me love you and let me make you mine.* Swallowing down that sentiment wasn't easy. "Swear you'll call me if anything happens."

"I swear." Smiling, she paused in the doorway. Softly, she said, "Thank you for caring about me, Kam. You make my heart happy."

Aw, damn. It took two quick breaths before he could say, "You make my heart happy, too."

Glory closed the door, but he waited until he heard the lock. As he started out to his SUV, someone asked, "Moved in, huh?"

Kam turned, and spotted Nosy Old Lady Simmons, still in her flowered housecoat and slippers, standing on her front stoop. "As much as she'd allow, ma'am."

Wonder of wonders, the woman cracked a smile. "I hope you're behaving."

"Only as much as she makes me."

At that, she cackled a laugh, waved him off, and headed inside.

Huh. Had he won over the neighbor? He'd take every bit of help he could get.

Once he was out of the driveway, he called Tanner.

"What's up? Callie's heading out in a few minutes."

"I know; she told me. Glory's home alone, so I'm glad she won't be long."

"Hold on." Tanner muffled the phone, and when he came back, he said, "Callie will take off now."

Relieved, Kam nodded. "I'm glad. Glory is hell-bent on doing things on her own, but if she so much as moves her pinkie, she flinches."

"Broken ribs are no joke."

With that covered, Kam filled him in about the call to Mike. "He's insane, and that makes him even more dangerous."

"You think he's still here in town?"

"Or somewhere nearby. He said he heard about her wreck from others talking in a store, so he's not far." In his gut, Kam knew Mike was too obsessive to go back home and get on with his life—without Glory. His biggest fear was that the bastard would never give up. "Think you could check around, see if anyone knows of the white car, or if they've seen Mike? I talked with the cops, but they can't be everywhere at once."

"They're better now. You know that, right? The cops who accused me back in the day . . . They knew my dad and made assumptions. I guess the ill will from too many run-ins with him carried over to me. As an adult, I've dealt with a few of them on behalf of kids, and they're okay. They do what they can."

Within the law. If Kam found Mike first, he'd deal out his own justice, and the law could have whatever was left. "Sure, I get it. I'll feel better if the people we know are also scoping out the area."

"I'm on it. I'll talk to Liam first, see if he's able to place that white car."

"Thanks. He and Nell might be going to Glory's later to set up a run for PB. If he finds out anything, I'd rather he tell me first."

"Same. I'll let him know. And, Kam, if you need anything, I'm here."

Meaning if he planned to kick ass, Tanner wanted in on it? Grinning, Kam said, "Not the kind of day I have planned, but I appreciate the offer."

He got to work shortly after that and finished up without a hitch. The customer was happy and wanted to chat, so that took up a little more of his time. He'd been checking his phone every twenty minutes and, so far, hadn't heard from Glory. He didn't want to pester her, not when he sensed she was waffling between wanting him around and wanting to live on her own. If he tipped the scales, it'd be in his favor, not the other way around. She wanted some time alone, so he was determined to give it to her.

Next was Putt-Putt with the kids, and he had to admit, he had a blast. The ages ranged from eleven to seventeen, with seven kids in all, not counting Liam and Nell who helped to organize by pairing up with the older kids.

One of those kids, he couldn't help but notice, looked miserable. Repeatedly, the boy cast his gaze at Kam. Each time, Kam smiled back but it didn't seem to help.

Shoulders slumped, clothes unkempt, and expression guarded, the boy looked as if he had more than he could handle. Several times Kam saw him in whispered conversation with Liam. Hopefully, he could find out more about the situation soon. If he could help in some way, he would.

Just then, a twelve-year-old girl swung at the ball and missed, and when some kids laughed at her, she looked ready to throw the putter. Kam jumped in, soothing tempers and redirecting anger using the methods he'd learned while helping out with Tanner. His own angry youth often gave him a good perspective to go by, but then, he hadn't experienced it as a girl and had no idea if her reactions would be the same. Hostile, yes. Petulant, most definitely. Yet, she also seemed keen to take part.

If Glory were here, she'd probably have some good insight, and if not—because he couldn't quite imagine Glory ever hissing at anyone—then she'd likely be good at understanding.

Rather than single out the girl, Kam addressed all of them with his instructions. "Understand, I'm a lousy Putt-Putt golfer, so I'm sharing what I've been told. There are plenty of times when I hit the ball too hard, not hard enough, bounced it in the wrong direction, or missed it entirely."

To his surprise, the girl rolled her eyes and then cracked a smile—with no hissing. He'd call that great progress.

The rest of the golf game went well. Even better when he took the kids to Ed and Ted's for burgers and fries, the brothers declared it was on the house, and even threw in scoops of ice cream all around.

While the kids all stuffed their faces, Ted called Kam over.

"This is above and beyond, Ted. I'm happy to pay if you—"

"Looks who's talking about above and beyond." He waved away the offer of payment. "I like what you're doing, and I like that your girlfriend suggested we take on some of the kids to mentor."

Girlfriend. That seemed like such a bland, tame word for all the things he felt for Glory, but he couldn't expect Ted to say "the love of your life" or "the one who's changed everything," so he let it go. Leaning on the counter so he could keep an eye on the kids, who now took up five booths on the far wall, Kam asked, "So that's working out?"

"We have a gal helping Ed cook. She's as cantankerous as him, so they keep each other entertained. Also have a boy waiting tables after school, and another who helps clean up at night. Can't get a lot of kids to work so hard these days, but I swear, the ones recommended to us are great. For the most part, they show up on time. Got their first paychecks and acted like it was Christmas. Made Ed and me want to do more." He lowered his voice. "The one who cleans up had a black eye a few nights ago. Worried me sick, but he wouldn't tell me anything about it. Told me to mind my own business."

Damn. That happened a lot, too often really. "Jot down the name for me and I'll see how I can help."

Having already written it out, Ted handed him the slip of paper and then clapped him on the shoulder. "Thanks. You're a good man, Kam. One of the best."

Even after Ted walked away, Kam stood there, left blank by the casual praise. He thought of Tanner as a good man. But himself?

Did others, besides Addie and Tanner, really see him that way? He thought of Tony, the customer from earlier, who'd wanted to stand around and chat. He'd offered a lot of compliments on Kam's welding skills, especially with metal fabrication. He could do things others couldn't, basically build a part needed for an engine, as he'd done for Tony's antique tractor.

That didn't make him a good man, though. It just made him good with his hands. Of course, thinking of his hands had him thinking of Glory . . . and a text came in.

He glanced at the screen, saw it was her, and swiped to open the phone.

FYI, doing great. PB is awesome. Callie visiting. All is well. Have fun & don't rush.

Feeling absurdly happy, he sent her a kissing emoji.

She sent back three.

Grinning, he sent one more reply.

Wrapping up soon. Home in an hour.

Before he could send it, he rethought his wording and changed *home* to *back*. He wouldn't claim her house as his. It was an accomplishment for her, and she was due all the credit.

Glory didn't have the same qualms.

Get home safely.

When he heard a hiss, he glanced up and saw that the same girl from earlier was now ready to throw hands with the two boys sitting across from her, so he hurried in her direction. On his way, he noticed that Liam and the downtrodden boy had moved to a booth by themselves, and they seemed to be engaged in a serious discussion.

Time to wrap it up.

Plenty of napkins were passed around, and it took some prodding on his part for all the kids to get settled in his and Liam's rides. The boy he'd been talking with, plus one more, rode with Liam, and the rest all piled into Kam's SUV. He checked and double-checked that they all wore their seat belts. By specific design, the angry girl sat in the front passenger seat. They weren't far from the halfway house where he'd return them, but he let her choose some music to play, then put up with everyone's heckling him over what they called his "old man jams." Ha! He was only twenty-six, not exactly a grandpa.

It wasn't until later, after he'd gotten them all returned, inquired about the boy Ted had mentioned, and found out what he could about the girl, that Liam approached him. He was outside, only a few yards from his ride, and Kam noted that the other boy was nearby, too, looking both fearful and sullen.

"I know you want to get home to Glory, but could I have a few minutes?"

Kam put a hand to his shoulder. He had massive respect for Liam, for all he'd accomplished despite the challenges, and would do his best to never let him down. "You can have as much time as you want." Glory would understand.

"Thanks." Liam glanced back at the boy, who appeared resistant to the point of bolting.

To keep it casual, Kam leaned back on the outside wall, his stance relaxed. "Nell staying here tonight?"

That diverted Liam for a moment. "Most nights, actually. She can't go home when her uncle's there."

Since Kam already knew about the abusive uncle, he asked, "Need some help with that?"

"No. She'll stay here until she's eighteen, then she's moving in with me."

Though he didn't know if that was a great idea, Kam just nodded. "Could be Callie's house will be ready by then." She and Tanner were turning it into another community home for at-risk kids. They'd learn skills like tree farming, working with chickens, goats and horses, as well as more basic things like budgeting their money, cooking, and managing a household.

"Maybe," Liam said. "That's not what I wanted to talk about, though."

"Okay."

It wasn't like Liam to hesitate so much. Lower, in a near whisper, he said, "I need your promise that you won't lose your shit."

Kam stared into his earnest eyes and suddenly, somehow, he knew. He looked again at the boy, and damned if the kid didn't look panicked. Drawing a bracing breath and tamping down on a surge of suspicion, Kam nodded.

"It's not his fault, okay? You have to hear it all."

Yeah, he'd hear it, and then he'd decide what to do. "Let's

do this." When they started toward the other boy, he straightened, his fight-or-flight posture obvious.

Kam held up his hands. "Everything is cool. We'll just talk, all right?"

His eyes went glassy, his jaw locked, but he nodded and braced himself.

Liam cleared his throat. "Kam, this is Kirby. He has a little sis and he's been doing everything he could to make extra money. The plan was to make enough to fly his sister to a friend's place in Indiana, then pay for her upkeep while she's there."

"I take it that hasn't been going well?"

Kirby worked his jaw. "He hurts her. I have to get her away."

So much pain-filled desperation filled his words that Kam's heart broke clean in two—and he thanked God that he'd never had a sister during the worst times of his life. That would have made everything so much harder.

Much softer now, truly comprehending, he said, "We can help with that, okay?" Whatever it took. "Is she in danger right now?"

Kirby shook his head. "She's here." He nodded at the halfway house. "When he finds out, though, he'll get her back—"

"We won't let that happen." Somehow, he'd figure it out. He never wanted another kid to be hurt the way he was.

Running both hands over his head, Kirby said, "I'm sorry, man. So fucking sorry. I didn't mean for her to wreck."

Shock ran through him, making his heartbeat stagger. But the sincerity was there on the kid's face, too. He looked miserable and broken, like he expected to get destroyed, and that got through to Kam. "We're talking about Glory?"

"The woman in the red car, yeah."

Desperate kids did desperate things. He knew that, because

he'd once been desperate, too. Kam clasped his shoulder, as much to ensure he didn't take off as to offer comfort. He needed two big breaths before he could say, "I believe you." With that said, he asked, "Did Mike tell you to tail her?"

Stunned speechless, Kirby stared at him. "You're not pissed?"

He was pissed all right—just not at Kirby. "You said you didn't mean for her to get hurt, right?"

"Swear to God, I didn't. I was just supposed to follow her, but the roads are tricky and I was afraid I'd lose her. He wouldn't pay me if I lost her."

"Why did he want her followed?"

"He didn't say, but he wanted me to stick close—close enough to spook her. He lost his shit when I told him she'd crashed. I was going to call the cops, but I didn't know if they'd arrest me, and then my sister wouldn't have anyone—"

"Easy." It seemed to Kam that Kirby was ready to implode with a mix of terror and guilt. "Take a breath, okay? No one is arresting you."

"He said he's going to kill me if I don't get her to meet me at a park. He's crazy. I didn't know it at first. Tailing her seemed easy—and I needed the money. But I can't do anything else for him."

"No, you can't. She's hurt, Kirby. Broken ribs, injured shoulder—"

Right there, in the middle of the walkway, Kirby started to crumple. He wrapped his arms around his head and his knees went weak.

"Hey." Liam caught his arm, but already Kirby's sobs were welling up.

Knowing the boy was on the ragged edge made this even harder. "Let's sit in my SUV." Kam led them both there. He needed all the details; he needed to ensure Kirby and his sister were safe.

And then he needed to get his hands on Mike so he could make the bastard pay.

Glory was in the backyard with PB and flinching only a little as the dog tried to race back and forth, each time running out of leash. Liam and Nell hadn't yet been over to create the run, but she didn't mind. She enjoyed this time with her dog-ter.

Plus, since Callie had left only a few minutes earlier, Glory had the opportunity to test herself—without witnesses—to see what she could accomplish.

Apparently, not much, but hey, she was outside in the fresh air, she had her dog with her, and Kam was living his life instead of playing babysitter. The twinges of pain were insignificant compared to the things that were going right.

"Oh, dear God."

Recognizing that voice, Glory turned to her neighbor's house. How was it that Glenda Simmons was *always* outside to see her, whether she was leaving, returning, or in this case, walking her dog.

She couldn't wave because she held the leash in her right hand. Actually, she couldn't do much of anything except smile her gruesome smile and say, "Hello, Mrs. Simmons. How are you?"

"What in the world happened to you?"

Subtlety wasn't Nosy Old Lady Simmons's forte. "I was in a car wreck. Totaled my beautiful little Mustang."

To her complete and utter shock, Simmons hiked up her housedress and deftly climbed over the low fence that enclosed her yard. Glory couldn't blink. She couldn't even get her mouth to close. "Um . . ."

"Country girl, you know. Been climbing fences all my life."

"But aren't you . . ." *Old*.

Simmons chuckled. "In my seventies? Yes, I am. Lived here for forty years and I've gone over the fence plenty of times." Slowly, Simmons knelt down to greet PB. "Aren't you a cutie? I used to have a little rat like you." Glancing up at Glory, she said, "That's one reason for fence-climbing. Had to retrieve my Scottie a few times. That's his name, not the breed."

"Scottie? How cute. This is PB, short for Peanut Butter. She's my dog-ter." Explaining before Simmons asked, Glory said, "As in dog-daughter. Dog-ter."

"Oh, I love that. How sweet." Even more slowly, Simmons got upright again. "That right there, kneeling and standing again? Way harder than getting over a fence."

"Well, as you can see, I can't do either right now."

"I see you're stiff as an ironing board. Hurt your back?"

"My ribs, actually, and one shoulder." She rushed to add, "I'll be fine, and I'm already feeling better, but family . . ." It struck her then: They truly were all family, or same as. Callie, definitely, but now Tanner and Addie, too. And Liz.

Kam. Kam was *everything*.

Simmons smiled at her. "Those blessings have a tendency to hover, don't they?"

"They really are blessings." She said it as much to herself as to her neighbor.

"I know it well. You haven't met them yet, but I have kids who come to visit. Two daughters and a son, with their families." She eyed Glory. "Your family is the rich folks, right? Church was buzzing about it."

"The McCallahans, yes. My aunt and uncle, and my cousin."

"And that handsome young man who's staying with you?"

So, so nosy, but in a sweet way. "He's Kam Norwood, brother to Tanner Patrick."

"Ah, yeah, I heard Addie Willis raised them?"

Here she was, outside for the first time in days, aching from head to toe, grateful that PB had decided to loll in the grass, and her neighbor wanted to gossip. "Do you know Addie?"

"I hear good things. That older boy replaced a few trees for me once after a storm. They live in the rural area, so I don't run into them often. Always seemed nice, though."

"They're the nicest."

"Well now, you might be biased since you have that young stud hanging around."

Hmm. Kam really was a young stud. "I don't mean to be rude, Mrs. Simmons—"

She fanned the air, as if to rid herself of the comment. "Call me Glenda. And your first name is?"

"Glory."

"That's unusual, but really pretty."

Before Glory could thank her, she'd taken the leash.

"How about I help you back into the house—I can see your mouth pinching a bit and I'd like to think it's from discomfort. Not that I want you hurting, but better that than you disliking my company so much."

"Oh, I don't mind your company at all. It's been nice chatting." For Glenda, PB trotted right along, her folded-over ears bouncing, her tail wagging.

Glenda somewhat trotted, too, actually, and it was all Glory could do to keep up.

"I suppose I should slow down a bit. I've been dying to see the place. Saw the movers carrying in all that nice furniture—almost as nice as the man candy you have coming and going." She winked.

"Yes, indeed." The best man candy ever. "Kam has been incredible. Always really, but especially since my accident."

"The man's smitten. Anyone can see that."

Smitten? "You really think so?"

"He hasn't told you?" Turning back to her, Glenda chortled. "You need to come right out and ask him. Bet he'll surprise you real nice."

"You really think so?" Would Kam commit to a long-term relationship?

"Better yet, tell him how you feel first."

Her mouth opened, but nothing came out. Tell Kam that she loved him? Did she dare? "Is it obvious that I'm . . . *smitten*, too?" Just saying the word made Glory feel silly.

Glenda gave her a superior frown. "You haven't told him how you feel, have you?"

"No?"

With a pitying shake of her head, Glenda got them moving again. "You, my dear, are madly in love. Why deny it?" She opened the back door and then stepped aside so Glory could enter first.

Knowing Glenda was curious about the house, she found herself avoiding the question and instead explaining away the lack of outdoor furniture. "I haven't done anything with the terrace yet, but I'll get to it when I'm able."

"Dodging? Fine, I'll play along." After Glenda stepped in, she looked around with genuine interest. "It's beautiful. And you know, the terrace is the perfect place to share morning coffee with that handsome man of yours."

Glory bit her lip. *Is he mine?* "You really think I should go first?"

"Women are no longer on the sidelines. If you want him, you should go after him. Why make him do all the work?"

Allowing herself to be led along with Glenda and PB, Glory considered that. "He really has done a lot of work." Having an unbiased person around was nice. "Even before my wreck, he helped with things around the house, and he repaired a window that got broken."

"Men are handy to have around, even outside the bedroom. Never let anyone tell you otherwise."

How odd that Glenda's outrageousness put her more at ease. Possibly because her personality was so like Kam's. "Don't undo PB's leash yet. I'm trying to teach him to follow protocol. I can't bend to him yet, so I want him to know to get on the couch first." Gratefully, she sank onto the cushions.

"After I see you settled, I'll get out of your hair."

"There's no rush; I'm enjoying myself."

"If you mean that, I could sit and visit a while."

"Yes, please."

Cautiously, Glenda took a seat at the opposite end of the couch and then patted the cushion beside her. PB jumped right up. "What a good dog-ter." She unhooked the leash and gave PB several pets.

Sighing, Glory relaxed back as much as she could. Honestly, she'd probably overdone it for her first day out.

"You look like you could use a drink. Point me in the direction of the kitchen, and I'll take care of it."

Wow. Once Glenda got started, she came on like a tsunami. "I'd appreciate it."

Glenda bounced right back up again. "Mind if I peek at the rest of the house, too?"

"No looking in drawers or closets," Glory said with mock sternness, already feeling comfortable with this particular neighbor. "Otherwise, I don't mind at all."

An hour later, Glory was still enjoying herself. Who knew Nosy Old Lady Simmons was such fun? PB adored her and spent a lot of time going from one end of the couch to the other before finally settling with her head on Glory's right thigh. With only a tiny bit of discomfort to her ribs, she was able to idly stroke the dog's soft ear.

"Well." Glenda stood with a stretch, which had PB shooting to her feet. "I need to get back home. I'm going to leave my phone number with you. I'm sure your man—"

"Kam." More and more, she thought of him as hers, especially after her long chat with her neighbor.

"Will be home soon, but if you need anything at all, let me know."

Knowing she'd have to secure the door, Glory clumsily hauled herself upright, too. "No more climbing fences, okay? You almost stopped my heart."

"Got your attention, didn't I?"

They said their farewells at the front door. It was a little tricky, keeping PB from getting out, and Glory realized that would be another issue. Would she have to leash him before answering the door?

All in all, it had been a wonderful day—except, now that she was alone, she realized Kam was late, much later than he'd said he'd be. Given everything that had been happening, his sudden lack of communication worried her.

She frowned as she settled back on the couch, then texted him.

Running behind?

. . .

Glory frowned as the screen showed him texting, but nothing came through. Her thoughts went to Mike, how unbalanced he'd sounded, and her worry quickly turned to very real fear.

13

Could the day get any longer? Out back, where they'd found Tanner working on the tree farm, Kam stood beside Kirby while they went over what had happened. If he could have handled this on his own, he would have. But Tanner had more extensive experience and better contacts.

The sun was starting to sink in the sky, leaving behind peach and orange hues. The day had cooled, and here among the trees, the air smelled fresh and clean.

As Kirby struggled to keep it together, especially against Tanner's darkening frown, Kam wrapped up his explanation of the situation.

Still scowling like the devil himself, Tanner put a hand on Kirby's shoulder. "First, we'll figure it out, okay?"

Kirby looked ready to piss himself.

"Dude, you're making him nervous. He doesn't get that you're furious at the situation, not at him."

Tanner didn't even spare Kam a glance. "I'm angry at all of it. Angry that Glory got hurt—that she could have been killed. Angry that none of us knew what was going on with you and your sister. Beyond fucking furious that Mike is hanging around and causing this type of trouble. But, Kirby, I mean it." He gave his shoulder a slight shake. "We're on it, okay?"

Warily, Kirby nodded. "I really am sorry."

"I know. It sucks when things are out of our control. Siblings are important." He slanted Kam a look. "I've one of my own."

"That goes both ways," Kam replied.

Nervously, Kirby glanced back and forth between them before a small grin, barely there, took the trembling from his mouth.

See, this was the magic touch Tanner had, knowing how to relate to kids in a way that got through to them. He seemed to have an instinct about when to curse, when to whisper, when to make physical contact, and when to keep his distance, all depending on the kid.

Damn, he admired his brother a lot. "What we need from you is your word that you won't do anything like that ever again. You need money, Kirby, you come to us, and we'll help you figure it out the legit way."

Bobbing his head in fast agreement, Kirby said, "I swear."

Kam nodded once in satisfaction.

Now, with that settled, Tanner asked him, "Shouldn't you get in touch with Glory? You've been gone the better part of the day. Or do you want Callie to run over there again? She will, you know."

"I'll call her now." He, too, patted Kirby's shoulder before saying, "I'll be right back." He'd need to return Kirby to his car, since they'd ridden over together.

As Kam walked off, he heard Tanner say, “Now, I want to talk to you about a better job opportunity, and tomorrow, I’d like to introduce you to someone who can help with your sister. No, don’t get spooked. She’s a terrific person from a local organization. I trust her, and I want you to trust her, too.”

Knowing he’d done as much as he could for now, Kam headed toward the house. He’d say hi to Addie, give her a hug, and then call Glory on his way home. Instead, as he neared the back porch, he found Addie and Shara chatting.

That drew him up short. *What the hell?* “Shara?”

With giant tears in her eyes, her mascara leaving tracks on her cheeks, Shara hiccupped.

Could this day get any longer? Manning up, he stepped forward to deal with this next issue, and his phone dinged with a message.

Nearly groaning, he pulled it from his pocket and saw it was a text from Glory.

Running behind?

He should have called her before now, should have at least left her a message, but he hadn’t known how to explain any of it. He wanted to be sitting with her, close enough to touch her, because he knew she was going to feel guilty over the pressure Mike had put on Kirby.

She wouldn’t hate Kirby, wouldn’t blame the kid any more than he did. And wasn’t that amazing? He had so much faith in her, in her big heart and understanding nature, that he didn’t have a single doubt.

He started a reply—and Shara landed against him, nearly knocking the phone from his hand. Quickly, he levered her back. “What’s going on?”

Addie, God bless her, joined them. She even took Shara's arm and eased her away. "She's had an upset."

To be safe, Kam took a hasty step back. Shara looked ready to grab him again. "Okay, let's hear it."

"You hate me, don't you?"

Her wail was pitiful—and annoying. Glory was at home with broken ribs and a jacked-up shoulder, and she didn't wail. "I don't hate you. I just don't understand what's going on."

Out of nowhere, Addie produced a tissue that she pressed into Shara's hand. "Mop up, honey."

Turning her back on him, shoulders hunched, Shara wiped her face and then loudly blew her nose. Still, without facing him, she said, "I'm sorry, Kam. Sorry that I ever bothered you."

And with that, she quickly started away.

Addie sighed. "Go on. I'll rescue you in a few minutes."

Glaring at Shara's back, he jogged after her. "Unfair. You don't get to come here, put on a scene, and then race off."

"Ha! I can do whatever I want. It's no longer your business. You won't even care if I'm gone for good."

That was too over-the-top dramatic to dismiss. Gently, he caught her arm, halting her rapid retreat. "You and I are friends, Shara. *Only* friends, but friends help when they can, so tell me what's wrong."

Groaning, she turned toward him again.

Good God, all that tissue had done was wreck her makeup more. How much did she wear, anyway? Squinting at her, he detected paler flesh beneath beige smears, blotchy blush, mascara streaks, and something shiny blue . . .

"Stop it," she wailed, covering her face and sobbing

"Hey, come on." Despite his frustration, pity welled up. "Whatever it is, it can't be that bad."

"It's worse." Again, she swiped at her face with the tissue, which was swiftly deteriorating.

Too bad he didn't carry a hanky on him. "Take a breath. That's it. If you have a dry spot left on that tissue, give your nose another blow."

"I have napkins in my car."

By silent agreement, they headed to the driveway.

Kam's thoughts were all over, mostly trying to think of ways he could expediently—and safely—get her on her way. Right now, she shouldn't drive. Not until she got control of herself and calmed down.

Opening the passenger door, she reached in and snagged several napkins off the console. She scrubbed over her face, blew her nose again, smoothed down her hair, and released a shaky breath.

Over her shoulder, she gave him a cautious glance. "If you start staring at me again, I'm going to sock you."

"I think I'm better prepared this time." Trying for some errant humor, he visibly braced himself.

With a small smile, she turned—looking better, not as messy, but with very red eyes and a pink nose. "You always were a comedian."

"Glory says I'm outrageous."

She huffed. "Yes, that, too, but always in the best ways."

Would Glory agree with that assessment? He hoped so. He was growing anxious, knowing Glory was still waiting. "What's happened, hon?"

"I think I really screwed up and now I don't know what to do."

"Tell me and I'll see if I can help." That is, if he didn't have to help right this minute. He didn't like that Glory had been flying solo for most of the day—especially not while she was hurt.

Not when he wanted to be there for her.

Shara leaned back on her car, her gaze on her feet. "There was a man . . . He was sitting alone at the bar, so I went over to talk to him."

"Looking to hook up?" He wasn't one to judge.

"I was exploring the possibility. You'd already rejected me, and I had this stupid idea of getting even."

Definitely off the mark, because he didn't care who Shara slept with, as long as it wasn't him.

"He was a snooty guy, in a hilarious way. Like he was from the wrong century or something. Too proper. I don't remember our exact conversation, but he told me he was in love with someone else."

Those damn prickles of alarm attacked him again. "What did he look like?"

Lifting one shoulder, she said, "Tall, slim. He had dark hair, but I think it was dyed. Like . . . it didn't match his eyebrows. Pretty sure he was wearing contacts too, because his eyes didn't look natural."

Mike. "What did you do, Shara?" If she'd said or done anything that would help Mike, he'd—

"He encouraged me to go after you. To . . . throw myself at you? He said when you accepted what I was offering, your girlfriend would realize you weren't worth her trouble. I don't know. Something like that. I'd had a few drinks and wasn't really thinking clearly." She frowned at him, as if it were his fault. "Anyway, that's why I've been coming on strong. At the time, what he said made sense."

"No, it doesn't make a bit of sense." Jesus, he hated stuff like this. Taking Shara's shoulders in his hands, he bent down to see her face. "Ruined makeup aside, you're a gorgeous woman. Funny, too, and easy to be around when you aren't playing games."

"Don't you just mean easy?"

"No, I don't mean that. You're a healthy woman and it's great that you like sex." He sure as hell liked it, too, but from now on, he wanted only Glory. "The last thing you need to do is chase a guy. Any man who doesn't want you isn't good enough for you, anyway."

Her gaze searched his. "Even you?"

"Especially me." He didn't plan it, didn't even give it a lot of thought before admitting, "I'm in love with Glory."

Eyes flaring wide, she stared at him.

Huh. Saying it out loud somehow made it more substantial. Real. Validated. Kam wanted to say it again, but to Glory, not anyone else. "You don't ever need to play second best."

"See, that's the problem. You're such a nice guy, it's easy to fall for you."

"You haven't," he pointed out.

"No, I guess not or I'd be extra-crushed right now."

Relieved on that score, he let out a breath. One catastrophe averted. "So what did this asshole do that has you sobbing?"

Her lip started to quiver. "He called me a worthless slut."

Anger swirled in Kam's gut—for Shara, who he really did consider a friend—but also for Glory, because he just knew this was another angle, like the threat to Kirby. Old Mike was really spreading himself thin, apparently without a single concern of getting busted. Maybe he thought changing his hair and eye color would take care of that, but Kam would recognize that smug, pretentious ass on sight. It was absurd for Mike to think otherwise.

Did that make Mike less dangerous—or more so?

"Who gives a fuck what he says? If it's who I'm thinking it is, he's a total creep."

"He's worse than a creep," she admitted quietly, guilt adding misery to her sadness. "Please don't hate me, Kam."

Dread had him clenching all over. "Why would I?"

"When Leon said he needed some reliable but desperate guys to hire for a few odd jobs, I told him about the halfway house."

"Leon?" he asked, and then with fresh alarm, "You told him where to find kids who are fighting for an ounce of stability?" Yeah, rage was there. Not hatred, but it was a thoughtless thing for her to do. "You sent him to the shelter?"

"I just . . . I suggested he might find some boys there who were willing to work."

"Jesus, Shara . . ."

"I know!"

"Do you? You have any idea what those kids have been through?"

Shame turned her face bright red and filled her eyes with a new well of tears. "That was before I knew how awful he is."

Hoping to avoid more sobs, he got her back on topic. "Leon, huh?"

After a hiccup and a loud sniffle, she nodded. "That's what he said, but he hesitated at first, so I think he made it up." She twisted the napkins in her hands. "I'm not quite as gullible as he figured."

No, but she'd still gone along with him, until things were completely out of hand. It took two tries to pop the tension from his neck. The day that had started out so well had gone to hell in a heartbeat. "Did he connect with anyone from the shelter?"

"I don't know."

It was probably how he'd found Kirby. "Anything else to share?"

Her pale throat worked as she swallowed nervously. "He . . . He said if I didn't get you away from Glory, I'd be sorry." Her gaze came up to meet his. "Kam, I believe him."

* * *

Glory stared at the blank phone screen. Why wasn't he texting her back? A million awful scenarios winged through her thoughts, escalating her worry until she couldn't take it a moment more.

She called her cousin.

Callie answered on the second ring. "Hey there, what's up? Everything okay?"

"I don't know."

"Glory?" she said, now with sharpened concern.

"No, don't—that is, I'm fine. Just sitting here on the couch with PB."

"Is the dog giving you problems? I knew it was too soon to leave her with you."

"She's an angel." A furry angel, ready for a long nap after the visit with Glenda. "The thing is . . . Kam has been gone all day. He texted a while ago, saying he'd be here in an hour, but it's been at least two, and now he's not replying, and I'm starting to worry—and, Callie, if he's right there by you, don't you dare say anything."

"He's in the yard. He was talking to Tanner, and it looked serious. He had a boy with him."

She knew he'd taken a group of kids for an outing. Had something gone wrong? Now she felt selfish. "I hope everything's okay. Don't bother him. I just had a bad feeling, that's all."

"No reason to worry," Callie said. "He's definitely into you. You know that, right?"

Fighting a smile did her no good. "He seems to be." But soon, she'd have to hit him with a lot of heavy stuff that he might rather avoid. Things like love, parental responsibility—long-term commitment.

Callie's rude snort came through the phone loud and clear.

"Let me peek outside to see if Kam is still out there. Oh, wait. Here's Tanner."

"Don't say anything to—"

"Where's your brother? He's not returning Glory's text."

In the background, Glory could hear Tanner's deep voice, but she couldn't make out the exact words.

"What do you mean, he's with Shara?" And then, "Well, why was she crying?"

Closing her eyes, Glory vowed to have a serious talk with Callie about sharing *everything* with her husband.

"No way. Seriously?"

"Seriously what?" Glory demanded.

"Hang on. Addie's here now, too."

Frozen with mortification, Glory groaned. She did not want Kam's family to know she was checking up on him. "When I get you alone, Callie, you're in trouble."

"You're on speaker," Tanner said with amusement. "No threatening my wife."

Fresh embarrassment heated her face. "She was my cousin before she was your wife."

"Your sister," Addie corrected. "That's what she is."

"My sister-cousin?"

"Just your sister. You were raised together. That's all the distinction we need."

"Decreed by Addie," Callie said. "That's good enough for me."

"While I have you," Addie continued, "I just rescued Kam. And, honey, it was a rescue. Shara has herself all wound tight about something. Poor girl was sobbing like a baby."

Glory wrinkled her nose. "I'm guessing Kam consoled her?"

"He treated her like a friend, because that's all she is."

Tanner interrupted to say, "Kam's calling me now. I'll tell him you miss him."

"Wait, no!"

Callie and Addie laughed.

"Sorry, sis," Callie said. "He's already gone. I'll chat with you until he gets home, though."

"No, thank you, you traitor." Deliberately excluding Callie, Glory asked, "Addie, why is Kam calling Tanner?" *Instead of me?*

Callie's snickers continued in the background as Addie explained. "Probably something to do with whatever had Shara sobbing. I convinced him to head out and call Tanner on his way home because I know he wanted to get back to you. Shara is still out front, so he likely wants Tanner to speak with her about whatever is happening."

"Wait. What's happening?" Callie demanded. Glory heard Callie muttering, her voice fading away.

With a huff, Addie said, "I swear. I raised good, honest boys, so neither of you need to worry about what they're up to."

A mother's defense. Glory loved hearing it. Somehow, these three individuals had created the absolute best family ever. Would Addie be happy to be called Grandma? For a certainty, Liz wouldn't like it. But Callie . . . She'd be the most wonderful aunt ever.

"Callie shouldn't worry. She's married and Tanner loves her."

After a beat of silence, Addie asked, "Is that what you want, honey? To marry Kam?"

Oh, dear God. She shouldn't have said that—especially not to Addie. A dozen replies came to her, some laughing it off, others full of denial, none of them appropriate. She finally settled on a small but honest truth: "I want Kam to be happy." *With me*, she could have added but didn't.

"He wants you to be happy, too. We all do."

"I am." Blast, she'd said that too fast, then had to laugh at herself. "Even with a few aches, I'm very happy, I promise." Deliriously happy most of the time, especially when she was with Kam.

With a smile in her tone, Addie said, "I'm glad."

To further cover up her faux pas, Glory added, "I was just worried when he didn't return on time. You know, with everything going on."

"I'd have worried, too. He should be with you shortly, but I'm happy to chat until he gets there."

"No, that's okay." She didn't want to take up more of Addie's time. "Thanks for explaining everything."

"Let me know if there's anything I can do, okay?"

Always so generous. "I'm going to take PB out now. Maybe we'll wait in front for Kam. That way, the dog can get her excitement out of the way before we come in."

"You be careful now."

"Yes, ma'am." Smiling, Glory ended the call. After hooking the long leash to PB, she worked her way off the couch. It seemed the more she moved, the easier it got. Still with a measure of discomfort, but loosening up all the other little aches gave her some relief.

To keep PB in a pattern, she went out the same door with her, let her piddle twice, and then shuffled her way to the front to await Kam. PB liked this new area to explore, and she spent some time investigating everything. When she finished, she came to stand beside Glory, her beautiful brown eyes so soulful, her flopped-over ears adorable.

"I wish I could bend down and pet you, baby girl. And I can't wait for the day when I can pick you up. Not just yet, though."

She barely got out the sentiment when Kam's SUV pulled down the street and turned into the driveway.

Suddenly, PB showed a whole new side of herself. Lunging at the car, she strained at the end of her leash, which gave Glory a yank that sent a breath-sucking ripple of pain through her ribs. Yapping and growling, PB continued to put on a vicious show until Kam hurriedly left the SUV.

PB's outrage transformed to undiluted excitement, and that was almost as bad.

"What's wrong?" Kam's long strides brought him quickly to her side, so he could take the leash.

It still took Glory a second to speak. "I got jerked a tiny bit, that's all. I'm okay."

He stared at her, worry keeping his brows together. "What are you doing out here, Glory?" As he spoke, he bent to lift PB into his arms. The dog was beside herself, licking his face and nuzzling at him.

Glory wished she could greet him like that, too. "It's a nice day, I've enjoyed being outside, and I figured PB and I could wait for you out here. I spoke with Addie, so I knew you wouldn't be long."

"And you missed me?"

How was she supposed to answer that?

"Stop analyzing," he said with grin, "and just tell me what you're thinking."

Fine, if he wanted the truth, she'd give it to him. "Yes, I missed you. A lot. But I'm also glad you got out to do your own thing. And I'm glad I got to do my own thing, too."

"You're really okay?"

"Perfectly fine." As much as she could be with broken ribs. "It was all going well until PB didn't recognize you. I had no idea she had such a vicious streak."

"She's a protective girl." Then, his voice dropping to a silly, sweet tone, he said to the dog, "Aren't you, baby? Yes, you are. Such a ferocious guard dog. The prettiest, too."

PB ate it up.

Grinning, Glory watched him carry on. "I'd wanted my own kiss, but now that you're covered in dog slobber . . ." she teased.

He put PB on her feet, lifted the hem of his shirt to wipe his face, and then leaned in for a soft smooch. "Get used to it, baby. PB is a lovebug."

"When she's not being protective?"

"It's a great quality in a dog, even in one so small." He kissed her again. "It's been a hell of a day, and I have a lot to tell you, so how about we head in?" With his arm around her back, he led her along.

"I have a few things to tell you, too." She started with how Glenda had climbed the fence, wrapping up with what a wonderful neighbor she turned out to be.

"I wish I'd seen that." Inside, he insisted on making them both sandwiches for dinner, and she insisted on sitting at the table again. "I'm glad you'll have someone nearby, just in case anything happens."

"Not that I'll rely on a seventy-five-year-old woman."

"Hey, she's close enough to lend a hand until I can get here—or Tanner, Callie, or Addie."

"Addie's only a few years younger than Glenda."

He paused with a pickle chip almost to his mouth. "Damn, that's right." The reminder turned him solemn. "I forget—or maybe I just don't like to think about her getting older."

"She always seems younger because she's so active. Other than her feet hurting at Callie's wedding, she never complains."

"Compared to Liz, who complains a lot."

"Usually at me."

He grinned with her. "Now I better understand, but at the wedding, it was making me nuts how she kept nitpicking at you."

"It's her way of giving me attention, I think." Since her accident, she'd reevaluated many things. "She's been so different lately. Really thoughtful."

"She loves you," Kam said simply. "She looked ready to lose it when she saw all your bruises."

Yes, she had. "Unlike Addie, she's not great at coddling, so she offers to bring me makeup to cover the bruises, or a stylist to fix my hair." It amused her to see Kam's frown. He looked as fierce as PB. "She also picked out comfortable clothes for me, and you know she's offered me everything from a recliner to a new car."

"The car," he said, shaking his head. "Can't believe you turned that down."

Glory wrinkled her nose. "Leased through the company, so it'd basically be hers, and I know she'd pick something classic in black."

"I take it that's not your style?"

"Mostly I just want to handle it myself. I have insurance; the car was totaled. It'll be fun—once I'm ready—to go car shopping." That'd be well over a month from now, but still. "I hope you'll go with me," she added.

"I'd love to."

Did that mean he was thinking long-term, too? Before she made her grand confession, she wanted to understand what had kept him away. Glory ate one last potato chip, drank the rest of her lemonade, and met his gaze. "Now that we've covered all the small talk, you said you had things to tell me?"

"I do, but I'm going to make it brief, okay? Once I put these dishes away, I need a long shower, and then, lady, I want to cuddle on the couch with you."

"Sounds good to me."

"Then I'll start with Kirby and finish up with Shara." He told her how he'd seen Liam and Kirby talking, how he'd known something was wrong, and about the confession Kirby had made.

Once he got started, Glory could only listen in dismay. Good God, she'd brought so much trouble to this wonderful little town, all because she'd accepted a few dates with Mike.

He said, "I felt pretty certain you'd understand."

"Poor Kirby." Yes, she understood. Mike was even viler than she'd realized. "Will you and Tanner be able to help him?"

With a slow smile, Kam stared at her. "Somehow, I knew . . ." He left his seat and came around to her chair, bending to kiss her forehead, her temple, the side of her neck. "You always lead with your heart, don't you?"

Right now, her heart was pounding. "You haven't gotten to the part about Shara, yet."

"I was so pissed at her earlier, but now, here with you . . ." He sighed. "Shara is in it up to her neck." Pulling out the chair right beside her and taking her hand, Kam went through the mess blow by blow.

If she'd thought things were complicated with Kirby, Shara's involvement was worse.

Glenda had suggested she should tell Kam how she felt, but how could she do that now? There was far too much going on without her also throwing out declarations of love.

His fingertips touched her chin and guided her face around so he could see her eyes. "Babe, we're going to handle this, okay?"

What could she do but nod?

"You don't look like you believe me."

"I'm worried. I feel terrible for Kirby, and I feel bad for Shara—even though she tried to steal you away."

Kam's smile went crooked. "Her attempts were doomed to failure. I'm still here with you."

Because she was a mess, and he was the kind of man who always wanted to help? Or because he loved her a little, too?

"You're looking at me funny." Kam stole a soft kiss. "You know Shara is just a friend now, right?"

A friend who wanted to sleep with him, but she trusted Kam. Shara, not so much. How could anyone resist him? Even now, with numerous aches and a heavy dose of worry, she wanted him. Pretty sure she'd always want him.

Lightly, Kam eased her hair behind her shoulders. "I want you to get in the habit of opening up to me. Can you do that?"

"Maybe."

"So tell me what you're thinking, and then I can reassure you."

Fine. He wanted the truth? She notched her chin higher. "I look at you and pornos play in my head."

After a second of surprise, that slow sexy smile of his widened. "Have you ever seen a porno?"

"Only one." Heat rushed to her cheeks, but she gave him the truth, anyway. "Callie found some racy stuff and showed me. We huddled together and watched the whole thing."

"The whole thing?" His brows lifted. "How long was it?"

In a hushed whisper, she admitted, "Three minutes." It still embarrassed her to remember how silent she and Callie had been while viewing it.

"Three whole minutes?" he mocked in a scandalized whisper. Then with a snicker, "Did you enjoy it?"

"No." Her lips twitched. "But when it ended, we laughed like loons."

He chuckled just hearing about it. That woke PB and she immediately raced over to him, her tail swinging, her soft ears bouncing.

Glory watched jealously as Kam lifted the dog to his lap, stroked her back, and gave her a kiss on top of her head. She'd been right to have her dog come home. Everyone who met PB loved her.

"Maybe we can watch one together sometime."

"One what?"

"Porno."

Eyes flaring, Glory felt a new wave of heat crawl up her neck. "No."

"Then maybe, once you're up for it, I'll just show you a few things I've seen."

Now that had promise. In fact, her heart pumped a little harder.

And suddenly, without giving her mouth permission, before her thoughts could even weigh in, she heard herself state, "I love you, Kam."

They stared at each other, his eyes widening, hers holding steady despite her misgivings.

Painful seconds ticked by before he whispered, "Say it again."

Surprised satisfaction, maybe a hint of desperate disbelief showed on his face, but no alarm or uneasiness. In fact, his green eyes now looked incandescent with heated emotion.

Throat dry and pulse racing, Glory said, "I love you. I didn't mean to fall in love with you, and I know it's not what you want, but—"

The press of his mouth on hers cut off her explanation.

Then she got a swipe of PB's tongue.

Laughing, Kam apologized and set the dog back on the floor with a few pets and an apologetic, "Sorry, girl, but this is serious stuff. Let's get you a quick treat, okay?"

PB turned an excited circle, then followed Kam when he went into the kitchen.

Glory sat there, very unsure of herself, listening to Kam's low murmur to the dog until he got her settled. She heard his steady footsteps returning. Should she take it back? Apologize for blurting it out like that?

With a glowing smile, Kam returned. For a moment, he just looked at her, his expression pleasantly bemused. "Let's get you comfortable."

"I'm fine," she objected. More than physical comfort, she needed to know how he felt about her declaration.

"Easy now." Continuing to smile at her, he helped her to her feet, kissed her again, and then got her moving. "I have a million things to say. I just need to collect my thoughts. No, Glory, don't frown." Another kiss, and then one more.

Soon as his lips left her, she stated, "I'll frown if I want to."

"Sure you will." This time, he kissed her temple. "That's okay."

Did he have to look so pleased with himself? If it wasn't bound to hurt her, she'd have elbowed him. Hard. "I'm going to the bathroom. You have five minutes to . . . do whatever it is you need to do."

"Yes, ma'am. I'll be ready." The smile brightened to a grin. In fact, he gave a short laugh. "Need any help?"

Shooting him a deadly glare didn't faze him. Having no idea what to make of that, she slowly made her way down the hall. "I'm going to brush my teeth, too, then yes, you can help me change into my sleep shirt." Irked by his smug happiness, she added, "It's been a long day. I might just turn in early."

Kam stood there in the hallway, watching her. Right before she would have shut the bathroom door, he said, "Glory?"

She looked at him.

"I want to do this right." Running a hand over the top of his head, he laughed again. "Just give me a few minutes, okay?"

Do *what* right? Reject her? Leave her? Confess his own love? "Sure. Take all the time you need." She closed the door with a resounding click, but she still heard his laugh. He sounded happy, damn it, and she had no idea what it meant.

Laughter wasn't the reaction she'd expected. But then, everything with Kam had been different. Unique. Special.

She sure hoped he made good use of those minutes.

14

Finally, fresh from his shower, wearing only boxers, and semi-prepared for her big disclosure, Kam eased into place on the couch next to Glory. Eyes closed, she either feigned sleep—or ignored him. He understood that.

After a really rotten day, she'd figuratively knocked him on his ass. Caught between laughing over the thrill of it, the rush of desire to hold her close, and a terrible fear that he'd somehow misunderstood, that she hadn't meant love as in "good times and bad," but rather, that she loved having him with her now, when she needed the help.

Of course, she'd done all right on her own today—as he'd known she would.

He knew she loved the sex.

She definitely loved his family.

But him? Could Glory really love him?

If so, a rotten day couldn't end any better than that.

"Hey."

One blue eye opened, looking mean.

Wasn't easy to keep his overjoyed smile at bay. Hell, he'd grinned through his shower. Even while brushing his teeth.

But this was serious, life-altering stuff. "I had so many plans."

Both eyes opened and she turned her face to better see him in the dim light. "I know, and I won't interfere—at least, not more than I already have. Loving you doesn't change anything."

The hell it doesn't! "It changes everything." By her own admission, life was different now. He wouldn't sleep until she understood that. "Now let me explain, okay?"

Stubbornly, she faced forward again. She even closed her eyes and tried for nonchalance when she said, "Fine. Have at it."

He watched her a moment and decided she wouldn't interrupt. "For a while now, I knew I wanted to get my own place. I talked to Tanner about it once, but he couldn't imagine ever leaving the tree farm, or the house we helped to remodel and expand."

Nothing. She didn't blink. She barely breathed, but he also knew shallow breaths were easier on her ribs.

"As a kid—before I moved in with Addie—I was told I'd be just like my dad."

Lashes lifted so she could gaze at him with her unique brand of quiet sympathy.

For once, he didn't mind. Talking about his folks was always difficult, but it was easier here with Glory. Everything was easier with her.

Except for seeing her pain. Everything he'd ever dealt with paled in comparison to that.

"I was supposed to be a drunken abuser like him. A cheater without morals. My mother would take a belt to me, saying if she didn't, I'd be just like him, but it didn't matter. Every day, she reminded me that I looked like him, sounded like him . . ." God, there'd been times when he'd hated her so much.

"Kam." Glory reached for him, but then he saw her tense up.

"Shh. Just be still." Taking her right hand, he laced his fingers with hers and rested their locked hands on her lap. Needing to be closer, he leaned in and nuzzled her cheek. Glory smelled so sweet, like a woman. Like *his* woman. Her pale hair, hanging loose, felt soft and cool against his cheek.

"Dad encouraged me to hit her back. Sometimes he'd pound on me, saying it was to toughen me up, to teach me to fight. I never understood why the two of them took out their bullshit on me instead of each other. I mean, Dad hit Mom sometimes, and she'd throw things at him, but it never felt the same."

"You're nothing like them."

That fierce declaration put another smile on his mouth. "No, I'm not, but for the longest time, even recently, I've worried about it. Even though they are dead, I want to prove to them—"

"And to yourself?"

"That I am different. Better." Being the bighearted person she was, he knew Glory understood.

"You are." Her hand tightened on his. "I want to hug you so tight right now."

"You can in a month or so." He thought about that, then decided to test her. "We have the rest of our lives, right?"

"Do we?"

Not the answer he wanted, so he gave one of his own. "Yes." He was sure of it.

"But your plans?"

Easy enough to explain that. "I didn't realize it at first, but everything changed when I met you."

"You didn't even like me when you met me. You made that clear enough."

"I didn't know you. I thought you were lazy and stuck up." Leaning back to see her, he caught her dejection. "Don't look like that. I didn't understand at first, but it didn't take me long to start wondering at my own misconceptions."

"Great. How long did you have that awful opinion of me?"

Actually, it had taken a long time before he started to really understand her. Skipping her question, he said, "You want to know the dicked-up part?"

"It's all . . . dicked." The word tripped off her tongue in a funny way. "So sure, feel free. No reason to spare me now."

By being herself, she amused him. Turned him on. Made him feel things he'd never felt for a woman. "Even when I didn't particularly like you, I couldn't help wanting you, and I couldn't stop watching you."

Skepticism arched her brows.

"It's true. I'd see you, think you were being snooty, and I wanted to strip you naked and kiss you all over."

"Ha! You are such a paradox."

"I'm as clear as water."

Her disagreeing sidelong look was sharp enough to pierce. "Sure. Muddy water in a pond, maybe." After a second, she added, "A pond fed by a murky river, so it's always changing."

Kissing her was as essential as breathing so he leaned in to take her mouth in a soft damp claiming of lips and tongue. Irked as she might be, Glory took part. She even gave him a low moan for his efforts.

Now that they both labored for air, he was able to tease again. "If I'm sometimes unclear, it's your fault. I was fine, intent on my agenda, then bam! This hot chick—*you*—arrived and changed everything. I thought I did a fair job of resisting, but at the wedding, I couldn't stop tracking you in that sexy one-strap dress. Lethal—that's what it was. At least to my piece of mind."

"The strap was designed to hide my scar."

He hadn't realized that at the time and knowing it now was like a kick to his conscience. "All anyone saw was a gorgeous woman, constantly on the go, making it all work."

"I had so much fun at that wedding."

A detail-oriented person like her would love the challenge of putting on a society wedding within the limited resources of Hoker, Kentucky. "You didn't disdain Dan's hall."

"Mr. Fellows is a sweetheart, and he was so helpful while I got things set up."

"The place is small and not up to your standards."

Insulted, her brows pinched together. "You really believe that?"

"No denying it's small and dated. My ass got pinched on those cracked plastic chairs."

"Poor baby," she said without an ounce of sympathy.

"Hey, I like the hall just fine; it's definitely good enough for Hoker, but you can't deny that everything about the place is ancient."

"News flash, Kam: I am now a part of Hoker. Bought the house and everything."

Could she be any sweeter? "Yes, you did." And somewhere along the way, she'd taken residence in his heart. "I thought you had high standards like your aunt and uncle, but you were great with Dan and his staff. You charmed Ed and Ted, too."

"I love their diner. I look forward to eating there again." She glanced down at herself. "When I'm more mobile."

That reminded him that he hadn't yet told her about them hiring a few of the kids, as she'd suggested. He'd get to that soon.

"You wrapped your car around a tree and your primary concern was about a stray dog."

"I was so afraid I'd hit her. That would have made everything so much worse."

Worse than broken ribs, a jammed shoulder, cuts and bruises? To Glory, yes. Kam touched her face, a face he found incredibly beautiful whether she was fully polished with her makeup applied and her hair styled, or as she was now, tired, concerned, with greenish bruising and puckered stitches. "When I told you about Kirby, I knew you would be concerned for him because that's the type of woman you are—the type who cares with her whole heart."

Optimism widened her eyes. "I do?"

How could she not know? "You're so caring it scares me sometimes." Forestalling more questions, he put his forehead to hers. "Not since I was a kid, fresh at Addie's, have I been this unsettled. Back then, I'd sometimes cry myself to sleep."

"Oh, Kam." She kissed the bridge of his nose, then his mouth. "Thank God you had Addie."

"Yeah." He'd certainly been blessed with some amazing women in his life. "She'd come into the room and just sit quietly with me. I'd curse her, tell her I hated her, but she said she loved me, anyway. She didn't ask questions or pressure me, either. She'd just say that I was home now and I'd always be safe and loved." Remembering filled him with warmth, both embarrassment at the pain in the ass he'd once been and gratitude over the love he'd received. "Addie promised me that it'd get better—and it did. I realized I wouldn't have dared to cry to my mom or dad. It would have infuriated them, because Mom thought I deserved it, that she was trying to better me, and Dad would have seen it as a weakness." Thinking about it usually put a vise on his windpipe.

Not this time. Not with Glory. "For different reasons, they

both thought I was no good. That's when I knew Addie was different, that she'd given me a chance, and I should take it."

Without her moving, without her revealing a frown, he felt Glory's intent sharpen, like the air right before a lightning strike. Keeping his gaze fixed on hers, he anticipated her reaction. One thing was certain: She never disappointed him.

Anger lowered her voice and stiffened her usually soft lips. "They were ignorant and cruel, and they didn't deserve you."

That summed it up nicely. "No?"

"Don't you dare let them influence you, not in any way. Know that you're a good man. An *incredible* man." She clutched at his hand, her eyes desperately convincing as she whispered, "Know it in your heart and in your head, because you *are*."

Evidently, she believed it, so did he really have to go out of his way to prove it to her? Maybe not. "I've never shared that, Glory. Not with anyone. Even as a kid, it shamed me." Now, so many years later, it still left him prickly with unease.

"You can tell me anything. I'll always keep your secrets safe."

Love was there in her eyes, and in the earnest way she spoke. It was another reason to love her.

Lightening things a little, he promised, "I don't cry myself to sleep anymore, just so you know. That ended after only a few months, thank God."

Subdued, she didn't share in his humor.

Right. Best to get on with it. "The thing is, the memories, the need to be better . . . that's still there—except I don't think about it as much when I'm with you."

"Then stay with me," she urged softly, pressing another kiss to his face.

Do this right, he reminded himself, so he got back on track. "I thought I had my priorities lined up. Independence, so I could be my own man. Respect from others, so they'd know I was nothing like my folks. Even now, wanting to be with you, I figured I'd keep my apartment and get it fixed up."

"But, Kam—"

"I needed you to know that you had options."

"What do you mean?"

"You could kick me to the curb and not feel bad about it." Because he had options, too. He was self-reliant, and he didn't need her favors. He didn't need help from anyone.

What a dumbass he'd been.

"I would *never*," she said, affronted by the very idea.

So freaking cute. For the sake of her seriousness, he kept his smile at bay. "But you could. You bought a house, moved in, and you were all set to live on your own until I finagled an invite."

"I never saw it as finagling."

"Are you kidding? The way you made me work for it?"

"I didn't want you to feel obligated."

"Guess we've danced around each other enough, huh? So here goes. That apartment means nothing to me. I love your house, everything about it. If you want me to stay here—"

"I do."

"Then I'd love to stay with you. But I pay my own way. I don't have the same resources as the McCallahans, but I have a decent savings account, my job is solid, and someday, I may even take over the business. I have a retirement plan." He cupped her face. "I have options, so you have options."

Her lips started to curve . . . but then her gaze shifted away and her warm sigh touched his mouth.

Kam sensed her gearing up for something. "Hey." He recaptured her gaze, then held it in his own. "What's wrong?" He was about to tell her he loved her, but her mood had definitely shifted.

"Do you remember, at the hospital, when I said you and Addie might hate me?"

Without knowing why, the question put him on edge. "By now you should know you were wrong."

The way she dampened her lips drew his attention. "I need to tell you something."

Okay, forget kissing her right now. This sounded serious. "Is that so?"

"It's something . . . big. And important. I should have told you before now, but I . . . So much has happened."

Needing to brace himself for whatever was about to come, he sat back. Given her injuries, Glory couldn't do the same. She looked small, fragile, and painfully vulnerable. "You love me," he said. It seemed important to reiterate that.

"Yes, I do."

Just as he'd hoped, hearing it again helped to ease the gripping tension in the back of his neck. He released a tight breath, knowing he could handle anything else. Once he learned what he was up against, he'd take care of it.

After smoothing her silky hair behind her ear, he let his fingertips drift around the injury on her cheek, and tipped her chin his way. "No time like the present, right? Whatever it is, we'll deal with it." Right now, he was as happy as a man could be. He wasn't about to let anything change that.

Maybe if she'd suspected the day would go like this, Glory would have been better prepared. She'd planned on Kam getting home after a nice outing with the kids. They'd eat, chat, and then she'd tell him that she loved him, just as Glenda had suggested.

Instead, Mike had struck again—twice, apparently—and her regrets were adding up. She was both afraid of what might happen next and equally determined to level with Kam. He deserved to know about the baby.

What a jumbled bunch of confusion.

When she hesitated, he said, "I won't hate you, and Addie doesn't hate anyone."

"No, she doesn't. At the hospital, I blamed my melodrama on the meds, but all I'd had was Tylenol."

A puzzled frown settled into place. "It's not melodramatic to be upset after a bad wreck, especially with your injuries."

How unfair to keep him worried, waiting. Well, no more. By staring into his eyes, she was able to borrow some of his strength, enough to get out the words. "I'm pregnant."

An arrested expression froze on his face seconds before he reared back and stared at her midriff. A series of reactions flashed by in rapid order. Disbelief, consternation, humor, shock. His attempt at a smile didn't quite make it. Neither did his frown.

Glory cleared her throat. "I know it's a surprise."

"It's . . . something." He couldn't seem to get his attention off her belly. "You aren't joking?"

"Would I joke about that?"

"Probably not." He sucked in a big breath, held it, then blew it out with a whispered, "Pregnant? You're sure?"

The hard pounding of her heart should have hurt, but instead, it just left her nervous. "They checked me at the hospital." She was so unsure of her next steps and what to do. Kam said he wanted to be with her. But that was before he knew it wasn't just her.

She would be a mother.

He would be a father.

"I thought about telling Callie, but I couldn't. Not before I told you."

He audibly swallowed. "So no one knows? I mean, besides you." He added with suspicion, "Since the wreck?" Then he shook his head. "No, you're right. It's been chaotic."

He was probably in shock after the way she'd just thrown that at him. "Miserable timing on my part, I know. You've already had a rough day—"

"But it wrapped up with you saying you love me." His face went blank again. "No wait. Guess it's wrapping up with you telling me you're pregnant, right? And you knew before we even left the hospital?"

"You seem hung up on that part." And he sounded on the ragged edge. "I wanted to tell you, I swear." She wanted to shout it to everyone. "Between the wreck and my injuries, and stupid Mike causing trouble . . ."

"Hey." His hand, big and warm, settled against her cheek. "I get it, babe. It was a lot coming at you all at once."

How could he be so understanding? She didn't even understand herself. "Still, that's no excuse."

"I'm just sorry you've been dealing with this all on your own." His thumb brushed her lips, and he leaned in to lightly kiss her, then stared at her middle again. "You didn't even tell Callie?"

"She's so happy with Tanner and her new life, and I don't want to bring my problems to her."

New worries filled his green gaze. "A baby is a problem?"

"Your baby," she explained, in case he hadn't understood the ramifications.

"Yeah, I figured."

His even tone and the mild way he said it further confounded her.

Glory stared at him, lost to his thoughts, having no idea how he felt about it. "Kam . . ."

"It happened in the front hall, didn't it?" Relaxing back into his seat, he settled very near to her. "We stepped in the door and immediately got carried away."

Deadpan, she said, "Oh, good. You remember."

His mouth quirked into a grin. "Remember, think about, and relish." He skimmed a kiss over her cheek, her jaw, and up to her ear. "You rocked my world. It was like a fantasy come to life. I'm sure when I'm too old to get it up anymore, I'll still be remembering it fondly."

Good Lord, she'd just told him they'd be having a baby, and he wanted to joke around?

Drawing back again, he looked at her. "Answer me, Glory. Will a baby be a problem for you?"

Adamant, she shook her head. "No." The love she already felt for the life growing inside her left her no doubts. "It's everything else that worries me. Not the baby," she hurried to explain. "I can afford it."

"I assumed so."

"I've already considered ways I can adjust my schedule. That is, once I'm able to go back to work."

"Then let's start with the biggest worry. Mike, I assume?"

Yes, Mike scared her. She didn't know who else might get hurt before he was out of her life. She didn't know when he'd show up, what trouble he'd cause, or when it would end.

At this particular moment, though, Kam was her biggest concern. He'd just agreed to give up his goals, his apartment, and she'd tossed something new—and very serious—at him.

"I love your family, Kam. You know I don't have one of my own. I have Callie's mom and dad, and I love them, but it's not the same."

By way of agreement, he said, "Liz isn't the nurturing type."

She never had been, though she'd been amazingly attentive with Glory's recent injuries. "Addie's been so kind to me, and Tanner is like the brother I never had."

"Just so we're clear here: I'm not your brother."

She choked on a laugh, then flinched at the discomfort. "Believe me, I'm well aware."

"Hey, don't do that." Helping to readjust her, he fixed the pillow behind her and straightened the quilt over her legs. "No emoting in painful ways, okay? I can't bear it. When you hurt, I hurt."

That caused her to snort.

Grinning, he continued, "Okay, so I don't feel your physical pain, but I swear, babe, it devastates me, so let's keep this discussion calm and even." His large palm cupped over the slight curve of her belly, lightly caressing. "There's a baby under those broken ribs, and I'm certain he doesn't want you hurt any more than I do."

"Do you want a boy?"

"Or a girl."

"Well," she said, "odds are good for either."

This grin was bigger, with pleasure overtaking the residual shock. "Addie won't hate you, not ever, so forget that."

"I've brought so much confusion."

"No, that's on Mike, not you. Plus, Tanner loves Callie more than life, and in every way possible, she considers you her sister. We're all glad that you're here with us and not facing Mike on your own." He kissed her temple. "Tell me the real problem."

No one could be that obtuse. "I'm not married."

"Like that's a requirement." The snarky comment felt like a slap.

A tiny flame of annoyance ignited. Was he being deliberately mean? "I've been a disappointment my entire life! First, to my parents, then to Callie's parents. I don't want to disappoint them again."

"Fuck 'em." Despite the dismissive words, his touch remained gentle, his smile more so. "Tell me the problem."

The tiny flame flared brighter. *"You."* Her voice rose and her breath huffed. "You're the problem!"

As if he'd known all along what she would say, he nodded. "So we're clear, I've always wanted my own family."

"You have Addie. You have Tanner."

"A mom, a brother, and now Callie as a sis." Nodding his agreement, he added, "I thank God for them every single day." His intent gaze moved over her face. "It's not the same as my own little family, though."

Her eyes widened. "You're telling me you want the baby?"

"Damn right I do."

"But . . ." She wanted to ask, *Do you want me?* The words got stuck in her throat.

When she said no more, his expression turned guarded. "Do *you* want the baby?"

"Yes." Until she saw his shoulders relax, she hadn't realized how stiffly he held himself.

"Do you plan to marry me?"

Next to wanting her baby, she wanted that the most. Marriage, her own home, an opportunity to show the world how a baby should be loved, how family should be. "Is that what you want?"

"I love you, Glory. Of course, I want to marry you."

Her world changed, all her irritation evaporating, crowded out by pure joy. "You love me? Really?"

"You being who you are, how you are—I never stood a chance."

Her smile came with a small, flustered laugh. "I'd like to both smack you and kiss you."

The sincerity of the moment kept his own smile at bay. "I vote you just go on loving me."

"Guaranteed, but . . ."

"But nothing."

"I'm such a mess. Largely out of commission, with a dirtbag hot on my heels. And look at me."

"I love looking at you."

That made her heart flutter. "I mean . . . I know I look awful."

"Silly, Glory. Your appeal isn't only your very pretty face. It's those eyes that always look vulnerable but also ready to take on the world. The mouth that begs to be kissed, even while giving me a hard time."

She smiled.

"And that. The smile that always reaches inside to poke at my heart."

"I don't poke."

His level look said otherwise, in the nicest possible way. "It's also you, Glory, the sister who always has Callie's back. The woman who thinks about a dog when she has broken bones and cuts. The caring soul who immediately forgives a kid who landed on the wrong track even when it caused her pain."

Is that how he really saw her? She felt her eyes growing damp, knew tears would only make her look worse, but these were happy tears, and she couldn't seem to control them.

"The daughter," he continued quietly, "who loves, even when the pseudo mom offers more criticism than care."

"Liz has been terrific lately."

Pleasure curled his mouth. "Loyal, sexy, strong—and now carrying my baby." One hand covered her stomach. The other cradled her cheek as he leaned in to kiss her. "Everything will be fine; you'll see."

"How can you be so sure, when I'm so unsure about it all?"

"Easy. If we're together, I can figure out the rest."

She frowned at him, kissed him, and said, "You mean *we* can, right?"

"Yeah." The intimate smile showed in his eyes, if not on his mouth. "That's exactly what I meant."

Kam had doubted that she'd be able to sleep. He'd doubted that he would sleep. But here it was, morning already, and he'd only stirred awake when PB stretched.

Once settled together on the couch, the dog had joined them. Funny how much Kam adored the little pooch already. She was a cute, smart thing, quickly learning that she needed to be easy around Glory.

He hadn't lied about feeling her pain. If he could have taken it for her, he gladly would have. Seeing how slowly she still had to move, how shallowly she breathed, and the bruises . . . She'd healed a lot, proven by how she'd gotten around yesterday, yet parts of the left side of her body remained badly bruised. It amazed him that only two ribs had fractured.

"Hey, sweetheart," he whispered to PB, stroking a hand down her back and then rubbing her velvet-soft ears. "Need to take a leak, huh? Me, too." Trying not to disturb Glory, who slept on, he set the dog on the floor and then got to his feet.

Glory looked boneless, slumped as she was against the corner of the couch, carefully propped in place with soft pillows so she wouldn't unnecessarily jar her ribs or shoulder. Her tangled fair hair half concealed her face, but he could see her pink lips, slightly parted, and the fading bruise that remained on her left cheek. One lax hand rested over her lap. As if reaching for him, her right hand was on the couch beside her.

They'd both slept more soundly for a change. Only once had he been awakened by her movements, but even then, she hadn't fully stirred, merely shifted a tiny bit. He hoped that meant she was indeed healing, her pain lessening a little each day.

The love he felt for her was enough to level him. And now there was a baby, a tiny son or daughter, binding them together. Glory had been carrying that weight on her own. It was his fault that she hadn't immediately trusted him enough to share with him. He'd fix that somehow.

She was it for him, the one woman he wanted to love for the rest of his life.

Yet, somewhere out there, Mike was plotting something. It was enough to make his muscles clench.

Knowing he couldn't keep PB waiting, he snagged his phone off the end table and gave a pat to his thigh. PB fell into step with him. He detoured to the bathroom, saying, "Sorry, girl, but me first." Next, he stepped into the extra bedroom and pulled on flannel pants but nothing else. He didn't want to push his luck with the dog, but he also didn't want to face Mrs. Simmons in his boxers.

So far, PB had been terrific about going outside, but no reason to take chances, so he was ready in under a minute. After hooking the leash to the dog's collar, he led her out the back door. The dew-wet grass, in need of a cut, smelled fresh. Even this early, the September air felt muggy. It'd be another scorcher for sure. When he glanced up, he thought it might also be stormy. He imagined Glory sweating and grinned. She'd probably hate it, but to care for the dog, she'd face the heat.

That reminded him, he needed to speak with her about using extra care. Maybe it was the need to hold on to his happiness, but he had a bad feeling that things with Mike were spiraling out of control. With that thought in mind, he checked the time on his phone, then called his brother.

Tanner answered with, "Everything okay?"

"Yup. Just taking PB out and figured I'd check in."

"Got it. I don't know if you saw the weather report, but we'll have storms all day, so I'm buttoning things up around here."

"Need any help?"

"Nope. But you'll be pleased to know that Kirby is coming by again. After talking with him a while, I've decided to hire him myself."

A slow grin snuck up on Kam. "No kidding? How'd that come about?"

"I needed someone, and he needs the help—not just financial, but someone who's involved."

No one better than Tanner. "You need help with the tree farm? Why didn't you say something?"

"You've got your hands full with your own job and helping Glory. Besides, I like the idea of spending more time with Kirby. Kid is super skittish and I get why. His mother's boyfriend has no business being around kids."

Familiar dread settled in Kam's stomach. "How bad is he?"

"Mostly verbal abuse with the girl, but he's laid hands on Kirby a few times. We both know how that goes."

Yeah, unfortunately, he did. "It accelerates, starts happening more often, and each time gets worse."

Lower, Tanner growled, "I'd love to teach that man a valuable lesson."

"Me first." Why the hell did some adults have to be such fucking assholes? It wasn't hard to be good to a kid. In fact, for most, it was a natural instinct.

But there were still too many cruel people in the world, those who preyed on anyone smaller or weaker because it made them feel superior—or just because they enjoyed it.

Tanner blew out a breath. "The only upside is that he has a stepdad who's been trying to help out. Kirby loved the stepdad. He'd been around a long time, until the mom found a new boyfriend, then the stepdad was booted out."

"Divorced?"

"Would you stay in that situation?"

"No." Trust was a valuable commodity, ranking high on his list. "You think the stepdad might be the answer?"

"I spoke with him last night. He loves both kids. Never had any of his own and said he considers them his."

Awesome. Finally some good news.

"From what Kirby told me, he was a great dad for a decade. I spoke with our contacts, and they're going to see what they can do. Kirby's old enough to make up his own mind. He could move in with his stepdad tonight."

"But he won't leave his sister." Kam understood that.

By way of explanation, Tanner said, "She's only twelve, petite, and she's scared of the bastard. She loves the stepdad, though. He's the only father she'd known for a decade."

With PB leading the way, Kam wandered the yard. "Until that all gets worked out?"

"The boyfriend is out of town for a few days, so we have some wiggle room." Tanner hesitated, then said, "I told Kirby he could bring his sis along if he wanted. Callie said she'd show her around, introduce her to the chickens and goats, then later, we'd all check on the horses. But now, with the storm, not sure how that'll work."

"Where's their mom?"

"Sleeping. She works late at a bar and then sleeps away the weekend."

Rough—not that Kam would excuse her. Parents should protect their kids, period. "Let me know if you need anything."

"I need you to enjoy your Sunday. They'll all be over to visit today, but Addie said they'd keep it brief. Says you're due an actual day off, and I agree. Callie just wants to check on Glory, then she'll head back here."

Keeping news of the baby to himself wasn't easy. Despite

the seriousness of Kirby's situation, imagining how Tanner would react put a huge grin on Kam's face. Addie would go bonkers, for sure. No telling how Liz would react.

Glory hadn't shared with Callie, so he'd hold it together, too. "Hard to relax with Mike still out there."

"The bastard will trip up soon. The cops are looking for him, and now both Kirby and Shara are on to him."

That part bothered Kam a lot. "I don't like it. It's too damned dangerous for them."

"Kirby has our numbers and knows to call if he sees anything fishy," Tanner reminded him, then added, "Seemed to me that Shara was spooked enough to lay low for a while."

"Guaranteed." Shara was terrified, as much by what people would think as the threats Mike had made against her. "I wish she'd go to the police."

"I'm not sure what good it would do. The cops are already doing all they can."

PB finished investigating the yard, did her business, kicked some grass on it, and was ready to head in.

The idea of scooping dog doo-doo had him grinning again. Seemed Glory had him on a roller-coaster ride of feelings. "I'm new to this."

"This?" Tanner asked.

"Caring so much about a woman." With only PB looking at him, he still shrugged. "Worrying about some things, anticipating others. Enjoying most."

With an amused grunt, Tanner said, "You're handling it better than I did."

It . . . being love.

"If it helps, it gets easier."

"It'll be easier when Mike is out of the picture." Allowing PB to lead him in, Kam mused on love. Love for Glory—and love for the baby they'd have. "If you hear anything, let me know. Otherwise, I'm heading inside to start my coffee."

"We'll touch base every few hours. Try to relax and enjoy a day off for a change."

As if Tanner ever took a full day off. Shaking his head, Kam disconnected, looked up, and spotted Glory standing just inside the door. Her hair was sleep-rumpled, her eyes still drowsy, but she smiled at him.

He hoped to see that particular look from her every day for the rest of his life.

15

Teeth grinding and fists flexing, Mike strode from one end of the house to the other. Each step amplified his impatience. Even now, Glory should be with *him*, but instead, she was with another man.

She dodged him. Cut him out.

She believed him capable of awful things.

Damn right he was capable—but only if she let him down.

Only to those who deserved it.

Briefly, he squeezed his eyes shut. He couldn't, wouldn't let this happen. Not again. Thoughts of Jenn haunted him, and at the same time . . . excited him.

Finding one perfect woman shouldn't be this challenging. He'd failed with Jenn, but he wouldn't fail with Glory.

Remembering Jenn, how she'd last looked, the gurgling sounds she made, assured him that he had to get to Glory now. No more waiting. Going through that level of disappointment once was bad enough—not that he would balk at what he had to do.

Glory would either measure up, she'd understand and accept their connection and what he needed from her, or he'd deal with it. Today.

The slashing of rain against the window drew him. As he lifted aside the blinds, a great flash of lightning ripped across the dark turbulent sky, followed seconds later by the rumbling growl of thunder. Perfect timing. The weather would hinder others, making it easier for him to get to Glory.

Her choices would be slim: She could either accept her destiny—or join Jenn in hell.

To get the ball rolling, he packed the few things he had with him and set the suitcase by the garage door. He gave the rented house a cursory glance but didn't see anything out of place other than overflowing garbage. So what? He wasn't a housekeeper. He was a man of means who usually had others serving him.

It was because of Glory that he was here, slumming it in this outdated, humble home in a town just outside Hoker, Kentucky. The mere thought had his lip curling.

More than ready to put it all behind him, he picked up a new prepaid cell phone and called Shara. Three rings sounded, then four, and his rage ratcheted up. Jenn had once dared to ignore his calls.

Worse, Glory had his number blocked. *For that, she'd pay.*

Did Shara now dare ignore his calls? Images of the three women floated in and out of his vision. Glory, a blonde. Jenn, raven-haired. And Shara—who didn't measure up to either of them, with her plain brown hair . . .

Why, that miserable little bitch—Mike caught himself. With the new number, Shara might not know it was him. Certainly, she wouldn't deliberately avoid answering. She, at least, was rightfully terrified of him.

Unlike Jenn, who'd grown insulting at the end.

And Glory, who pretended indifference to their obvious connection.

He was still stewing, fury expanding to every pore of his being, when he heard a tentative, "Hello?"

The fearful squeak of Shara's voice grounded him back in reality. Amused, even mollified, he smiled. "Shara, Shara, Shara. You took an awfully long time to answer."

"Leon?" she gasped. "I . . . I didn't realize . . ."

God, he was sick of hearing that alias. "If you'd known it was me, you would have answered right away?"

"Yes." Then with bitterness: "You didn't give me a choice."

No, he didn't. He'd told her in explicit terms the consequences of snubbing him. Glory got by with it while she came to grips with things, but any other woman, especially a useless bitch like Shara? If she tried it, she'd find the same fate as Jenn.

Mood lightened, he stood by the window looking out. "You went to Kam, didn't you?" It was an easy assumption. Terrified women naturally sought a protector. Very soon, Glory would seek him.

"I . . . No."

"Shara," he scolded with silky menace.

"I mean, yes, I did." A small sob escaped her. "I didn't know what else to do!"

He smiled at her uncertainty. "You want this over and done with, don't you?" When she didn't reply, likely unsure of what he meant, he steered her along. "I assume you'd like to get back to your life with me out of the picture?

"Yes," she breathed in a rush. "I mean . . . What do you want me to do?"

"If I tell you, you'll do it?"

A load of hesitancy preceded her whispered, “Yes.”

“Perfect. I’m sure we can wrap this up in no time at all. But remember, Shara, if you cross me, I will end you. No one, not a cop, not a boyfriend or a bodyguard, will be able to protect you. One dark night, you’ll wake up from a deep sleep and find me there. Do you understand me?”

Tearful now, she whimpered, “Yes.”

Satisfied, Mike got moving, grabbing his wallet and a rain slicker. From the garage of the rented house, he stowed the suitcase into the black SUV he’d *borrowed* from a friend who was out of the country. No one would recognize it, and no one would link it to him. The house wasn’t rented in his name. The car wasn’t his. The few people he’d dealt with—Shara, the grocery store clerk, the young man at the phone store—knew him only as Leon.

As he drove away from the house, he accepted that Kam might be a problem, but he couldn’t prove anything. Shara would be too afraid to assist him, and if not, then he’d kill her. Easy-peasy.

Gleefully, he acknowledged that he’d thought of everything.

While he drove, he spent several more minutes taunting her. Shara deserved it for letting him down, but now, finally, she’d be useful.

When he’d gotten near enough to his destination, he said, “Meet me in the park.”

“The . . . park? But it’s storming.”

“You won’t melt. Park by the south entrance. I’m in a blue sedan,” he lied. “Once you arrive, you’ll join me.”

Breathing more heavily, she stammered, “Join you?”

“So I can pay you for your trouble.”

“You . . . you won’t hurt me?”

“Not unless you disobey me. Show up, collect your money, keep your mouth shut, and you’ll be back to your usual abysmal life in no time.”

Audible breathing carried through the line. And then finally, "Okay."

"Fifteen minutes, Shara. No more than that or you'll make me angry." With that last threat given, he disconnected—and grinned.

Knowing Shara would turn to Kam again, and that Kam would try to set him up, he cautiously drove toward the street adjacent to where Glory lived. To avoid running into Kam, he took his time. He wanted the bigger man gone before he arrived. He had to time this perfectly.

This was his chance to get to Glory. At first, he'd been worried about her injuries—injuries she thought he'd carelessly caused. For that alone, she deserved a little pain, plus her broken ribs would make her easier to control.

Once Kam headed to the park, he'd be far enough away that Mike could grab Glory and get out of town.

She'd be alone. Vulnerable.

It would be *their* time—and she'd learn what it meant to belong to him.

"Are you absolutely certain you don't want me to bring in a stylist for your hair?"

Knowing how her hair looked, Glory barely hid her grin. Poor Liz struggled more with Glory's unkempt appearance than Glory herself. It wasn't that she liked being messy, but Kam truly didn't seem to mind, and that made it matter less to her. Just being her true self, in attitude and looks, was nice for a change. Very relaxing.

Holding humor at bay became especially difficult when Addie said, "Leave her be, Liz. She's dealing with enough without worrying about her hair." Remembering how they'd laughed at her last time, Addie added, "Even without it being styled, it's still cute."

"Thank you." It amazed Glory that Addie and Liz had become such good friends. In every way, they were very different women. Today, Addie wore her usual jeans with a loose-fitting pink T-shirt. A breeze had mussed her gray-streaked blond hair but her blue eyes were as mischievous as ever. Liz wore a chic designer sundress that fit her toned body to perfection. Her hair, cut in an asymmetrical style, remained perfect, as if a breeze wouldn't dare disrupt it. Her blue eyes, darker than Addie's and showcased with subtle makeup, assessed everyone and everything, most specifically Glory's hair.

With a smile, Liz stroked a hand along Glory's crown, smoothing back a wayward tress that kept falling forward. "I miss being able to give you suggestions."

"Don't you mean orders?" Callie said from the kitchen.

Liz sniffed. "Glory, at least, always listened . . . Unlike that one."

"That one, Mom?" Callie stepped into the living space with a taunting grin. "I'm your *daughter*."

"Well, I've always thought of Glory as my daughter, too." As Liz said it, she finger-stroked Glory's hair, still trying to manage it. Shooting a sharp gaze at Callie, she added, "The daughter who *listened*."

The teasing went on around her, but Glory was blank, thunderstruck by Liz's sentiment. *I've always thought of Glory as my daughter, too.* Was it true? If so, why hadn't Liz said something before now?

Coming into the house with PB, Kam glanced her way and then did a double take. He'd already removed his rain jacket and shoes, and he had PB wrapped in a towel. In a single swift glance, he took in the situation and quickly nosed closer. Without an explanation, he handed the dog to Callie, edged his way around Liz, and seated himself beside Glory.

The storm had left his face dewy and his hair damp. He

smelled of the fresh outdoors, and she wanted to curl into him. Instead, she smiled. "You don't have to run to my rescue."

"No, but I missed you." He leaned in for a kiss, and a second later, said to Liz, "Love the quilt."

The compliment redirected her from Glory's hair. "It perfectly matches her decor, don't you think?"

"It really does. Now when she sleeps out here, she'll look so stylish."

Totally missing the irony in his words, Liz beamed. "Exactly." Chin elevated and smile satisfied, she stated to Kam, "We McCallahans can deal with anything and still look classy."

From the kitchen, Addie called, "Liz, come in here with me and leave those lovebirds alone while we finish lunch."

Rushing, Liz explained, "Addie needs me," and off she went.

"You're a wizard," Glory whispered.

"Nah. I just have a way with women."

She nearly choked on her laugh.

Seeing that they were alone, he asked, "What was the problem?"

The words seemed to lump together in her throat. "You'll think I'm silly, but Liz made a comment about me being her daughter and it . . . surprised me."

That sexy mouth of his curled. "More like it left you gobsmacked—but in a good way?"

"Yes."

From the distance separating them, the voices of all three women blended together with Callie's being the loudest and most hilarious. Laughter followed.

Accompanied by a thunderclap, the realization came to Glory. "I'm blessed with an amazing family."

"We both are. They're not traditional, but they're still pretty damned awesome."

"Until I met you, I never realized—"

His phone buzzed in his pocket. "Sorry," he said, and lifted a hip to get it out. One glance at the screen and he frowned. "It's Shara."

Fear grabbed hold of her. "Oh, no."

"It might be nothing." With a swipe of his thumb, Kam answered the call. "Shara, what . . . Hey, slow down."

Glory struggled to sit forward, one hand clutching Kam's forearm. He readjusted the phone and helped her.

"Okay, shh, no, it's fine. You did the right thing. Yeah . . . *no*, don't go. Lock yourself inside. Yes, I'm sure." Agitated, he stood. "Is anyone there with you? Call your folks or a friend and have them come stay with you. I'll let you know what happens. Right. I promise. Okay, you, too."

The second he shoved his phone in his pocket, Glory knew he was leaving. "What is it? What's happened?"

"Callie?" he called out, and given the urgency in his tone, it didn't surprise her that her cousin came running.

He helped Glory from her seat. "I have to go. Right now."

With her thoughts in a blender, Glory grabbed for the first concern. "Is Shara okay?"

"Yeah, but she got a call from Mike. He told her to meet him at the park."

"When?"

"Now, basically." He strode to the foyer to get his shoes and rain jacket.

"And instead she called you?" While trotting behind him, Callie retrieved her own phone from her pocket. "I'll call Tanner right now. If I hurry, I can get there before Kirby and his sister arrive."

Worries bombarded Glory. "Mike's unstable and that makes him dangerous."

"I know, babe." Shoes in hand, he pressed a firm kiss to her mouth. "I'll be careful, and I'll call the cops on the way."

"This could be a trap."

"Could be," he agreed, "but it's also our best chance to get the bastard."

Addie and Liz had joined them and they both looked frightened. Addie shook it off first. "We're both parked in the driveway, blocking the garage. You can't get out until we move."

"Take my car," Liz said, already rushing for her purse.

Stymied for a split second, Kam stared after her. "Your BMW?"

"It's a car," she said. "Only a car." She pressed the key fob into his hand.

Glory jumped on that. "Remember, Mike is fond of car accidents. He probably knows what you drive, but he won't expect Aunt Liz's car."

Accepting that logic, Kam wrapped his fingers around the fob and thanked Liz.

Addie grabbed for her own jacket. "I don't want Callie alone, so I'm going with her."

Liz hitched her chin high. "I'm staying with Glory." She rounded on Glory. "I'm *staying*. Don't argue."

"No," Glory said, taken aback by her vehemence. "I won't. I'll be glad for the company."

The agreement took the starch out of Liz's spine and she scooped up PB, who'd been dancing around them. The dog seemed very unsure of what was happening.

Against her furry ear, Liz said, "It'll be okay, precious. You'll see."

Glory wasn't sure if she was convincing the dog or herself. Never, until this moment, had she seen Liz talk to an animal, much less show it so much affection.

With her phone to her ear, Callie said, "Tanner will meet you at the gas station right before you get to the park."

"Sounds good." Kam briefly slid his hand to the back of Glory's neck. After a long look, he touched his mouth to hers. "Try not to worry. I'll let you know what's happening the moment I'm able."

Numb with fear, she nodded, and seconds later, everyone but Liz was gone.

Another boom of thunder shook the house and put Liz into action. Still holding PB, she raced to the front door and secured it. When she turned, she made an obvious effort to put Glory at ease. "Food is ready. Addie made enough for everyone, but now it'll just be us. Where would you prefer to eat?"

Putting a hand to her unsettled stomach, Glory said, "I don't think I can—"

"Yes, you can." Remaining in her no-nonsense mode, Liz put down the dog and swept past her. "Addie went to the trouble of making a lovely brunch, so we will eat it."

Lightning strobed against the windows, a crack of thunder right behind it, and everything went deathly quiet. With a yelp, PB scuttled over to cower by her feet, then proceeded to growl.

"Poor baby." Liz rushed over to get her. "Now we have to eat. If we don't, the food will be ruined." As if to tempt her, she said, "Chicken salad on whole wheat bread—the bread was my idea. I got it from a lovely little bakery that's been here since I was young. Addie also made avocado salad as a side, and homemade brownies for dessert. Oh, and she even brought along fresh lemonade."

"It sounds delicious." Struggling to compose herself, for Liz and PB, Glory agreed to enjoy the meal. After all, she was eating for two now. Carrying her phone with her, she headed to the dining room table. "PB likes to rest under the table when we have dinner, so let's eat here."

"Perfect," Liz said. In rapid order, she gathered PB's blanket and a chew, bent low to put them under the table, then helped Glory to get seated.

Though it was bad manners, Glory set her phone on the table right beside her plate. No way would she miss Kam's call.

PB, being the best dog-ter ever, got comfortable, but every so often, she still issued a low, nervous growl. Thankfully, the storm quieted some. The rain continued in a steady downpour but without the accompanying fury.

Once Liz had served them both, she sat at the table across from Glory. "So. You and Kam?"

Despite her jitters, Glory noted the motherly way Liz asked the question. "He's wonderful, isn't he?"

"He's not at all what I planned for you." She glanced around the house. "None of this is—but then, Callie's life isn't what I anticipated, either."

"It's better," Glory said, ready to defend her cousin.

"Indeed. The connections here are substantial. Genuine." Liz forked up a bite of avocado salad, then paused with it held aloft. Both her voice and her expression displayed contentment. "Callie is happier than I've ever seen her. Who knew feeding goats and petting chickens would be so good for her?"

Callie knew. "This is where she's meant to be."

Thoughtful, Liz said, "Frank and I were happiest here, when we were still planning our future. Things seemed so much easier then." A quirky grin made her aunt look younger and far more carefree. "We were too busy surviving, living on tight budgets and getting our business off the ground, to worry about what anyone else thought." Sighing, she added, "And now we're back, and we're both more content than we've been in years. We're closer, too." After a moment, she said, "I think Frank was meant to be here as well."

"And you, Aunt Liz?"

She gazed across the table at Glory. "I feel younger, rejuvenated even." Her lips tipped up in a smile. "Addie feels like a lifelong friend. Heaven knows, she doesn't hesitate to correct me. You know what's equally nice?"

"What?"

"She accepts me for who I am, and she loves me as a friend. She told me so."

"Well, of course she does."

"I've made so many mistakes, but Addie told me all moms are flawed and she pointed out how amazing you and Callie are. She said that's to my credit."

Nodding, swallowing back a few tears, Glory said, "It's true. You gave us so much and showed us how to be strong women. How to be independent and smart about our choices."

Liz's gaze softened. "Now I just need to learn how to respect those choices."

They smiled at each other, and Glory decided that Hoker really was the place to be—for all of them. "You don't approve of Tanner?"

"Of course, I do. He makes my daughter happy, and I've never seen a harder working man."

Coming from Liz, that was high praise. "And Kam?"

Being brutally honest, Liz shrugged. "He's not what I would have chosen for you, but for such a muscular young man, he has a gentle heart. I see it in how he treats Addie, how he cares for the animals, and the respect he shows to Frank and me. Plus, he's steady and levelheaded, certainly determined, and . . . he clearly loves you."

Glory's heart felt big enough to burst. "Yes, he does."

"There's one more thing." Liz took her time, taking a bite of her chicken salad sandwich before explaining. After a drink of lemonade, she patted her mouth with a napkin.

"Well?" Glory asked, her curiosity ripe.

Liz leaned in to whisper, "He is an extremely *gorgeous* young man."

For a few seconds, her worries were forgotten. "That he is."

As they ate, Glory checked her phone often, but she hadn't yet heard from Kam.

Both women were silent when PB made it clear she had to go outside. The rain continued, and Glory didn't look forward to getting soaked, but she couldn't ask her aunt to handle the chore.

When PB whined again, she knew she shouldn't wait any longer. The dog was nervous and she might have an accident. Glory wouldn't be able to clean it, and no way could she ask Liz to do so. Just serving a meal was more than her aunt was used to. Plus, PB had been really great about her house training and Glory wanted to build on that, not lose ground.

Excusing herself from the table, and taking her phone with her, Glory went to the couch to attach the dog's leash. Kam probably hadn't even made it to the park yet, and once he got there, he'd be busy. Even if the police didn't arrive at the park right away, he'd have Tanner for backup. She had to believe that it'd be okay.

There were no cars in Glory's driveway, and none parked on the street in front of her house. Perfect. Feeling brazen, Mike parked two houses down to avoid drawing notice, but it was probably an unnecessary precaution. With the sheets of rain coming down and the occasional cracks of lightning across the sky, everyone was safely inside.

Everyone but him.

Jenn had brought him to this . . . No, *not Jenn*. Glory. He gave a mental shake of his head to clear out the old memories.

This was about Glory and her transgressions, the ways that

she'd let him down. Jenn was forever gone now, he reminded himself—just as Shara would be once he was finished with her.

But that would be later. For now, he had to get Glory.

Buffeted by wind and rain the second he stepped out of the SUV, Mike kept his head down. Water washed over the sidewalks. Thick storm clouds darkened the day until it seemed more like evening.

Deciding to approach her house from the back, he pressed forward. Movement to his right drew his attention. With a quick glance, he noticed an older woman peering out the window of the house next door. Without acknowledging her, he continued on, as if he were heading home. No reason to deal with nosy neighbors.

With that thought in mind, he went to the other side of Glory's yard, where the neighbor wouldn't see him. To his utter shock and gleeful satisfaction, he found Glory there. She stood just inside an empty terrace, holding the end of a long leash attached to a small mutt, who was busily sniffing the grass along the edge of pavers.

His heart thundered as satisfaction swelled.

Finally, he had her.

When his cell phone rang, Kam glanced at the screen and almost ignored the unfamiliar number. He'd be at the gas station to meet Tanner in only a few more minutes. With the weather so bad, he'd driven slower than he wanted to, but he wouldn't chance a wreck that might cause him to miss this opportunity.

On the third ring, he answered and put it on speaker. "Hello?"

"Get back home. Now. Glory needs you."

His blood froze in his veins. "Who is this?"

"Glenda, damn it, the neighbor. I got your number from the tree farm website. I'm telling you to get here now."

Pulling into the next driveway to turn around, Kam asked, "What's happening?"

"A man snooping around, that's what. He headed straight for Glory's house, but when he saw me looking out my window, he didn't go to her front door. He went around the side."

"Shit." Warning bells blared in his head. "I'm on my way."

"I saw you leave, so I knew you couldn't have gone far. I'll call the cops next, but hurry—and be careful!"

She disconnected, and Kam dropped the phone to the cup holder in the console and pressed on the gas. Scenarios sped through his brain. He thought to call Tanner, but didn't want to slow down to do that.

And Old Lady Simmons! Did the woman miss nothing? Right now, he could only thank God that she was so vigilant. If they all got through this, he'd kiss the old gal in gratitude.

As the tires of the BMW went through a puddle, water sprayed out in an arc. He'd trust his heavier SUV more in this weather, but he was still making good time. He sped around a corner and slid but quickly righted the car. He risked pushing through a stop sign, already seeing that the roads were empty. He'd be there very soon—but would it be soon enough?

It had to be. He couldn't lose Glory.

Not now. Not ever.

Standing inside the covered terrace, Glory avoided the rain while PB did her business right along the pavers. It amazed her that the dog, despite her nerves, would brave the weather.

Then again, it probably hadn't been the weather that had spooked her. It was more the tension from the humans.

PB had been homeless, Glory reminded herself. Her poor dog-ter had lived outside, suffering the elements—even weather like this—without shelter, and without anyone to love her.

That knowledge, along with her worry for Kam, conspired against her. Her chest tightened and her nose tickled with the threat of tears, but she fought off the emotional upheaval. The last thing the dog needed was more of her moodiness.

PB did look at her a few times, then she hurriedly piddled and started back. Before the dog could reach her, Liz stepped outside with a towel. "I'm going to dry this little baby for you."

Hearing the word *baby* made Glory's heart trip, but she quickly recovered. "You mean PB. Yes, I'm sure her paws, belly, back . . . Well, everything is probably wet."

Liz grinned. "No problem." Going to one knee, she briskly took the towel over PB's wet fur. The dog loved it.

Never before had she seen her aunt with an animal, so she'd definitely never witnessed her toweling one dry. Awed by the novelty of it, Glory smiled down at them.

When movement in the yard drew her attention, Glory glanced up—and there stood Mike.

The sight of him rocked her foundation, making it impossible for her to move. Mike, *here?*

He was supposed to be at the park. Kam was headed there to confront him. But instead . . . The puzzle pieces finally snapped together. It had all been a ploy to get her alone. Except she wasn't alone. Aunt Liz was here, and now she was at risk, too.

Mike's narrowed gaze darted everywhere, seeing and discounting Liz. He wore a chilling smile, until he took in Glory's injuries and unkempt appearance. Facial features contorted into a mask of disgust, and he lost his smile.

The intimate scrutiny sucked all the air out of her lungs.

A slow deep breath didn't ease the restriction in her chest—a restriction that had nothing to do with injured ribs.

Could he hear the erratic thundering of her heart?

Given her physical shape, she didn't stand a chance of running. But even if she could, Liz was still down on one knee with PB, oblivious to the danger.

Lunging at her before Glory could do more than gasp, he finally gained Liz's and PB's attentions.

"You should have been alone. It would have made everything much easier."

The little dog went wild, snapping and snarling.

Poor Liz dropped back on her tush. "What in the world?"

"Shut up," Mike said, as he roughly jerked Glory around to lock her back against his chest. The rough handling sent piercing pain lancing through her.

Liz scuttled to her feet. "Stop that! *You're hurting her.*" Barely maintaining her hold on PB's leash, she reached out.

And Mike wildly swung his fist at her face.

Glory gathered enough breath to scream, but she wasn't loud enough to be heard over the storm. In reaction, Mike crushed her closer, stealing her breath and sending agony through her shoulder and ribs.

With the way her vision blurred, it took her a second to realize he hadn't struck Liz, had in fact missed her, but only because Liz had fallen back again, harder this time, landing mostly sprawled on the floor of the terrace. PB got free and immediately clamped her teeth onto Mike's leg.

Cursing, Mike loosened his hold enough to kick at the dog. He missed, PB darted back to bite him again, and Mike lifted his foot to prepare for a stomp.

Glory grabbed him. With both hands.

Where she found the strength, she didn't know, but her pain became secondary to protecting PB. In a guttural snarl of her own, she snapped, "Don't you *dare*."

It was as if her words froze everything else in the room. PB went still. Liz blinked. And Mike stared at her as if he'd never seen her before.

"Jenn?" he whispered, his confusion evident.

Wondering if he'd lost his grasp on sanity, Glory searched his bewildered eyes. "Who's Jenn?"

Only a second later, the fog cleared and he viciously gripped her arms, yanking her to her tiptoes. "You will not speak to me like that, Glory. Do you understand?"

Yup, the stabbing pain returned in a rush, but at least PB darted out into the rain. Mike wouldn't be able to hurt her, but would she get lost? Injured?

Struggling for every shallow, agonizing breath, Glory wheezed, *"Please . . ."*

Excited approval curved his mouth. "Yes, that's better. You will do exactly what I tell you to, isn't that right? You'll be more malleable this way, not so mouthy. Don't worry. I'll take care of you—once we're away from here." He licked his lips and whispered, "I can't wait to get you alone."

"If you had any furniture out here, young lady, anything at all, I would use it to bludgeon this cretin. A wrought iron side table would be especially helpful right now. Or even a potted plant."

With Glory still suspended in Mike's hold, they both peered at Liz.

Her aunt half sat up on one hip, brusquely rubbing the shoulder she'd landed on. "Take that as a lesson to always finish furnishing your home, inside and out. If you'd needed assistance, you should have told me so."

Her complaint was so nonsensical in the moment that Glory gaped at her through the haze of nearly unbearable pain.

Then Liz brutally kicked outward, nailing Mike right in the knee.

His leg awkwardly buckled, and he fell half out of the terrace and into the rain—almost taking Glory with him. She couldn't stop the raw, broken groan that ripped from her throat, made worse by the way Liz caught her. Even shallow breathing was awful, and her shoulder screamed in pain.

"I'm sorry, Glory. So sorry," Liz crooned to her, petting on her as much as she'd petted PB. "Here, rest back against this support beam."

The world swam around Glory, fuzzy grayness closing in. *I cannot pass out. If I do, what will happen to Liz?*

"Easy. Easy now," Liz said. "Kam is here. He'll take care of everything."

Kam? The blurriness receded and she became aware of hard thumps and brutal cracks of fists on flesh. Cradling her arm and trying not to move a single inch, Glory opened her eyes enough to see Kam throwing hard, fast, relentless punches that kept knocking Mike back. He tried to defend himself, but it was like a puppy up against a pissed-off wolf. For every punch Mike threw, or tried to throw, Kam hit him three times. His jaw, his gut, left, right . . . Where had he learned to fight like that? Other than Mike's grunts and groans, both men engaged in silence.

After another particularly vicious punch to the temple, Mike's head snapped back, his eyes rolled up, and his legs crumpled under him. He landed hard on the soggy ground. Kam stood there, heaving, his hands balled into impressive fists, his feet braced apart while the storm blew around him.

Belatedly, he knelt down, ripped away the rain slicker, and searched Mike for weapons. He found a short length of rope and immediately was enraged again. He looked deadly, but all he did was bind Mike's hands behind him.

God, Glory loved him so much. Barely able to get out a sound, she whispered, "Kam."

Amazingly enough, he heard her. His gaze cut to her, and

his nostrils flared. In an instant, he was on his feet and striding toward her. "You're hurt?"

So badly hurt, but she whispered, "No."

The intrusion of sirens drowned out the storm, and suddenly, several cops were there. Liz left Glory to shout explanations to the officers from beneath the terrace. She made it very clear that Kam was a beloved member of their family, and "*this other man*" was a vile intruder who'd hurt Glory.

Liz summarized things as only she could, with a lot of adjectives to describe Kam's heroism and numerous insults toward Mike's intrusion.

Now in his drenched shirtsleeves and regular khakis, Mike screamed as two officers tried to lead him away. "You're mine, Glory!" His face was bloodied, bruised, and grotesquely swollen in places.

But then, hers had been too after the wreck, all because he'd obsessed over her. She didn't blame Kirby and never would.

Mike had instigated all of it.

She stared at him with as much disdain as she could muster.

Struggling against the officers, he shouted again, "She's mine!" He twisted back to say, "We belong together. You know that, Glory. Tell them."

Instead, she turned away.

"No, damn it! You're not like Jenn. *Tell them*."

That was the second time he'd mentioned Jenn, making Glory wonder if the woman was his last obsession—and whether she'd survived it.

Dripping from head to toe, his shirt stuck to his body and his knuckles bloody, Kam brought her gaze up to meet his. "Tell me you're okay." Reddened eyes looked her over.

Glory summoned a small smile. "I am now." As Mike's voice faded away, the release of mind-numbing fear stole the support of her legs, and she slumped against him.

"Glory?" Gently, he held her, kissing her hair, her ear. "Honey, I'm soaked."

"I don't care." His wet hair dripped onto her shoulders, and yes, her ribs continued to thump, and her shoulder radiated pain into her neck and collarbone, but she needed Kam's strength now.

She needed him. Always.

He drew back, then bent his knees to look into her eyes. "The baby?"

A wobbly smile joined her tear-stained face. "The baby is fine."

"Baby?" Liz rounded on them. "Did you say *baby*?"

Glory nodded.

Face going white, and then suddenly flooding with wild joy, Liz shrieked.

She startled the cops as much as she did Glory and Kam.

Arms spread wide, she reached for Glory, but Kam intercepted her—and got swept into her jumping joy dance.

Laughing pained her, but Glory couldn't hold it back. Never had she seen her aunt like this. Her wild performance wasn't dignified, and in fact, it was goofy. She kicked up her feet, bouncing wildly around the confines of the terrace, making the most ridiculously happy faces.

When she finally released Kam, it was only to throw both fists in the air and shout her happiness.

Kam started laughing, too, but he said in an aside to Glory, "Addie looks a little overwhelmed by the excitement."

"Addie is here?" She turned slightly to see Addie and Callie, with Tanner between them.

"I think they just arrived."

One hand to the wall, the other over her heart, Addie both cried and smiled. "A baby *is* exciting," she said. "The best kind of excitement. The kind that makes you happy from the inside out."

"Glory?" Callie approached her slowly, her gaze roving all over her, again and again. "Oh, my God, Glory. We're having a baby?"

Glory barely tempered another chuckle. "Yes, we are."

With extreme gentleness, Callie embraced her. "A baby," she breathed.

"I know."

A second later, she stepped back and demanded, "Why didn't you tell me?"

Figures that would be her cousin's first question. "I had to tell Kam first."

"And that just happened last night." Putting a hand to Glory's cheek, his thumb brushing over her lips, Kam said, "Our girl was keeping that all to herself."

"Well, not anymore," Tanner said, joining them with a towel, which he held out to Kam. "And definitely not in this family."

Family. Glory hurriedly looked around. Cruisers with flashing blue-and-red lights were at the curb. Two police officers headed toward them while others stood by the car where they'd put Mike in the back seat.

Nowhere did she see her dog. "Kam, PB ran off! At first, I was glad, because then Mike couldn't hurt her, but in this storm—"

"Shh. She's fine," he told her as he stripped off his saturated shirt, dropping it with a sodden plop to the terrace floor. "Just as I pulled up, I saw Glenda taking her in. She said she'll hold on to her until we get this all wrapped up."

"Thank God." With that settled, every ache swamped back in on her. Elation did, too, because finally the drama with Mike would end. He wouldn't be able to disrupt her life anymore. "I need off my feet, please."

Everyone came at her at once, but they all backed off when Kam said, "I've got her."

His strong arms came around her, offering her support, just as he'd done from the start when Mike had shown up at Callie's wedding. His warmth enveloped her, and the scent of his skin filled her head with every slow inhalation. *Mine, mine, mine*, her heart chanted with every steady beat.

He led her to the living room, and when they reached the couch, Kam carefully helped to get her situated.

Addie showed up with a cup of tea. "It'll warm you."

She realized she was shaking, but it was more from nerves than cold or pain.

Liz pressed her way in to spread the beautiful new quilt over her legs.

Tanner, a big brother to the end, pulled Kam aside to check his bleeding knuckles. "Looks like you got in some good hits."

Kam muttered something she couldn't hear, but she saw the way Tanner grinned. "You need to talk to the cops yet. They're waiting, because they know us, but their patience won't last long."

Callie slid onto the couch beside Glory, saying, "Tell me everything. When is our baby due, do you have any names in mind, and are you and Kam tying the knot, because, Glory, I want you happy and I know he'll make you happy."

Kam had already done that. She was happier than she'd ever thought possible. Even better, he'd expanded her family—not only through the baby they'd have, but he'd brought her closer to her aunt, and now she'd have a brother and mother-in-law as well.

When two cops stepped into the room, Callie gave up her inquisition—for now. Glory knew her cousin would be back to it in no time, and that was okay. She wanted to share. Finally, she could share her love with everyone.

The police separated them to give their stories, but Kam didn't go far. From the dining room, he could still see Glory, and in between giving details, he'd smile at her or frown in worry. It was by listening in that she learned Glenda had seen Mike creeping around and had gotten Kam's number from the tree farm's website.

One cop had already been at the gas station where Tanner waited for Kam, so that's how he'd heard the news. On his way to Glory's, Tanner had called Callie, so she and Addie had shown up.

Apparently, that's how it would be now. When one of them needed something, they'd all pull together.

To the older officer questioning her now, she said, "He mentioned Jenn a few times, once confusing me for her. I think he's . . . unwell, and I'm afraid Jenn might be a previous obsession."

"We'll look into it," the officer said, making another note. He also noticed her remaining bruises, which were now a muddied yellow and green. "Do you need to go to the hospital?"

"I was injured in a car accident, and I'm not quite healed up yet. You should have a report on that actually." She gave him the name of the officer who'd dealt with them.

"Thanks." He made more notes.

"I don't think Mike did further damage. Mostly, he just manhandled me." And scared a decade off her life. For a few moments there, she'd feared his insanity would cause terrible violence—not just to her, but to Liz and PB, too.

Just then, Kam crouched by her seat. He took her right hand and kissed her knuckles. "Hey, you okay?"

The officer politely stepped away.

Kam had been through enough on her behalf, and she was ready to move on. "I was thinking about family, actually."

"Fibber." They could both hear Liz's dramatic recounting of how she'd kicked Mike to rescue Glory. It was told with flair, making them both smile.

Sighing, she admitted, "I was so scared."

Kam tightened all over. "I wanted to kill him."

Aware of the police still nearby, she shushed him. "You wouldn't do that."

"No," he said, "I wouldn't. Once he stopped fighting back, it just . . . sickened me."

Tears gathered in her eyes, not for herself, but for Kam's discovery. She tightly squeezed his hand. "You're a good man, Kam. Nothing like your mother and father. You would never abuse a defenseless person, not even a worm like Mike."

"It was tempting."

Hearing that for the joke it was, she grinned. "He was no match for you, and you realized that." In case he misunderstood, she added, "You did enough to ensure my safety—and Liz's—and thank God for it. My ribs . . . I don't know how much more I could have taken. Plus, he planned to hurt PB."

"I should have slugged him one more time."

The tears spilled over, but they were happy tears now. "Thank you for saving me. For caring." Her voice caught. "And for loving me."

"Always. For the rest of our days, Glory. I'm going to take very good care of you."

She'd take good care of him as well. He was the best man in the entire world, and he was all hers.

"For now," he said softly, "I want to take you to the hospital. Shh, I know you're okay. I do. But it'll make me feel better."

Loving him as she did, she agreed.

16

There was no better place to gather with friends and family than in the diner. Ed and Ted were thrilled to be filled to capacity, but they also took part in the engagement party.

Kentucky had gotten their first big snow, but after all, it was now mid-November, so snow wasn't unexpected. It had taken a lot of resolve, but Glory had gotten back in a car, first for prenatal care, now that everyone knew about the baby, and later to have her injuries assessed. It gave her a great deal of satisfaction to have the orthopedic doctor agree she could regain use of her shoulder without surgery, but she still did the light exercises that helped to keep the discomfort at bay.

Driving definitely made her nervous, but she wouldn't lose her independence just because of two nasty wrecks. Kam had given up his apartment and moved in with her without reservations. After his encounter with Mike, he no longer questioned himself, and he no longer felt he had anything to prove.

"After all," he'd said to her, "since I didn't mangle Mike, I must damn near be a saint." She had laughingly agreed.

The few things she'd ordered for his apartment were now at her house, and in the spring, they'd have the terrace beautifully decorated.

It had taken Kam a good long while to stop hovering over her, especially after Mike's background was exposed. Jenn was an ex, and when she'd tried to break things off, he'd brutally murdered her. Thankfully, her remains were recovered, so her family had closure, and Mike would never again be a free man.

For a while there, no one had wanted to let Glory out of their sight, but it was no-nonsense Addie who'd set them all straight—*after* she'd gained Glory's vow to always be exceedingly careful.

Kam kissed her forehead. "You, Glory McCallahan, soon to be Glory Norwood, have turned into a very low-key woman."

She waved to Glenda, Addie, and Liz, seated together at one booth, and then to Nell, Callie, and even Shara, seated at another. Dan Fellows, who'd been thrilled that they'd be using his hall for yet another wedding, sat with her Uncle Frank at the bar, laughing at whatever Ed said when he handed them their food.

"I love it here. I love that Ed and Ted have gotten so involved in helping kids who need it, that Shara is now a friend, that Liam and Nell are part of our lives. I love that Glenda gets regular visits now from Liz and Addie. I love my house, I love planning my wedding, and most of all, Kam, I love you."

His warm green eyes showed happy contentment. "To think I once considered you stuck up."

Laughing, she lightly punched his ribs and got a quick kiss in return. No one understood her as well as he did, not even Callie.

Tanner came through the door, allowing in a dusting of snow carried on a cold wind. Liam and Kirby were with him, and so was Kirby's sister. Glory knew the girl was twelve, but she was so petite that she appeared even younger. These days, she was all smiles.

Not long after Mike was taken into custody, Kirby's stepfather had shown up with great news—depending on your perspective. To Glory, it was amazing and it appeared the kids were adjusting well to their new circumstances.

Their mother's abusive boyfriend had been involved in a serious drug deal while traveling in South Dakota, and for now, they were keeping him, with a possible prison sentence pending. The mother had taken off to be with him, giving the stepfather permission to keep the kids.

The courts, under the circumstances, allowed an emergency hearing where they listened to each child explain their preferences. At the little sister's request, they'd awarded the stepfather full custody of her. Kirby had accepted his invitation to move in as well. Now they were thriving—and it was due in large part to Kam's intervention, Tanner's connections, and the fact that really amazing people cared.

Yes, there were disappointing parents in the world, some who were overwhelmed, some misunderstood, and too many who just didn't care. But there were loving parents, too—whether blood-related or not.

That thought drew Glory's gaze to Aunt Liz. Addie laughed at something she said, and Glenda snorted at them both.

When the door opened again, Glory turned and saw Kirby's stepfather, Rich, entering the diner. He gave her a friendly wave before following the kids to the only available booth.

Not long after securing custody, he'd come by to personally thank her for giving Kirby a chance, and to apologize for all she'd gone through. But she gave her own apology in return, because Kirby had been drawn into Mike's sick plans.

Mike's obsession with her, his twisted belief that she was perfect, had caused a lot of harm, but Glory thought it had also been the impetus that pushed her and Kam together, and for that, she was grateful.

Tanner strode over to say, "I invited them, Rich included."

"I'm glad you did. He's a nice guy, and obviously, the kids are crazy about him."

"He's solid," Tanner said, "and he's offering to help where he can with any kids needing guidance."

"They're part of Hoker now." Rich had relocated so the kids could still attend their schools and keep their friends. He didn't want to disrupt their lives any more than necessary. Glory hugged Tanner, something she'd missed doing when her ribs and shoulder had taken her out of commission. "I want all of Hoker to celebrate with us."

"I'm glad you're a part of our family, hon." Tanner kissed her forehead and moved on.

"This time next year," Kam said, hugging her from behind, one hand on her still-flat stomach and his chin on top of her head, "we'll have a little one with us. The celebrating will be different."

"Even better?"

Kam was thoughtful a moment, then he turned her to face him and framed her face in his hands. "For me, every day with you is amazing, no matter what. I can't imagine it getting any better, but tomorrow, I know it will be, and the day after that."

Such a beautiful sentiment. "Because you love me, and I love you."

His slow smile stole her breath. "Everything changed when I met you. For so long, I thought you were perfect."

That made her scowl, because Mike had thought the same. "I'm *not*," she assured him.

"I agree." He touched a brief kiss to her mouth. "You're wonderfully flawed, but you're still perfect . . . for me."

That was more like it. "What do you say we join this party? After all, we have a lot to celebrate."

He nodded. "The rest of our lives, together."

★ ★ ★ ★ ★